I0690035

Because He's

My Guy

A Contested Possession Novel

Sasha Avice

Copyright © 2023 by Sasha Avice

All rights reserved. No portion of this book may be reproduced or used in any manner without the prior written permission of the copyright owner, except for the use of brief quotations in a book review. For permissions contact sasha@sashaavice.com

This is a work of fiction. All of the characters, incidents, and dialogue, except for incidental references to public figures, places, products, or services, are imaginary and are not intended to refer to any living persons or to disparage any place or company's products or services. Any resemblance to actual persons, living or dead, or events, are entirely coincidental.

ISBN: 978-1-7635380-1-6

Cover by Cate Ashwood Designs.

Edited by Copy by Kath.

Newsletter

Subscribe to my newsletter via sashaavice.com for regular updates on WIPs, new releases, and thoughts on writing.

You'll receive two free novellas upon sign up.

Just want the books? No dramas: hit unsubscribe after you've downloaded them.

This one's for my Sasha

1

♥

GEORGE SETTLED INTO HIS couch as the 2020 Australian Football League draft got under way on his flat screen TV.

"Well, that's my cue," Joq said and got up.

George cracked a grin at him.

"Not gonna watch?" he asked rhetorically.

Joq rolled his eyes. He rested his hand on George's thigh as he leaned down to kiss him goodnight, his dark blue eyes shining with sarcasm. "Not even if you paid me."

George kissed him back, a quick press of lips before Joq straightened and moved away, his lean frame blocking George's view of the TV.

George craned his head around him gathering up his book, laptop and beer bottle from the coffee table so he could still see.

"Night," Joq said.

"Night, babe," George smiled up at him before quickly fixing his eyes back on the TV.

Joq snorted a laugh.

"Shut up," George said around a smile and settled in as Joq shuffled out of the room, his bare feet quiet as he went up the stairs.

George always watched the draft. He was excited to get eyes on this year's touted number one pick: Finnegan Flynn. He'd made a habit of seeing the prospects play in person since he was drafted number one himself ten years ago. Trips to the country games to watch the A leagues and the juniors, the state league games whenever he went interstate. He loved the feel of the smaller clubs—hot meat pies and shitty beer, every man and his wife with an opinion, sometimes even a half decent opinion.

He'd missed seeing Flynn play though. The first time he was up that way, Flynn was injured. The second, his game clashed with Flynn's.

"Alright, and here we have the first pick..."

George leaned forward to grab his low-calorie beer.

"Now, it's no secret they'll be taking Flynn, you'd be nuts not to take Flynn in this market..."

The camera cut to a young guy in a suit. George's hand stopped around the bottle. The caption told him it was Finnegan Flynn, eighteen, prospect from the Sharks. He was smiling, a small thing, his eyes alight. A gorgeous girl leaned in and said something against his ear. His smile widened to show teeth as he turned to her and whispered something back.

He was striking—tan skin, messy blonde hair with shocks of white through it. It was unruly even though it appeared he'd tried to tidy it because it sat down awkwardly, flat on the sides. He smothered his smile and George could see he was trying to appear professional, but his big eyes—crinkling in the corners—reflected the light and shone.

"Fuck me," George said under his breath as he gripped his beer and sat back. He hadn't had a visceral reaction to a guy like that in a long time. Probably not since he was a teenager.

"*Flynn is a real catch for the AFL*," the presenter went on, "*he could have had an equally promising career in surfing with all those junior titles—*

The presenter cut off as the League CEO appeared. "*Okay, here's the number one pick...*"

Flynn's name was called and he stood, jerked the lapels of his suit jacket down in a clumsy movement. The girl next to him stood and hugged him, kissed his cheek, a woman on the other side of her came around and did the same. Flynn gripped them both back tightly; the woman said something against his ear and he leaned back to beam down at her. He moved away from them and jogged up the stairs, his smile blinding, his gait awkward in the way of a boy growing into that enormous body, that potential, but his handshake was firm and sure as he took their President's—Jim Mason's—hand, and accepted the jumper.

George remembered to sip his beer after Flynn had left the stage.

He picked up his phone and shot off a text to Ally, the team PR manager. He'd get Flynn's number. Welcome him to the team. He was the captain, that was a totally normal thing to do. He hadn't thought of it when Lacy was drafted number one, but well, Lacy was a different kind of guy, sure of himself and crazy in equal measure. He didn't need welcome messages from fawning captains.

He got an unusually effusive reply from Ally with Flynn's number—Ally wasn't usually effusive about anything.

He added the contact, pulled up messages and wrote: *Hi*. Deleted it.

Yo. Deleted it. Jesus, what was he, a frat boy?

Welcome, here if you need me. Deleted it. Too informal. And insane.

Welcome to the team. Here if you need anything. George Creed.

He deleted George. No, too formal.

He deleted Creed.

No, then Flynn wouldn't know who it was.

He added his surname back and hit send.

"Jesus fucking Christ," he said to the empty room and threw his phone on the coffee table.

They had the number seven pick. He needed to focus on that. They were yet to fill the glaring hole Jack Reaver left when he got himself traded back to Fremantle. Flynn would help, but it wouldn't hurt to add someone else to the front end.

He looked at his phone. The black screen.

Jesus, what had he been thinking? Kid like Flynn would probably have a thousand texts from friends, adoring girls—and guys if he swung that way—which George was not touching because it was ludicrous, even if Flynn did, it was totally irrelevant.

His phone lit up and beeped with a message. Another two came in quick succession.

George's heart pounded and his whole body went tingly. He scooped up the phone and told himself to get it together. His smile grew at all the messages coming through under Finnegan Flynn.

Holy shit!

George laughed.

Sorry.

Hi!

Call me Finn.

And thnx!!! Gonna take you up on that.

George's stomach fluttered.

Seriously.

So tell me if you were just being nice or you gonna hear from me.

George's smile was so wide, he was glad Joq never watched the draft because he'd struggle to explain it.

Not just being nice.

Message anytime.

Shit, is that flirting? No, of course not, he's being welcoming, he'll need to have Flynn, Finn, in hand for team dynamics, for—

I SO will.

George huffed a laugh. He felt warmth spreading from his stomach down to his groin, which was ridiculous; he was exchanging texts. And he needed to reply.

Good. He hit send.

The message bubble popped up. Disappeared. George took a swig of his beer. There was no good way to reply to 'good'. Why'd he send 'good'?

I look forward to it. He sent before second-guessing himself.

He finished his beer in one go and got up to get another one. Jesus, Finn was probably realising what Scotty—the team's number one ruckman and George's long-suffering BFF—told everyone about George: beyond the media circus and his mad football skills was the world's biggest fucking dork, the least cool person anyone could meet, insufferable in his earnestness.

He sat down with his fresh beer and felt terrifyingly nervous to look at his phone. What if Finn hadn't replied?

His phone lit up.

Me too.

George exhaled, all the tingling in his limbs racing along his skin.

He tucked his phone under the couch and decided to bail while he was ahead.

He'd meet Finn in less than a month and he needed to develop some chill before that occurred. He could not be mooning over an eighteen-year-old like a sketchy loser. Joq would mock him until the end of time if that happened.

He settled back and continued watching the draft. He'd missed the number seven pick, so he'd need to check that. The camera cut to Finn sitting with those women—they must've been his mother and sister—his eyes on his phone on the table before his sister nudged him. He glanced up into the camera and smiled, warm and professional, but bashful too, caught.

George decided to finish this beer in one go as well.

2

WHEN GEORGE GOT THE news Finn wouldn't be joining them that season due to osteitis pubis—a debilitating groin injury that'd need at least a year to rehab after rest and debating whether or not to do surgery—the disappointment he felt was so profound, it defied reason.

"Sucks, babe," Joq said from where they were sitting outside by the pool. Joq had most of his concentration in his book, but George knew if he needed to talk about it Joq would set the book aside.

But what would he say? He didn't understand why he was feeling so intensely about it, and he had no idea how to express that.

"It really does," he said. "We need to fill that forward pocket. Fucking Jack, and Finn would've been perfect, have you seen him play? I downloaded some games, shitty filming, but you can see enough."

He clicked his mouth shut. That was a rant.

Joq dropped his book and raised an eyebrow. "You're gonna have to let this thing with Jack go at some point, it wasn't personal."

George shook his head too vehemently. This wasn't about Jack. All these feelings? This had nothing to do with Jack. He seized on it.

"It felt pretty bloody personal, after all that work we put in to get him where he was the golden centre of the team—

His phone pinged and Finn's name flashed on the screen.

Joq picked up the slack. "I'm just saying, it wasn't easy for him. He knew he'd be disappointing you..."

George tuned him out. His phone buzzed with another message.

They'd been texting every week since the draft. Finn had mentioned the lingering effects from the injury, but George guessed even he didn't realise how bad it was. They'd mainly discussed team dynamics, good places to eat in Melbourne, and Finn had opened their first thread with, *but seriously, what's Lacy really like???* George had snorted and excused himself from a team lunch with teammates who lived in Melbourne to go and answer.

"... and I think it'd mean the world to him if you made the first move." Joq finished. He was giving George the look that said George was being a dick but Joq was his boyfriend and he was trying to be on his side, but could George make it a bit easier, maybe, please, thanks. Joq could pack a lot into his handsome face; a lot of quiet judgement in those fine features.

For once, George wasn't really interested in defending himself against it.

"Yeah," he said, and cleared his throat. He grabbed his phone and stood. "I'll think about it."

"You do that, and get me a beer on your way back, please?"

"Course," he focused on his phone, went inside and looked at the message.

I reckon you heard? This sucks so bad.

George leaned against the counter. It really did. The team needed Finn.

He read the second message as another one came in.

Is it stupid I feel so disappointed? Like, it was gonna be Xmas tomorrow and someone just told me it's not gonna be for another year.

George's lips quirked. It felt exactly like that.

Sorry, u prob busy and im being stupid.

George typed quickly: *Not stupid.*

He took a deep breath: *I feel exactly the same. Like someone stole Xmas.*

He hit send and sucked in a sharp breath. That was probably too much.

Thanks came back with a lot of smiley faces and prayer emojis.

I know it should be about the game, playin in the AFL you know?

George read that and frowned.

Course he sent back.

But is it stupid im most disappointed about having to wait to meet?

That crazy warm, tingly feeling started up all over George's body again. It really was getting ridiculous. But. He had a rule as captain: face your fears, don't let them control you, and always tell the truth. Finn was putting himself out there and George could honestly say he felt exactly the same, so why shouldn't he?

Sorry again, im bein stupid and maudlin. U prob got a big superstar life not worrying on meeting the new rookie, eh?

George shook his head and typed quickly: *No. I'm most disappointed about that too.*

He hit send and then needed to walk it off in his kitchen. Right, Joq needed a beer. George needed a bloody beer.

His phone buzzed. He scooped it up.

Good.

His phone buzzed again. A laughing emoji.

Not good, but good like, im not out being stupid, just was really looking forward to hanging out, you know?

Me too. George sent that quickly. *Got to tighten up your marking.*

Finn took a spectacular mark, but he knew that comment would diffuse whatever weird energy was starting to seep in and sure enough, Finn came back with a series of laughing emojis and some comments on George's blooper reel from over the years. George was surprised by how well Finn knew it. He settled in and defended himself.

"How's that beer coming?" Joq called from outside.

George startled and glanced up. "Coming."

Joq gave him a lazy smile and returned to his book.

"Group chat?" Joq asked when George came out with his beer. He was smiling up at him, relaxed, his eyes fond, a familiarity in the look exchanged between them. After ten years and change, he knew Joq better than anyone, and he didn't think he'd ever outright lied to him. He didn't know why he wanted to now. It's not like he couldn't flirt with another guy. Hell, he could fuck a different guy every week if he wanted to and it was totally cool. Joq certainly did.

So why did he find himself saying, "Yeah, trying to organise this pre-season BBQ."

"What's to organise? You do the same thing every year," Joq accepted the beer, smiled up at George, his eyes squinting against the sun.

"You want your sunnies?" George asked.

"Oh, yeah," Joq looked around. "Summer's finally coming I guess."

George's phone buzzed several times in quick succession.

"Geez, just order the meat and get the salads catered," Joq said.

"Yeah," George replied and went back inside.

Summer might've arrived, but it was still warmer inside, the clean lines of his kitchen and open plan dining area absorbing and holding the sunlight filtering into the room from the open patio doors and floor to ceiling windows. He leaned his hip against the kitchen bench, his back to the outside and looked at his phone.

Hell of a mark in that final though.

I mean, you lost, but still, you shouldn't have.

And what was up with your hair?

George chuckled. This kid.

My hair? Are you fucking serious? He hit send. His heart fluttered with nerves—he liked Finn's hair, he hoped Finn got he was joking. Of course he was joking, this was normal ribbing.

Hey now, my hair's awesome. Best feature, came back with a series of smiley faces.

George wanted to tell him his hair was one of many of his best features, but that was definitely too much. And he needed to bring it back to the game. They weren't doing anything wrong, texting like this, and yet he couldn't shake the feeling of something not right in it either.

Make your footy your best feature. He sent that before he could second guess himself. He frowned at it—was it too cold?

He needed to bail. He needed to get out when he started to feel like *this*—this unnameable excitement and terror all at once.

I gotta go organise a team BBQ, he sent over Finn's message bubble coming up. It disappeared.

Oh, course, sorry, popped up a second later.

All good, he replied.

Please tell me to fuck off if I keep messaging. Don't wanna overdo it.

George took a deep breath. Tell the truth, he told himself.

But maybe not the whole truth.

I like your messages. Send them whenever.

There, that was better than: *message me all the time, I love hearing from you, it makes me giddy.* And: *I hate hearing from you for that same reason, you make me nervous and I don't understand why.*

"Still messaging about it?" Joq said from behind him.

George almost dropped his phone. He slipped it into his back pocket.

"Yeah, bloody Scotty, throwing a spanner in the works over beer selection."

"He drinks bourbon," Joq replied.

George glanced over at him. He was pulling stuff out of the fridge for dinner, his smile that same fond, familiar one. There was a shared warmth between them in that smile. George returned it and ran a nervous hand through his hair.

"You know what he's like, being difficult. Can I help?"

His phone buzzed twice against his ass.

Joq snorted a laugh. "Uh, no, but you could go get us some wine? I'm making fish marinated in lemon and dill."

"Course," George slid up alongside him at the bench and wrapped his arm around his waist, kissed the sharp angle of his cheekbone, ran his nose along his jaw. "Sem sav?"

"Hmm, yeah, or maybe the Barossa chardonnay if they have it."

"Course."

He pressed another kiss to Joq's temple and headed out.

He was in his car, the engine idling when he checked the final messages.

I like your messages too was waiting for him with a fucking heart eyes emoji, which George was embarrassed to admit made that warmth flood him, made his limbs tingle.

Talk soon was under that with a winking face.

George typed his two-word reply very carefully and terrifyingly self-consciously.

Can't wait.

He threw his phone on the passenger's seat and flexed his fingers a few times. Jesus, get it together, he berated himself.

3

♥

TIME ACCELERATED OUTWARDLY AFTER that. It always did when he was gearing up for a season. Meeting his nine to fives—the team training schedule, physio appointments, ice baths, meetings, video review—and in his case, obligations as captain and the media go to person. Every day was packed and he shouldn't have had an idle moment.

But in his mind, time dragged and he was unsettled. A year. A whole fucking year. He'd pumped the brakes on messaging with Finn as much as he could. Rationed it to once a week.

He'd written and rewritten the message to put some structure into their exchanges so many times he was terrified the sentence had lost all meaning and Finn would think he'd lost his mind when he finally sent: *message on Sundays?*

Oh yeah, course! Came back straight away.

Quickly followed by: *sorry, but good, you gotta tell me if im bein too much.*

George had swallowed. Finn wasn't the one being too much. Clearly, the kid was a fan and more than that, a good kid who was finding common ground with a fellow player, a senior player. There was nothing wrong with what they were doing.

But George was driving himself crazy worrying he was giving off a vibe. He wasn't sure what that vibe was, but it wasn't good, he was pretty sure.

Not too much, he'd written carefully. *Just want to give you my full attention. Getting busy.* He sent and hoped it was toeing the right side of the line of normal, captain-like advice.

He'd gotten a smiley face in return and nothing more.

He'd waited for Sunday like a school kid waiting for Friday.

Finn never made the first move.

George didn't like that, but he was grateful for it beneath the disappointment.

When he caught himself calculating that a year meant fifty-two exchanges while he did beach training that first week, he had to physically shake himself.

"You good?" Scotty asked.

"Yeah, yeah, fucking sand," he replied and shook his head from side to side to remove the non-existent sand from his hair.

"You love the sand," Scotty replied and ruffled his hair.

"Yeah, yeah," George smiled and took the head pat.

He grabbed his phone after training. His heart sank when he saw nothing but the usual texts from Joq, Jim, his sister, his mum.

Fifty-two weeks, he thought, and told himself to stop being fucking ridiculous.

They made the eight that season, but bombed in the first game of the finals. George was disappointed, pissed off, but he was elated too—next season. Next season they'd have Finn.

When he got the message from Finn—*need to do another year with the Sharks*—he had to sit down. He was sitting on his couch, looking at the blank screen.

"Hey?" Joq called as he came in the front door.

George sat up, cleared his throat and tossed his phone on the coffee table. "In here."

"Why're you sitting in the dark?" Joq asked and flicked on the light.

George flinched.

"You alright?"

"Yeah, just..."

Joq came and sat next to him. "What happened?"

"Nothin'," George tried to smile. "Just, we suck, you know."

Joq shook his head at him. "You know that's not true, c'mon. The Hawks are on fire, no one's gonna stop them."

"Yeah," George smiled for real. Joq was right of course. And George knew that: they weren't a shit team, there was simply a better team.

But he couldn't come out and say he was crushed because his superstar rookie was out for another year. His reaction to the news was not normal. He knew that for sure.

He shoved it down. He reframed it. It was good. He'd have another year to rethink this. He was being stupid. He needed to take control of the situation.

And for the next nine months, he kept their exchanges as professional as possible. Finn followed his lead.

When he got the message to confirm Finn would be joining them the following season, he had his phone in his hand in front of his locker, and he turned to Scotty beside him and grabbed him in a headlock.

"Fucking boom!" he yelled as he shook him.

Scotty laughed. "Jesus, man, what is it?"

"Nothin', nothin'," George gave him another shake and let him go.

"Retirement party plans?" Scotty grinned over at him. "You get James Blundell confirmed to play?"

"Ah, shut it," George said and shoved him. "He's awesome."

"Yeah, a real winner."

"Well, how about you then, got the Hilltop Hoods on speed dial yet?"

"Hey now," Lacy interrupted them, "the Hoods are the shit."

"No one's taking advice from a man who wears a crushed velvet suit to the Brownlow's," George replied. The ceremony for the best and fairest player of the season had been a few weeks before and George still couldn't get the purple monstrosity out of his brain, and that was even with the drag queen in a bright orange ball gown Lacy had brought as his date.

"That suit was the fucking bomb," Lacy replied, grinning. "Also, since you're gonna be my coach next year, I reckon you better start bein' a bit nicer to me, gotta get me in hand." He winked.

George snorted. That was never going to happen.

He waited until he got home to message Finn.

He didn't even care that it was Friday. Finn would be here soon. Fuck the Sunday only rules.

Fucking finally, he wrote and sent.

His phone started ringing in his hand for a video call. He almost dropped it. Finn's name flashed on the screen.

"Hello?" he asked as he accepted the call and was met with the very alive, very animated face of Finn and his blinding smile.

"Hi," Finn said around his white teeth. His smile turned bashful. "Sorry, hope it's cool that I'm calling? I just got all this, you know, energy," he laughed. His hair fell in his eyes and he dropped his gaze. "Sorry," he said again.

"What're you sorry for? It's fucking awesome," George replied. He was smiling closed-mouthed but he wasn't fooling anyone, he was just trying to hold it all in. "And call anytime, it's good, talking face to face."

Finn looked up again. "Not just on Sundays?" he asked, smile cheeky.

George blushed. That never happened to him. Well, rarely, fuck you, Scotty; that was one time and he was meeting James Blundell, sue him.

But right now, he was lost for words as he drank Finn in—his beaming yet shy smile, his eyes that were surfer blue against the beach tan.

"Sorry about that," George found his voice. "I just thought we better ration it or we'd be talking every day."

"Yeah, no, I get it, got shit to do, people to see, probably a super-secret hot girlfriend who'd get pissed if you're on your phone all the time," Finn replied.

George huffed a laugh at that. "Uh, no. No girlfriend."

He thought of Joq. Of how oddly close Finn was to the truth. He did have a super-secret hot boyfriend. But that was so secret the word 'secret' didn't feel like enough.

"When do you arrive?" he asked to stop that line of questioning and not for the usual reason—normally, he avoided the topic of his sexuality as much as possible because he hated outright lying but he wasn't about to tell the truth—now though, he didn't want to talk about being in a relationship with someone else when he was talking to Finn. He didn't know why, but it made him uncomfortable.

"November."

"November when?"

Finn grinned. "Haven't booked the flight yet, but I gotta be there for pre-season so probably like the fourteenth?"

"So, two months, give or take."

"Yeah," Finn said.

"Yeah," George replied.

"Give or take," Finn repeated. He dropped his gaze and his arm moved like he was picking at his pant leg. It was blindingly sunny where he was, the garden behind him bright green against it.

"Where are you?"

"Home," Finn looked up again. "I still live with my mum most of the time. And my sister when she's not at uni."

Finn had mentioned them in their exchanges.

"From the draft?"

"Yeah. It was pretty boring for Mum and Soph after I got picked, but they were good sports about it, they know I like it," he smiled again. It was a self-conscious smile, but there was a quiet confidence there too.

"It's good to see who's coming up, where they're going," George replied.

"Yeah," Finn said with more enthusiasm than his previous comment. "That's what I reckon. Plus I know a lot of those guys."

"Draft class," George nodded along knowingly. "Scotty's my best mate and he still won't let me hear the end of getting number one over him that year."

Finn snorted a laugh, his body shaking and eyes shining. "He's got to be kidding."

George smiled. "You never know with Scotty. Have you got a place sorted yet?"

"Was gonna do it when I got there. Where are you based, if that's, sorry—

"Finn, you're probably gonna come round at some point and you can ask me anything. I got a place in Toorak."

"Isn't that like, hella fancy?"

George shrugged. "I guess, but it's mainly for privacy."

"I was thinking St Kilda, maybe Fitzroy," Finn said.

"That'll work," George said around a smile. "I'd go Fitzroy over St Kilda, more central, less problems." He wanted to tell Finn to get a place in Toorak, but that was stupid—young guys were better off amongst it, not tucked away in fancy suburbs behind electric gates and high walls.

"Mum's gonna come down and help me look, otherwise I'd ask you," Finn grinned.

George chuckled. "I suck at that stuff." It was true. He'd picked his house, but all the style in the place was Joq's. He'd probably live in a prison set-up if left to his own devices.

Finn looked off camera, still smiling, head nodding, something self-conscious in it. It wasn't that unusual—most rookies had some hero worship coming into the league, and George got the feeling he was reading more into the shyness than was actually there.

Still, he found himself saying, "But I'd be happy to help if your mum doesn't cut it."

Finn looked back at him, his smile out of control, his expression so animated. "I'll let her know she's got some competition then."

"You do that," he settled back in his chair, held the phone up. "It might be worth thinking about the travel times, so time it when you pick a place—the distance to the training paddock, the stadiums."

Finn nodded along. "Yeah, that's a good idea."

"You gonna be driving?"

"Probably not?"

"Hmm," George thought about it. "Lacy lives around Fitzroy, maybe look into getting lifts. I'll send you his number."

"Lacy always shows up?" Finn asked, surprised.

"Always, don't believe the media. He might be a party boy, but he never misses his nine to fives, not once," George said. He always felt an odd defensiveness around this. Probably because he'd been asked so many questions about it since Lacy got drafted.

"Oh, sorry, I didn't mean like…" Finn dropped his gaze, shook his head.

"No, I didn't mean. It's just, in general, don't believe the media, okay?"

Finn glanced up. George had a flashback to that fucking article, the feeling of pure terror when it came out and there was his nineteen-year-old face on a list with other athletes from around the world under the crass headline: *Are these guys gay and too afraid to come out?* He reckoned Finn was too young to remember that, even though the article had circulated a few times since then, inching closer to the mainstream every time, but then there was something in his look when he met George's eyes.

"Yeah, no I get it," Finn said. "I'm not like, you know, on the same level as you guys, I got my endorsements from the surfing but, yeah. Anyway, Soph's already banned me from reading comments on my socials and shit."

"Smart. Don't read that shit. Get yourself an inner circle and the team, that's it," George said firmly.

Finn nodded, his expression serious. "Will do."

They lapsed into silence and it should've been awkward, but it wasn't. George found himself drinking Finn in, and Finn seemed to be doing the same, his smile warm and open before he cracked up quietly.

"What?" George asked lightly.

"Nothin', just weird you know? Talking in person finally."

"Weird good?"

"Yeah, real good."

"Good."

Finn grinned. "So you got—

"George?" Joq called from downstairs.

George glanced away, fumbled the phone.

"Busy?"

"Ah, yeah, got a dinner," George smiled, it felt strained.

"Cool," Finn took it in stride.

George didn't want to hang up.

He got up, held the phone to his chest and called down the stairs. "Be there in a sec, just on the phone."

He clicked the door shut and brought the phone back. "I better go."

"Yeah, course," Finn tilted his head to the side, his smile easy on George. "Big super star life, eh?"

George scoffed. "Hardly, you'll see."

"Can't wait."

George reckoned he would soon enough. So why didn't he want to hang up?

"Hey, I mean it, call anytime, alright?"

Finn's smile widened, it was disarmingly shy. "Yeah?"

"Yeah, course. I'm gonna be your coach, I wanna know if anything's up with you."

Finn's smile dimmed, turned professional. "Yeah, course."

"I just mean—

"No, I get it, I get it. Gotta keep you in the loop."

"Yeah, but also," George sank back into his office chair, "it's a big transition and you're already news and I been there, so. Call if something's on your mind."

"Alright," Finn replied, nodding seriously and taking it to heart. "I will."

"Good," George said gruffly.

Finn laughed. They held eye contact and George didn't know what to do with it.

"Alright, I better."

"Yeah, course," Finn replied.

"I'll talk to you later?"

"Yeah, definitely."

"Okay," George said.

Finn laughed. "I'm not gonna hang up first."

George huffed. "Why not?"

"'Cos you're my coach," Finn replied, faux-seriously.

"Fair, alright. Later, Finn," he said.

"Bye, George," Finn grinned.

George ended the call, his smile out of control.

Jesus. He had a crush. On a nineteen-year-old rookie. Well, Finn would be twenty by the time he arrived, but that didn't make it any better. It was not good. Not good at all. He needed to get that under control and fast.

He got up, phone clenched in his hand and went out of his office.

"Joq?" he called as he came down the stairs.

"Out here," Joq called back.

George found him beside the pool. For a second he thought about telling him. Joq would tease him, laugh about it. And why not? It wasn't like they hadn't laughed about some of Joq's hook-ups, though George couldn't remember any being so young. Still, it wasn't like he hadn't seen the glint in Joq's eye after he'd clearly fucked some guy who'd rocked his world. It was fine. It was allowed.

"Wanna go out for dinner?" he heard himself asking instead.

"Yeah? Where you thinking?"

"Scotty was talking about that sushi place in Richmond, reckons he can get us a table if you want to try it?" he came over to him, slipped an arm around his shoulders where Joq was sitting at the patio table. He ran his hand along his neck in a caress. Joq leaned into it.

"Sounds good."

"Cool, I'm just gonna shower and change," George leaned down to kiss him.

Joq met him, surprised.

They fucked on the regular, a healthy amount George thought, and he was always tactile, but he guessed it'd been a while since he came over for a kiss, a real kiss.

He broke away. Joq looked up at him, his eyes opening, and smiled.

"Right, shower," George said and booked it for the house. He shot off a quick text to Scotty.

Joq huffed a laugh. "Take your time."

George didn't think that was a good idea. He felt like he needed to be around Joq. He needed to feel what they had. He couldn't understand what this need was. But he had a lot with the upcoming season and Joq was a great sounding board, so as he stripped off and got in, he focused on what he'd bring up at dinner.

4

♥

FINN TOOK GEORGE'S INVITE to call anytime at face value and called every few days. Being a footy player as well, he intuitively knew the best times to call; after nine at night being one of his favourite slots.

George had to fight the butterflies every time Finn's name flashed up on the screen.

He avoided telling Joq who it was.

"Team shit," he'd say as he left the living room, the bedroom, the back patio to go take the call in his office.

He was answering the call and clicking his door shut now, Finn's beaming face coming into view as he spoke.

"Flights are booked."

"Yeah?" George grinned. "When?" he asked as he kicked out his office chair and sat down.

"Fourteenth. Two weeks," Finn was smiling so hard, he was practically bursting with it.

"Fuckin' beauty," George replied and huffed a laugh. "God, it's gonna be a great season."

"Hmm," Finn said and glanced away. "Hey, can I talk to you about something?"

"Anything," George leaned back.

Finn didn't go on—he seemed nervous.

"Finn, you can talk to me about anything. I'm your coach, door's always open and all that," he said in what he hoped was a warm yet authoritative manner. He was working on it.

Finn nodded, twisted his lips to the side in what George had learned was the smile he gave before he delivered a line that would disarm George. That look scared and excited George in equal measure.

"Yeah, I know, but this might be like... I dunno, talking about something I might not talk to a coach about," he said.

George frowned. "You should be able to talk to your coach about anything."

"Including where I like to put my dick?" Finn quipped.

George got caught between a laugh and a choking sound. Before he could reply, Finn was on it.

"You reckon I could chat to old Kenny about that?"

He was referring to the veteran Sydney coach—three-time premiership winner as a player and then three as a coach up at Brisbane; he'd taken the mantle for the new Sydney side the year before and taken an interest in Finn, going up to his Sharks' games and working with him on his form. He was also at least eighty. Old school. Man of few words. A real pain in the ass on the media circuit according to the inside gossip when George went on the talking heads shows where Kenny gave nothing but clipped responses and pissed the presenters off no end.

"Yeah, maybe not," George managed.

He didn't know how to tell Finn maybe he shouldn't tell George about that either. But with the surprise fading he felt an odd irritation creeping in.

"Yeah, so," Finn glanced away. He was sitting on his bed in Byron, reclining on a pillow covered in bright tropical plant prints against black. Unlike George, who stuck to his office, Finn liked to move these conversations around—backyard, beach, lounge room—George had met his mum and sister briefly when they came in the room.

This was the first time George had seen him in bed though. He was shirtless, his hair mussed, but his eyes were nervous, scared even. That's what made George pull it together. Okay, players might not talk to coaches like Kenny about this, but he was going to be the kind of guy they could. Well, maybe not Lacy—he didn't want to know—but Finn, okay.

"Girl troubles?" he asked as evenly as he could. "If it's about moving down with you, I'd recommend taking it slow, seeing where you're at first."

Finn laughed, something disbelieving in it. "Uh, no. Not girls."

George waited.

Finn met his eyes, held his gaze. He was definitely nervous, but he was steady.

Oh.

"Guys," George supplied.

Finn looked over the top of his phone, jerked his chin and said. "Yeah," slowly. "You reckon that's alright?" he asked quietly, eyes fixed ahead.

"Yeah?"

Finn looked back. "Yeah?"

"Well, yeah, good."

Finn laughed. "Good?"

"You know what I mean," George huffed a laugh. "Jesus, rook, kinda throwing me a bit. But yeah, good. Good for you I mean."

"Good," Finn smiled shyly and looked down, his hand moving like he was picking at his bedspread. "I thought I was into girls, you know? I thought like, when the guys would talk about tits and shit, I was like, yeah, they're nice. But then I was at this beach party, just some kids from school and some other guys, some tourists, joined us. And like, this guy, he was super fucking hot and I kept, you know, looking at him?"

George nodded to let Finn know he was listening. He didn't know what to say. He was on the edge of his fucking seat.

"And well, anyway, stuff happened and we ended up alone on the jetty and he kissed me and I was like, oh, fuck yeah, this," he waved his hand around, eyes focused elsewhere like he was reliving the memory. He looked at George. "Sorry, is this too much?"

"No," George said firmly. It was making him feel conflicted—fucking elated, which was ridiculous, it's not like he was going to do anything with Finn, but he was also, shit, jealous? Who was this random dude? And when Finn said hot, how hot?

"Anyway, so yeah, not into girls," he rubbed the side of his nose.

"Well, that's not a problem, just uh," George wondered how to phrase it. He had a flashback to that awful article. To the first time it came out when he was nineteen, his shock then his fear. It was based on a rumour that was true; a truth accidentally spoken in a private conversation by Alistair's sister when gossiping ears were present in her hair salon. George had been with Alistair all through high school; it'd felt like the most natural thing in the world, going back to his place to fool around whenever they could. But after the article came out, he couldn't think of them without anything but shame, a kind of dirtiness tainted with regret.

"Just?" Finn asked, so trusting.

"Just, no one's out. So."

Finn shrugged. "Yeah, well."

"Are you planning to come out?" George felt a paralysing terror wash over him at the thought of it. He gripped his phone.

"Nah, not unless, you know," Finn smiled again. "I'm not really seeing anyone or anything, it's kinda not relevant at the moment? But I just wanted to tell you, so, you know."

'*Not unless, you know,*' what? George wanted to ask. Not unless Finn had a boyfriend? Was that what he was implying?

"What about you?" Finn asked.

"Huh?"

"You got someone?"

George shook his head 'no' in response; it was so ingrained by this point. He'd been with Joq for over a decade, but he had his reply to this question down. '*No, focused on footy at the moment.*' And to the ever-present: well, maybe you haven't met the right girl, yet? He'd reply, laughing: '*yeah, maybe.*'

But Finn nodded along, his smile widening. "Maybe now that you're retired? After footy you always said in interviews."

George huffed a surprised laugh, but of course Finn would've seen his interviews.

"Yeah, maybe," he rubbed the back of his neck. "Coaching is still footy."

Finn grinned. "Yeah, it is."

"Best to focus on the footy for as long as you can. A relationship could get in the way of that," he said a little too firmly. Alright, George, settle down.

Finn took it to heart though. "Yeah course, it's not like I got guys lining up round the block."

George scoffed and spoke without a filter. "I find that hard to believe."

Finn gave him the cheeky smile. "You'd be surprised. Soph says I'm 'unapproachable'" he added the scare quotes and laughed, "and I'm certainly not hooking up with the guys sending me dick pics in my DMs."

George choked out another laugh. "No," he managed, "I'd give those a miss."

Finn grinned, but he was blushing, his hand scratching his bare chest like he wasn't aware he was doing it.

"Feels good to tell someone in footy, someone on my team," he mumbled after a while.

"I bet," George replied. He didn't know. He couldn't imagine it. No one knew about him outside of Joq, his immediate family, Jack—ex-teammate, and the people from back home, his town, and the latter was in a vague, leave it alone kind of way.

"I'd like to have someone one day," he flicked his eyes up and met George's, something pointed in it. "When I was deciding on footy and surfing, it was kinda one of the reasons I was leaning towards surfing."

"There's no out surfers," George replied. He didn't think?

"Nah, I know, but it'd be the easier road, wouldn't it?"

George rubbed his chin and thought about it. "Maybe? Not as reliable financially unless you make it big time though."

"I woulda made it big time," Finn grinned.

George laughed. He liked that, the confidence—at this level, you've got to back yourself. Never at the expense of the team, but as part of the team.

"Why'd you go with footy?"

Finn tilted his head to the side and did that smile again. "I guess once I got on the track to be drafted and then it looked like I was gonna go to you guys, like, the scouts kept coming, I looked at you guys and thought," he shrugged and looked off camera, then directly into George's eyes again, "I thought 'that's where I was meant to be'."

"Yeah," George said gruffly. He cleared his throat. "It's getting late."

Finn looked sleepy. George was wired as fuck; he needed to go for a run or do some laps. He never wanted to hang up, which is why he knew he needed to hang up.

"Yeah, sorry, I keep bugging you," Finn smiled and sat up. The phone jostled with the movement and George got a sweeping view down Finn's chest, to the low slung boardshorts he was wearing, a glimpse of his dick against the material.

"No, you don't," George said roughly. He didn't know what was wrong with him. But he needed to get off the phone. "I just know you gotta get some sleep. I'd stay on here all night if you let me."

Finn laughed and righted the phone again. "Yeah?"

"Yep. So I better go."

"Okay."

Finn smiled sleepily and George huffed. Jesus Christ.

"Night, George," Finn said after a moment.

"Night, Finn," George replied and ended the call.

He gripped his phone and sat forward in his office chair.

Jesus Christ. So, Finn was gay. That was just... George barked out an incredulous laugh. He needed to do some laps.

He went downstairs. Joq had the TV on but he was reading a book.

"Hey," Joq said as George passed the room. "That took a while."

"Yeah," George waved his phone around. "I gotta burn off some energy."

Joq raised his eyebrows, dropped his book down. "Bad news?"

"Nah, just," George rubbed the back of his neck. "Team dynamics, usual shit."

He went down the hall before he could say more.

"I'm going to bed soon," Joq called after him.

"'Kay, see you in there," George yelled and went outside.

He stripped to his boxers and dove in. It was cold. Good. He needed to shock himself, wake up, calm down. Something.

5

♥

GEORGE WOKE UP BECAUSE something was buzzing. He rolled over and saw the screen of his phone lit up, watched it vibrate on his bedside table.

Joq groaned next to him. "Who is it?" he mumbled.

George rolled over and picked it up.

Finn.

It was almost one in the morning.

George panicked.

"Go back to sleep," he whispered to Joq. He yanked the phone out of the charger, went out of the room, and closed the door softly behind him before accepting the call.

"Finn?"

"Hey, sorry, sorry," Finn said, his breaths panicky.

"Shit, Finn, are you alright? What happened?" George asked as he went downstairs, then further down the next set of stairs to the games room near the garage, carefully closing each door behind him.

"Shit, sorry," Finn said again.

It was dark where ever Finn was. And he wasn't making eye contact; he was looking away, looking terrified.

"Finn," George said firmly. "Talk to me. What happened."

Finn sucked in a breath and looked at him. "I'm scared," he said softly. "I didn't know who to call. I shouldn't have called."

"You should always call," George insisted. He sat on the couch in his games room. "What are you scared about? Did something happen?"

Finn shook his head and looked down. He was sitting on the ground, the night black behind him, his bare knees up, the phone held between one hand while the other one gripped the wrist with the phone tightly.

"What if I'm not good enough?" he mumbled to his feet.

"Not good enough?" George asked bewildered. "You went number one for a reason. And you're killing it with the Sharks."

But Finn was shaking his head. George realised his hands were shaking.

George had gone number one as well—he remembered being nervous, but this looked like panic.

"I'm a fucking liability. My body, and my contract, shit," he shook his head. "Sorry. You don't need this shit—

"Yes, I do," George cut in firmly. "Look at me."

Finn glanced up, but dropped his gaze again quickly.

"Finn."

He looked up. "Sorry, I'm. Fuck, I'm so embarrassing."

"No, you're not," George watched him and smiled through a short huff. "You're fucking incredible and everyone worries about their body, everyone."

"Did you?"

"Ah, yeah, course, didn't you hear about that concussion? Thought it was all over, the fucking headaches. And don't even get me started on how worked up I used to get over the skinnies in those early years," George said and smiled at the memory. He was nowhere near in the league of Scotty when it came to the skinfold tests they did to measure body fat at preseason training—Scotty tubbed out every offseason and scored a hundred, which was shocking: the average player was fifty to sixty. George was always hovering in the top end at sixty—but the difference was, Scotty never worried about it, whereas George would score just above sixty and hyperventilate until the trainer told him, "Given your build, mate, a sixty is fine, good even." George didn't want to be good. He wanted to be perfect.

"I don't reckon you're gonna have any trouble in that department," he smiled pointedly and Finn laughed, which was George's intention.

"Yeah, my skinnies are always good, last one was thirty-nine, but like, my fucking groin. What if it keeps happening? What if I'm like an every-other-season player 'cos I gotta keep getting surgeries? And then what if other shit happens, which it will," Finn said, his face twisted.

"Okay, that's a lot of what ifs," George started, swallowing a little ways back on the thirty-nine in the skinnies—that was cut.

"Yeah, and then there's my play," Finn kept on before George could get it together to keep speaking. "What if I'm one of those guys whose only good in the farm team? What if I don't measure up against real players? I've already got bloody McCarthy from Brisbane tagging me on the regular and he says I'm a pansy ass who ain't gonna cut it in the league," Finn went on.

George shook his head. McCarthy was an old friend of his—came up on the Victorian country junior sides together—and he was an infamously good tagger for a reason.

"Finn, that's his job, to get in your head, throw you off your game, and you know that. Why're you letting him?"

Finn blew out a breath. "I know, but like," he glanced up, "what if he's right?"

"For fuck's sake," George said sharply. Finn raised his eyebrows. "I'm only gonna say this once, alright? And you're not gonna tell anyone else on the team I said it, alright?"

Finn nodded warily.

"You're the best fucking player I've ever seen. Hands down. You will go all-Australian, you will go down as a GOAT, I have no doubt in my mind."

"Come on, what if—

"If," George cut him off. "If you get out of your own way. It's all ahead of you if you want it. Maybe some injury ends your career early."

George crossed himself and Finn cracked a smile.

George went on. "You can't control that and you'll do something if that happens, maybe surf, it's not like you need to be all that tough to do that. Probably be good for your injuries."

Finn scoffed, his smile was widening though.

"Probably be good for your little pansy ass," George said with a grin.

Finn gave him a sarcastic look, but he couldn't hide the way his eyes were shining, the smile there. "Yeah? Tell that to Pipeline."

George smiled. He did not have the balls to surf, but rather than get into that he wanted to keep this thing on track. "What brought all this on?" he settled back.

Finn sobered and looked away.

"Did someone do something to you?" George sat back up and gripped his phone. He would fly up to Byron and clock them.

Finn shook his head, dropped his eyes again, his hair falling in his face, but George caught it when he mumbled. "Nah, nothing like that. It's embarrassing."

"Finn, I once called an official meeting with Waugh, remember when he was our coach?"

Finn peeked up and nodded.

"And formally told him he needed to take the captaincy off me 'cos I'd booted one out on the full in that week's game."

Finn smiled.

"Under pressure."

Finn giggled.

"Hard not to boot on the full under pressure," Finn said.

"No shit." Kicking the ball out of play while being mobbed by opposition players and creating a potential turnover was a stupid thing to do, but hard not to do in those circumstances.

"Whaddid Waugh say?"

"Told me to get the fuck out of his office."

Finn cracked up. George grinned.

Finn shook his head and looked to the side. "I was watching your last Grand Final."

George nodded. That'd been a good game, rough, lot of heat. He waited for Finn to go on. Finn didn't.

"And?"

Finn shook his head again. "I dunno, it was so physical and you were like, *so* good."

George felt embarrassed. He didn't remember that game like that—he was good, but it'd been a hot fucking mess, a contest from start to finish and once the adrenaline wore off, he hurt, everywhere.

"You're just as good," he replied.

"No, but like, the fights and shit," he looked at George. "I'd get taken out in the first minute and that'd be that."

"If someone takes you out like that, then they'll have seventeen other players gunning for their blood for the whole game, mark my words, and every team knows that."

Finn nodded.

"Finn, you're not on your own. You won't be on your own."

Finn nodded again, but his eyes looked glassy.

"What's this really about?" George asked. He felt like something was clicking into place.

"Nah," Finn smiled, but it was sad. "I'm just being stupid."

"Hmm. I don't reckon you are. I reckon this is all normal. Plus, unlike me, you've had to wait two years. Lotta time to worry," George said, but he had the feeling there was more to it.

"I should let you go back to bed," Finn said.

"Not until I know you're gonna be alright."

Finn sighed. "Yeah, thanks. Sorry."

"I'm gonna ban you from apologising to me," George said.

Finn opened his mouth, closed it, and smiled sheepishly. He looked unbearably cute with his charming, guilty face.

"Good," George said. "I wanna know you're alright before I hang up."

"It's one in the morning," Finn replied.

"No shit?" George raised an eyebrow and grinned.

"You've got shit to do tomorrow."

"So do you."

Finn shook his head. "I'm alright, seriously."

"I got nowhere to be right now. Tell me about your day, surfing?"

Finn smiled. "Nah, no swell plus not a lot of time with training."

"It's offseason, just gotta keep in shape."

Finn shook his head. "I been training proper."

"And you're worried? Do you know what Lacy is probably doing right now?"

"What?" Finn's expression cleared and he leaned in.

"I can't say for sure, but if I had to guess—he rolled out of the locker room when we finished the season into a sea of booze and parties and he'll ride that wave into the locker room for preseason. Last I heard, he was in Amsterdam, possibly Berlin."

Finn laughed. "Man, but he can play, eh?"

"Oh, yeah, great player, real head for the game. But he knows how to unwind."

Finn nodded like he got that he needed to get that.

"So what'd you work on today?" George asked

Finn tilted his head to the side. "You really wanna know?"

"I really wanna know."

"Okay," Finn smiled gratefully and then detailed his training program, his long, tan fingers moving into the shot as he got excited.

George settled in and listened, offering tips every now and then.

He could see the night turning light blue under the garage door by the time they hung up.

6

GEORGE HAD TO GO up to Sydney for a preseason weekend the league put on for coaches and management. It was, in theory, to celebrate and welcome the new Sydney side joining the league. In practice, George felt like it was a dick measuring contest under the pretence of social functions—dinners, watching a cricket match, meetings about rule changes.

And, as the youngest coach to take the mantle, and doing it from playing—without doing years as an assistant first—every other guy wanted to take his measure and remind him he was going to fall short. He caught the side-eyes, the incredulity at his presence in the odd handshake, the implication he was not meant to be there, he'd failed to do his time.

From everyone but Kenny.

George was standing at the buffet on the final night, his flight booked for later that evening—thank Christ—trying his best to avoid getting any more doubt into his mind by dealing with these assholes. It felt like a form of tagging—at least, that's what he was telling himself—and he was debating having a spring roll when he heard a scratchy voice behind him.

"Creed."

George turned. "Kenny."

Kenny extended his hand and George took it. Kenny didn't smile as he shook George's hand, but it was like he was smirking on the inside. He was ancient—maybe past eighty by now, pushing ninety even—and it showed in his wrinkled face, his white hair, his hand that felt like tissue paper. But he was still in great shape—tall and slim—and his eyes had an aliveness to them, a twinkle like he was peering into your soul when he smirked at you.

"Hear you're gettin' my boy Finn tomorrow," Kenny said and took his hand back. He glanced at George's plate. "Have the spring roll for fuck's sake, ya still training aren't ya?"

He was a perceptive old fucker too.

George huffed a laugh. He grabbed a spring roll and wiped the oil from his fingers on a napkin.

"Yeah, flying down tomorrow, presser in the afternoon."

"Good," Kenny said and made himself a plate of carrot and celery sticks, a slice of the low-fat quiche. He stared George down when he caught him looking but didn't explain himself.

George followed him when he moved away from the buffet to a little table.

"Don't worry about these assholes," Kenny said at the same time as George asked if he wanted him to get him a drink.

"I'll get my own drink after I eat," Kenny said and bit into a carrot stick.

"I'm not worried," George replied and sipped on his low-calorie beer.

"Yes, you are," Kenny shot back.

George fiddled with his collar. "Probably the normal amount for a new coach then."

"You got a good head for the game?" Kenny asked.

"Yeah, course."

"That was rhetorical, I know you do."

George nodded and smiled. He ate his spring roll.

"Anyway, I didn't seek you out to pump up your tyres, you don't need it. You're gettin' Finn."

"Yeah, lookin' forward to it, he's a hell of a player."

"Yeah, he is. One of the best natural abilities I've ever seen, and he's got a work ethic to rival anyone in the league. We wanted him, but you know how these things go," Kenny stared George down again.

"I don't reckon we're looking for a trade."

Kenny cracked a smile. "No shit. Not why I'm talking to ya."

George smiled. He knew that. His heart was beating a little faster talking about Finn.

"You met him yet?" Kenny asked.

"Not in person, we spoke on the phone." Bit of an understatement. They'd been texting for two years and speaking every few days for months.

Kenny grunted. "You might know it then, but I'm gonna tell you anyway. You're gonna think he's getting in his own head too much, getting in his own way."

George nodded. "Yeah, I noticed that."

"He's not," Kenny said and finished his quiche.

George waited for him to stop chewing.

"He's not?" George prompted as Kenny wiped his fingers on a napkin.

"It ain't him," Kenny looked up. "He's got all those, whaddya call it? Shit online."

"Socials?"

"Yeah, that dumbassery these kids do now. Got a lot of fans. Already got some endorsements from outside the league," Kenny went on.

George knew about those in an idle way. Finn was an up-and-coming superstar, and he'd had interest from the surfing world from a young age as well as football. It made sense he had endorsements. George just wasn't sure what they were and what Kenny's point was.

"Point is," Kenny went on and George was grateful for it, "he cops a bit of shit on there from assholes who live in their mother's basement. Kid takes it to heart. So," Kenny straightened, "I'm just giving you a heads up. Finnegan got more focus and talent than anyone we seen in this game since maybe yourself, Jack, few other kids, Lacy if he could get off the piss, but he lets shit from the outside get into his head and that's what'll tank him, not him."

George frowned. "Why doesn't he just not look at it?"

Kenny cackled. "Who you been playin' with lately, son? I can't even get my grandkids to put those fucking things away in church."

George laughed. He didn't have any socials and he had an iron will about not looking at any media because of that article—he'd given himself a rule early on and stuck to it since. He really didn't want to know.

"I reckon that's part of the problem. So, if he's spiralling, I'd ban him from it for a week, get his head clear."

"Alright, thanks," George said.

Kenny grunted and went to move away.

"What's the other part?"

Kenny looked over his shoulder and grinned. "I reckon that's the kind of shit like we used to say in the navy—don't ask, 'cos it ain't none of your goddamn business."

And then he was wandering over to loom into a conversation with Selly and Wagner—Victorian coaches—and George watched as they turned self-conscious in whatever they'd been going on about.

George drained his beer and tapped his phone. He'd be early, but he figured he might as well head to the airport. Aside from that nugget of intel from Kenny, this trip had been nothing but a head fuck and a pain in the ass.

Joq's phone rang out. George looked at his screensaver—him and his sister at the Brownlow's the year before, her beaming face and George trying to hold back his grin after he told her to settle the fuck down, it was just the Brownlow's—absolute pain in the ass for most guys because you had to sit there all night and behave while there was the world's most open bar. But Cara loved it, loved getting a night out away from the kids and 'the old ball and chain' as she called Barry; always with a wink, an ass tap. George was happy she'd found someone so perfect for her.

The screen went dark and George contemplated calling Finn. It wasn't that late and George knew Finn would be up, but he was flying down tomorrow. He probably had family stuff. A going away party, though he hadn't mentioned anything. He could be all up in his head like Kenny said.

George was tapping out a text—*Busy?*—and about to hit send when his phone rang in his hand. Joq.

George answered it. "Hey."

"Hey, thought you'd be in the air by now?" Joq asked, tinny and breathless down the line.

"Delayed," George replied, looking out at the tunnel leading to no plane.

"You wanna talk—

"Sorry, you're busy," George rushed out—the panting, of course Joq was hooking up. He always did when George went away. It gave him a rush of the usual mixed feelings—horny, obviously, Joq had given him enough explicit details over the years and George had fucked him about it enough times now it was a hair trigger; but it made him feel an odd shame, which was a feeling he never examined; and finally, a gruff desire not to discuss it unless it was in the foreplay way in the bedroom.

"Nah, just a hook up," Joq said as he caught his breath.

"Any good?" George asked kind of shyly, kind of like he always did. This was the play.

"You know I don't kiss and tell." George could hear the smile in Joq's voice.

He snorted. "Since when?"

"Since I'm still lookin' at the guy's ass," Joq quipped and George shut down.

"I'll let you go then," he replied. He didn't want someone overhearing him, getting any hint of who was on the other end of the line. Joq met guys through an app for fuck's sake—there was no trust there.

"I'm kidding. What's up?"

"Nothin', just delayed," George replied, he wanted to get off the phone.

"Hmm," Joq said, his breathing more even. "You're nervous."

"I'll talk to you when I get back," George got up and stood at the window, watched a plane land.

"He doesn't know who I'm talking to."

"Joq, don't," George hated even the thought of risking it.

"Fine, I'll talk in code. You meet him yet?"

George breathed steadily. He was nervous about tomorrow. He'd called to talk about anything else, anything to deal with the nerves. But Joq knew him and he trusted Joq; he wasn't going to say anything to some random guy and George felt like a balloon needed to burst inside him, he felt like he needed to speak to a friendly voice after a weekend of tension and competitiveness.

"Tomorrow," George said. "I don't envy him." He thought about what Kenny said, about all the media attention, management meetings about their incoming superstar and using his image for the good of the club—which was code for, how can we milk this guy's magnetic social capital? All of this before Finn had even joined the team. George might not have socials, and he might avoid the footy news as much as possible, but he wasn't living under a rock. He knew Finn was being scrutinised as the second coming and that kind of chatter came with a terrible fear—everyone pumping you up before you'd even played a game? Well, it took a special kind of headspace to not let the imposter syndrome get to you. Add to that the other attention he got for his looks, his body, his bankable 'image' and he was under a lot more pressure than guys back in George's day.

"Babe, come on, it's different now—

"It's worse," George snapped because Joq had no idea what Finn was about to be put through.

And it certainly wasn't right of him to put that on Joq.

A plane was being fixed to the tunnel. "We're boarding. I'll see you at home." He ended the call before Joq could say anything else and pocketed his phone.

Well, that call made him feel like shit. He didn't understand why—he and Joq were good, solid, and Joq knew better than anyone George could be abrupt if he didn't want to discuss something, if he couldn't put his feelings into words.

And besides, Joq really was busy; knowing him, he'd fuck the guy again before meeting George at home. It was good, that Joq had that; aside from anything else, George didn't bottom, and while Joq liked both, George knew from the way he talked he really enjoyed giving it to someone as well.

George felt that hair-trigger tingle again and thought of Finn. He wondered for a second if Finn was a bottom. He had the height and build for a top, but there was something in the unexpected shyness, the way he'd drop his gaze and look up at George through the fall of his hair.

And okay, George, he said to himself. *Not fucking going there.*

The call for first class came through the PA and he made his way to the attendant, flashed his boarding pass and gave a media approved grin to the guy when he said, "Mr Creed, welcome aboard, if you need anything, you let me know."

As he buckled his seatbelt and accepted the water from the star-struck attendant, he ordered his mind to stop thinking about Finn in any context beyond a player. George had an iron will, he had control of his mind. People thought it was talent that'd made him the player he was. It wasn't. It was this. He decided what he thought about. He decided what he felt. He was in control.

7

♥

As GEORGE SHOOK HIS hand out and tucked it into his suit pocket, he thought again how he wished he'd been able to meet Finn in person privately first. But here he was—in the wide corridor under the stadium, milling around with management, his two assistants—Kurt the Cruncher, fitness expert, and Todd the Tactician for tactics—as they waited for Finn to arrive.

Ally from PR and their President, Jim, lifted their heads to the side and looked to the glass doors leading into the corridor at the same time. Ally actually smiled—showing her little teeth—and Jim straightened, his beanpole figure stringing taut, his smile an effusive grin.

George couldn't see through the doors from where he was standing, but he sucked in a quick breath, took his hand out of his pocket and shook it just as the door swung open—Jim was pulling it as Finn pushed on it from the other side.

George's first thought was *He's bigger in person—tall, built, but not as built as he's going to get.*

His second thought was: *Sunshine.* A stupid thought, but it was the best way to explain what he was seeing—the sun-bleached hair from surfing, the tan, but more than that was the instant warmth in the room when he appeared in it. He immediately knew why Finn was getting endorsements—he was charisma in a bottle.

Finn was shaking Jim's hand, smiling politely, lifting his head as soon as—George could tell—was polite to look around.

It was ridiculous, but when Finn's gaze landed on him, his smile turning to a full-blown grin, George felt his heart pound and his face stretch to return the smile. Finn broke the look and went back to shake the hands of several board members, to greet Ally, to quickly pump Todd's hand, his eyes drifting to George again as he said, "Looking forward to what you got in store for me."

"Gonna put you at half-back, feeding to Lacy first," Todd was saying.

"Oh, sweet," Finn looked back to Todd, then turned fully to George.

"Finn," George said and it sounded deeper than usual, like George had something caught in his throat.

Finn laughed, delighted like he couldn't help himself, and he beamed as he took George's outstretched hand. "George."

Finn's palm was warm and firm, and George felt electric, distracted, by the feel of their skin touching.

"Finally," George said without thinking.

"Finally," Finn replied, still grinning and watching him so completely, his eyes were fixed on George's like he was trying to peer right into him, and George watched him right back as if to say, *look all you want, I hope it measures up.*

"Right, shall we get this show on the road," Jim came over and clapped George on the back.

George let Finn's hand go and turned to Jim.

"You two at centre, George, you know the drill, and Finn?"

Finn turned to him, but he stayed close, his body a line of warmth at George's side.

"They're gonna ask about the injury, pester you a bit about being a disappointment as our first choice since you're only now arriving."

George tensed. Fuck them if they said that, he'd like to see any one of these geezers play a game of professional football.

"Yeah, no worries, I've been expecting it, all good," Finn replied.

"Right," Jim smiled, relieved and kind. He clapped his hands together and led them out.

Finn stayed right beside George and just before they stepped into the room, into the noise of a bustle of reporters and cameras, he leaned closer to whisper, "Do you think I can tell them to go fuck themselves?"

George cracked up, and he turned to look at Finn grinning back at him.

"Maybe not just yet," George said under his breath as they stepped into the room. "Save it for the game, say it with your play."

"Roger that," Finn winked and George watched as he donned what George recognised as the media personality—welcoming but guarded.

George followed him to the table and sat to his left. He leaned forward and cracked his water bottle, took a drink as Finn leaned back beside him. George was used to this as captain, but this was his first time as a coach. He sipped the water, focused on the feel of it wetting his dry mouth, soothing his throat. He focused on the feel of the grooves in the lid as he screwed it back onto the bottle. He straightened his spine, clasped his hands and looked out at the room, kept his face carefully blank.

Ally turned on her microphone at the lectern to the side of the table, the noise giving a short crackle into the room; it worked like a signal and the chatter died down, the eyes that were already forward and on them flicking to her, then back to them—assessing, categorising, turning them into headlines and words on a page.

Ally was small, plump, probably late twenties with small teeth and a large forehead; okay at her job, physically unimpressive with her limp black hair and pasty skin; and yet she scared the shit out of everyone on the team with her foreboding presence. But right now, she was absolutely beaming. It was so incongruous to how she normally seemed and George deduced it was Finn; Finn was so likeable even scary-Goth-Ally was smiling.

She began with introductions, some quick remarks about the team's excitement for the season, and a few pointers about what was off limits. George focused on her voice—friendly, yet kind of mean—and breathed deep through his nose.

A slight tap on his thigh forced him to glance back. Finn was watching him—leaning back in his chair, casual as you like, his full lips smiling closed-mouthed. George quirked his lips in return and had to stop it from turning into something more.

Jim was talking now: his excitement for the season; his hopes now they had a fresh young coach who loved this team, knew this team, knew the game; the addition of Finn, who was the missing piece they needed.

And then the questions began.

Soft at first. How George was feeling. How Finn was feeling. How was the offseason?

"Will you be heading to Bells, Finn?" the reporter from *The Herald* asked. Cameron. George liked him—he always stayed on the game, never went into gossip, and he seemed genuinely interested in the players as people. George was also pretty sure he was gay, which made no difference either way, but sometimes George got the feeling he knew George was too.

Finn laughed at the question and sat forward. "I'll get the footy schedule sorted first, but yeah, I reckon if there's a big swell and it's my day off, well, pretty hard to resist that call."

"Do you worry about further injury if you continue to pursue big wave surfing though?" the reporter from *The Sun* cut in. George hated this guy. He was the opposite of Cameron—every question was really a headline waiting to happen if the player said the wrong thing. Jack had been particularly bad at getting caught out by him, and Jack was the most well-behaved, innocent player they had. Lacy, on the other hand, never gave the guy so much as an inch of ink, and he was the complete opposite of Jack.

"Well, it's not like I'm planning to surf Nazaré and if I'm unlucky enough to get taken by a shark, I reckon I'm going to have bigger problems than whether or not I can play footy," Finn replied laconically.

"Like being dead," George said and stared at the guy.

Finn cracked up. George glanced at him. "Yeah, that," he said and whacked George on the thigh again. George held eye contact, felt a flush of warmth at finally being with Finn in person, before remembering where he was.

The questions moved on to actual play, the plan, and George fielded those with Todd and Kurt. Then the wanker from *The Sun* launched into Finn about being "injury-prone", but Finn took it all gracefully and seriously, basically explaining that the surgery had worked, the rehab had worked, he was as good as new.

"I think he's gonna surprise you all," George answered the next question directed at Finn because fuck this guy, seriously. "He's certainly better than me, got a better head for this sh-... stuff as well..." George smiled at the slip up, but made sure he stared the guy down. He felt Finn laughing beside him and glanced back, shot him a smile.

"Yes, about you," one of the guys from the talking heads footy show said, "There's been a lot of talk about whether or not you're ready for this. Care to comment?"

George focused on the guy and delivered the line he'd been practicing. "I understand and appreciate the concern, I do, and I get this is an honour and a privilege to get the coaching gig straight out of playing, but I love this team and I will do my best by them. I will not waste this opportunity, mark my words."

"Plus, he knows the guys, the team, better than anyone," Finn piped up and George glanced back at him; Finn was focused on the reporter, his gaze steady, and with his hair sticking up everywhere he appeared the perfect picture of relaxation. "The way I see it, that can only be an advantage, to already have the room."

Jim cut in with his defence of their choice and George focused on him. He felt warmed through at Finn defending him and he was right—George did have the room.

"So you two just met this week?" George's favourite reporter asked.

"In person, yeah," Finn answered for them. George met his eyes again and Finn watched him as he went on. "But we been facetiming for a while now, texting, that kind of thing."

George nodded. "Yeah," he refocused on the room; he needed to frame this as what it was—a captain then a coach welcoming a new player, nothing sketchy in it. "I reached out after the draft, then again after he got the call up and we kept in touch. Thought I could offer a few pointers."

Finn tapped him again and George couldn't help himself—he shot him a grin.

"A few pointers, he says," Finn finally sat up as he laughed. "Think he was more worried about all this than me."

George had to speak around his smile. "Hey now, it's a lot of pressure and I didn't hear you complaining when you called at midnight with every panicked thought a man can have."

"That was one time!" Finn exclaimed around his laughter.

"Anyway," George cleared his throat and made his face blank—this was all feeling a lot like flirting; he needed to get it back on track, it was about the footy. "It's been good to finally meet in person, see what I'm dealing with."

He felt Finn's hand on him again and at this rate, George was going to have the warmth from it burned into his skin and his face stuck in a blinding smile. At least Finn was grinning too.

Thankfully, they moved on to how the team was planning to use Finn, and that he could answer; that, he was really excited about.

By the time they were stepping back into the hallway after the presser, George was relieved and elated.

"That went well," Jim said, smiling at George and then Finn. "Really well, good job, guys."

"That jerk from *The Sun*," George said, "as if he could play a game of footy, who's he think he is questioning Finn's athleticism?"

Jim gave him a wry smile. "You know he's gotta do anything to sell a paper, even make it up if that's what it takes."

"Yeah," George looked at Finn who was already watching him back—they were of a height and he was close; not so close as to be awkward, but about as close as he could be without it being odd and George liked it, liked the feel of him beside him. "You don't listen to that bullshit, alright?"

Finn quirked his lips. "Got it, coach."

George smirked. "Come on, let's meet the team—I know they been dying to meet you."

Finn's smile widened, showing teeth. He tucked his hands into his pockets. "Lead the way."

They stepped into the tunnel.

"Maybe we should add surfing to the fitness regime," Kurt said, deadpan.

"Yeah, head on down to Bells in a storm, send all the guys out, film it," Todd replied equally dry.

"Post it on the socials," Jim said seriously.

Finn started laughing and George grinned at him as they walked side by side.

"Guys, please don't make my life harder," Ally said, but it was clear she was trying to repress a giggle.

"I don't know, Ally," Jim replied, "think of the visuals."

"Can you imagine George on a board?" Todd asked.

"Hey now, I can learn," George replied.

"You're way too chunky," Kurt said.

Finn cracked up.

"I'm in great shape!" George defended himself. He was. He was just solid; not an ounce of fat on him, but he was always going to be a wall of muscle, not the cut lines of Finn.

"Yeah, you are," Finn laughed. "It's great cardio."

George was smiling at him, his head slanted to watch as Finn extolled the virtues of surfing for fitness. He was so focused they were practically on top of Joq by the time George noticed he was there.

"Joq," he said, surprised. He felt embarrassed, like he was doing something wrong. But he wasn't. He was sure of it.

"George," Joq replied, cool as always, looking good in his black suit, his Nordic features calm. And yet George could see the smile he was repressing.

"This is Joaquin, Joq," George explained to Finn as Finn stayed by his side while everyone else kept moving. "Runs surveillance in the stadium."

"And you must be the great Finnegan Flynn," Joq said and extended his hand.

Finn huffed, but he was smiling as he took Joq's hand. "It's Finn," he flicked his eyes to George, back to Joq, then to his dress shoes.

"Your parents called you Finn Flynn?" Joq asked as he pumped Finn's hand.

"Yeah, they're assholes," Finn replied around a shy smile and dropped his head.

George felt Joq sizing him up; he knew Joq was damn good at assessing character, at reading people. He didn't understand why it made him feel uncomfortable.

"We better keep moving," he said to head that off. Joq raised a subtle eyebrow at him; George gave him a quick, gruff smile—a blink and you'll miss it exchange between them.

"Yeah, yeah, course," Finn said. "Nice to meet you, Joq. See you round?"

George knew the question was polite, but Finn still giggled when Joq replied: "You'll find me lurking in the shadows, yeah."

Joq's face broke into a real smile; George was both glad and nervous to see it.

It was always awkward seeing Joq in public. He was used to it—the awkwardness—and they both knew how to play it, but on this occasion, it felt more like the nerves of ten years ago, minus the thrill.

"Alright," he said and placed his hand on Finn's low back and made a subtle gesture to get them moving. "Time to face the team. Later, Joq."

"George. See you later," Joq said from behind them.

"Alright, game face, rook, they ain't gonna go easy on you," he said close to Finn's ear.

Finn grinned at him just as they pushed the locker doors open.

Every head swung their way as George held the door open for Finn to enter, let it clang shut as he stepped in behind him.

"Look at this fuckin' superstar," Lacy said and a few guys cracked up.

"Finn," George said then looked around the room—everyone was there, getting dressed in training gear, standing in front of their lockers or sitting on the floor and stretching —"these are the shit cunts you'll call team mates."

Finn cracked up and George got a few laughs and boos.

"Nice suit," Cary said to George. They'd started a year apart; Cary was a brilliant ruckman in Scotty's absence, and he showed no signs of retiring.

"Ah, shut it," George said and guided Finn to his locker. "Here. Settle in. Get changed. I'll see you out there in twenty."

George reluctantly left him to it. He had to shake that off because he was here to do a job—probably the most important job he'd ever have and he had a wall of doubters and haters he needed to knock down. He should've been focused on that, not the soft drawl of his superstar rookie as he answered a few well-meaning sledges.

He left them to it to go change and thought about making some time after practice to chat with Finn, make sure he was settled in okay, that the search for a place was going okay. He pulled out his phone and texted Joq not to wait—he'd get Kurt to drop him later—but his phone buzzed immediately. Joq was going to wait. And well, that was probably for the best.

George was sitting in his office—which was still surreal to think about, to be on this side of the desk, but he figured it would grow old eventually—and the feeling of exhilaration from the training session with Finn on the team was still coursing through him. He needed to write down his thoughts immediately. It was never a good idea to build an entire team around a single player—for obvious reasons; if you lost that player you were fucked—and he had no intention of doing that. His motto was simple: team first, individual second. But watching Finn, streaking past defenders; seeming nonchalant but then finding another gear; leaping and using Cary's back to launch himself up and take the mark, well, it was hard not to feel inspired.

He was jotting down his thoughts for the upcoming team meeting, trying to remember a quote about the diggers in Gallipoli when a soft knock on his open door made his head swing up.

"Sorry," Finn said around a soft smile.

"What've I said about apologising to me?" George sat up, then stood. "You good? Come in, come in."

Finn shuffled into the room, stuffed his hands in the pockets of his soft looking black tracksuit pants, his smile turning shy. "You're not busy?"

"Never too busy to talk to a player," George reassured.

Finn came to stand in front of the desk, tilted his head to look at George's open notebook. "Game plan?"

"Pep talk," George replied.

"Yeah?"

"Yeah," George tapped the page for something to do. "I've got a team of great players, but I need a great team. And it's my job to see it and then make you lot see it too."

"Hmm," Finn looked up without moving his head from being tilted down; it made his eyes seem bigger, his little smile seem sly; his tan skin smooth but creasing slightly with the movement as he looked directly at George. "Like an army."

George grinned. "Exactly. You want to sit?"

"I don't want to disturb you if you're on a roll," Finn straightened, flexed his fingers in his pockets.

"Nah," George waved at the seat, "I was just getting started, sit."

George sat and watched Finn do the same across from him, his hands still tucked in his pockets, his smile endearingly shy again.

"So, what's up?" George asked, keeping it professional.

Finn looked at him, tilted his head to the side again, then shook it. "Nothing, just, haven't had you to myself yet and," he glanced away, blew out a breath like he was embarrassed, "I guess I just wanted to say hi," he looked back at George and pulled his hands out and fiddled with his pant leg, looked at it, "which actually sounds pretty stupid now I'm here saying it."

"Not at all, I know what you mean," George sat forward and rested his elbows on the desk. "I was kinda hoping, well, thinking, this morning, it would've been better if we met before the press conference."

"Yeah?" Finn looked up. "Same."

George grinned at him. "So, hi Finn, I'm George, your new head coach."

Finn laughed. "Nice to meet you, George, I'm Finn, your new half-back."

They watched each other for a moment, smiling, and it was awkward but it wasn't—it was... it felt... good. George liked being in the same room, he liked being around Finn.

"So what you got so far?" Finn said as George asked, "You find a place yet?"

They laughed and Finn answered, "Yeah, Mum's set on a place in Fitzroy. Les offered to get a place with me, which," Finn leaned back and ran a hand through his hair, "I can see the appeal, but I dunno," he looked at George, "kinda want my own space for a change."

"Yeah, I get that, I did that at first too, then got a place with Scotty for half a season"—after that article came out, he didn't mention—"and then I bought my place"—and he also didn't mention because he and Joq decided to get serious and move in together.

"Better living alone?" Finn asked, still smiling.

George had to pause for a second. Of course everyone assumed he lived alone. It's not like he lived in a heavily trafficked area and no one was actually stalking his place, and his neighbours were as wealthy and private as he was—no one noticed or cared he lived with Joq, that he had been living with him for a long time.

"Yeah," he said after a beat.

A question flashed in Finn's expression, like he noticed the hesitation, but all he said was, "I don't reckon I'll last, I love company too much, but I figured I should do it at least once."

"Yeah," George readily agreed to change the subject, "you can always room with one of the guys down the track."

"Or move in with my boyfriend," Finn replied.

George startled. He hid it—he was sure he hid it—but he was shocked by Finn talking so openly about something like that. And what boyfriend?

"So you seeing someone then?" he recovered and asked as neutrally as possible.

"Nah," Finn smiled and watched George closely. "Not yet, I just mean," he shrugged and looked at his leg again, picked at his pants, "if it happens."

George jerked his chin in acknowledgement. He knew he needed to say something supportive, but the words wouldn't come. Finn looked nervous.

"Anyway, sorry," Finn went to stand, "Soph's always telling me I'm a classic for too much information, you're busy."

"No," George shook his head, "I think it's great, I'm just..."

Finn was half out of his chair, but he was waiting patiently on what George was about to say.

George needed to get it the fuck together. "I'm just not used to anyone being so open about it around here," he smiled warmly, re-assuringly. "It's good. You're good. Everything's good."

Finn huffed a laugh. "Good."

George blew out a breath. Christ, sometimes talking with Finn was like doing a really intense workout—he felt it, he had to concentrate so he didn't fuck up, and he was just, all there.

"So, you got a particular army you want to use to inspire us?" Finn asked.

George smiled and hoped the smile hid his gratitude at the subject change—if Finn was going to talk so openly about being gay, George needed to go away and do some preparation for that.

"Viet Cong," George said. "Hoping to organise the team preseason trip there for next year."

"Yeah?"

"Yeah, so maybe I'll save it 'til then and talk about something to do with Gallipoli," George picked up his pen and tapped the pad.

"Heavy," Finn smiled over at him.

"Too heavy?"

Finn sat up like he knew George was really asking and George got the feeling he liked it.

"Maybe? Like, I get it, you want us to have each other's backs, yeah?"

"Yeah," George nodded along, "and if one goes down—

"We all go down."

"Yeah. Too cliched?"

Finn tilted his head. "No, it's good," he said slowly. "Like, 'cos I surfed too, I get it, it's totally different—that's all you, just you and the wave, like, nature and you," he laughed at himself, "I'm making no sense."

"No, I get it. You're competing against yourself."

"Yeah," Finn brightened. "Whereas footy, it's about the guys, it's about us as a group."

"Do you like it better than surfing?"

Finn squinted like he was there—the ocean, the oval—"I like both for different reasons. But I reckon one of the best parts of footy is you're not alone. Going for something on your own, it being all on you? That's awesome and like, fulfilling in a deep way, like, something in your heart that's like, all yours, it feels good," he smiled sheepishly. "Does that sound too gay?"

George laughed. "Well, you are gay, so..."

Finn grinned and thankfully took it as the joke it was intended to be.

"But no, I get it, that's like training on your own," George went on.

"Yeah, whereas with footy, it's about everyone stepping up and sometimes you gotta sacrifice your glory for what'll make the team win."

George jotted that down. "So, maybe I need something less heavy that says that to start."

"Yeah, like, freedom marches and shit," Finn rubbed his nose, scrunched his face up and looked away. "Maybe too battle-like. I'll think about it."

George huffed. "I think I just hijacked your coach talk."

"Nah, I came in to get to talk in person, so, success."

"Yeah," George replied. "You got dinner plans?"

Finn's smile dimmed. "Yeah, Mum's here, but maybe—"

"Oh, no, of course," George stood. "You should spend time with your mum before she goes back home."

Finn stood as well; he fidgeted with the drawstring on his pants and looked flustered. "But do you wanna maybe, some other time?" He flicked his eyes up. "With me?"

And was he asking to get dinner? Or was he asking to go out-out? Like a date?

George swallowed. He absolutely could not go on a date with Finn for a million reasons, but a hysterical thrill went through him at the thought of it: he wanted to say yes.

"I'd like to do this again," he started.

"Yeah, for sure," Finn backed up towards the door; he was blushing and looking anywhere but at George. "I better go, Mum's waiting," he tripped on nothing, turned around and called over his shoulder, "Okay, yep, later, bye!"

George was left standing in the empty office, his heart pounding and his body tingling with nerves. Did Finn know he was gay? George wasn't stupid—he knew all their texts and calls were, well, not flirting, but it was clear they got along, liked being around each other. It was like when you meet a new guy on the team and you just click. But it was a leap to go from that to dating, to assuming someone was

gay. But maybe Finn knew about the article and he was interpreting this friendship—yes, George reassured himself, this was
a friendship, maybe skirting the edge of what was appropriate
between a coach and a player for friendship, but still a friendship—maybe he was interpreting it as something more?

He sat back down. The thought of Finn maybe trying to ask
him out—if he hadn't been in the room for that, he'd think it was
preposterous. In fact, it was. That hadn't just happened.

'*Hero worship*,' Scotty always used to say sagely when one of
the new guys got flustered talking to George for the first time and
George was left bewildered.

Of course. George laughed, embarrassed. As if someone like
Finn—Christ, gorgeous and kind Finn, who was unexpectedly shy
in one-on-one conversation, which made for such an endearing
contrast to his competent presence on the footy field—as if he
would be asking out an old has-been like George. Shit, George was
a decade older than him. Retired. Boring. He wasn't ashamed of
his one-track mind, but he was who he was.

He shook his head and stood.

He'd probably missed Joq. He'd get a car.

He needed some time to think, to get his head clear before he
got home.

George stepped out of the building into a fine mist of rain, which
was a welcome relief in December and typical of Melbourne.

He saw Joq standing by the sole car in the parking lot and felt relieved. Joq smiled as George walked over and something in the familiarity made him feel settled in a way he hadn't expected—he thought he needed time to himself, but this is what he needed; a reminder that he had someone, that he didn't need to be getting flustered over a twenty-year-old rookie for fuck's sake.

"You didn't have to wait," he said as he came up to the car.

"Just finished myself. I told you," Joq replied and unlocked the car.

George grunted to hide his relief. He got in and sank into the comfort of Joq's car seat, let the trance music flow over him as he gazed out the window at the city whipping by. He thought about the training, how everyone looked coming back from the offseason. He thought about it to avoid thinking about Finn and the buzz under his skin from being around him. It was weird, but being around him, and then not, felt like withdrawing.

But he had a team to coach and three big holes to fill: Jack going back to Fremantle still needed to be dealt with, leaving a hole with the player getting on ball out of the ruck and down forward—Finn would fill that role. And now he was thinking about Finn again. The ruck, Cary was solid, so Scotty leaving wasn't a problem, but they'd need a back-up—

"I saw your press conference," Joq said suddenly. George stilled in his thoughts and his body. He felt like that was private, which was a ludicrous thing to think—how could a filmed press conference for television and the internet be private?

"Yeah?" he asked after a while; might as well get the conversation over with—he looked at Joq's profile. He was focused on the road, his face calm like he was just making conversation because of course he was.

"Not all of it," Joq glanced at him. "What?"

George shook his head. "Nothin', just the usual bullshit." He didn't want to discuss Finn if he could avoid it.

"So, Finn seems alright," Joq said as he pulled up to the gate.

George grunted and focused on the gate; if he didn't engage, Joq would drop it.

"What?" Joq asked as the gate rolled open slower than usual—it was the same, but it felt slower, maybe George should call the gate people and get it checked out. "You seemed to like him," Joq went on.

"Course I like him, he's on the team," George replied and focused out the window.

Joq cracked up and George whipped his head around to look at him. Joq was losing it—and George read everything he needed to know into that laugh, into the way Joq was looking at him knowingly.

George frowned, but his smile was taking over; shit, but it was embarrassing.

"Oh my God!" Joq exclaimed. "Old man's got a crush!"

"Can you just park the car?" George shook his head and continued to try and hide his smile.

"You do," Joq whistled and parked the car. "Pity he's too young. And he's one of your players. Oh, and you never fuck around."

"Yeah," George unclipped his seatbelt and mentally added that it was also a pity there was no way in hell this crush would be reciprocated and even if it was—fucking around with a twenty-year-old player on his team? That crossed so many lines, just the thought of bringing that into his carefully-ordered world made him anxious.

Still, he could see it through Joq's eyes—as someone able to fuck around on the regular, able to measure other guys as potential fucks? Yeah, Finn was about as close to the dream as it got. It was nice to think about it like that, to share it with Joq in a never-going-to-happen fantasy way.

George leaned back into the car and smirked at Joq. "More's the pity," he said as he leaned over the console to kiss him.

He felt Joq's smile against his lips and George realised he was in the mood for a nice, hard fuck.

His arousal simmered all through their late dinner, as they got ready for bed, and by the time George was sliding in next to Joq he couldn't hold back—he braced himself over him, kissed him roughly and raced through getting Joq ready, rolling him onto his hands and knees and slicking his dick up with lube.

He pushed to the hilt in one thrust, his hands gripping Joq's hips tightly. He pulled out all the way and slammed back in and groaned at how fucking good it felt. He was so keyed up, he felt it everywhere, he started slamming into Joq so hard Joq slipped to his elbows. George tightened his grip and pounded him harder, let his eyes slip closed and lost himself to the incredible feeling, his breathing rough. The tightness around his dick was incredible, the waves of pleasure as he pounded roughly into that wet heat tingled up his body and his mind flashed to an image of Finn in the locker room after training—shirt-less, smiling good-naturedly yet bashfully at the teasing from the guys. George groaned and fucked Joq harder. He felt it when Joq started jerking himself off and that ratcheted it up for him, the thought of him taking his pleasure from the pounding.

"Yeah, get yourself off, baby," slipped out.

He felt Joq tightening up around his dick and yanked him back against his groin, really gave it to him as he chased his orgasm, the thought of Finn getting twisted up in his mind as he kept going, as he felt it rushing from his groin through his whole body.

His orgasm ripped through him and he rode it out, slamming in as deep as he could go, groaning loudly. He pulled out, ran a hand over Joq's back and fell back. Between one panting breath and the next, one guilty thought of what he'd been thinking about—Finn, violating him like that in his mind—he passed out.

8

♥

GEORGE WOKE UP AND it was still dark. He rolled his head on the pillow. 3:32. He was wide awake. He thought about Finn. He thought about fucking Joq the night before. He felt embarrassed. He slipped out of bed and went to the shower. They had beach training at 5:00, but a quick thirty-minute run on his own would do him good.

Joq stirred and groaned as George came back and got dressed. George leaned down, planted his hand beside Joq's hip.

"Go back to sleep," he whispered.

"Where you goin'?" Joq asked sleepily.

"Training," George said and kissed the top of his head—he needed to get out of there; he felt self-conscious, thinking about the way he'd fucked Joq the night before.

He went to pull away, but Joq grabbed him by the collar and kissed him for real.

George huffed but allowed it; when Joq tried to deepen it, George felt something uncomfortable stir in his gut and pulled away.

"Bit early," Joq said as George headed for the door.

George paused. It was. He couldn't explain that he needed space, he needed the ocean and his feet on the sand and a good hard run to get rid of the jitters, to right himself.

"Beach," he replied. "Go back to sleep."

He stepped into the dark hallway and headed down the stairs to grab his car keys on the way through to the garage.

It was pitch black when he stepped onto the beach—a long stretch of sand to his left, the port and industrial area to his right, and dead in front, the inky blackness of the bay crashing onto the shore, the dapples of white foam bright as it washed up and dragged back.

He took a deep breath, and as he let it out, headlights washed over him from behind. George glanced back; most guys dragged themselves to beach training. Who would come this early? But even as he thought it, he knew.

"George?" Finn's voice asked at the same time as the car door opened.

The asphalt crunched under his feet and the air felt like it moved to accommodate him.

"Finn," George replied, his surprise morphing into a smile. "You're early."

Finn came alongside him; it was dark but George could see the curve of his lips, his mussed hair, his bright eyes focusing right on George's.

"Used to it," Finn said around a smile. "I like getting a run in before we start, borrowed Mum's rental."

George chuckled at him. "Crazy. You got a whole day of training and you wanna get in some extra time?"

Finn's smile was sheepish. "Yeah, well, I still got those first day nerves and like, I just love the beach. What about you? Getting in the zone?"

George bumped his shoulder with his own. "Was gonna go for a run actually."

"And you're mocking me?"

"Yeah, yeah, you wanna then?"

Finn knocked his shoulder against George's, then started stretching. "You reckon you can keep up?"

"Oh, I'll keep up, reckon that's the other way round," George replied and quickly stretched his hamstrings, his groin. He'd been pretty lucky in his body—aside from the concussion and a few minor things along the way, he wasn't plagued by a single paralysing injury that returned to haunt him every season.

Finn laughed. "Thataway," he nodded at the left.

"Lead the way, you're gonna need a head start," George dropped his foot back from his ass and bounced in place for a few beats.

Finn shot a smile over his shoulder and took off.

George took off after him.

Finn was fast, but George already knew that. The question was: did he have stamina yet? George quickly came up alongside him and matched his pace. Finn was setting a pace right beyond what George was comfortable with, but that was the zone he liked to work out in and so having a running partner push him there was a godsend.

"This it?" he panted out.

Finn's laugh got caught in the wind, but George heard him well enough when he replied, "You wanna go, old man?"

"Old man?" George was fondly affronted. He accelerated.

He could feel Finn charging behind him, watched as he streaked past him and ate up the flat of the sand, skipped through the push of water like it was nothing.

George marvelled at his speed. But he knew it couldn't last indefinitely, so he increased his pace incrementally, held the line behind the sound of Finn's feet splashing in front of him, the vague outline of his body, the top of his blonde head a beacon in the dark.

Sure enough, he was beside him again within minutes, meeting his panting grin with his own.

"Feelin' good?" he asked.

"Yeah," Finn beamed.

They settled into a pace, still faster than George would normally do, and ran the full length of the beach. They went beyond the jetty and stopped by mutual agreement before winding up in St Kilda.

"God, I'm feeling that," Finn said as he braced himself on his knees and caught his breath.

George tried to laugh but he was panting too much. He sucked in a pull of air and stretched his arms.

"Feels good, but," George eventually said. He looked at Finn. "To feel it."

"Yeah, no, for sure," Finn straightened, planted his feet and stretched his inner groin. "If you're gonna do it, you better come back in with nothin' left."

George cracked a smile. "My thoughts exactly." He watched Finn stretching out his groin. "That still bothering you?"

Finn looked up; there was enough wind that his hair was flying around his face, flicking into his eyes. "I can play on it, no problem."

George dropped his arms. "Not what I asked."

Finn shook himself and straightened. "Sorry, it's become a nerve, you know?"

"I hear that, but I'm not accusing you here, just asking as a coach. I know you know your body," George looked out at the water. "And I know you know what you're willing to play through and I'll never get in the way of that, but you gotta keep me informed or else I can't protect you."

He could hear Finn catching his breath beside him, calmer now, but still heavy enough to be audible. The horizon was lighting; soon there'd be the first hint of the sun.

"It comes and goes," Finn said.

George looked at him.

"I can play on it when it comes. It hurts, but," he shook his head and looked away. "I can play on it."

"Alright."

Finn looked back at him. "Alright?"

"Yeah, Finn, it's your body and your career, I'm just here if you want guidance with that. Been around the block, you know," George smiled.

Finn nodded seriously though. "Thanks."

"Yep," George rubbed the back of his neck. He'd gotten a lot of star-struck young players over the years; none unsettled him quite like Finn. "You ready to head back?"

"Course."

Finn ambled alongside him and George couldn't help nudging him again. Finn glanced up, his smile small and shy; it made George's heart flutter. He looked away.

"Better take this one easy, I've got a training session I've nicknamed 'from the pits of hell' to prep for the fitness tests," he said.

Finn chuckled and they set off, easily matching pace, breaths in sync as they ate up the sand and watched the first hint of red-orange burn at the horizon. Their feet slapped the sand, splashed in the water when it skirted just high enough, their voices a panted conversation as they talked about who was a possible ruckman to fill the back-up, about who was about to come out of contract. Every now and then their arms brushed, a bump of fabric on skin, skin on skin.

Kurt had brought the playlist and speaker. George cracked a grin at him when the notes from the opening scene of *Top Gun*—the first one—flowed over the players assembled on the beach, mingled with the seagulls screeching and circling, drowned out the waves crashing on the shore behind them.

"Right," George clapped his hands and grinned. "Cone to cone, burpee at each, then here," he pointed at the next set of cones, "suicides," he pointed further up the beach, "and here, interval running—sprint, jog, sprint, building, you know the drill."

"Fucking hell," Lacy muttered.

"That's the spirit, Lacy," George said.

Some of the guys looked at George, muttering under their breaths, while some guys, like Finn, looked at the course with excitement.

"Well, get on with it," George waved his hand at them.

"Motherfucking fuck," Cary said but led the guys to the first drill.

"Who wins Grand Finals?" Kurt yelled.

"Good players?" Lesley—probably their best defender—asked as he got lined up with the rest of the guys.

"No, dumb-ass," Kurt said. "The fittest team. We're gonna win it and you wanna know how?"

Lesley looked around, his face begging for someone else to answer that, but everyone was yawning and avoiding eye contact. "By being the fittest?"

"Yes!" Kurt shouted. "We're gonna run over every other cunt on that field, you hear me?"

That got a few wide eyes on him. A few guys bouncing on their feet.

"Yeah," Lacy answered for them. He grinned, wild and mean. "Fuck yeah." Lacy just needed an opportunity to start some shit and he was in.

Kurt took out his whistle from under his shirt, set up a timer on his phone. "Well, get your fat asses moving!" He blew the whistle.

The guys took off in a puff of sand.

George came alongside Kurt. "Good pep talk," he said.

"Whaddya call that, Cary? This isn't an old person's home—run, run, run!" Kurt shouted before turning to George. "Thanks."

"You got everything set for the fitness? Nance coming in?"

"Yeah," Kurt said, both their gazes fixed on the guys belting through the sand. "She's excited to get her hands on Finn for the skinnies."

George laughed under his breath. Dr Nancy Brewer had been the team chief of sports medicine since before George started; George used to like to kid her that one of these days she'd be up for sexual harassment, to which she grinned, winked, and always said, "You wish." It was quite disorientating coming from a sixty-plus-year-old woman. George always got a kick out of how she made the guys blush, especially since it wore off on him in about the fifth year.

"He looks good, doesn't he?" Kurt asked.

George focused on Finn—a good metre ahead of everyone else, his face contorted with exertion but there was a hint of glee in it too. "Yeah, he's got some superhuman gene, I'm sure of it."

"Nah," Kurt replied and glanced at his phone, "Eight more minutes, ladies!" he shouted, then dropped his voice back to talk to George. "That there is hard work and surfing, you know he was doing comps since he was twelve? You should check out the videos, he was good, even back then."

George focused on Finn tearing it up on the suicides. Finn looked over like he felt the gaze—he grinned, whip-fast and free—and George had to subdue the urge to grin back. He got that fluttering feeling again and looked away, focused on Lacy, who was also already on the suicides. And he was also tearing it up. He talked a big game about slacking, but that was never the case—next to Finn, he was the fittest guy out there.

"Lacy looks good," George said.

"He always looks good," Kurt replied. "Sometimes I imagine what he'd be like if he gave up the other shit."

"Hmmm," George did too. But then you had to wonder if the partying was why he could go so hard on the field, it was a balance.

The guys were on the third obstacle with two minutes remaining. They had a swim after this—out to the buoy and back—and then a beach run to finish before they headed back to the facility for showers, food and fitness tests. George would then have a clear idea of what he was working with post-offseason. Looking at Finn and Lacy, Cary, who was the eldest guy out there with brand new triplets at home and yet he still made it look easy, he felt a quiet excitement that he was looking at something good. He also needed to think about captain since Cary had begged off on account of the new babies. Lacy was the natural choice—he was the best, he was a team man, and he had the room—but the media would crucify George for it, which he resented, but he didn't need the headache.

George was walking down the tunnel with Todd after they got back from the beach, all of the players dressed and ready to go out on the field.

"He's got speed, and I watched the Sharks' games, he's good off the feed, so let's see if he's got some chemistry with Cary and Lacy," Todd was saying.

It was the obvious set-up and of course it's what they'd try. God, George hoped they had the chemistry—that kind of power and speed off the centre bounce? It'd take a defensive wall to stop them. The only problem was everyone else would predict that's what they'd do and spend their preseason building the wall.

"I know you gotta select a captain and I reckon with Cary out, Finn's eventually gonna be the choice, but the dilemma is selecting someone to fill the years before then..."

Todd was still talking when George felt a prickling on his skin, an awareness in the cavernous space of the tunnel. He looked up and saw Finn coming towards them. It was electric, the feeling he had seeing him, a giddiness he needed to get under control, but it was beyond his control not to let out a half smile, not to respond.

"Let's chat to Cary after this," he said to Todd. "See what he thinks, who he reckons might work."

"Sounds good," Todd replied as he peeled off for the tunnel that'd take him out to the oval.

George walked straight for Finn; Finn was already smiling at him, stretching his face wider the closer he got and George answered it with a wider smile now they were alone.

"That was from the pits of hell?" Finn asked. "Reckon it was barely a simmer."

George laughed, surprised. Finn dropped his gaze, hiding his answering smile, hiding his pleasure at making George laugh by kicking at nothing on the floor with his footy boot.

"Noted. Next time I'll tack a bike ride and marathon on the end," George said and bumped Finn's shoulder to get him to look up. He wanted to see Finn's eyes, to look him in the eye; he liked that, and he realised he still hadn't gotten past the thrill of seeing Finn in person after texting and facetiming for almost two years. There'd been camaraderie over the screen, but in person it felt warm, soft. He couldn't help himself from touching—reaching out and grabbing Finn's wrist and sweeping his thumb up and down the skin.

Finn looked up.

"You make us all look like amateurs," he didn't mean to say that, but it was the truth. He leaned close as he dropped Finn's wrist and spoke against his ear. "But save something for the season, you'll still make my debut look like a pale comparison."

George moved on down the tunnel, tucked his hands in his pockets, still smiling; he could hear Finn's disbelieving laughter behind him, imagined he was turning to head for the field.

He glanced back.

Finn was watching him, expression clear, eyes shining; but his smile dimmed to self-conscious and it did something to George's whole body, made his stomach flip like maybe something was here. He couldn't have stopped the reassuring smile he gave Finn if he tried.

He returned his focus to the door, to the steps to his office, to his training notepad. He needed to focus—he did not need to be crushing on his rookie.

But he was beginning to think this was... bad. He thought about Finn's shy smiles, his nervous look just before he cracked a joke, and he realised he did have it bad.

He couldn't remember feeling like this, ever. He'd been with two guys: Alistair and Joq. He loved both of them, no question. But he didn't feel like the first twenty-four hours of meeting them reorientated his entire worldview. They didn't make him feel like he was inside his own personal snow globe that someone kept shaking, and the snowflakes falling around him in a constant shimmer were warm and bright—as delightful as they were unsettling in the middle of summer.

The notepad in front of him was a picture of the oval, the positions, names scratched in, plays to run. George drew on his iron-will—his oldest friend, the weapon in his arsenal that'd gotten him into the league, won it all, and got him this coaching gig—and with that force, he told himself to put this ridiculous crush out of his mind. It was impossible. And absurd. He needed to get over it. And fast.

9

"So, I saw the press conference," Joq said that night while they were having dinner.

George took a deliberate sip of his water—the press conference was a press conference, of course Joq saw it, of course he wanted to discuss it, George always used him as a sounding board.

"Yeah?" he asked as casual yet interested-in-your-professional-opinion as he could.

"Months, huh?" Joq asked.

George kept his feelings of doing something wrong to himself—he wasn't, he was sure of it—and focused on the line he'd been rehearsing since he started to get the feeling he was maybe getting in over his head: "It's true what I said, thought he could use the support."

"Hey, I think it's cool of you," Joq replied easily, "but I was thinking..."

George looked at him, waited, and kept his expression carefully neutral. Inside, he was panicking and preparing his defence simultaneously—Joq already knew he had a crush, they could laugh about it. In fact, the more Joq mocked him the better. That'd really put this out of his head, turn it into something else and George could have this at home—a joking refuge and a space to get over it.

Joq didn't go on. George wanted him to get on with it so they could get to it and that'd be that. "You were thinking?"

"We should have Finn over for dinner?"

"Why?" George couldn't fathom a world in which that would be a good idea. It was not what he'd been expecting at all—why on earth would Joq want that? George absolutely did not want that. He couldn't think of a worse idea than inviting Finn in more, until he had this under control.

Joq raised both eyebrows. "He should know we're together," he said like that was an obvious point.

It most certainly wasn't!

"What? Why should he know that?" George stood. He needed to get away from this conversation—the last thing in the world he needed was Finn to know he had a boyfriend. And hold up, his brain interjected, isn't the last thing he should know was that George was gay? Yes, that too, he told himself. Finn knowing any and all of the above was the last thing he needed or wanted. Christ, he didn't want it, he couldn't have it; if Finn thought or knew that, he might pick up on George's crush. A decade older, past it, crushing on him? Finn would be put in the world's most awkward position. No way.

Joq was looking up at him, genuine confusion in his expression. "Because he's gay and you're friends?" he said like it was also obvious.

"He's not," he started and didn't bother to finish. If Joq knew, he knew. George didn't care how, Joq seemed to have an inkling for it since he fucked around so much—or at least that was George's theory—or he was testing a hunch and lying was pointless. "He doesn't need to know about us. Why would I tell him that?" he changed tact.

He cleared the plates and went inside. He needed to get away from this conversation. He wanted to be around Finn in the way you wanted to constantly be around someone you found yourself really liking, which was why he absolutely did not want Finn in his space any more than he needed to be until he had a handle on this infatuation. He focused on rinsing the plates, stacking the dishwasher. He needed to get this idea out of Joq's head. He needed to not be crushing on his rookie. He grabbed a beer and went back out, determined to put his foot down.

"You should tell him," Joq insisted before George could speak.

"I don't see why," he answered honestly—what would it help?

"You said it yourself, he needs the support," Joq replied readily, reasonably. It was part of why George loved him actually—he was reasonable, steady, and he wasn't ashamed of being gay. George had always loved being around that—it made him feel like maybe he was okay too. "If he saw this," Joq waved his beer between them, "he'd see what was possible."

With another guy, George's mind supplied. Finn would see what was possible with another guy. The thought made him angry and sad, which was confusing and irritating and not relevant because Joq was right. When Finn came out to him, it was clear he wanted something like this. A boyfriend.

He sighed, sipped his beer and looked at the pool. It would actually be the right thing to do.

"I'll think about it," he said.

"Yeah?" Joq asked. George could hear the smile in his voice.

He huffed an irritated breath at himself. Of course it was important for Joq too—sometimes he forgot how much he stole from him, keeping him locked up in here with him, not sharing their relationship with the world. Someone else knowing? That meant something for Joq. And George could and should give it to him.

He smiled, quick and small, and hoped it conveyed all that. He sucked at talking about this and he appreciated that Joq let him get away with that.

10

♥

FINN WASN'T STUPID. He liked George. Liked him-liked him. Liked him in the *I've got a crush on my idol* way, then in the *Oh my God I can't believe he's texting me and now we're texting every day* way (until George rationed it, which Finn understood, he was coming on too strong). And somewhere in there it went from a crush on his idol and it'd be awesome to bang him in the idle way everyone dreams about banging their idols—he'd had similar jerk-off sessions to Kelly Slater and Mick Fanning—to *He's no longer a cut-out in my head, he's a real person. And he's kind and supportive and funny. And when we talk, he really watches me, I feel like he sees me, the real me, and he likes what he's seeing and I like that, the way he holds eye contact and listens so carefully.*

Point was, Finn was not stupid and he knew his crush had morphed into something that felt a lot like falling in love. He'd never been in love before, but he didn't think it was the kind of thing that needed explaining—when you felt it, you knew it; it was a part of being human.

He was aware of the article. Of course he was. He was an athlete with the potential to enter two major sports in an elite capacity and he was gay. He kept an eye out for this shit. The stuff on George though was uncertain. Real gossip realms. Some rumour from some girl who knew the sister of the guy George was supposedly banging when he was a teenager in his home town? And then a bunch of stuff about how he never had a girlfriend, took his sister to the Brownlow's—well, that was all potentially using evidence to say what you wanted it to say, wasn't it?

Finn hoped, again in the idle fantasy way, but he knew it was not his business, it was no one's; George Creed was still George Creed, one of the greatest of all time and if he was gay, well, that was his business.

Then he got to know him. And his idle fantasy turned to full-blown hope. And the way George held eye contact, the way he couldn't hang up when they talked? Finn had a strong feeling not only was George gay and maybe, hopefully, as into Finn as Finn was into him, but maybe, possibly, in a world where all Finn's dreams come true, George would go out with him.

Finn's attempt to ask him out for dinner was a flaming disaster. But, Finn reasoned that George had good reason to hold him off—rookie and coach hooking up? Yes, that would be bad. He just needed to talk to George though, to tell him plainly: I'm into you, I think you might be into me too, but I can wait. Maybe. Or maybe we could do this on the down-low.

God, the thought of it gave him hives. It was crazy. He wasn't going to say that.

He was sitting in front of his locker, the first week of preseason training hitting the midway point and he was absolutely loving every second of it. The door clanged open and George walked in. Finn's heart gave a thump and a flutter of nerves skittered up and down his skin.

"But for real, Finn, you gotta get out of Fitzroy and come have a drink with us at rooftop in the city," Lacy finished up what he'd been saying.

"I'm keen," Finn smiled at him, but his awareness was on George rolling the whiteboard to the front of the room. He looked at George—because he couldn't not when he was in the room—and it did him in, made him feel achy in the best way: George in his training gear—the workout pants hugging his firm ass and thighs, the team polo opening invitingly at his throat, his brown hair brushing the collar of his shirt in wavy, soft-looking wisps. Ever since Finn had seen it on FaceTime, he'd wanted to run his fingers through the strands.

George glanced up and caught Finn watching him. Finn felt the same charge shoot through him that was becoming familiar—pure attraction, a connection—he was definitely feeling it, but he didn't know if George was too or if he was making that up in his head because he was. George gave him a quick smile though, a smile like he couldn't help himself. Finn grinned back.

"Right," George said looking around the room, his voice gruff and expression serious. "Listen up."

The voices died down and everyone focused on him, gazes darting to the board and back.

"These are the positions we set up over the last two days, how we're gonna start the season," George tapped the board and everyone murmured assents. It was a good set up. They had a few holes, they had a way to go to assure chemistry, but it was about as good as you could set a field with this team.

"I don't give a shit about this," George rubbed everything off the whiteboard.

There was some nervous tittering, a few shared looks. Finn was riveted.

Once the board was a blank slate, George placed the eraser on the ledge with a soft thump.

"You know all of this, you know your positions, you know the importance of fitness. Kurt's been shouting at you that we're gonna run over every other team and he's gonna keep shouting it until you hear it in your sleep," George looked around and guys watched him back, nodded their heads in agreement with various levels of enthusiasm.

"Todd's got you running the drills to give you the edge on each play and he's going to make you do it again and again until those plays are burned into your muscles and you execute them without thinking," he went on, paused on Lacy.

"I already got that shit in my limbs," Lacy quipped.

"No shit," George gave him a quick smile. "Which is my point. None of that alone is why we're going to be the best team this season."

George paused, glanced around. His eyes skimmed over Finn and for a fraction of a second Finn felt like his gaze tripped, like it wanted to stay but couldn't, or like with Finn in the room, he was firing on all cylinders.

Yes, Finn had it bad.

"I want each and every one of you to tell me why you want to be the best team this season."

Silence.

"That wasn't rhetorical," George's smile was indulgent; the coach mask slipped for a second to reveal the friend and player he had once been with most of these guys.

"Because we wanna win the Grand Final," Cary replied, like it was obvious.

"Why?" George asked.

"Whaddya mean why?" Cary asked. "That's what we're here for."

"Okay," George said, "but why does it matter? Why do you want to win it all? Just to win?"

A few guys exchanged looks. "Because it feels good to win?" Les—the rookie defensemen asked. Yes, Les and Lesley on the D, Finn smiled to himself as he looked at them sitting next to each other on the other side of the locker room.

"It does," George agreed. "But what I want each of you to do is go away and ask yourselves this question until you get an answer that makes you feel so fucking pumped you could go out on the ground right now and play full out for eighty minutes. And even if it made you gassed, you could play another eighty," he checked each guy's expression, cleared his throat. "Why are you here? Why do you play? And I want your answers by tomorrow morning."

"Because we get paid a lot," Lacy shot back.

A few guys laughed.

"Could get paid a lot doing other shit and you wouldn't be putting your body on the line, you wouldn't be beholden to a schedule that took you away from your kids, your partners, your pets."

"Can we get an example?" Les asked.

Finn hid his smile. Les was every inch the eighteen-year-old who did well at school.

George stared at him. Les fidgeted.

"Alright," George replied and tucked his hands in his pockets and straightened. "Why do I coach? I had a stellar career, I could've easily retired and taken the media job I got offered. It paid a fuck tonne more, the schedule was better and I wouldn't have a pack of assholes after me saying I'm gonna fail, I'm too inexperienced, and all the other shit I'm sure you've seen. So why'd I do it?"

"'Cos you love it," Finn blurted without thinking.

George smiled at him. "I do. But that's not the only reason why. When I dug down, I found my why: I don't feel more alive in anything else in my life. Being part of a team, watching it come together, being a part of it? For me, that's about as much fun and fulfillment as I can get from life. Putting together a team that works, that pushes beyond limits, that's a cohesive unit? The thought of pulling that off drives me, I can't imagine anything better. That's my why. So," he looked at Les again, "what's yours?" He looked around and grinned. "You got twenty-four hours. Now get your asses out there, I wanna see ten laps, full out and then we'll begin."

There was groaning.

"Finn, a word," George said as everyone filed out.

Finn's heart fluttered as the guys gave him shit.

George waited until everyone was gone.

"Is everything alright?" Finn asked at the same time as George said. "Sorry, didn't mean to make this seem so serious."

"Sorry," Finn said, though he didn't know what he was apologising for.

"You're all good," George said over the top of him again.

George huffed and Finn smiled anxiously.

"Right, I just wanted to see if you wanted to come round for dinner?" George asked.

"Yeah?" Finn couldn't believe it.

George's expression was stern yet he seemed nervous underneath that. Finn felt a weird uncertainty in the vibe.

"Yes, I've got this," George looked over Finn's shoulder, "house-mate, a pool, BBQ, good set-up," he rushed out after putting a weird emphasis on 'housemate', "and I wanna make sure you feel welcomed, feel like you know you got a place you can go when you need it, away from home I mean."

Finn was so elated at George asking him around, he didn't dwell too much on the inkling he had that something was off about this invite.

"I'd love to," he replied because he really would.

George exhaled and glanced at him. "Great. Friday? We'll head to my place after training."

"Sounds good," Finn said. Because it did.

"Alright, get your ass out there," George said and smiled at him for real, properly met his eyes.

Finn laughed, surprised. "Yes, coach," he jogged to the door, felt George behind him. He looked over his shoulder. "I love being in a team, giving everything as a team. I love how it feels when we all give everything we've got for each other. That's my why."

George smiled softly at him. "That's a good why."

Finn felt flustered, his smile was bashful and he heard himself say, "Yeah," weirdly, before he headed for the field.

The guys were coming past on a lap as Finn jogged out to join them.

"You owe us another one," Lacy grinned at him.

"I reckon another two unless you just got your ass handed to you," Cary went on.

Finn laughed. "How about I give you three?"

"Show off," Lesley panted.

"Is that everything you've got?" Kurt shouted.

"Don't do it, Finn!" Les shouted from the back.

"I've gotta do it!" Finn accelerated. He felt Lacy match him and the others push up behind them—he didn't go as fast as he could, but just fast enough that everyone would be going faster than they normally would.

When they got back in, George shot him an approving nod and Finn's stomach flipped even though he was completely gassed.

"Teacher's pet," Lacy said under his breath and nudged him.

"Ah, shut it," Finn replied.

Lacy grinned knowingly at him and Finn dropped his head, placed his hands on his hips, sucked in pulls of air.

"Nothin' to be ashamed of," Lacy murmured.

Finn glanced at him, suddenly terrified—he was so fucking obvious.

But Lacy winked. "He's hot as fuck."

Finn huffed a shocked laugh.

"Not my type," Lacy went on between sucking in pulls of air, his smile turning sly, "but I wouldn't say no, if I like, didn't know his dull personality."

Finn giggled, relieved. "He's great."

Lacy made gagging noises. Finn gave him a playful shove.

Kurt shouted at everyone to get into position and it finally caught up to Finn what Lacy just told him. It was a roundabout way to put it out there, but it was out there. As they got into position for a practice match later, Lacy jogged past Finn down to the forward pocket, Finn taking his spot outside the huddle where the ruck would happen; they made brief eye contact and it was normal, two teammates exchanging a look, and the normality of it made him feel steady in a way he didn't know he needed.

11

FINN HAD NEVER TAKEN so much time to decide what he was going to wear. He'd pulled out all his shorts and shirts in his new apartment and spread them on the bed. He knew he was being ridiculous—it was a casual BBQ with George and his housemate—and all of Finn's shorts and shirts looked about the same. But some were nicer, he thought as he picked up the tailored shorts he'd gotten in Sydney before he moved down. But were they too nice? Was this a boardshorts and singlet affair? Would George want to go swimming and then as Finn breached the surface George would swim over to him like he couldn't help himself and kiss him?

Finn laughed, shook his head at himself and tossed the shorts on the bed. He picked up the ones he got in Brisbane when he went on a shopping trip with Soph. These ones were in between casual and fancy—cream, almost grey, a nice cut, stylish but not as obviously styled as the other ones. He folded them carefully. As for the shirt, a button-up was needed but did he want to go the blue one, the Hawaiian, or the pinstripe? He tilted his head and glanced at the alarm clock. He had time. An embarrassing amount of time. He'd barely slept, which was amazing since training at this level for only a week was already handing his ass to him, but he was so excited his brain had supplied him with endless scenarios and fantasies all night.

"Blue," he said to himself. "Soph would say the blue."

He wanted to call. To tell her about this new development. She knew he was crushing hard on George, but until now it'd been something she mocked him for in the '*never gonna happen*' way. He wasn't sure he wanted to dissuade her until he was sure it could be something that was actually going to happen.

Plus, he didn't want to jinx it. And Soph would tell their mum and that was fine, he told his mum everything anyway, but she'd want to meet George and she wouldn't embarrass him but he wasn't ready for 'meeting the boyfriend' until he knew if this thing he was feeling was maybe possibly real. He wasn't convinced it was—there was just no way—but he couldn't stop himself from hoping.

He carefully folded the shirt and placed it with the shorts in a clothing bag and got ready for training.

By the time George came over to him at the end of the day—after Finn had showered and changed, styled his hair, applied just the right amount of deodorant—Finn was glad he'd just done the most intense training session of the week because it meant all that nervous energy was muted.

"You ready?" George asked.

They were the only two people left in the locker room.

"Yeah," Finn hoisted his bag over his shoulder and smiled; he felt it straining his face.

George gave him a crooked smile and Finn realised he liked this smile, it was the one George gave him when he thought Finn was being awkward in his own head and George couldn't believe he was awkward ever. Finn had seen this look a lot.

"It's dinner, no need to look like that," George bumped him.

Finn ran his free hand through his hair and busted out a self-deprecating laugh.

"The great George Creed is taking me home for dinner, give me a sec to like, be nervous," Finn replied.

George scoffed. "Dunno about great," he nudged Finn to get him moving, "but there's certainly nothing to be nervous about."

George's voice faltered at the end and something about it pinged Finn's instincts. Maybe George was nervous? Was that a good or a bad thing?

George changed the subject to the training they'd just done and Finn piped up with his opinions as they made their way to George's car. It was nice—black, a new looking Ford Ranger—and Finn couldn't help his laugh.

"What?" George asked as he looked at Finn over the roof of the car, his expression curious—it made him look young.

"Nothin', just. You can take the boy out of country Victoria, eh?"

George laughed. "Ah, shut it, what're you gonna get yourself? A hybrid Tesla?"

They got in and Finn laughed to cover his embarrassment. He was actually.

George cracked up. "You totally are."

"What? It's good for the environment."

George started the car and peeled out of there.

Finn liked being in the confined space with him—it felt like a warm little bubble, comfortable yet charged. The streets were lit up with cafes, restaurants, bars, the street lights bright, the energy of Melbourne gearing up for a solid Friday night.

"So what's your housemate do?" Finn asked looking over at George.

George tensed—it was almost imperceptible, but Finn was attuned to him in the way you got when you were so into someone you noticed absolutely everything they did.

"Works at the stadium, actually," George said after a brief hesitation. Again, Finn thought his response would be normal if Finn wasn't watching him with that complete focus.

"Yeah? That's cool, can share lifts and stuff."

He was about to ask what he did exactly when George cut him off.

"Cary can't captain this season 'cos of the triplets," he said.

"Why?" Finn asked. It's not like he needed to bring them to training.

George glanced at him and gave him a look like he was thinking the same thing. "Yeah, I know, bit of a foreign concept for us without kids, but like, it's a lot of work, he doesn't wanna put it all on Julie and take this on as well."

Finn nodded. "That makes sense. Me and Soph are twins and Dad shot through when we were like, not even one. I reckon Mum could've used a hand."

"Shit, sorry, I didn't know that?"

"It's all good," Finn shrugged and smiled at George's profile. "Mum's awesome. But who're you thinking? Lacy's the natural choice, but..."

They wound into a classier looking neighbourhood.

George shot him a smile. "My thoughts exactly. Lacy's the perfect choice, except for the 'but'."

They pulled up at a gate, George hit a button and it whirred to life.

"You reckon he'd ever straighten out so he could take the leadership?"

George chuckled. "No, never. He likes his lifestyle."

They drove in and wound up in front of an impressive two-story house.

"Fucking nice," Finn said.

George took a deep breath and cut the engine. Finn glanced at him. Now, Finn was no expert and he couldn't understand it, but George seemed reluctant.

"Yeah," George replied, his eyes out the windscreen on his very impressive home. "My housemate, you met him, Joq?"

"The surveillance guy?" Finn remembered—seemed like a chill dude, handsome in that fine-featured way, like a Nordic villain in a Bond film or something.

"Yeah," George replied. He glanced at Finn, then looked away. "He's looking forward to meeting you properly."

"Okay," Finn said as George got out of the car. Finn realised what George was saying. Again, Finn wasn't stupid: he knew he had a lot of fans from his social media stuff, from his endorsement shit, hell, even from his surfing comp days. So this Joq was probably a fan. If that was the only reason George was inviting him over that was disappointing, but then George had said he wanted Finn to feel welcome, to have a place away from home so it probably wasn't just that.

He was close behind him when George spoke again. "Besides, what kind of role model would we be setting for you rookies if we made Lacy the captain?" he asked, picking up the previous conversation.

"He's a hell of a player," Finn replied as George opened the door.

"We might as well buy you the coke and ecstasy and hand it out at training," George went on, deadpan.

Finn cracked up laughing. George was smiling at him over his shoulder as he led him inside. The place was nice—minimalist but impeccably decorated in neutrals with perfectly framed pictures on the white walls, an artfully placed indoor plant that reached to the ceiling, a white couch with carefully thrown cashmere blankets in cream and tan. It looked stylish, clean, and reeked of money well spent. Finn was impressed, but something about it didn't feel like George. He didn't know George well enough to think that though—maybe this *was* George?

He followed George into an open-plan kitchen-dining area, took in the pool with lights on, the palms, the cabana beyond the window.

"Hey, babe," came from the kitchen and Finn felt a hit of surprise. He instantly thought it must've been some in-joke, but when he glanced at George, he looked too surprised.

"Hey," George said. "You remember Finn."

Joq gave George a strange look before coming over to them, his eyes rolling and his hand extended. "Uh, yeah."

Finn felt Joq's palm in his and smiled, but it was a practiced media smile, a smile he gave when someone asked him about his injury and he knew he needed to act nonchalant and conceal how he really felt, which was terrified he was never going to get better.

But Joq smiled warmly and Finn felt himself relaxing. Joq was even more handsome like this—in casual pants and a white shirt, his lean body displayed like someone who worked out for maintenance, took pride in their appearance; Finn got the feeling he was self-possessed and Finn liked that, he liked being around people like that.

"And you remember Joq, from surveillance," George said.

Finn watched as Joq suppressed a flinch, grinned and replied, "A bit more than that."

Finn took his hand back and waited for an explanation. He felt like something awful was dawning on him; he felt out of his body and embarrassed all at once. He was going red. No one said anything. He looked around and decided he needed to say something, to act normal, to not act like the guy who had come over hoping to what? Fuck some other guy's boyfriend? Oh, God. No, don't think about it yet.

"This is nice," he heard himself say.

"Like you haven't got nicer in Byron," George said and tapped him on the ass. Finn wanted to look at Joq, to see what he thought of that, but then footy guys tapped each other on the ass all the time. "You want a beer? Joq gets the low-cal stuff."

Finn watched as George smiled at Joq—who was? he was?—Finn shook off the questions. He needed to get through this dinner before he examined what was happening here.

He took the beer George handed him and drew on his years of talking to the media—he'd been doing it since he was twelve, since he won his first surfing comp at Bells—and smiled as he replied. "True, Byron's pretty nice, eh? But this is still pretty sweet."

George herded him to the door and Finn stood alongside him and watched the pool. His heart was racing. He took a sip of beer.

"I've never been to Byron," George said. Finn could hear the way he was trying to sound normal.

Finn bumped his shoulder and tried to convey reassurance. "You'll have to come visit. It's actually the best, I'm just tryin' to be nice."

George laughed and bumped him back. Finn had to return the bump if for no other reason than to get rid of his panicky energy. George returned it and smiled at him. Finn laughed, giddy; their eyes caught, held and it felt like they exchanged an understanding that this was awkward, but it was okay too, like they were trying to reassure one another. Finn knocked George again and they got into it, laughing like they were stoned.

"I will knock you down," George said.

"You can try, old man," Finn replied, giggling when George gave him a firmer hip and shoulder.

"BBQ!" Joq said from behind them and Finn startled.

He looked at Joq in the kitchen. He was backlit by the soft glow of the kitchen lights, his blonde hair almost white, his eyes serious on the pair of them.

"I've got to cook the BBQ," he said and it was a normal thing to say, but everything about this felt like everyone was pretending to be normal.

"Hey, no, I can do that," George said and left Finn's side. "Finn can help, try and get some meat in his hippy ass."

Finn laughed, it was closer to genuine because over the couple of years they'd been talking he'd realised George was terribly earnest and therefore sucked at sledging. He'd heard the hippy insult many times before. He did his best to ignore the meat in his ass implications.

George inclined his head for Finn to follow him out to the BBQ. It was a newer-looking model, clean, and George got it going and picked up their conversation from the car.

"You got any good feel for the leadership group?" George asked. Finn looked at him; he was genuinely asking for Finn's opinion.

George held the eye contact and smiled; the question in his eyes without the words. "What?"

Finn shook his head. "Nothin', just like, you really care what I think?"

"Yeah?" George said and nudged him as he turned the flame on, scraped the non-existent mess off the plate. "You're in the team, amongst it, and you don't seem completely inept."

Finn chuckled. "Thanks. Good to know I'm a cut above useless."

"Now let's not get too carried away," George said as he placed the meat on the BBQ, poked it with the tongs as it sizzled. Finn could feel the joy in his words, and he could hear how he was trying to tamp it down.

Finn was still partially caught on the questions he had about what was going on here, caught in a kind of denial—maybe he was mistaken, Joq wasn't George's boyfriend, was he? But as he met George's smile, it became infectious; George was a bubble of happiness in person and Finn found himself slipping inside it every time he was around him.

Finn shoved him. "Yeah, don't look at my high school transcripts," he shook his head at the memory—but how did anyone expect him to give a shit about Shakespeare and the bones in the skeletal system when he was training from five every morning and then picking it up again until nine at night?

"I'm sure you woulda done better if you weren't working to go pro in two sports," George nudged him and Finn couldn't help his grateful smile. Of course George would get it without Finn having to say anything.

"Yeah, as for Captain," Finn tilted his head to the side and thought about it. "Jack would've been perfect."

"Don't get me started," George said and turned the steaks.

Finn laughed at him. "Yeah, he said you were pissed."

George gave him a surprised look. "You know him?"

"Yeah, he came up to Byron one summer before I got drafted. We used the same trainer," Finn replied. It'd been a great summer—Jack was awesome. Jack was also gay and made Finn feel like maybe he was going to be alright—playing professional and just, as Jack put it, "Keeping it to yourself, it's no one's business unless you want it to be."

"Really?" George seemed really surprised; and a flicker of annoyance was there too.

"I reckon if he knew it was gonna piss you off so much, he might've reconsidered," Finn tested how far he could go, "I mean, if he knew you were gonna throw the world's biggest tantrum over it."

George laughed, surprised, and shoved Finn. "I did not throw a tantrum."

"Yeah? You just stopped taking his calls and speaking to him because you were busy?"

"Yes," George said gruffly but Finn could see he was trying not to smile.

"You coulda rationed him to once a week," Finn went on, trying to hide his own smile.

"Ah shut it," George gave up and smiled at him. "You know I only did that because I woulda been on the phone to you all day, every day."

Finn couldn't help it—he beamed and felt caught again in those big brown eyes meeting his; it felt like it was just them when George looked at him like that, it felt like it was something. But it clearly wasn't.

Finn looked away. "Reckon it's ready."

"Yeah, and we still got no captain," George started taking the meat off the plate. "Can't believe you're friends with Jack."

"Ah, quit sulking," Finn reached up and shook his shoulder.

George shook his head and smiled at him from under the hair in his eyes.

Finn felt caught again in that look and had to look away.

"Come on, let's eat," George said.

They brought everything over to where Joq was already sitting at the head of the table, drinking a glass of wine from a half empty bottle. George herded Finn to a seat to Joq's left and went and took his own opposite. Finn felt Joq's presence in the way he felt like he was being examined—as if Joq could see every filthy thought Finn had had about George and was smirking at him like, *I get it, my boyfriend's hot as fuck*, but there was an undercurrent of surprised annoyance there too. Or maybe Finn was projecting. He glanced at Joq as George spoke and Joq looked completely normal—handsome, at ease in his home.

"Looks good," George was saying.

"Looks the same as it always does," Joq replied and refilled his wine glass.

And Finn got a flash of images of their life together—home cooked meals by the pool, a fucking relationship? He was still rebelling at the idea. But he couldn't help the wistful longing it brought up in him—he wanted that, he really did.

"Then that's a sweet set-up," he replied and accepted the salad bowl George handed him, caught again in George's orbit and unable to do anything but tell the truth he just thought. "BBQ by the pool every night, home-cooked food."

"What're you eating? Take-out?" George asked him.

"Mainly, yeah, but I been getting those boxes too with the recipe and all the shit. My mum set it up," Finn replied. His mum had drilled the 'food is medicine, your body is a temple' mantra into him and Soph since they could talk and even his take-out was healthy.

"You can cook?" Joq asked.

Finn felt himself reddening—it was awful; Joq made him feel off-kilter, the uncertainty of what he was in the middle of, of what he was sure Joq could see, made him uneasy.

"I can follow a recipe," Finn replied like he was a school boy who'd been called on to answer a question and he really wanted to get it right.

"Very open to instruction," George agreed and smiled reassuringly. Finn was grateful for it.

"Alright, well this is not a training drill. It's family dinner, so eat," Joq said flatly and Finn heard and felt the implications of 'family dinner' like a slap.

There was a brief awkward silence, the sound of Joq swigging his wine, and Finn dropped his eyes to his plate.

"Oh, come on," Joq said and Finn tensed.

He felt Joq looking at him.

"You know we're together, right? We're trusting you with that," Joq said.

And if he'd felt 'family dinner' like a slap, that there was a body blow. He drew on his calm beneath the roar of heartbreak that what he thought was going on here was not, and he was so fucking stupid, as if George invited him over to what? Go out with a twenty-year-old rookie? Of course George was gay—fantasy come to life!—and shacked up with one of the hottest, coolest dudes Finn had ever seen.

"Joq," George said and his knife clattered to the plate. Finn wanted to tell him it was fine, he got it, he needed to know.

Finn glanced up at Joq—those eyes cool, yet trying to be inviting—but all he could feel was George watching him.

"I know that now," he said and looked to George. George was giving him an odd look—did he not want Finn to know?

He looked back at Joq. He didn't think George would've told him he was gay—he didn't know why he knew that, but he was certain that if Joq knew it was because he'd figured it out himself.

"You know I'm gay," he said to Joq.

"Yeah, I figured that out," Joq replied apologetically. "I'm not trying to out you. Sorry," he shook his head. "I'm trying, very badly, to say it's okay and we're here if you ever need us." He was being sincere, Finn got that much. So maybe he didn't realise how much of a raging boner Finn had for his boyfriend? He fucking hoped he didn't. He was so embarrassed. But he wanted to be sure too, he wanted to hear George say it.

"So, you're like," he glanced down at his plate and told himself to say it, to get the confirmation he needed. He looked up and between them. "Really together?"

"Yep, twelve years," Joq replied.

Twelve years? Finn couldn't process that. They'd been together since he was eight? And now he really felt like a child.

"Oh," he said lamely. "That's cool."

"It is," Joq replied firmly.

Finn nodded to himself and did his best to digest this. One thing was for sure, he needed to go away and get all thoughts of George being with him like that out of his stupid head. Another thing? He saw this house, this dinner, this relationship and ached for it.

"Must be nice, having someone," floated out of his mouth before he could stop it.

He sat up, grabbed his beer and had a sip. "I've basically accepted I'm never gonna get laid again until I retire."

He smiled at George as he said it—the sly smile guys used in the locker room when they knew they just delivered a good line. It was also the truth—he'd thought maybe, if George was into him. Because that would be the perfect set-up, wouldn't it? Someone else in the same situation. There was no way he could fuck someone outside the bubble. And there was no one else he was interested in.

George shook his head, smiling out of control at the line. "Well, it's not like I get as much dick as this one," he nudged Joq.

Finn heard the words and didn't understand.

"Oh, shut up," Joq finished his wine.

Was George saying Joq gave it to him a lot? Finn thought he was going to need a carton of beer if they were going to get into that much detail, he really was.

"We have an open relationship," George said to Finn. "We can't be out 'cos, you know. So," he shrugged and cut into his steak before looking up, straight at Finn, "it's a compromise."

Finn stared at George, trying to process that while remaining cool on the outside. So, was George actually interested, but in casual sex?

"Oh," Finn replied, he could feel his face flaming and against his will his dick was interested. "Cool, cool. Cool," he said as he focused on his food.

Thankfully, George changed the subject to taking a trip to Vietnam to check it out for the training camp the following year, and Finn felt a pang when Joq talked about tagging a trip to Thailand in there and he and George shared an easy smile, a memory, but George quickly brought them back to the Kokoda Track, to getting inspired by the Australian prisoners of war, their bravery and comradery, and Finn managed to breathe through the rest of the dinner.

"So, you really fuck other guys?" Finn asked as they waited for his car. He'd had four beers, the perfect amount to eliminate his nerves and just ask.

George raised both eyebrows at him, but it seemed like he was more shocked at being asked a question like that outright than Finn asking specifically.

"Sorry," Finn shoved his hands in his pockets and looked around the tree lined street—it was beautiful, dark and quiet—"I shouldn't... It's not my business."

"I never fuck other guys," George said.

Finn glanced up at him because he couldn't not. He was totally confused again.

"Look," George said, he ran an agitated hand through his hair. "It's hard for Joq, being with me. I can't be out and so this is a compromise."

"The compromise is your boyfriend gets to fuck other guys because you want your privacy?" Finn asked.

George looked at him. "Sort of? I mean, he puts up with a lot, being with me and," he waved a hand at the street, "he wanted this, so that's what we decided."

"But you never fuck other guys," Finn said again; he was really feeling those beers.

George didn't look at him when he replied. "Not yet."

Finn watched him; his heart was going to pound out of his chest. But he didn't want a casual fuck, if that was even what George was suggesting? He looked at the street again and blew out a breath.

"Sorry," George said. "This was meant to make you feel like, you're not alone and I reckon I've just dumped a lot of shit on you. You can forget all about this, okay?"

Finn laughed incredulously. He glanced back at George. It was dark, but the streetlights made George seem blue, and his earnest expression was clear as if it were day.

"I can forget my footy idol is gay? That he has a hot boyfriend he lives with in domestic paradise and oh yeah, his boyfriend goes out and gets dicked down on the regular by other dudes because you want your privacy?" Finn rambled out and realised he sounded kind of mad. Because he was mad. Who gets someone like George and fucks around? But it was none of his business. He glanced at his phone. "Where the fuck is that car?"

George grabbed him by the shoulder and squeezed. "Finn."

Finn exhaled roughly. Shit, he needed that touch, he didn't realise he was so shaky.

"Sorry," Finn said to the ground. "This is really none of my business. And Joq seems really cool, you're lucky."

George huffed a laugh. Finn met his eyes. He was so close.

"I want it to be your business. I mean," George shook his head and took his hand back. "I mean, I told you because I want you to know. I want you to know it's okay."

Finn frowned. "Do you know it's okay?"

Headlights washed over them from the top of the hill.

"Thanks for dinner," Finn went to meet the car as it pulled up.

George grabbed his wrist and pulled him into a hug.

Finn gripped him back—surprised, but he melted into it, it was perfect, their bodies pressed together everywhere, it was exactly what he needed.

"We good?" George asked against Finn's ear.

Finn squeezed him. "Yeah, thanks for telling me."

George let him go and stepped back.

Finn got in the car and greeted his driver—Mohammed, the app said—and proceeded to ask where he was from, what he really did, and gave George a quick wave as they pulled away. He saw George in the side mirror, standing on the street, watching the car disappear.

He listened as Mohammed told him about how he was an engineer back in Pakistan, but he had to requalify in Australia to work and Finn nodded along; he'd heard several versions of this story, and he was stuck on a few things back there. Was probably going to be stuck on them for a while.

George was gay.

George was in a relationship but he could fuck other guys if he wanted to.

George was not the one who wanted Finn to know that.

It was the last point he paused on. That dinner was Joq's idea. George never planned to tell him any of that, hell, as far as Finn could tell, George didn't even want Finn to know he was gay.

As he let himself into his apartment, he made a decision to leave it the fuck alone. He liked George, really fucking liked him, but that was the problem, wasn't it? George wasn't available in the way he wanted him.

But it was probably for the best, he reasoned as he got ready for bed; he needed to focus on the footy, and him and George needed to be professional.

He lay on his back and stared at his ceiling. The street was noisy outside his room—the sounds from the parties spilling out of bars and clubs onto the street up the road—and he felt the emptiness of his place.

He thought about George's face when he'd said, "Not yet," his eyes fixed away from Finn, his expression shy. Finn didn't think he'd get that image out of his head for a while.

He thought about how he did not want a casual fuck. Not normally and especially not with George. Soph told him it was okay to play the field before he settled down and he told her not everyone was as much of a slut as she was. "More's the pity," she'd wink at him and he'd tell her to stop grossing him out. He missed Soph just then like an ache. He missed his mum and his home. But he'd never tell anyone that—imagine the ribbing if he admitted he was homesick and lonely and the only time he felt okay was when he was around George?

George. Who was gay. And had a boyfriend. And a nice place. And who Finn could absolutely not casually fuck.

He was never going to fall asleep with all these thoughts racing around in his head. He usually jerked off when he was like this. But lately whenever he jerked off, he thought about George. And could he still do that? Was that wrong?

He imagined George pulling back from that hug and their eyes meeting; George leaning in and kissing him hesitantly, kissing him with the shyness he'd had when he said, 'Not yet.'

Finn groaned and rolled onto his stomach, he got his hand around his dick and started to slide it up and down. It was dry but it didn't matter—he was keyed up so fast it took him by surprise—he imagined George pushing him against the wall outside his place, slipping his hand into Finn's shorts and jerking him off, kissing him, telling him he hadn't done this with other guys before but God, how could he not when Finn was interested?

"*How can I not touch you?*" he imagined fantasy-George saying, and he came with a loud groan, the intensity of it ricocheting through his body.

"Fuck," he said to the quiet of his room. He needed to get up and shower. He passed out.

12

♥

PRESEASON TRAINING HIT ANOTHER gear after that and George put all of his energy and focus into it. When he saw Finn in the locker room the Monday morning after the dinner, he gave him a quick smile and Finn smiled back, something reassuring in it, and George felt like he could breathe. Someone knew. Well, Jack knew because Joq had told him, and all weekend George had ruminated on whether or not Jack knew about Finn. And if Jack and Finn had fucked around. And that pissed him off no end, so he decided to channel all that energy into coaching. It was the kick up the ass he needed—he could not be dragged into some gay footy soap opera fretting over where his hot rookie put his dick or who might be putting their dick in him. Which made him even madder.

He was grateful for that smile though, he really was.

"Right," George called everyone to attention. "You've all given me some pretty good reasons why you want to win this thing. After training and video review, we're gonna work on how you can keep that in the forefront of your mind."

He looked around the room, most of the guys nodding along, Cary included, and that meant a lot. George had known the transition from player to coach and the success or failure was going to be measured by how well the guys he'd played with took it. Cary was all there for it, and Lacy had backed that up with an odd intensity in the why exercise. It'd taken George by surprise. Lacy had two gears: chilling off the field and vicious gun on the field. So to see him totally animate when he said: "I play because it's life. It makes me feel so fucking alive. It's like, there's life when you're not playing a game, all the stupid shit you gotta do and I feel like a corpse walking around and then I hit the field and time slows, right? I'm all there. It's life. It's fucking life. I wouldn't give it up for anything."

The guys exchanged a few glances at that, but no one looked mocking, just as shocked as George.

"Right, well, that's a pretty good why," George said.

"Yeah," Lacy nodded, still oddly animated, "It fucking is." Then he sat.

George might think he was high, only he knew he'd never come to training in that state. He knew he partied, but he also knew he scheduled it so it didn't conflict with the footy schedule. And he knew he used masking agents to beat the drug and alcohol tests—courtesy of Scotty telling him, because Lacy told Scotty and George just didn't want to know. Lacy could play. That's all that mattered.

The point for now was, everyone focused on their why, everyone had shared their why, and as a team, they committed to helping each guy achieve that. They would elevate—as a team—for each other.

"So, what're we doing?" Lacy asked now.

"We're going to meditate."

There was nervous laughter.

"Really?" Cary asked seriously.

"Really," George replied.

"I don't think I can turn my thoughts off," Les said, looking worried.

George hid his smile. This kid.

"That's not the point, you'll see. Now get on out there and we'll do it after. Get everything out on the field, it'll make it easier," he finished.

He caught Finn's eyes as Finn headed out and the soft, approving nod he received made his stomach fill with butterflies. He did not need approval from his twenty-year-old rookie for fuck's sake. But man, he liked getting it.

He stood with Kurt as they ran through drills. He realised as he watched the players that this was what he was going to have to do. He wasn't in denial—he knew the conversation he and Finn had on his driveway had a subtext and that subtext was, *are we gonna fuck?*

Now, in that moment, George had been full of beers and giddiness and all, *hell to the yeah*. Joq did, why shouldn't he? He'd heard the warning in Joq's voice when he came back in, when Joq said, '*But surely you're not thinking...*' and at the time he'd been thinking, *That's exactly what I'm thinking*.

He woke up sober the next morning and the reality of that crashed into him like a freight train. He wanted Finn, wanted him like he'd never wanted anyone.

He watched him now, racing down the field, his hair catching sunlight, his laughter as he launched and took a mark, and thought he'd do a lot to get to touch him, to kiss him, to have him in every way.

Which is why he absolutely couldn't. He had way too much with the coaching to worry about.

And it took him until Sunday night to arrive at the real reason—he couldn't just fuck Finn. Not in a million years. And a guy like Finn? He was destined to shack up with a younger guy, someone perfect, someone infinitely better than George. And as George sat in his living room, watching the afternoon sun cast the room in a soft glow, he realised if he got involved with Finn, that reality would crush him.

Meeting Finn's boyfriend? Christ, the thought of it made him so anxious, so angry, so oddly ashamed, he had to put a lid on this.

And so, he did. He shrank his whole world to training, to turning this team into an unstoppable unit. He remembered what he had with Joq—he had a great boyfriend who put up with his shit and took good care of him. He needed to go back there, to his mindset before he saw Finn at the draft.

He had a well-ordered life, clear goals and a stable home life. That's what he was focused on.

Fortunately, it seemed Finn had drawn a similar conclusion, George thought as they wound up the meditation exercise. It'd been a mixed success—with some guys unable to stop laughing, others telling them to '*shut the fuck up*,' while Les was fretting over not being able to quiet his mind, and no matter how many times George told him it was about watching his thoughts, detaching from them, not stopping them, the worse it seemed to get for him. George had only just managed not to laugh when Les looked seriously worried as he whispered: "But I am my thoughts."

Finn hadn't made a sound. Sitting cross-legged, palms resting on his thighs, George would've thought he'd gone to another astral plane if it wasn't for the quirk of his lips listening to George trying to reassure Les beside him.

As everyone filed out of the room with variations of: "Thanks," "Is this going to be a regular thing? Do I need to practice?" and some muttering about missing the point, George saw Finn hanging back, ostensibly shaking out his legs, rolling up his mat.

"All good, Finn?" George asked once they were alone in the physio room.

"Yeah, just wanted to mention something," Finn smiled.

And it was then George realised they'd both decided to be professional about this. There was something in that smile—it was warm, but it was closed off too, it was the smile of a player talking to their coach. And every interaction except that first reassuring smile so far that day had been firmly in that realm—a player and a coach. George knew he should be relieved—and he was, he was doing it too—but he felt hurt too. It hurt to see Finn withdraw from him. He needed to get over it.

"What's up?" George asked.

"It's about Les," Finn said and came to stand in front of him.

"He'll get there," George replied. "He's just gotta stop taking everything literally."

"Yeah, nah, not that," Finn grinned. "You know he got told to gain some weight?"

"Yeah, muscle, bulk, he's too skinny," George indicated for Finn to walk with him.

Finn came up alongside him, his voice warm and professional when he went on. "Yeah, well, he's been uh, eating nothing but Nutella."

"What?" George shot Finn a look. Finn was trying not to laugh. He appeared to be doing his best to appear like a good teammate, but he looked adorably young for a second as he met George's eyes around suppressed laughter.

"Yeah, 'cos it's all fat and sugar? So he figured it'd be a fast way to gain weight, but now he can't shit," Finn explained.

George pressed his lips together to hold in his laughter.

Finn was grinning when he went on. "I found him... Well, let's just say I heard him somewhere and he was in a lot of pain and then he told me why."

George started laughing.

"I reckon you better get the nutritionist to have a chat with him," Finn finished.

"I reckon I need to get the nutritionist to move in with him," George shook his head.

"Or that," Finn chuckled.

"Thanks for letting me know," George said as they arrived at the locker room door. George would head to his office, while Finn would head inside and get his bag and go home.

"Yeah, course," Finn smiled over at him. "I mean, I can give him some pointers, but I feel like this calls for a professional."

George shook his head again, still laughing. He wanted to reach out and bump Finn with his shoulder. It still felt warm, being around him; he entered Finn's orbit and it was where he wanted to stay.

He took a step back and turned for his office. "I'll get Nance on it,"—that'd scare the shit out of him—"Have a good night, eh?"

"Yep," Finn smiled at him, his hand on the locker room door. It was still warm, yet professional, but it was also strained. "You too."

George headed for his office so he wouldn't have to keep looking at it.

It was for the best. And he was sure if he kept his promise to himself to simply be Finn's coach, and to be a friend in the whole 'it's okay to be gay and play' he'd found himself dragged into, then it would fade with time. Especially now it was clear that Finn had reached the same conclusion.

It would be fine. Everything would go back to normal.

George sat at his desk and looked at his photos—him and his sister at the Brownlow's, him and the team when they won the last Grand Final, him and his parents at his draft—no Joq in any of these ones, for obvious reasons, but he had a picture of them together on his bedside table at home. It was a good picture, the pair of them looking smart in their suits before they went to a function for Joq's dad, an ex-Olympian's fundraiser. It was the kind of thing George could be expected to attend if he felt like it, and he loved Joq's dad, found a special comradery with the Olympic swimmer. It'd been a good night.

He had a great life. He was happy. And training had gone well.

He spun in his chair and looked out at the empty oval, the lights still on, the seagulls flocking in for the night. He wondered what Finn was doing for dinner, if he was meeting up with other guys or eating at home alone. He wanted to text him something teasing about it. Which is when he realised they hadn't texted all weekend. And that hurt the same way getting a hip and shoulder when you weren't expecting it hurt.

So, it really was like that. Good, George said to himself and spun back to his notes, this was good.

13

GEORGE WENT INTO THE zone after that. He had the preseason to whip these guys into an unbreakable unit, and by God, he was going to do that. While seeing Finn still gave him fucking butterflies and made him feel like a teenager, the longer the careful space they were keeping between each other went on, the better George got to know him, and the more he liked him. Not like that! But as a young guy, as a player. Finn would hang back a few times a week to ask questions, offer his opinion, and give George a heads up if something needed to be escalated. The latter never crossed a line—it was always within the range of what a coach should know without breaking confidence—and George really liked that.

Finn caught him on one occasion as George was heading for his car.

"George," Finn called out as he jogged down the tunnel.

"Finn?" George stopped and waited for him. "What're you still doing here?"

"I thought of something," Finn replied around a grin as he came to stand in front of him. He was dressed in street clothes—tailored shorts and a nice button-up, like he was going out, which of course he was, it was Friday night and he was probably the hottest bachelor in the state.

"You heading out?" George asked without thinking.

"Oh," Finn's smile dimmed as he dropped his gaze and plucked at the shirt. "Yeah, getting dinner."

"Did you need something?" George asked because he didn't want to know if Finn was dating someone already. He totally could if he wanted to. And he was freshly showered, shaved, dressed in his best summer clothes, smelling amazing and George didn't want to know.

Finn looked at him again, the professional smile slipping under George's question. "Sorry, it's nothing," he jerked his chin at George's bag. "Heading home?"

"Yeah," George said. "Tell me what you thought of."

Finn fidgeted. "Now I'm gonna say it, it sounds stupid."

"You could text it?" George said without thinking. But they'd stopped texting. The only reason Finn really had to text him was if he was sick and going to miss training—Finn was never sick and he never missed training.

Finn smiled like he was thinking the same thing—*But we don't do that anymore*.

"I was just thinking, should we walk?" Finn started to walk down the tunnel.

George followed. He couldn't help himself—he bumped Finn to get him talking.

"What were you thinking?"

Finn glanced over his shoulder, he was blushing, something adorably shy in his gaze. "Just about the individual for the group thing? Now it seems stupid, but I was thinking about like, schooling fish. I watched 'em a lot when I surf and the way they move? Like, they move as one. I dunno, it's stupid," he dropped his head and tucked his hands into his pockets. "You and Joq got dinner plans?"

George suppressed his surprise at hearing that question—just like that, out there, at the stadium—and answered it. "Joq's either cooked or gone out, I'll find out soon enough. What're you thinking about these fish?"

Finn smiled at him like he was grateful for being indulged. "It's actually kinda depressing? But they move as one for protection, you know? One moves, they all move, and like because they're a huddle, it's harder to pick them off. But like, what got me thinking about it was how they don't think about it. They're that tight, that in the moment. I dunno," he laughed and looked up at the sky, "it made sense at one this morning when I was thinking about it."

"You were up at one?"

"I was in bed, but I couldn't sleep."

"So you decided to count fish?" George took the gentle shove Finn gave him. "Such a beach bum. I usually work with sheep, but I can see it, what you're saying."

"Yeah?"

"Yeah, no one fish is greater than any other fish, all move for the goal."

"Yeah," Finn said.

"I reckon the only problem is—

"Fish aren't cool."

George smiled. "I was gonna say predators, but yeah. We need that, but like, something to inspire violence. Not actual violence—

"Blood lust," Finn finished.

They were at George's car.

"I'll keep thinking on it," Finn said.

"Do you need a lift?" George asked. He imagined dropping Finn at a hipster restaurant where some hulk would come out and meet him for their date and regretted asking.

"Nah, gonna get the tram, meeting Les in the city. I'm gonna introduce him to the wonderful world of salads and smoothies, then maybe grab a coffee."

George flashed him a grin—hugely relieved, but also—"You know you can tell me if you're really heading to a bar, a club. I did when I was your age."

Finn tilted his head to the side. "I don't wanna get on it for no reason. We're really getting coffee. I wouldn't lie to you."

George felt like he'd just been called out. He was embarrassed.

"No, of course," he rushed out. "Well, have fun," he finished but didn't get in his car.

"You too," Finn replied and rocked back on his heels. "I'll come up with a predator."

George smiled at him. He liked the way his mind worked, the way he was looking at George like he was really going to go away and ruminate on this until he had the answer.

"You want my job?" George asked.

Finn laughed. "Not for all the money in the world. If this doesn't work out, I'm going to uni to study like, business or something."

George smiled at him. "Or something."

"Yeah," Finn backed up. "I better go. Have a good night," he said awkwardly then tripped as he spun around and headed for the street. He righted himself quickly, jamming his hands in his pockets and focused on the sidewalk.

George watched him go and reassured himself that this was good. Finn's idea was good. He focused on how to find a blood lust animal that schooled.

Then there was the time Finn was waiting for him the week before the season opener. They'd settled on wolves for the analogy, after a lengthy conversation in the carpark near George's car about the merits of orcas and magpies before settling on wolves. George was impressed by how much Finn seemed to know about all these animals. Finn had smiled sheepishly and said he'd just been looking it all up for this.

"Finn," George breathed out as he exited the building now and saw Finn leaning against the wall, one leg cocked, phone in hand and engrossed in the screen.

Finn startled and broke into a smile. "George," he said and pocketed the phone.

"You good?"

"Yeah, just a bit," Finn shrugged and walked over. "Excited?"

"You should be," George replied and hoisted his bag over his shoulder. "First game is the best."

"Yeah, and we're really coming together, it feels good, feels like we could be something," Finn went on.

The lights in the carpark lit up Finn's face—his smooth skin, eyes that always seemed so animated, that watched George so closely—and George wondered for a fleeting second if he was ever going to get over it.

"If not this season, then next," George replied.

"You reckon we can't go all the way?" Finn asked. It wasn't an accusation, it was a genuine question.

"I reckon we gotta see how we go once we're under pressure. Sometimes guys who get the theory of team first lose the mentality once we're in an actual game," George said.

Finn tilted his head to the side—it was the slightest, quizzical head movement, and he did it a lot, it made his hair fall out of his eyes—"Like they forget and go for glory."

"Exactly, plus we still got some holes, we need another ruckman, and you're gonna surpass what Jack was bringing, no doubt about it, but we gotta see how it comes together in a game. You know they been studying you in ways like they never would've studied Jack."

He made no move to go to his car. These carpark chats seemed to have found their own parameters—they'd stand under the lights outside the doors, greet the security guard if he came by, and talk until George had to cut it short because he simply had to, or Finn would cut it short because he had somewhere to be.

"Yeah, I'm not worried about that for the first game. No way any of those Sydney boys can catch me," Finn said around a sly smile as he shoved his hands in his pockets.

George laughed. "I reckon you're right about that."

Finn's smile widened and turned genuine.

And now was when George needed to go.

"You need a lift?" he always asked, even though the thought of Finn in his car, so close, filling the space with his gorgeous smell, drove him kind of nuts. But Finn always said:

"Nah, gonna get the tram."

"You know once you're playing that might not be a good idea anymore," George headed for his car, Finn beside him, close enough George could feel his presence.

"Meh, we'll see, I can handle myself."

"I know, but it can be a lot, and I don't like the idea of you alone around that," George stopped at his car. "You'll probably need a lift then." He didn't know why he was pushing this when he really couldn't do that.

"Lacy's always offering," Finn shrugged.

"So why haven't you been taking him up on it?" George asked as he unlocked his car and threw his bag in.

"You know," Finn trailed off. George looked up at him; Finn's eyes were looking out at the street, his hands still in his pockets. He met George's eyes and smiled. God, he was gorgeous. "I better," Finn jerked his head at the street, "See you tomorrow?"

"Course," George replied.

"'Kay, night, George," Finn said as he backed up, still smiling, something embarrassed in it.

"Night, Finn," George replied and watched him turn and stroll down the street.

"Fuck me," George said under his breath once Finn was gone.

So, this was still bad, George decided once he got into his car, but it was better than it had been. And the season would start and Finn would have to go with Lacy and that would be the end of the carpark chats. Good.

14

Before a game, before a surfing comp, Finn was one of those guys that got in the zone with a precise routine. The same smoothie, then oats with fruit, put headphones on and blare his 'get fucking pumped up' mix as he entered the stadium, then a warm-up, massage, get dressed, finish warming up, all with the headphones on. He didn't talk to the other guys. He visualised, saw exactly how it was going to go—clean passes, soaring marks, fingers finding the ball like glue, and goals that sailed through the middle.

He looked up when George entered the locker room and slipped his headphones off. He'd been there, in his zone, for several hours and this was always when he came out of it; when his coach addressed the room, or with surfing when he grabbed his board and headed for the water for his heat.

It was like re-entering the world after being far away.

George was assessing everyone, his face seemingly blank—but Finn was getting to know him and underneath that, evident in the tiny uptick of his lips at the corners, he was fucking pumped. And that made Finn pumped.

Finn grinned when George's eyes landed on him and George didn't return it, but his eyes seemed to shine a little brighter.

"Right!" George clapped his hands. "What are we gonna do out there?"

"Hunt as one, win as one!" the boys shouted.

"Fucking boom!" George walked out again.

His job was done, now it was on them.

They jogged out of the room, down the tunnel, and onto the sunny field, the stadium packed—a sell-out, fifty thousand fans.

Finn felt a flutter of nerves. Lacy jogged alongside him.

"Take 'em in now, get it all out, then pretend they're not here," he said as they matched pace.

Finn jerked his chin. "Got it."

"I mean, unless you score and some shit cunt rival supporters are giving you shit," Lacy smiled at him. "Then you remind them whose fucking church this is."

Finn laughed and Lacy took off, marked the ball Cary kicked towards them and took two more strides before belting it right through the middle.

He did as he was told—looked around the stadium, took in the huddle of girls screaming for him (how did they not know he was gay?)—and gave a quick smile before jogging over to where George was waiting and the other guys were assembling.

The stadium was loud around them, and Finn was aware of the opposition huddle, could hear Besson riling up his players. He stood at the back and watched as George regarded each player seriously, like he had confidence in each man.

"We've worked our asses off in preseason," he said and a few guys nodded. "We've recognised we're a unit, no man is greater than the team."

More nods.

"And most importantly, we know why we're here," George went on, his voice never going above conversational. He had a deep voice, and his cadence when he put on his coach voice was commanding yet calming. Finn felt like it was a voice that trusted them.

"Then there's only one thing left to do," George said. He smiled, quick and sure. "Take what's yours."

The guys cheered and George turned and headed for the coach's box. They fanned out into position. Cary, who was acting captain until they settled on someone, lost the toss and they accepted kicking into the wind for the second and fourth.

Finn felt a knock at his shoulder. "Your mum says hi," a nasty voice said.

Finn ignored him. He knew who it was—Carr, their top-D-man, which meant they were already tagging him.

"She takes it like a pro," he went on and shoved Finn.

Finn almost laughed—mum sledges, seriously? He focused on the ball. Cary won the ruck and Finn exploded into the open to grab it. He raced past the fifty-metre mark and clocked Lacy in the pocket to his left—watched as the defender pulled him back—and took a split second decision to line up and take the shot. It sailed straight through the middle and Lacy was the first one jumping onto his back.

"Fuck, yeah! Finny!!!" Lacy screamed in his ear as the other guys rushed him—hugs, taps, and a grinning shoulder shake from Cary.

They went back to centre and then it was on—Carr upped the sledges, hit him harder—Finn ignored it, focused on the ball. He was copping it from other players too—he ignored it. He'd worked hard all summer to put on more muscle and it insulated him; plus, he only had eyes for the ball, the game. The rest of the team were the same and they were tied at half-time.

Finn jogged in behind the main group and George met him coming in.

"And you were worried?" George asked quietly around a grin, his notepad up and covering his mouth.

"Ah, shut it," Finn replied and hid a sheepish smile. It was embarrassing now to think about.

They turned together and jogged down the tunnel.

"You alright?" George asked quietly just before they went into the room. "Carr's got them all gunning for you, we can take a run at them if you want."

"Nah, I got it," Finn said as George held the door open for them.

"Yeah, you do," George clapped him on the shoulder as he went by to address the room.

Finn felt the touch warm him through, even felt it once George had let him go and he had to shake himself—that wasn't happening and he'd been good, he'd been professional, kept his promise to himself to let it go. He focused on George telling them what they were doing well, what they needed to watch.

"And Finn reckons he's got Carr in hand," George said around a gruff smile.

"Yeah, he does!" Lacy shouted.

"Right, stretch, drink, break the tie—this one's ours," George said and left them to it as he made his way around the room to talk to each player.

He crouched down in front of Finn. Finn ignored the swoop of butterflies when he watched George's hair fall into his eyes, the slight wave to his brown curls.

"You reckon you got another one in you?" George asked around a private smile.

Finn smirked. "I reckon I got two."

George huffed a laugh and shook Finn by the boot. "Good. Between you and Lacy—

"This one's ours," Finn finished for him.

George smiled. Finn smiled back. The moment stretched on and thankfully Les slamming the door startled them and it broke.

In the end, Finn belted another two. And when Lacy insisted everyone go out to celebrate and George agreed wholeheartedly, well, Finn couldn't see any reason to say no.

"I fucking love this song!" Cary shouted.

Finn watched George crack up—he was at Finn's elbow, standing at the bar at the rooftop garden bar, and Cary was dancing, awfully, real white man horror show, to 'We Built this City.'

"He's like the Manchurian candidate," George said as he refocused on Finn.

Even through the beers, Finn felt butterflies at the gaze, at the proximity.

"Huh?" Finn asked eloquently.

"Cary," George jerked his chin at him. "Every time this song comes on, he starts dancing like that, then he'll stop and won't dance again. Unless someone puts this on again."

"Maybe we should try it," Finn replied and drained his beer.

The barman was in front of him instantly. He was cute and he'd been flirting with Finn in a joking way when they arrived, and in a quizzically serious way as the night wore on. George had been doing the rounds and drifting back to Finn all night. Finn was aware of where he was in the room like a line connected them; and each time George drifted back to him, he felt flustered in a way he tried to cover by getting invested in the conversation with Les, then Lacy, then the barman.

"Another one?" the—admittedly gorgeous—dude asked now. He was lithe, lip pierced, covered in tattoos, and his tan skin was set off by bottle bleach blonde hair. He had an accent—Spanish? Portuguese?—and Finn liked the way it sounded.

"Two," George answered over Finn's shoulder from where he was leaning with his back against the bar facing the room. "And one of those cigars, please."

"Coming up," the barman smiled at Finn, held eye contact as he poured the beers.

Finn laughed and dropped his gaze. Sue him, he liked being flirted with—not that he'd do anything with the guy, fuck no, he could just imagine the headline: *Finn Flynn has a blinder and celebrates by getting railed according to anonymous Brazilian source.* That's where the accent was from, he was pretty sure.

"Are you Brazilian?" he asked the guy.

The guy smiled, surprised and pleased. "I am. Most people think Spanish," he slid the beers over and leaned on the bar. "How did you know?"

"Surfed with some Brazilians," Finn replied.

"Ah yes, Brazilians are excellent surfers," the guy said, insinuating Brazilians were very good at other things as well.

"I've got these ones," George cut in and the guy looked at him.

"You're running a tab," he straightened, winked at George, "but I'll get the cigar."

Finn focused on George, who was shaking his head; he smiled at Finn as he took the cigar, lighter and cutter from the bartender when he came back. "You wanna head to the balcony?"

"Yeah," Finn said.

"Come see me before you go," the bartender called as they moved away.

Finn smiled over his shoulder as he followed George to the balcony.

They came to a stop at the railing, placed their beers on the ledge as George unwrapped the cigar.

There was an awkward silence. Finn tried to think of something to say. He was falling back into the George bubble and the beers weren't helping.

"Be careful if you're gonna hook up with anyone outside the system," George said, eyes focused on cutting the tip off the cigar.

"Huh?" Finn asked.

George flicked his eyes up. He had the look of a captain telling a player something they didn't want to point out but had to.

"That bartender wants to hook up with you," George said. He was speaking quietly, not that anyone else was around. "I'm just saying, be careful. If you do something with someone who hasn't got what you've got to lose, you better make sure you've got an NDA."

"Is that what you did with Joq?" Finn couldn't believe he just asked that.

George looked surprised and the coach mask slipped away. He lit the cigar, but he seemed to be really focusing on it. Finn wanted to take the question back.

"Sorry," George said at the same time Finn said, "I shouldn't have said that."

George smiled at him, something almost sad in it. "It's none of my business. I just want you to be safe."

"I'm not gonna hook up with that guy," Finn blurted.

George's smile transformed and Finn swore he looked relieved.

Before he could reply, Kurt appeared with three glasses of whiskey and the talk turned to the game, to how they could run that play against the team the following week.

Finn drank too much, and he was a giggling mess, Lacy's arm around his waist when he went up to the bar for final call.

The bartender was serving someone else, but he grinned over at Finn, and Lacy cackled. "Get it, Finn."

Finn blushed and dropped his gaze. "I'm not gonna do anything."

"Fuck, why not?" Lacy asked, affronted and loud. "I would. Christ, dude's a ten."

Finn knew he should be looking around, making sure nobody could hear them, though to be fair, everyone would pass it off as a joke. They always did.

"Alright," came from behind them. Finn turned and met George's smiling face. "I'm taking you home," he said to Finn.

"Not yet, Creed," Lacy shot back. "My boy here's having another and we're getting the number of that tall drink of water," the bartender was moving towards them. "Oh hello, here he is," Lacy beamed at him.

"I reckon we've all had enough," George replied, but his smile was friendly as he directed the remark at the bartender. "I don't want the wrong headline in the morning."

"You know what your problem is, Creed?" Lacy turned to him.

George grinned. "Yeah, yeah, I care too much about headlines," he focused on Finn and explained. "Lacy's been bitching about this for years."

Lacy scoffed. "It's true! Live in the moment, Georgie and fuck the haters!"

"Can I get you another one?" came from the bar.

"Yes," Lacy said as George said, "We're good."

"Finn?" Lacy asked.

Finn could feel George beside them; he checked in with him.

George shrugged. "If you want another one, we can do that," he said and Finn could see he really meant it. But his head was spinning and if George was offering to get him home, he'd take that.

"Nah," Finn said and extricated himself from Lacy.

"You suck," Lacy turned to the bartender. "Double fist me, my good man," he winked.

Finn listened as the guy laughed at Lacy and double-checked Lacy was still drinking soda water and vodka—Finn was going to give him shit about that later—before he called over to Finn. "You come back and see me anytime."

Finn looked back and smiled, too drunk not to. The bartender grinned. George nudged Finn to get him moving as he told Lacy, "Todd's still here, he'll get you home."

"All good, boss," Lacy grinned then leered at Finn.

"Right," George said and got them walking.

The stairs were moving.

"The stairs are moving," Finn said as he leaned on George.

George's arm came around his waist and Finn sank into it, felt everywhere George was laughing.

"How much did you drink?" George asked.

"Lacy wanted to do shots. Tequila," Finn replied.

"You're gonna feel that tomorrow," George herded him onto the street. He was pulling his phone out. "What's your address?"

"Umm," Finn frowned at him.

George stared at him, waiting. Then he laughed. "Give me your phone."

The street was busy, and Finn felt George shuffling them to a dark alcove in front of a closed shop.

Finn giggled and dug around in his back pocket for his phone and handed it over.

"You wanna unlock it?" George asked. He was so close—Finn could smell him, musk and cigar smoke.

"Twenty-one, eleven, zero, two," Finn said, well, slurred.

He could feel George's eyes on him.

"Your birthday? Really?"

Finn giggled again.

"It's like you want everyone to know your business," George said and did something with the phone.

"Nah," Finn leaned his weight on George. It felt nice. "There's nothin' on there."

"We've texted a lot," George slipped the phone back into Finn's back pocket. It was perfunctory, but Finn liked that too.

"I saved 'em in a secret folder."

George didn't reply and through the haze Finn wondered if he just said too much. "No one would know what it is. It's called tide records 2020, 2021, then 2022 and like, no one's gonna look at old tide records."

"You saved them?" George asked.

Finn met his eyes. It felt charged; and even though he was drunk, he was self-conscious.

"Yeah, lotta good training advice," he mumbled.

"Yeah, course," George replied. Was Finn imagining his disappointment? Before he could ask, George went on.

"I ordered us a car, can get you dropped off first."

He leaned against the shopfront window next to Finn.

Finn leaned on him. "I'm so drunk, but like, I could've had another one with Lacy."

"One game in," he jostled Finn. "You gonna be like this every time you have a blinder?"

"Nah," Finn sank into his side. "Just this once. And if like, we win the Grand Final."

"Don't jinx it," George nudged him again and stayed close. "It's probably for the best, you cannot handle your booze."

"Hey, fuck you, I'm tight," Finn replied and tried to shove George, which resulted in him almost toppling them both sideways.

George's arm came around his waist and hauled him up. "Yeah, you could walk a real straight line," he chuckled softly and held him against his chest.

It felt so nice that Finn sighed. Right. He couldn't be doing that—he pulled back and forced himself to lean against the glass, a careful space between them.

He felt George doing the same beside him, carefully respecting the distance. He hated that George had clearly come to the same conclusion he had—they couldn't casually fuck. Even though, technically, they could, Finn thought, suddenly vicious. He'd been having this thought spiral sometimes—who gets someone like George and fucks other dudes, who does that? He was about to ask but thankfully George spoke first.

"That bartender was hot," he said. It sounded weird.

Finn looked at him. George glanced at him and looked away—he seemed to be trying to be cool? Supportive? Finn didn't know why, but it pissed him right off.

"Maybe you should fuck him then," Finn said.

"What?" George asked. "Why would I fuck him?"

"Why would I?" Finn asked and stared at him.

"I... Sorry, I," George ran a hand through his hair. "I suck at this."

"At what?"

"Being like, a gay support system," George said quietly.

Finn cracked up.

"What?" George asked, but he was smiling again.

"Nothin', just yeah, you do," Finn shoved him gently. "Please don't."

"You don't want me to be your gay support system?" George was grinning at him now.

"I really, really don't," Finn laughed.

George looked like he was about to say something else when his phone buzzed. "Car's here."

They didn't talk on the way to Finn's place, but when they got there, George got out with a "Just a sec," for the driver.

Finn waited.

"I'm just gonna make sure you get inside alright," George said and tucked his hands in his pockets.

Finn's heart clenched and he smiled. "Thanks."

"Yep," George smiled softly back and jerked his chin. "Well go on then."

Finn laughed and crossed the lawn to the gate that'd take him up the stairs to his place.

"Night, George," he called before he went in.

"Night, Finn," George called back but didn't get back in the car.

By the time Finn was in his apartment and looking down at the street, he saw the car pulling away.

15

*M*Y HEAD'S FUCKING KILLING *me*, was waiting for George on his phone when he woke up.

He was still half-pissed himself, and he grinned as he tapped out: *Swimming helps, come over?*

Yeah? Came back immediately.

Yeah. Bring coffee.

He got a laughing emoji and *on my way* and couldn't stop his smile.

He rolled out of bed, grabbed his board shorts and a t-shirt. He padded down the stairs and found the place empty. He vaguely recalled Joq stirring when he came in; he didn't recall him leaving, but then he remembered he had plans with his uni buddies and felt relieved. He hadn't been thinking of Joq at all when he invited Finn over and now, when he realised he'd have the place to himself, a weight dropped off him. Then he felt immediately guilty. So what if Joq was here? In fact, it'd be better if he was, he reasoned as he got himself the jug of cold water from the fridge and a glass. He chugged three glasses and then made a smoothie. He was just finishing it when the intercom crackled to life and Finn's voice came through, '*George?*'

George clicked the gate open and went for the front door, his smile taking over his face.

Finn was grinning manically back at him as he walked up the driveway—two takeaway cups of coffee from a fancy place in each hand, wearing board shorts and a hoodie with nothing underneath, his feet wedged into shoes with the laces undone.

"You just get up?" George asked around his grin as Finn came closer.

"Yeah, but I been awake for a while," Finn smiled as he handed over the cup.

"That'll teach you for trying to keep up with Lacy," George replied. "Come in, Joq's out." He didn't know why he tacked that on the end and felt guilty again. But that was stupid—he wasn't doing anything wrong, and he wasn't going to do anything with Finn at all, even though he totally could if he wanted to.

"Cool," Finn replied easily though, like he couldn't have cared either way, and that was good too. Finn might be here now and it was just the two of them, but they weren't doing anything and they seemed to be on the same page with that.

George held the door open and Finn went past him, ducking his head around a smile before waiting just inside the door for George to go first. He let the door fall closed and it was an odd moment—the two of them inside the foyer, alone. George was in that weird space where he was hungover but still kind of drunk.

"Right, swim," he said awkwardly, but Finn snort-laughed, also nervously. George couldn't help his grateful smile as he went by him, couldn't stop himself from brushing his hand over Finn's hip to get him to follow. Finn turned into the touch and stayed close and God help him, but it felt electric.

He led them out to the pool, to the shallow end, the white marble an austere match with the high white walls framed by perfectly trimmed hedges. George sat on the edge and dropped his legs into the water as he took a sip of his coffee, Finn following suit. It was a beautiful morning—the sky clear, the sun warm but not hot, a gentle breeze lifting the palms that flanked the cabana to their left, the house quiet to their right.

"Shit, this is good?" he said as he sipped.

"Yeah," Finn lifted his face, still at an angle so his hair was falling in his eyes, which were bloodshot and black smudged, hungover, but they seemed bluer for it, and they were looking right at George, looking into him, warm and happy. "There's this epic place at the end of my street. They even use Bonsoy, I couldn't believe it."

"This is soy?" George asked.

"Yeah, dairy's shit for your immune system."

George scoffed and kicked the water at him. "Says who?"

"My mum, man, it's true," Finn replied and splashed him back.

Right, his mum was a naturopath, of course she would be into hippy nutrition.

"Well, I never get sick, how do you explain that?" he teased.

It was Finn's turn to scoff. "You're an elite athlete with a team of coaches, nutritionists and physios looking after your health for over a decade?"

George smiled like a smug asshole.

"Also," Finn drained his cup and pulled his hoodie off as he went on, "you probably got good genes," he tossed the hoodie behind him.

George couldn't help the surreptitious look he gave Finn's body—the shorts were low on his hips and even sitting huddled forward, his abs were sharp, pronounced, his tan skin perfectly smooth, and there was so much of him—he was a large unit of perfectly carved muscle. George was no slouch himself, but damn.

"Look who's talking," he said without thinking.

But Finn laughed and George met his eyes, caught the blush starting up his neck.

George reached over and pushed him into the pool to cover his feelings about it. Finn went, his laughter getting caught in the water. George just had time to pull his shirt off before Finn grabbed him by the ankle and yanked him under the water, his hands working their way up George's leg as he dragged him down.

George went with it, opened his eyes and caught the blurry image of Finn watching him under the water, his smile blinding. He lunged forward and grabbed Finn around the waist and launched up, throwing him as they breached the surface, Finn's shout of laughter ricocheting off the high walls.

They wrestled for a while, joking about each other's lack of strength before that made the other prove said strength. George didn't know how long they'd been fooling around when he decided they needed to eat.

It was nice, nicer than it should've been, to have Finn across from him in the kitchen as he prepared steak and salad wraps, answered Finn's steady line of questions about his past games—which Finn knew extraordinarily well—and reassured him, again, his career was nothing like Finn's was going to be.

"I feel like your jinxing me, man," Finn said as they sat in the cabana and ate.

"Nah, I just been around, I know what I'm looking at."

"Yeah, but," Finn picked at a piece of lettuce sticking out of his wrap. "Your career was epic, I don't like you saying I'm gonna be better."

"But you are," George said because he obviously was.

"No, but," Finn took a bite and George waited for him to finish, watched as Finn watched the water and chewed, swallowed, turned to give George a serious look. "The way you talk sometimes, it's like you don't realise how good you were."

"Oh, well," George looked away. "Course I do, Brownlow and all that," he rubbed the back of his neck.

"No, George," Finn said seriously. George glanced at him. "You were fucking amazing, just consistent, solid. I never saw you have a bad game—

George scoffed. "I had so many bad games."

"No, you didn't, not by normal standards."

"Yeah, well," George shrugged. He knew his stats were good. He played every game like it was the most important game in the world. That didn't mean he couldn't have been better. And he never had the flashes of brilliance Finn had and would go on to have.

"That kinda consistency is what makes a great player," Finn finished.

George looked at him. He said that like only a twenty-year old rookie could, with absolute conviction.

"Don't dismiss the power of being an emotional player," George said. He'd thought about it over the years—looking at guys like Lacy and Sean Hiller over at Freo—sure, they had bad games, but when they were good? There was no one like them, they were untouchable, they played with the Gods; whereas players like George? Steady and good, but it would always be in the mortal realm. And George knew crowds came to see those guys, not the steady hands. Finn was going to be like that.

"Use it to your advantage," he went on. "And don't let the bad games, which will come, get you down."

"But they will," Finn said, dejected.

They finished their lunch and George bumped Finn's shoulder. "It must be so hard, being so good you get to sulk about bad games that haven't happened yet."

Finn snorted, but he smiled up at George. "Wait until they do, I'll be even worse."

"Like I said," George bumped him, "it must be so hard, being the best player and having a cry about not getting best on ground one day in some imaginary future."

Finn giggled and shook his head. "Come on," he stood, "I need to swim that off."

"You need to swim off a steak and salad wrap?" George replied but followed him.

Finn slid into the water, swam to the middle and George launched himself into the water next to him, making an almighty splash, their combined laughter ringing out as they got into another wrestling match.

They passed the afternoon like that—swimming, wrestling, sun-baking—and it was unbelievably nice. George didn't think about coaching, about all the worries he'd been carrying around, not once.

It was late afternoon when Finn's phone buzzed; they were lying side by side next to the pool when Finn got up to get it. George realised he didn't even know where his phone was.

"You need to go?" he asked.

"Nah," Finn smiled over at him before returning to tapping something out on his phone. "Just Les, wants to order shit and get me to try this new game with a few of the other guys."

"You should go," George replied and sat up.

"Oh, okay," Finn busied himself with his phone again.

"I don't mean I want you to go," George got up. "Just if you want."

Finn met his eyes like he was checking George's sincerity. He smiled. "Maybe later." He tossed his phone back on top of his clothes and walked towards George, casual as you like, smile sly, and George sucked in a nervous breath when Finn broke into a grin and pushed him into the pool, his hand wrapping around George's shorts so he toppled in on top of him.

"Oh, it's on!" George said as he breached the surface and grabbed for Finn to push him back under.

Finn wriggled free and pushed George under again and as George launched up, he laughed and shouted, "I'll get you for that!"

Finn swam backwards, George grabbed his ankle and Finn shrieked with laughter as George pulled him close and got him in a headlock and dunked him playfully. Finn came up—still laughing—turned, blinking water out of his eyes and launched himself onto George's shoulders, shoving him under.

George came up again when Finn loosened his grip, still smiling. Finn looked past George and his face flashed with surprise, or was it fear? George spun around and saw Joq resting easy in the doorway; he was smiling wryly at them, looking cool and relaxed in his tailored shorts and designer polo shirt.

"Hey," George smiled up at him. His heart was beating weirdly. "Where you been?"

"Lunch," Joq replied easily, his gaze assessing yet fond.

Finn swam over to the edge of the pool away from George. "Hi, Joq."

"Finn," Joq nodded an acknowledgement and his smile looked forced when he asked Finn about his night. Right, because Joq probably thinks George is going to fuck Finn because George hadn't brought Finn up again since that dinner. He'd made his resolve and then just gotten on with it.

"It would've been," Finn answered Joq's question, "if this one didn't make me go home."

And George couldn't let that stand and he felt a weird need to show Joq this was just buddies. "Hey now, rook. We're one game in. Gotta save it for the finals," he said and splashed him—it was a canned response, and as he and Finn got into it again, he felt like their wrestling was no different than what he'd do with Scotty, with any other guy.

Joq disappeared inside and they settled down. Finn lay on his back in the water and George reclined on the edge. Finn started telling him about his adventures introducing Les to vegetables, about how he missed surfing, and George leaned back and listened; he liked Finn's voice—deep yet soft, there was something intimate in it, which felt strange yet good around such innocuous stories. He watched Finn's mouth moving around the words, caught his eye every time he tipped his head back to meet George's eyes to check he was still there, still listening. *Where else would I be?* George thought.

"I'm pruning," Finn said after a while.

"You wanna get out? Have some dinner?"

Finn smiled over at him, closed-mouth, before looking away and getting out. "Nah, I told Les I'd get there eventually."

George didn't know why that felt like a lie. "Yeah, course," he said and followed Finn out. "I'll give you a lift."

"I can get a car," Finn replied.

"Or I can give you a lift," he smiled over at him as he watched Finn towel off, pull on his hoodie quickly.

"Or you can give me a lift." He shrugged, his smile small.

George grinned—he felt like he'd just won a round—and Finn dropped his gaze and headed for the door.

George got dressed, cast about for his phone, didn't find it, and went inside. He brushed his hand over Finn's side and smiled over at Joq sitting at the kitchen island with a beer and his phone out. "Gonna give Finn a lift," he said and got them moving.

"Oh, you didn't want to stay for dinner?" Joq asked, which is what George had been thinking. But he could hear the insincerity in Joq's voice. He really needed to talk to him.

"Nah, me and the other rookies gonna game and order in," Finn replied, friendly yet guarded.

"No junk," he said on autopilot—even though Finn would never eat junk, he knew that—and told Joq, "See you when I get back."

"See ya," Finn chimed in, dropped his head, and George followed him out the door.

They were quiet as they got in the car, quiet as they left George's place and Finn punched Les's address into the sat-nav, quiet until Finn changed the music.

"Steady on," George said and grinned over at him as some awful folk sounding music filled the car.

"This is the shit, I saw them live," Finn replied and settled back in his seat, his long legs kicking out in the space trying to accommodate his athletic build, his shorts riding up around his powerful, bare thighs.

George refocused on the road, grateful the weird tension had been broken.

"You and Joq got dinner plans?" Finn asked. It was a normal enough question, and Finn had asked it before; George didn't get why it made him uncomfortable.

"Just the usual," he replied.

"Nice," Finn picked at his shorts, looked out the window.

George wanted to say something—reassure Finn that Joq liked him. Ask him what they were having for dinner at Les's place. Get into a debate about the merits of interval training versus long-distance cardio. Hell, anything. But he felt that tension creep back in and he didn't know what to do about it.

"I really hope I get that someday," Finn said, his eyes still out the window. "Soph says there's more to life than a boyfriend, but I dunno..."

George felt his gaze on him and looked to check. Finn was watching him, an inexplicable smile on his lips, but it didn't touch his eyes.

"It's like you been living the whole dream all this time," Finn said.

George swallowed. It certainly didn't feel that way to him.

"It's hard," he said slowly, kept his focus on the road. "It's good, but it's hard. Stressful. The hiding."

He didn't want that for Finn. He thought about how stressful the past twelve years had been—the undercurrent of fear someone would find out and he'd have to do a press conference, talk about it, talk about where he put his dick for fuck's sake, see Joq get hounded. The familiar feeling of panic crawled over him, made him want to pull the car over and get out just so he could breathe, so he could run.

"Yeah, but," Finn said quietly, "it's not like you have to do it alone."

George focused on his breathing. Finn was right. Sort of. Joq got it and yet he didn't, while George preferred not to talk about it. So Finn was right; physically, he wasn't alone. But sometimes you could be with someone else and it danced along the knife's edge of companionship and a trap. He didn't want that for Finn. He really hated the idea of Finn with anyone, as childish as he knew that was, but he had to believe it would be better for Finn, even though he didn't believe that, not really.

"I guess so," he replied, a shortness to his tone he didn't mean as he pulled up outside the little house the sat-nav had directed him to. He cut the engine. "Not something you need to worry about just yet," he smiled over at Finn, tried to diffuse the tension he'd brought back and felt that rush of gratitude when Finn returned it, warm but reserved again, like he'd tucked a bit of himself away.

"See you in the morning?" Finn asked and George noted the tone; it was a very deliberate way to evade the conversation they'd been having.

"Course," George smiled at him, professional again.

"Cool," Finn smiled back. "Thanks for today," he opened his door and got out and then leaned back in, "I had the best time. I mean," his smile slipped back to the fun one, "you know what I mean."

"Yeah, me too," George smiled warmly. "Go, have fun."

"Yes, boss," Finn grinned, straightened, and closed the door with a soft click.

George waited and watched him pad up the stairs. Finn turned back and smiled over his shoulder while he waited for the door to open and George smiled before he started the engine, watched as Les let Finn in before he drove off.

The house smelled of cooked fish and felt warm and inviting in the way Joq always made it. George felt a sudden rush of gratitude for him—Finn was right, he wasn't alone and Joq made his place a home.

"Hey," he said to Joq as he went for the fridge to get his water. He didn't know how to say that to Joq without it sounding like he was saying something awkward. So, he just grabbed his drink.

"Hey," Joq replied, his usual unruffled self, still looking classic cool in his designer shirt, his eyes calm on George. "All good?"

"Yeah," George replied and went over to the table, gave Joq a firm kiss on the temple before he took his seat. "You know rookies."

"Yeah," Joq replied around a loaded exhale.

George looked at him and realised he was worried.

"I didn't," George tried to say it. Then he decided to drop it. Joq would see for himself he wasn't doing anything with Finn. "This looks good," he said instead, focusing on the marinated fillets, baked just the way George liked.

"You didn't what?" Joq asked.

George focused on cutting into his fish, getting some salad. He needed to say it; he hated that Joq was worried about all this and he could reassure him, so why was it so hard to say?

"With him. I didn't. It's a bad idea," he took a mouthful to stop himself from saying everything else.

It was absolutely a bad fucking idea: he'd never taken advantage of their arrangement because being with Joq made him panic, the thought of being outed as a couple was hysteria inducing enough. Never mind fucking someone else and adding another potential person who could out him to the equation. Joq would never out him, of course he wouldn't, but it wasn't always done on purpose, just doing it was enough. And George was attracted to Finn, he wasn't in denial about that, but he absolutely could not fuck a rookie, one of his players, that was absolute madness, that was a potential disaster of epic proportions.

"It is," Joq replied firmly.

George grunted his acknowledgement even though—even with all his knowledge that he couldn't—it pissed him off that Joq was so firmly against it. He'd lost count of the number of dudes Joq had fucked over the years. It never bothered him—it didn't—but he had a sudden irritation at the unevenness. But he wasn't going to start something over that; they had what they had and George had made his peace with it.

"How was lunch?" he asked instead. He knew these things were a mixed bag for Joq—always good but he'd be wistful about them too. George got it. Joq was way too smart to be running stadium security for fuck's sake. But he'd assured George it'd been his choice and he was happy, so George listened to him recounting what everyone was up to, laughed when he heard about his friends' adventures with all their kids, and held onto the certainty that he was doing the right thing not pursuing anything with Finn.

By the time they went to bed, he was telling himself he was glad he had Finn the way he had him, he got to have this friendship. It was enough. It was really good.

Joq leaned over and George met him, kissed him, said, "Good night," around a warm smile.

He listened to Joq sleeping beside him, his presence warm and familiar in their bed. His mind drifted to memories of Finn's hands on him in the pool, playful, the feel of Finn's skin under his hands. He watched the play of shadows on his ceiling, ran his thumb over his fingers and he didn't feel tired, not at all.

16

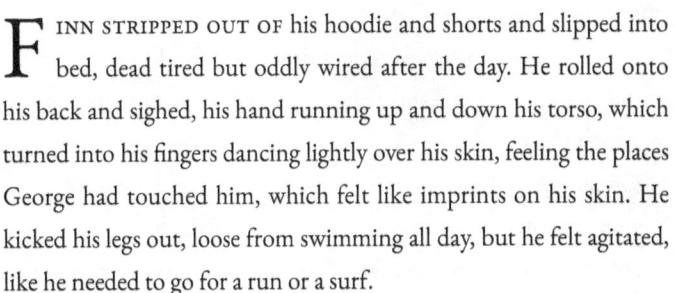

Finn stripped out of his hoodie and shorts and slipped into bed, dead tired but oddly wired after the day. He rolled onto his back and sighed, his hand running up and down his torso, which turned into his fingers dancing lightly over his skin, feeling the places George had touched him, which felt like imprints on his skin. He kicked his legs out, loose from swimming all day, but he felt agitated, like he needed to go for a run or a surf.

He glanced at his alarm clock. 12:03. He thought about texting George in a fit of madness and even scoffed out loud at himself. They might've done that again, but it was firmly in the friendzone.

He circled his pec with his index finger, rubbed his nipple and stared at the ceiling. He wasn't going to sleep. He drummed his fingers on his chest, rolled over and grabbed his phone and sent a message.

You up?

He watched until the screen went dark and sighed. It lit up.

Go to sleep.

He grinned and hit call.

"Why?" Soph whined when she picked up.

Finn laughed. "Why not?"

"I was sleeping," Soph bitched.

"Really?" Finn actually felt bad. "Sorry, are you alright?"

"Yeah," she groaned and Finn imagined her getting up, going into her little kitchenette. She was studying Environmental Biology at the University of Queensland and rented an apartment in Brisbane. "Just had an early morning doing all this tagging shit. What're you doing up?"

"Couldn't sleep," he rolled out of bed, found his trackies, tugged them on and went to make some herbal tea. He knew she'd be doing the same. He never, ever wanted any of the guys to know this was something he did at odd hours with her, or with his mum. Imagine the shit he'd get for it?

"Haven't you got training at ass o'clock? And you didn't respond to my message," she yawned, "good game, but you needed to punch Carr."

Finn laughed. "Sorry, we went out drinking and my phone was blowing up. And I'm not gonna get suspended, c'mon."

"Might be worth it. Shoulda heard Mum, I think she wants to fly down and punch Carr," Soph said and Finn heard rustling, heard her blowing on her tea.

He laughed. This is why he didn't worry about the mum sledges—these guys would be turned to stone with one look from his mum.

"Yeah, George offered to set the guys on him too," he got his tea and went into his living room, stretched out on his excessively large couch and glanced around at his house plants as he blew on his tea. "I told him I had it though."

"Hmm, George must've been happy with your game then?"

"Yeah," Finn felt an odd thrill just talking about George. "Yeah, I think he was."

Soph snorted. "Why wouldn't he be? Hard to miss him grinning in the coach's box every time you scored."

"Yeah?" Finn didn't know that. George never emoted, well, rarely, he was known as a cool head for a reason.

"Yeah, looked fucking chuffed. Well, for him anyway. So, drinking? Did you meet anyone nice?" she asked mockingly, then snickered.

"Shut up. No, *Mum*, there are no nice boys in Kansas," he replied and thought, well, there was one, but he wasn't available. "What'd you tag?"

"Oh, yeah, flying foxes..."

And Finn listened to her telling outrageous stories about tagging wily creatures until dawn.

"What'd you do today?" she asked around a yawn after she finished up.

"Y'know, just hung out with George, went swimming," he closed his eyes.

"Yeah? That's nice, I guess. He less boring in person?"

"He's not boring," Finn objected, his eyes flying open.

"I've overhead enough of your conversations; I didn't know anyone other than you could debate the merits of complex carbs versus high protein for that fucking long," she replied.

"It's an interesting discussion—

"Well, so long as you're having fun. You sound happy?"

He thought about his day. He was.

"I am."

"Good."

"Are you?" he asked.

"Course," she said.

"Good."

"Alright, I'm going back to bed," she said. "You should too."

"Yeah," he said and stayed where he was.

"Don't sleep on the couch."

"I won't."

"You are."

"Alright," he heaved himself up and sat forward, sighed.

"You sure you're good?" Soph asked, suddenly more awake.

"Yeah, course."

"I know we don't, you know," Soph said. We don't get all touchy-feely, Finn got it. "But you can talk to me about shit if you want."

"That's very generous of you," he said.

She laughed. "It is. I don't even let my friends talk to me about shit. But, you're definitely good?"

"Yeah, just," he sighed and decided to tell half the truth. "Home-sick."

She groaned. "Get it together, man."

He laughed.

"Me and Mum will be at the Brisbane game."

"Can't wait."

"Yeah," she trailed off. "Alright, well, I can't do anymore moody silences. Call me if you wanna talk."

"Yeah, thanks, you too," he said.

They said their goodbyes and Finn padded back to his room and got into bed.

He still couldn't sleep.

Training that week was good, fine, normal; Finn had been repeating some variation of this all week. Because while on the outside it was good, fine and normal, on the inside, he was spiralling.

It started with a niggle in his groin on the Monday morning. He knew it was all in his head and the groin was fine.

Then in training on the Tuesday, he missed an easy pass, which should've been an easy shot on goal and six points.

On Wednesday George stopped by his locker and asked how he was doing.

"Great!" Finn replied, too loudly.

George gave him a concerned look, but left him to it.

By Thursday, he had all three events cycling on repeat in his head and leading to absolute disasters—he was going to need another surgery; he was never going to kick another goal; and George was going to realise he was a total loser and end their friendship.

It wasn't surprising that his game that weekend was a disaster.

So, he did what he always did when he was feeling down: he looked himself up online and went through all the comments and messages on his social media. The majority were good, but they faded into the background as he read line after line, an endless tirade, detailing all his faults, ranging from *soft, spoilt, over-rated* to *pretty boy wanker, he should spend less time on his image and more on his actual game.* And then there was message after message of nudes, tits, some dick pics, invitations asking if he'd like to fuck. He didn't understand it, but those ones made him feel worst of all. One woman had even asked him to be her sperm donor, like, it was a legit request; it made him snort a laugh, but it made him feel like shit too.

He slammed his laptop shut and stretched out on his couch, the reel of insults running strong in his head, the weight of it holding him down on his couch. His phone pinged and he ignored it. He'd been ignoring it since the end of the game. He didn't even know why he turned it back on after the flight home. It started ringing. He ignored that too. It rang out and the room fell silent. He watched the afternoon sunlight play on his ceiling, listened to the sounds from the street up the road, the crowds moving in and out of bars for their Sunday sessions.

His phone rang again.

He ignored it.

It'd barely stopped when it started again.

"Fucking hell," he reached for it and hit answer.

"What," he said flatly.

"Finally. Fuck's sake, Finn. I was about to drive over," George said. He sounded like he was trying to sound mad, but he couldn't hide his relief.

Finn felt bad. "Sorry," he rubbed his eyes. "Didn't really feel like talking to anyone."

George was quiet, but his breaths sounded nice down the line. Finn closed his eyes and listened to them.

"Alright," George said after a while. "Just wanted to make sure you're alive."

"I'm alright," Finn's voice cracked.

"Fuck's sake," George huffed. "You're worse than a diva. What are you doing?"

"Not much," Finn said.

"What's not much?" George asked.

"Nothing, resting."

"Have you eaten?"

Finn sighed. "I'm fine. I'll," he let out a long exhale, "I'll be good as new tomorrow for training."

"Fuck training," George said.

Finn's eyes widened.

"You can't be taking one bad game this hard. Now," George blew out a breath, "I'll let you go if you don't wanna talk, but you gotta promise me you'll get off your ass, eat something good, and go and watch a comedy or something."

Finn cracked a smile. "You don't have to go."

"Yeah?" George asked. Finn could hear him smiling.

"Yeah."

"Alright, well, get up then, you can talk to me while you get dinner," George said.

Finn groaned but got up. He went into his kitchen and got out one of the boxes from the fresh delivery service.

"I'm gonna cook some eggplant thing with rice," Finn mumbled.

"Good, I'll tell you about the time me and Scotty went to Bali," George said.

Finn smiled again. "Not gonna lecture me on my game?"

"Not tonight."

Finn could hear him moving around—he sounded like he was in his office.

"Tomorrow then," Finn said.

"Do you wanna hear about this trip or not?"

Finn smiled for real. "Course."

"Alright, we'd just finished our first season, knocked out in the first round and we thought it'd be a good idea to go drink our sorrows..."

Finn listened, cooked, and by the time he was sitting down to eat, he was laughing for real.

The next game was worse. Finn was so far up in his head, he couldn't see straight. No one would know it—Finn had perfected his public image years ago, showing no real emotion, maintaining his easygoing façade, and his team were supportive, rushing him to shake his shoulder when he missed. Again. While George just shrugged like it didn't matter at all.

"It'll take time to build consistency," Kurt said sagely the week after that loss in the locker room. "Don't worry about it."

Finn didn't feel like he had time. It'd been two years since he'd been drafted; the time to prove his worth was now.

"Lacy," Finn said once Kurt was gone. "Wanna run some plays with me?"

"I do not," Lacy grinned at him. "Sorry, man. I got plans. But Kurt's right, don't let it get to you. I mean, are you trying your best?"

"Yeah, but—

"Then that's the only measure."

"Yeah, but everyone—

"Uh, whose everyone? Some shit cunt online? Some shit cunt who couldn't run to his letterbox never mind play eighty minutes?" Lacy scoffed and hoisted his bag over his shoulder. "Don't take your measure from those fuckwits, Finny. I'm out, we can run drills on Monday."

And then he was gone, the door clanging shut behind him and the room empty save for Finn, sitting in front of his locker, breathing in the dank smell and staring at the old brick walls. The white paint was peeling.

He needed to get up, go home, call his mum back. He leaned back against the metal and closed his eyes, kicked his legs out. His hammies hurt and that was good, that's what he deserved.

The door opened.

"Finn? What're you still doing here?" George asked.

Finn cracked his eyes open. "What're you still doing here?"

"Lacy told me you were in here being a sad sack," George replied and smiled gruffly at him.

Finn shook his head but he couldn't help his tired smile. Then he remembered George had a hot boyfriend and on top of the last two games that fact combined with his stupid crush felt like the biggest insult of all. He schooled his expression and leaned back.

"I'm good, just decompressing," he tried to smile reassuringly and felt it contorting his face.

"I think we're gonna have to have a chat about this," George went to sit down in front of him.

"No we don't," Finn sat up. "You can go, just go and have dinner with your boyfriend," Finn waved his hand.

George froze and Finn felt guilty, which was fucking stupid—George did actually have a boyfriend, it wasn't a lie or a secret between them, he didn't need to be here babysitting the bruised ego of his team's wasted first draft pick.

"This is where I want to be right now," George said quietly. "Can I sit?"

Finn leaned his head back against the locker with a soft thud and closed his eyes again. "Knock yourself out."

He felt the air shifting in front of him as George sat. It felt warm, nice; he wondered if he was ever going to stop loving the feeling of just being near George. And he couldn't have that.

"Won't Joq wonder where you are?" he asked.

He felt George moving, heard him huff like that was a stupid question. "We don't live in each other's pockets. He's got his life, I've got mine."

Finn slid his eyes open but didn't move his head. George was watching him, a strained smile on his face. Right, he probably didn't want to discuss his sex life with his stupid rookie.

"Sorry," he said. "It's none of my business. I don't know why I keep," he waved his hand and didn't finish that sentence—because what he kept doing was getting mad about it and he had no right. And on top of everything else, he really didn't need these feelings and he especially didn't need to be alienating George.

"It's gonna be a long fucking career if you take every bad game like this," George said, seeming keen for the subject change.

"It's gonna be a short fucking career if I keep doing this," he retorted.

George clapped him on the thigh and shook him. "You won't."

Finn's skin buzzed and he drew on everything he had not to respond to the touch. It set him on fire and he wanted so much more of it. George took his hand back as suddenly as he'd touched him. Finn did his best not to react to that too. George looked unsure for a second, which was weird.

"I'm alright," Finn said softly, "I just do this sometimes."

"I wish you wouldn't."

"I'm sorry, I know I'm a fucking pain—"

"No, I wish you wouldn't beat yourself up so much. I hate seeing you like this."

"I'll get better."

"No," George shook his head for emphasis. "I hate seeing you down, I could care less how many bad games you have, I wish you wouldn't take them to heart like this."

Finn nodded. He needed to get it together. "I'll get over it."

"When?" George asked.

"When I have a good game," Finn replied seriously.

George groaned, then he laughed.

"What?" Finn asked, he couldn't stop his smile.

"Nothin', just, didn't expect you'd be like this."

Finn sobered and sat up. "Yeah, well."

George grabbed him again and Finn froze.

"And I didn't think I'd find it so, I dunno," George smiled at him, his lips twisting to the side like they were sharing a joke. His hair was even longer, the wavy brown strands falling near his eyes, and his expression was happy, like Finn being a moody little bitch was delightful. "So charming I guess."

Finn snorted, disgusted. "It's not charming."

"It kinda is, I mean," George took his hand back again and stood. "You need a better way to work through it 'cos it's not good for you, but it's nice to see you're not perfect." He held his hand out.

Finn took it and let George pull him to his feet.

"I'm far from perfect."

"Me too," George replied and squeezed his hand. "And that's a good thing."

He let Finn go and stepped back. "Get your shit together, I'll give you a lift home."

And for once, Finn didn't argue about getting the tram.

He wasn't perfect and George thought that was okay.

Okay.

But nothing could've made the absolute clanger he had in the next game feel better. Right in front, no wind, a total set fucking shot and he booted it out on the full. The opposition fans went ballistic—cheering and sledging—and Finn kept his expression calm but inside, he was shocked, embarrassed, devastated.

He felt a rough shake on his shoulder as he jogged to join the huddle for the umpire to throw the ball back into play.

"Now you're really part of the team," Lacy said close to his ear. Finn glanced at him.

Lacy winked. "What? You reckon we haven't all done that? You're not special."

Finn cracked a weak, private smile between them. He couldn't recall seeing Lacy do that, but it was the thought that counted he supposed.

The rest of the game finished in a blur and he did what he'd been doing all week since George took him home: he called him. They'd been talking about anything but football and it made Finn feel better. He'd also promised George he wouldn't read shit about himself online. He constantly broke that promise, but George didn't need to know that.

Only this time, George said. "Come round, we'll sort it," and then told him he'd pick him up and hung up.

They spoke about anything but football on the way to George's place.

"You want something to drink?" George asked as they came inside and took their shoes and coats off.

"I'm good," Finn replied. He felt like they were alone in the house, but he wasn't sure and something about the thought of Joq being there made him feel like he needed to behave, to be on guard.

"Okay, sit," George said and herded him into the lounge room. "Joq's at work."

"Oh, be cool if he wasn't," Finn answered in what he hoped was a nonchalant tone but still felt like it had the vibe of a school kid hoping his friend's parents weren't around.

"Maybe, but we need to talk one on one, get this sorted, so, sit," George demanded again once they were near the couch.

Finn sat. George sat in front of him on the coffee table.

"Okay," George said and smiled at him in the coach way. "Talk to me. What's going on."

Finn huffed. What a stupid question. "You know what's going on, I fucking suck."

George shook his head. "History would say otherwise. What's happening up here?" he leaned forward and tapped Finn's temple.

Finn sighed and stopped himself from leaning into what was a perfunctory coach's touch. "I just, I can't" he shook his head and sat forward; he thought George would lean back, but he didn't, he stayed where he was, in Finn's space. Finn breathed out, shakier than he meant to, and dropped his gaze. "I keep thinking my groin is gonna get fucked again and then I'll be this player who played a few fucked games and got injured. Then I'll be out for the year for another surgery. And then I'll just be this dead fucking weight on the team, but everyone will be secretly glad to be rid of the pretty boy wanker who was good for nothing but one game and a few ab shots."

He threw himself back dramatically after he finished; he was too scared to look at George.

"Okay, no one thinks any of that," George started.

"That you know of," Finn gave him a pointed look.

George was trying not to smile. "Look, Finn, I might not know everything, but one thing I do know is what most guys on a team are thinking about. And most of us are thinking about our own shit, not a rookie finding his feet in his first year."

Finn thought about it. That was probably true, which made it so much worse.

"God," he groaned. "I'm such a narcissist."

George laughed. "Nah, you're just young and like I said, you're an emotional player, you've just got to figure out how to use it to your advantage."

"Lacy said I'm not special. After I booted it out on the full, he said, 'you're not special', everyone's done it."

George snorted. "Lacy has a way with words. He's also right."

"You haven't."

"Yes, I have. I told you about it."

"With no wind? Dead in front? Less than ten metres out? No, you were under pressure, that's normal."

George frowned like he was trying to think of a way to sugar coat it. "It's not really the point. Why don't you replay all the good moments?"

"I dunno, nobody else does and besides," he rushed on so George wouldn't ask about who nobody else was, "I'm never gonna get better if I focus on what I do well."

"Whose nobody else? Everyone's talking about your first game."

Finn gave him a derisive look. "I dunno who you're talking to, but no, they're not."

"You gotta get out of your head, it's all up here," George said and tapped his temple again. Finn dropped his eyes to the carpet—he liked the touch so much and he didn't want George to see that and read everything in his face. And he liked that George got he was doing this to himself—reading this shit and twisting it and making himself crazy. He liked that George got him.

"Hey," Joq said from the hallway and Finn startled back, felt George do the same.

Joq was in the entryway, looking suave in his suit, something apologetic in his smile. "Sorry," he said as if to confirm it.

"All good," George replied and straightened up, turning his attention more fully to Joq. "Didn't hear you come in."

"Hey, Joq," Finn said as he sat back and tried to smile.

"Wouldn't worry about the game. This one had some clangers in his time," Joq inclined his head at George and smiled reassuringly. Finn knew it was meant to be comforting, but it felt like a platitude, like an invitation to talk about it when the last thing he wanted to do was talk about it at all. But he smiled and George snorted like he was used to Joq giving him shit, but maybe that's not what was needed right now.

"Well, I'm gonna," Joq waved his hand at the back of the house and Finn assumed he was indicating the kitchen, implying food. "You guys want anything?"

"I'm good," George said.

"Nah. Thanks, Joq," Finn replied and tried to mean it. He felt bad, but he was just glad Joq was going away. As he listened to him moving further into his house, he felt terrible for thinking that and decided he was the one who needed to go away.

"I should go," he said.

"You don't have to," George said with a soft smile.

Finn sighed and sat forward, he looked at his feet because he couldn't look at that smile. And George still wasn't moving back when Finn entered his space.

"No, I should... leave you to it," he finished lamely looking at his feet.

"What I want to be left to is getting my best player out of his head," George said gruffly, but when Finn looked up he saw he was smiling like he was endeared by Finn's stupidity. Because Finn was stupid and useless.

"Yeah. Can't let everyone down," he replied.

"Hey now," George said sharply. "Fuck everyone."

Finn raised both eyebrows.

"This is about you," George said, eyes boring into Finn's. "You gotta realise one bad game, hell, fifty bad games doesn't change who you are."

"Think fifty bad games is gonna change who I am," Finn replied like George was being ridiculous—because he was.

"No, it doesn't. Fifty great games, fifty bad ones. You're still—"

"Still a pretty boy wanker who should spend less time cruising for pussy and cock with his thirst traps and more time playing actual football?" Finn cut him off.

George sucked in a breath, he looked affronted. "I told you not to read about yourself online," he said after a minute.

"Yeah, well, it's probably true," Finn dropped his gaze again.

"That's why you post that shit?" Now George sounded angry.

"Of course not," Finn's head shot up.

"Then why'd you say it's true?" George asked him.

"I dunno, lots of people message me about it."

"Is that what you want? To meet a guy that way?"

"What? No! Of course not."

"'Cos you're not gonna meet someone worthy of you if he's reaching out just 'cos of some picture."

Finn snorted. "Pretty sure I'm not gonna meet a guy anytime soon. And I dunno about worthy of me," Finn emphasised 'worthy' because that was a joke. "They're right. I'm just a dumb fuck-up with a nice face and good abs who could've been good at football if he spent more time on it and less on his fucking image."

George stared at him, his expression giving Finn nothing.

"You gotta know any guy who gets you is gonna be the luckiest son of a bitch in the world," George said after a moment.

Finn's heart fluttered. But he didn't believe it. "Stop trying to make me feel better."

"I'm not."

Finn just stared at him and George stared right back.

"You're a great player," George went on after several beats. "And yeah, you're easy on the eyes. But that's not all you are. That's not what makes you... special."

"What makes me special?" Finn whispered because he couldn't help himself.

"This," George replied softly; he tapped the side of Finn's temple with his index finger. "And this," his hand moved down and pressed against Finn's heart.

Finn felt his heart starting to pound under the touch.

"No one can touch this," George finished quietly. "Not unless you let them."

Finn leaned into the touch and watched George watching him back. He breathed and watched George do the same, his eyes never leaving Finn's. The moment seemed to break when George looked away, his eyes flicking to the side, something shuttering.

"And no fuckwit on some social media site is fucking worthy of it, you hear me?" George said in a different tone and the moment was broken.

"Now," George said and sat back, "what you've got to do is figure out a way to shut out the noise and just play again. And I reckon the answer's in your why—the team. Think about everything you do as being for the team..."

Finn nodded along because that was a good point, but his chest felt warm where George had touched him and he knew Joq was somewhere in the house, being George's super-cool boyfriend, but for the first time the thought of him didn't hurt.

"Yeah, okay," Finn said and smiled the first real smile he had smiled all night when George finished up with the new plan.

Finn didn't know how much longer he could go without touching George, kissing him. He never wanted to be this guy, but he was beginning to think he'd take what he could get.

17

♥

GEORGE SAW A DIFFERENCE in Finn that week in training—he was laughing with the guys more, focusing on how he could be a player for them from within the team. Not that Finn had been acting like an all-for-himself-glory-whore guy before, but he'd certainly started to take his shortcomings so personally it was debilitating to himself and the team.

Finn gave him a blink-and-you'll-miss-it smile as he jogged up the beach—his blonde hair catching sunlight and shining, his eyes bright and alive—and George gave him a quick smile back, a short exchange against the backdrop of bare feet thudding on thick sand, the waves crashing on the shoreline, the rest of the team moving as one as everyone grabbed their stuff and got back into the carpooling arrangements that got them there.

George glanced at Finn and Les getting into Lacy's car. He heard Les asking if Lacy could swing through a drive-thru to get breakfast, "Please?" he tacked on the end.

"You'll get fat…" Lacy was saying as he got in and Finn glanced up like he could feel George watching him, but kept on laughing at Lacy giving Les shit.

"Reckon we need to focus on blocking the corridor," Todd said from George's side and he tuned into their tactics. The West team visiting was a bottom side and should be pencilled in for the win; but after three losses and knowing the thing you had to watch with a bottom side was the fact they had nothing to lose and could come out with a blinder at any moment, George knew this was a game they needed to take seriously.

"Yeah, flood their forward line," George replied. "Focus more on suffocating them, kill any momentum and we'll be able to answer."

"Alright," Todd nodded along and headed for his car. "I'm gonna run it when we get back, pull everyone out of position."

"Sounds good," George replied and clicked his immobiliser. He saw Lacy gun it into a gap in oncoming traffic and shook his head.

They did win that game, which was awesome and the shot in the arm they needed, but Finn had another bad game—barely any possessions, and the shots on goal he did have got him nothing but messy turnovers. He'd been good in defence though, and George was pleased to see he could be relied on as an all-rounder when needed.

He wanted to tell him as much, but when he did the rounds, he couldn't find him. He figured he was in the showers and focused on chatting to everyone else.

The place was empty and quiet by the time he realised Finn must've raced through everything and left. Lacy had been one of the last to go, which meant Finn took the tram.

Good game, he fired off as a message and went back up to his office.

His phone pinged. *Is that sarcasm?*

No. Where are you?

Home. And that was another shit game.

How did you get home? George reclined back in his office chair, spun and looked out at the oval.

Tram. Don't change the subject.

George wanted to laugh but his worry for Finn on public transport overrode it.

Did anyone give you a hard time?

His phone was silent for long enough that George thought about calling.

Nothing I don't deserve, finally came back.

"For fuck's sake," George said under his breath. He hit call.

"I'm fine," Finn said as he picked up.

"And I'm officially banning you from public transport. What happened?" George asked.

"Nothin' much," George could practically see him shrugging. "Just some drunks talking shit, it was fine."

George tensed and his stomach dropped. "But it could escalate. Jesus, Finn. I can't enforce a ban on you but please, for me, please stop doing that, okay?"

Finn groaned. "Don't ask me like that."

"Like what?"

"Like it's for you."

"It is for me," George replied. "And it's for you, for your safety."

"I can handle myself," Finn replied.

"I know you can, but there's a difference between handling yourself against a couple of drunks and a whole crowd of them and you just," he blew out a breath. "Look, like it or not, you're a celebrity and there's shit you need to insulate yourself from, do you hear what I'm saying?"

"I have a responsibility to hear what the fans think," Finn replied, but there was something off about it. Like he wanted the punishment. If George didn't know better, he'd think Finn was a masochist.

"No, you don't. You have a responsibility to play your best. Operative word being your," George told him.

"Well, that's not happening, so maybe I need some incentive," he snapped.

"Right," George sat up, he needed to get this through that thick skull. "They don't own you, you hear me? You own you. This is about you. And I'm asking, again, please, for me, don't do that anymore."

"Ugh, fine," Finn said.

"Promise?"

"Fine, fuck, I promise, whatever. Now do you want to tell me about my game, coach?" Finn asked.

George stifled a laugh. "Well, yeah, good defensive work."

Finn snorted.

"It was. I wouldn't lie to you. You play like that, you build other aspects of your game. It's good for the team," George went on.

Finn sighed. "Yeah, I guess."

"You guess, while I know. Now stop being a sad sack and unwind," George finished.

"How am I supposed to unwind?" Finn asked after a beat. There was something loaded in the question or maybe it was George's imagination, but ever since that weird moment at his house, when he'd touched Finn's chest and they'd stared at each other, he'd been feeling like they danced up to a weird line. A line they absolutely weren't going to cross, but just dancing near it gave him a thrill and made him back off in terror.

"Hot shower. Food. Maybe a movie," George replied, a beat too late.

"What kind of movie?" Finn asked, a hint of humour in his voice.

George gave a breathless laugh. "I dunno, you do you, but Finn?"

"Yeah?"

"Just make sure it's something that gets you out of your head. You need to give yourself a break, okay?" George put on his best professional coach voice and he hoped it delivered.

"Yeah, yeah, okay. Sorry, I know I keep being…"

"You keep being a rookie in his first year in the league under a fuck tonne of pressure. This is all totally normal and you'll get there, okay?"

"Yeah, I guess."

"You will. And you come see me if you're getting down, alright? I mean it, this is normal. There's no magic switch or some fucking positive affirmation that'll make you skip this part," George went on.

"Were you like this?" Finn asked. George could hear the genuine curiosity; and he decided to answer honestly.

"Not about the footy," he blew out a breath. "I found my feet pretty quick and I was a big body, even back then, took the hits no problem and I'd played with a lot of those guys coming up. But," he felt like shit just remembering that time, but he knew telling Finn would help and he needed to find the words he'd never found before. For Finn.

"But, I was gay, right? I've always known that. Well, not always," he tried to laugh but it came out weird. "Let's just say when a guy knows what his dick is for, I knew what mine was for."

Finn didn't say anything, but George could hear him breathing down the line. Listening with full attention.

"Anyway, that… was tough," he finished inadequately.

"Yeah?" Finn asked softly.

"Yeah," George nodded; he felt like he was on the verge of a panic attack like he used to get back then. "I knew early I was gonna make it, gonna get drafted. And I knew I was always gonna be hiding too.

It was," he looked at the oval and remembered that first year, fuck, that article coming out, the absolute paralysing terror that his worst fears were coming to life—everyone would know and he'd be drenched in shame. Worse, he'd have to deal with it. To say he was in a bad headspace with all that in that first year would be an understatement.

"Let's just say sometimes I could be a real pain in the ass to be around," he finished.

Finn laughed. "Yeah?"

"Oh yeah." Christ, he thought back on it, the stories Joq could tell, Scotty—who didn't know, but knew something was up on the regular—well, it made what Finn was doing pale in comparison.

"So, you know," George finished. "It's okay. It's a lot. And believe me, you're doing better than I did."

"I doubt it," Finn replied quietly.

"No," George said. "Fucking seriously, Finn. I was a nightmare." He cringed recalling how he'd shut Joq out, how he'd sit in the locker room and try to act normal, and how that came off as cold, even rude sometimes.

"How'd you get past it?" Finn asked.

"How do you know I did?" George asked around a smile.

Finn chuckled. "Everyone knows you're loved in the locker room, come on."

"Yeah," George loved his team, so he couldn't deny it. "I just put everything into the game and shut everything else out. I still never watch the news, I figure if something bad happens, like aliens invading, I'll know soon enough."

Finn laughed. "And I guess you had Joq?" he asked hesitantly after a moment.

"Yeah," George replied because it was true enough, but at the same time, it was hard. He reckoned if he wasn't such a couples guy—and he was, he loved having a partner, a home—he might've been better off alone. And Joq made it easy for him; hell, even Joq's request to fuck around early on made it easier, made it feel like a fairer trade.

He didn't want to discuss that with Finn though. Something about it felt like the kind of example of a relationship he didn't want for Finn, which led him back to Finn being in a relationship with another guy and he was again accosted by the irritation the image of it inspired in him.

"Thanks for telling me," Finn said quietly, heartfelt.

George huffed. "To be honest, I feel like I just unburdened on you. I don't reckon coaches are supposed to do that."

Finn laughed again, warm and delighted down the line. "I won't tell anyone."

"Thanks," George replied gruffly. He felt like he was saying thanks for a lot more. And he needed to get off the line now. "Go and unwind. I'll see you on Monday."

"We've got the day off," Finn said.

"Right," George had forgotten. "Tuesday."

"Yep."

"But call me anytime you're getting up in that head, okay? I been there and it's okay."

"Okay."

"Alright," George smiled, a sense of relief filling his chest. "Now go on then."

Finn laughed again. "Night, George."

"Night, Finn," George forced himself to end the call.

He held his phone in his hand and looked out at the oval, the lights, the buildings lit up behind it and he felt a bit lighter himself.

Sunday turned into an all-day discussion with Todd and Kurt about how they could use this new defensive play to go all the way. George got the appeal, but in the end, he shut it down.

"It's a good tactic, but I dunno," he mused, rubbed his chin. He looked Todd in the eyes—he was older than George, had a hell of a head for the game but he had a heaviness that came with age and seemed to get heavier every year; and then he looked at Kurt, who was older too, but he vibrated with the energy of a Jack Russell—"Doesn't it kill the best part of the game?" George asked them.

"How you figure?" Todd said.

"Well," George threw his pen down, got up, and went in front of the whiteboard to where the oval was sketched. "The free flow of the game, running, making plays, hitting targets, scoring, that's what's," he looked at both men and shrugged, "for lack of a better word, beautiful. That's what's beautiful about football."

"I hear you," Kurt replied and sat up. "But when you're coming up against this Freo side, the new Sydney side, they're playing that and frankly doing it better."

"For now," George said.

Kurt smirked. "For now."

"So, let's not lose our ultimate goal and change our whole style just to win."

Todd tilted his head, scrunched his face up. "Alright, but we gotta do somethin' this weekend. But for now," he stood, "I got dinner with the missus and her family. Tuesday, let's run the defensive play and see where we sit with the offense mixed in."

George didn't realise how late it was. "Yeah, sounds good."

"Good," Kurt got up as well. "Don't stay here too late," he said to George in a way that could be patronising but he knew Kurt meant: 'we know you don't have a missus, doesn't mean you should be a workaholic.' George was used to it. George always brushed it off.

Once he was alone in the conference room, he wondered what Finn would think about playing all defence, suffocating your opponent, rather than focusing on a free-flowing offence. So he fired off a text asking him his opinion on Geelong during their Grand Final streak and how they dominated with the free-flowing, attack style of play. He got a series of excited responses, clips and opinions.

George smiled, sat back down and texted back and forth for a while, solidifying in his mind what he already thought.

He was at home in bed when he heard from Finn again, just a link to an article. It was mean-spirited and critical of everything about Finnegan Flynn.

George sighed. There was no point telling him to stop reading this shit. Again. So he texted one line: *Come over and workout with me tomorrow?*

Okay came back with a smiley face.

George was in the gym attached to his garage early the following morning. He'd converted the space, originally intended as a ten-car garage, into a games room, gym, bar and garage for two cars with all the trimmings when he moved in—it even had its own bathroom—and he felt good whenever he came down here. He'd been pushing it too hard that morning, trying to quell a nervous energy racing under his skin.

Talking to Finn about all that shit had cracked it open again. He wasn't the same frightened teenager, not even close; that didn't mean he wanted to change his situation in any way, be out. He could still hear the voices of the old guys back home, the farmers, the inflection in their tone when they said 'faggots.' It'd burrowed under George's skin like a splinter. He'd carried on with Alistair regardless, but that feeling of doing something wrong never really left him.

And then there was the anticipation of Finn coming over. He still liked being around him way too much, had a protective streak for the kid a mile wide. It made him antsy.

The gate bell rang and George dropped his weights and strolled over to the intercom. "Yeah?" He asked. He felt winded.

"*It's me,*" Finn's voice filled the room.

George clicked the gate open. "In the gym," he said into the intercom then opened up the garage door. He walked into the early morning sunshine, the light blinding off the white driveway, his breaths coming a little fast from the workout. The cool morning air chilled his skin against his sweat and he felt something flutter in his chest when he saw Finn coming up the driveway.

He had his hands tucked in the pockets of loose workout pants, his black hoodie a stark contrast to his hair, which was sticking up everywhere like he'd just rolled out of bed. He was smiling, but it was subdued.

George walked towards him and lifted his arms up on instinct. Finn met him—chest to chest—and rested against George's bulk as George reeled him in.

Finn rubbed his face against George's neck, his nose dragging up the skin of his throat as he spoke against George's ear. "They said I don't take it seriously."

George tightened his grip. George read it, but hearing it in Finn's broken voice almost broke something in him—those fucking assholes, there wasn't a player who took it more seriously.

"Fuck them, they don't know shit," he said.

Finn sagged into the embrace and George just held him. Finn still had his hands in his pockets, content to let George take his weight.

"I told you not to read that shit," he said softly.

"I know," Finn replied, rubbing his face back and forth, his breath fanning over the sweat in the hollow of George's throat.

And okay, George needed to take a step back. He did, but he didn't let Finn go, he kept him close with a hand on his elbow.

"Sorry," Finn said, his blue eyes staring into George.

"What've I said about apologising to me?" he squeezed Finn's elbow. "I reckon I'm gonna have to get that phone off you somehow. And the TV. And probably your laptop too."

Finn chuckled, but it was weak.

George was about to say something else when he heard Joq's immobiliser beep. He turned, but didn't let Finn go. He felt caught, but a part of him reasoned loudly that was ridiculous—he wasn't doing anything other than comforting his player who was under intense and intensifying pressure.

"Heading out?" he asked Joq.

"Work," Joq replied, something off about it. It made George feel bad, which made him feel worse.

"Have fun," Finn said to Joq and stepped away. George let him go.

He watched Joq get in his car, waved, nodded and then turned back to Finn.

"Shit, sorry," Finn said.

"What for?" George stood with his back to the driveway, listened as Joq reversed.

"I keep interrupting your like," Finn jerked his chin, "private life."

George shook his head and gave Finn a warm smile as he heard the gates slide shut behind them. He slung an arm around Finn's neck, made it deliberately bro-like, and got Finn moving into the garage.

"You're good. Joq's got work and I got us a workout. Gotta see what you're made of when it's a real challenge," he pulled Finn into a headlock and heard him huff a laugh.

"Alright, it's on," he said into George's armpit—it tickled.

George gave him a good shake and then let go, nudging him to the bike. "Warm up. I'm not gonna go easy on you."

"You don't wanna talk about?" Finn asked. He was pulling off his hoodie, half of what he said muffled under the material.

"I don't wanna give any more air time to a bunch of wankers making up shit for clickbait," George replied.

Finn popped his head free and smiled. "How do you even know that term?"

"Shut up and get warmed up, I know things."

Finn laughed but did as he was told.

It was a good morning, and after, while Finn drank a smoothie and George made them eggs, George listened to Finn talking about his sister's uni, and he watched as Finn finally smiled for real. George hoped he was finally getting that he was above all that nonsense. The thought of Finn beating himself up over so much bullshit caught him up so painfully for a moment he had to shake it off.

"... she's getting to do so much cool stuff, you know? She says it's a lotta hard work too, but I dunno, Soph's pretty lazy." Finn grinned as he finished.

George answered with a smile, but it felt forced. He was caught back on those articles hounding Finn. It felt like a whirlwind had blown up from the sidewalk and in a vortex of dust he was sucked back; but not scared, not this time, he was hurt. He saw Finn hurting and it made something in him hurt. He wanted to take it all away. Fix it.

He served the eggs.

"You alright?" Finn asked once George was beside him. Finn smelled good, like sweat mixed with his own scent.

"Yeah, just," he looked at Finn's eyes looking up at him, trusting and friendly, and he didn't want to lie. "Just hate those fuckers writing that shit about you."

Finn went from carefree to dejected so fast George regretted uttering the damn words.

"Shit," he clapped Finn on the shoulder. "I shouldn't have brought it up. It's all bullshit, all of it, you hear me?"

"Yeah, I know, but," Finn shrugged.

"But?"

"What if it's not?"

"It is," George said and squeezed.

"Yeah, but," Finn looked at his plate. "I did waffle between surfing and footy for a while, that looks like I don't take shit seriously. And then this damn injury—I am weak. And then..." he shook his head.

"Then what?" George thought he might as well get it all out.

"Then I am, you know... Or I can be happy or chill or whatever, it's why they used that photo. It looks like I'm not serious."

George gripped him tighter. He knew the picture. Finn was coming out of a gym in Byron, headband on, shirt off, grinning, but it was something about his posture—he looked so at ease. None of the writers came out and said it, but they were running that image in a series of articles questioning the way he went about his business, implying he wasn't working hard, suggesting he was having a laugh.

"They can twist everything," George ran the thumb from the hand that held his shoulder up Finn's neck, then kicked out his own barstool, letting Finn go but knocking his knee with his own as he sat. "But look, how hard did you work before that photo was taken?"

George already knew—he just spotted this maniac in his gym.

"Oh, I was so gassed," Finn laughed and glanced at George.

"Yeah, I know," he knocked their knees together. "But I get it, buying into it. They're writing shit and if you read it and overthink it, you can start to think, shit, maybe they're right. And in my case, they are right, but you know what I realised?"

"What?" Finn asked, he was watching George with rapt attention.

"It's none of their fucking business. Any of it. We're contracted to play a sport. They don't own us. And if they don't like the way we go about our business, they can turn the damn TV off," George said.

"Yeah," he knocked George's shoulder with his own and his eyes lit up. "Fuck those guys, seriously. You know I looked up one of them? Crawley, keeps gunning for me," Finn gave George the sly smile again, "he's so red and fat, I reckon he's gonna have a coronary soon."

George laughed and focused on his eggs. "Good."

Finn gave him a little smile, like a kid who'd just tested saying something and liked the result, his face scrunched up.

"Eat your damn eggs," George said around a gruff smile of his own.

Finn laughed.

They ate, eyes forward on the pool shimmering in the sunlight, the big palms and manicured gardens so green against the high white walls, their knees knocking every now and then as they debated Fremantle's chances, chatted about what they might get up to in Perth and it was so damn nice, George was surprised how late it was when he gave Finn a lift home.

It was weird, George thought after he dropped Finn off and came home to find Joq standing at the fridge with the door open, staring at it like it could answer some indefinable question, but since George had let some of his past out with Finn, started to actually talk about that article, he felt lighter.

He saw Joq standing there and felt a rush of gratitude for him so profound it almost bowled him over. Joq had stood by him, been his home without complaint for over a decade and George was beginning to realise just how lucky he was.

"Hey, babe," he said and walked over.

"Hey," Joq replied, eyes still fixed on the fridge.

George slid his arm around his waist and pulled Joq's side against his chest, bent down to kiss his temple. "We could just order in?" he said against his skin.

Joq blew out a breath and pulled away. "Yeah, I guess."

"Rough day?" George asked as Joq scrolled through his phone on the other side of the kitchen.

"Not really," Joq glanced up and gave him an odd smile—it was Joq, so it was a nice smile in his perfectly symmetrical features, his smooth skin crinkling but just barely; the man still had no wrinkles—his skin evened out as soon as he dropped the smile and looked back at his phone. "You want Thai?"

"Whatever you want," George replied and got himself a water.

Joq shot him another weird smile as he glanced up before looking back to his phone and typing something.

George realised what was odd about it: it wasn't real for one thing, and for another, it looked set to conceal whatever Joq was really thinking.

For a moment, George thought he should come out and ask—if Joq had something to say, he could just say it. But then George realised he didn't actually want to know.

"Be here in twenty," Joq said and threw his phone on the counter. "I'm gonna have a beer and watch some TV."

"Cool," George replied. He listened to the TV click on, the sound of the news filtering into the room, and grabbed his phone and headed outside.

They ate dinner at the inside dining table. It was a nice space—floor to ceiling windows with half the ceiling made of glass so it felt like a greenhouse jutting out onto the patio along the edge of the pool—and George always enjoyed it when they used it, enjoyed their dinners. But Joq was giving him nothing. He didn't seem mad, just distracted, his eyes going distant as George talked. He'd changed out of his work suit and he looked as hot as he always did in his white t-shirt and casual jeans. Combine his sense of style with his short blonde hair and Scandinavian ancestry blue eyes, his sleek body that belied those good genes from his Olympian dad, well, it was safe to say he got George riled up on the regular.

George came up behind him as Joq rinsed their plates after dinner and kissed the nape of his neck.

Joq huffed a laugh but extricated himself to get another beer. He leaned against the counter as he cracked it open and took a sip, his eyes on George. "So you think Cary will just stay as Captain then?" he asked.

George guessed he'd been listening to his inane dinner conversation then. He shrugged and shook off the weird vibe. If Joq wasn't going to talk about it, George sure as shit wasn't going to ask.

Later, when they were in their night time routine—Joq scrolling through his iPad and scanning all his news alerts for the day, while George finished up with a session of yoga before coming in and finding Joq—George caged him in from behind again, nuzzled the back of his head and Joq moved away from the touch by inching his head forward the tiniest bit, going tense. George got the message. What he didn't get was why.

"What's with you?" he asked.

Joq spun around. "Nothin'," he said. "Just not feeling it, I guess."

George looked at him—Joq's expression was blank—and raised both eyebrows.

"You?" he asked because come on. Joq liked to fuck more than any other guy George had ever met. Not that George had a lot of direct experience—he'd been with Alistair and then Joq—but based on what he'd made out over the years living and working with a team of guys and listening to their shit talk about getting laid, he was pretty sure Joq liked to get laid more than average, a lot more.

Joq dropped his gaze to his feet, but at least he smiled.

"You already get some today or something?" George asked. It was a regular joke, hell, it was what they used as foreplay, but he heard his accusation this time. He had no idea where it was coming from.

Joq's head whipped up. "Of course not. What? You think I'm double-teaming Cameron and Simo at work?"

George scrunched his face up at the thought—Cameron was a great guy, but he was typical of what you'd imagine someone working in a surveillance room would look like: large, pale, and plain; while Simo was scrawny and uncouth, a real tip rat. Joq started laughing and George could practically see him having the same thought George was and laughed as well.

Joq sobered. George still had his hands on either side of his hips against the bench, a careful space between them, but it didn't feel like either of them really wanted to close it.

"Sorry," Joq said, the first real flicker of emotion showing in his face all night. "I'm just," he waved his hand around.

George nodded. He got it—Joq's work could get oddly demanding since they had to deal with the—highly unlikely but still plausible—threats of some maniac deciding to make a statement with a bomb or some shit.

"All good, just road trip," George shrugged and moved away. That was their routine—they always fucked in the week before George went away—but if Joq wasn't feeling it, George was absolutely not going to push. If anyone got being up in your head about shit, it was George.

"Later?" Joq asked from behind him.

"Sure, babe," George said over his shoulder as he grabbed his phone and headed for the living room. He was always available to fuck, Joq knew that.

George clicked over to the footy channel and opened up his text thread with Finn.

The footy show was doing a post-weekend post-mortem of the round.

You watching this? He fired off.

Yeah, God Crawley is such a fucking dick, like he understands how to run a corridor, came back immediately.

George laughed and settled in.

In the media conference prior to the match, all anyone wanted to talk about was Finn. George had decided to make him sit it out and he was extremely glad for that decision right about now.

"Look," he said with a tad more coldness than he'd employed so far, "everyone on this team from the security guard to the President backs Flynn on this team and none of us entertain gossip from second rate mags designed to entertain old ladies getting their hair permed. Nothing against old ladies, but I think you see my point—you're asking me to comment on lies dressed up as entertainment not football."

He felt Cary jerk in surprise beside him, while Lacy didn't even bother to hold it in—he snorted out a laugh.

"Now," George went on, "if you've got a question about the match-up this week, happy to answer it. If not, we've got a plane to catch."

Thankfully, his favourite from *The Herald* had a legitimate question about what George thought of Fremantle's offensive firepower.

"Creed," Lacy crooned as they walked out, "kinda lost your shit in there."

"That was hardly losing my shit, Lacy, come on," George said.

"No, it was good," Cary said from his right as they walked, "with the way they're goin' on about it, you'd think Flynn had played bad for a few years, not a few weeks. Assholes."

Kurt appeared, nodding his approval. "Everyone's on the bus, 'cept Finn. Think he's still packing his shit."

"'Kay. Meet you on the bus," George said and headed to check on him. He had a feeling Finn was doing everything he could to avoid having to accidentally see the press conference, which was totally understandable.

Finn stood when George walked in.

George went straight to him and suddenly didn't know what to say. Finn looked outrageously good in his suit—he always did; it was perfectly tailored and there was something so appealing about his surfer-ruffian vibe being stuffed into it.

Finn gave him a nervous smile, but still didn't speak. George shook his head and smiled. For some reason he felt exposed, like there was something too honest in his smile. He reached for Finn's bag to try and cover it.

Finn's lips parted like he was about to say something and then stilled when George brushed up against him. The contact felt charged and George startled back with the bag. He felt caught out. But caught out for what?

"Sorry, sorry," Finn said, his voice husky between them, his hand running nervously through his hair.

George shouldered his bag. "Nothing to be sorry for," he said and hoped it sounded normal; he had a feeling it didn't, he heard how breathless it was.

He headed for the door and felt Finn behind him like a warm weight on his back. As Finn came alongside him in the tunnel, George nudged his shoulder gently.

"Press conference went well," he said.

"Yeah?"

"Yeah," George reiterated.

They didn't say anything else and when Finn went ahead of him onto the bus and took his seat next to Lacy near the back, George wanted to follow to stay near him and yet at the same time, he was grateful for a chance to catch his breath. He felt like he'd had the wind knocked out of him and he didn't understand why.

It was wet in the west when they touched down, and it got wetter in the lead up to the game. Driving rain that hit side on and stung. The harder the rain fell, the more George's excitement grew—Fremantle sucked in the wet, hell, both the West Australian sides did, but the Victorian teams didn't, and their team didn't especially.

He was beaming when he walked into the visitor's locker room, and the players beamed back.

"Well," he said when everyone fell silent. "Don't reckon there's much to say."

The guys laughed.

"Let's fucking hand it to 'em, don't hold back, expose every weakness, you hear me?" He smiled sharply. "Every weakness."

The guys cheered and ran out the door, down the tunnel and onto the field into the pelting rain. George jogged out after them, ran up the steps to the coach's box, Kurt and Todd right behind him.

"Jesus," Todd said as he shut the door. "Scanner says it'll ease up by the third, but I dunno."

George took a seat and surveyed the black sky—it was a vast ball of oppression, heavy with fat water above them. He smirked. "Don't think it's gonna matter."

George went down and addressed the huddle before the start of play. He felt an energy coming off the team, an excitement. If the rain eased up or not, he was right, it wouldn't matter—this one was theirs. He told them, but he didn't need to—they knew it, he could see it in their wet faces, their breathless smiles.

The rain was part of it, sure, but George got the feeling the guys were feeding off some sort of excited energy. They moved as one, unleashed and ecstatic in the rain.

Shortly after the first bounce, he watched as Finn scooped up the water-logged ball with his long fingers, hugged it to his chest and exploded into a sprint. He hit the fifty-metre mark—he didn't even need to give it a bounce because he was belting it off his left boot and it sailed straight through the middle for a goal.

"Yes, Finn," George said under his breath; he had his hand covering his mouth to hide his reaction from the cameras, but there was nothing to be done with the excitement, the relief, the sheer joy pumping through him as he watched Finn getting mobbed.

George flicked his eyes up to the TV screen and caught Finn's laughter as everyone hugged him, tapped him on the ass, rubbed his head.

"Maybe he just needed some rain," Kurt joked.

"He just needed one to get his confidence back," Todd replied.

"Yep," George affirmed. "He's a confidence player."

Which was proven when he got another one in the second. Between his goals, Lacy having an absolute blinder in the pocket and mouthing off at his defenders, even Les kicking a goal and turning to the guys with shock and pure joy as everyone jumped him, this one was theirs. It was the best kind of footy too—he could see how much fun the guys were having, felt it in the box with Kurt and Todd, and when the final siren sounded and they won it by 72 points, George felt a deep contentment.

The guys were jubilant in the locker room—soaked through, yet their skin steamed with the sweat under the drenching.

"Right," George called everyone to order. They settled, smiling, panting, watching expectantly. George took a deep breath. "That's what I'm talking about!"

Everyone laughed and cheered and got into the huddle to sing their anthem.

Afterwards, George told them if they were going out, not to go crazy, to remember where they were, and accepted it when most of the guys said they'd head to the casino, use the bar there as a meeting spot.

"You goin'?" George stopped by Cary's stall. Cary had begged off every outing and George got it—he'd had to take the captaincy and when he wasn't training, playing and captaining the team, he was doing everything he could to help Julie with the babies.

"Yeah," Cary smiled, tired but real. "Gonna call Jules first, she's gonna tell me to stop bein' a martyr and go out and enjoy myself for the both of us. She always says if she was in my place, she'd be shitfaced every fortnight," and he smiled wider.

George clapped him on the shoulder. "Good. Thanks for this, I know it's not ideal."

"Nah," Cary grinned. "You know Lacy's basically doing it, right?"

"Yeah," George replied. He did know that. It sucked he couldn't just do it officially. But the media would have a field day and besides, he wondered how Lacy would go if he officially took the role. He was the kind of guy who operated best under the radar.

"You comin' out?" Cary asked as he moved towards the showers.

George didn't mean to, but his gaze flicked to where Finn was having a spirited debate with Les about something, both of them gesticulating wildly and grinning like maniacs.

"Yeah, one beer won't hurt."

"Good," Cary replied and left him to it.

He was on his third beer when Finn found him breaking even at the blackjack table.

He wasn't drunk, so he nodded an acknowledgement as Finn came to stand behind him. "Flynn."

"Creed," Finn replied, his smile small and professional, and like it was about set to burst.

"You want my seat?" the guy next to George asked Finn effusively and started to get up.

"Oh, no. Not at all. Didn't mean to interrupt," Finn replied.

"It's really fine," the guy insisted. He was around George's age, fit, looked like a business type, and clearly well aware of who Finn was, who George was, though he hadn't lost his chill when George took a seat at the table.

"I can't play," Finn laughed.

"I'll teach you if you want?" George said.

"Yeah? But you sure you want?" he directed at the guy.

"Of course, of course," he grinned and cashed out.

"Sorry," Finn said to him as they swapped places.

The guy grinned at him, he looked a little breathless. Sounded it too. "Not a problem, great game by the way, great game."

"You a fan?" George asked.

"No," the guy shook his head and smiled sheepishly. "West Coast, but any team who belts Freo is a friend in my book."

"I hear that," George laughed.

"Plus," the guy went on, looking at Finn again, "can't quite believe I'm giving up my seat to Finnegan Flynn. Wait 'til I tell the guys at work."

George nudged Finn as if to say—*look at you superstar!*—and Finn smiled politely at the guy. "You want me to sign something?"

"Ah, selfie?" the guy asked, flushing.

"Sure," Finn replied and got to it.

The dealer cleared her throat.

"Right," George said as Finn muttered an apology and bid farewell to the guy who wandered off, looking at his phone.

The cards were dealt and Finn leaned in close and whispered against George's ear, "What the fuck am I doing?"

George laughed softly and shook his head, but then he quietly explained the rules, walked him through a few hands. Their shoulders brushed as they played and Finn kept shooting him little smiles under the fall of his hair every time he did well and sheepish smiles when he didn't.

George had that winded feeling again. He drank another beer and felt again the competing urges to stay as close to Finn as possible for as long as possible, and the need to get as far away as he could as soon as possible.

He needed to lock this feeling down, he really did. He forced his mind to focus on the feel of the cards in his hands—clean, crisp, thick—on the sounds of the pokie machines, bells ringing, stupid little tunes—on the smell of beer and the dealer's perfume.

It worked for a second, but then he was drawn back—the feel of Finn's bicep bumping his through the material of their shirts, the warmth every time they touched, a tingle of sensation he was desperate to press into. The sound of Finn moving beside him—a hand going through his hair, a huff of air when he laughed, the shifting of fabric as he adjusted his seat. And his smell—an understated cologne, just a hint of it mingling with the smell of his skin, which always smelled clean yet manly, like leather mixed with sweat but subtle.

"Right," he said suddenly. "I better call it a night."

He asked the dealer to cash him out.

"Oh, yeah, course. Me too," Finn said.

"No, you should stay, keep playing," George said and tried to smile encouragingly at him.

"Nah," Finn said and cashed out as well.

They fell into step as they made their way down the wide lane between the gaming floor and the bars, a normal space between them for two guys walking together.

"You wanna get a drink?" Finn asked, something shy in it.

George wanted to say yes so badly it almost bowled him over. Especially when Finn asked like that—like he was asking George, specifically, to go and have a drink with him, specifically, like a bloody date.

He was shaking his head before he answered for that very reason. "I'm beat. Old man and all that."

"Aren't you like turning thirty-one next week? That's hardly old," he said, his smile teasing and eyes bright.

"It is when you've played as many games as I have," George replied around a gruff smile.

Finn nodded, jammed his hands in his pockets. "I'll head back too then."

"You should stay, have fun," George wasn't sure he could handle sharing a car with Finn right now, never mind sharing an elevator, where they'd be alone.

They spotted Lacy at the same time. He was listing to the side, having an argument with some douche bros at a bar.

"Right, let's get him home," George said and went to intervene, Finn beside him.

"Yeah?" Lacy slurred up at the guys. "I reckon you shit cunts couldn't find a root in a brothel, never mind find the middle of the goal posts."

"Listen, you little—"

George stepped in front of the guy and hauled Lacy up, Finn on his other side.

"And we're out," he said to Lacy.

"I'm all good, Creed," Lacy said. "Just gonna have one more and finish talking to my mates here."

"You can have another one back at the hotel," George replied. He most certainly could not, but George had learned over the years telling him he couldn't have any more was like waving a red flag at a bull. "Okay?"

George watched Lacy's face scrunch up. He was a handsome guy in a weird way—nice olive skin, wide set eyes somewhere between the colour of whisky and brown, messy brown hair he intermittently shaved off or grew into a mullet; but his mouth was big with full lips and nice teeth save for the missing front one he refused to repair, and his nose was crooked from where he'd broken it twice so it'd been twisted the first time then set back to straight with a bump in the middle the second time. He was covered in tattoos, which gave him *that* look, but he was so kind under the bravado, the tattoos were like an afterthought.

His eyes were bleary now as he thought about what George was suggesting.

"We've got some beers going in my room," Finn said, picking up the game.

"Yeah," Lacy nodded. "Yeah, alright." He flung his arm around Finn's shoulder and let them drag him out. "Finny! Where you been?"

Finn laughed. "Playing blackjack with George."

"With George, eh?" Lacy leered like he'd forgotten George was there. George was pretty sure he was trying to wink.

He glanced over at Finn and saw a blush starting up his throat, redness licking his skin above his collar, his eyes fixed firmly ahead.

"And the you know, other blackjack people," Finn mumbled.

Lacy cracked up. Then he sobered. "Hey? Where's my drink?"

"In Finn's room," George said.

"Ah, okay," Lacy agreed.

They got him into a taxi, wedged on either side, and played a variation of the conversation all the way back to the hotel.

It was drizzling rain when they got out, a fine mist between them as they hauled Lacy inside and straight over to the elevators.

"Stay," George said as he pushed him against the wall between them.

Lacy slumped down and Finn hit the button for their floor before wedging back on his other side.

George caught Finn's eyes over Lacy's head and was about to snort a laugh when the soft look Finn gave him stopped him. It hit George like a terrifying invitation. Not even an invitation to fuck, it was more like an invitation into this attraction.

Finn looked away, embarrassed, his head shaking before George could respond.

They carefully avoided eye contact as they got Lacy into his room, got him into bed, and something about it felt like what George imagined parents felt like when they needed to discuss something and put all their energy into focusing on their kid to avoid it.

"Finny," Lacy said as he rolled over. "Get it, Finny," he cackled and curled in on himself. Then he passed out.

Finn was looking anywhere but at George when they got back into the hall, the door clicking shut quietly behind them.

"Well, night, George," Finn said, eyes on the carpet, one hand in his hair as he turned for his room at the other end of the hall.

George grabbed his wrist and squeezed. Finn went still. George did it to reassure him, he did it because he couldn't not. "Night, Finn."

Finn brought his fingers up and wrapped them around George's wrist awkwardly, desperately. He squeezed, his fingers clammy yet electric on George's skin. He pulled away just as suddenly and headed down the hall. George watched him go.

Finn glanced up just before he went through his door; he didn't smile, he just looked at George, something honest in his expression. George watched him back, his heart pounding in his chest.

Finn went into his room.

George went through his nightly routine back in his room on autopilot, his thoughts turning to a mantra: they couldn't fuck, they just couldn't. Even though.... Well, technically they could.

No. Finn was too young. He was on the team—a rookie on the team, what a fucking disaster. It was a terrible idea. It would end terribly. He could not, in any universe, just fuck around with anyone, never mind with Finn who made him feel, made him feel—

No. As he got into bed, stared at the ceiling, his heart still pounding, his dick half hard, an arousal tingling all over his entire body, consuming him, making him giddy, wide awake, desperate and terrified, he forced his mind to the game, to the team.

They could capitalise on this, he thought frantically, and he went far down that line of thought like a lifeline until he drifted into a restless sleep, his dick aching, but he refused to touch himself.

He had it under control by the time they touched down in Melbourne. The flight had been good—he'd thrown himself into a post-mortem of the game with Todd and Kurt and beyond a professional nod of acknowledgement for Finn at breakfast, he'd managed to avoid further contact. He was aware of him, aware of his bulk carefully tucked into his seat, his gaze resting out the window when George went by his row on the plane to use the bathroom; they didn't look at each other and that was good.

Joq was idling on the curb at the airport when George left the rest of the team at the bus, and he was flying high off his conversation with Todd and Kurt.

"Did you see it?" he asked as he got in.

"Some of it," Joq replied, his eyes fixed on the oncoming traffic, looking for a gap. "Nice win."

"Win?" George was affronted. "We destroyed them."

"It was wet," Joq replied as he pulled out, the indicator clicking in the car between them, Joq's focus firmly on the road.

George couldn't believe what he was hearing. "Wet doesn't account for a score like that, come on."

He watched the streetlights flicking by as they headed for the high-way, felt Joq glance at him, his body thrumming with the possibilities of making this into something. They never thought they'd be Grand Final contenders this year—too many holes and, honestly, there were better teams—but now all he could think was, *maybe*.

"Yeah, well, do it when it's not wet and I'll be impressed."

George scoffed because seriously? "You switch teams while I was away?" he asked. He knew Joq was fond of Jack but that was a ridiculous thing to say.

"No," Joq replied, eyes focused on the road as he accelerated. "I'm just sayin'."

George couldn't believe what he was hearing. They just played an absolute blinder, everything George had them working towards had come together beautifully in that game; it wasn't defensive and full of stoppages, it'd been a free flowing, forward attack and domination of their end. The ball barely made it into Freo's end the whole game.

It pissed him off that Joq was dismissing that when he knew how much it meant to George, how hard he'd been working.

"What's with you?" he asked, then added because he figured it was a fair question with an obvious answer: "Didn't you just get laid? You hung up after two minutes last night."

George hadn't been bothered by that—he'd been keen to get to the casino and meet up with the guys. And now he was here with Joq, he was ready—beyond ready in fact—to fall back into their post-away game routine. He squeezed Joq's thigh and felt a bolt of anticipation and arousal go through him. Yeah, he was ready to get right into the foreplay alright.

"No, I did," Joq replied and glanced at him, something cool in his expression, but George smiled invitingly, hoping to get this started. "Did you?" Joq asked.

George was hit with confusion, which rapidly turned to shame, then shock. "What?"

"Did you get laid?" Joq asked again.

"Of course not. Jesus, Joq," George was outraged by what Joq was implying, but he was also pissed off and frightened to have the thing he'd been working so hard to bury since last night just dropped in his lap like that.

"Sorry, I don't know why I—

"I said I wasn't..." George trailed off because words failed him. Everything buried exploded back to the surface. He couldn't think about Finn like that.

He stared at Joq and felt a surge of anger. Then he realised he wasn't angry at Joq, he was angry at himself, for being so weak, for letting this juvenile fucking attraction get to him so much. He was breathing roughly and he didn't know what to say.

"I know," Joq said with quiet conviction, which oddly made George feel better.

George sat back and turned his body away from Joq, focused out the window.

Joq's certainty made him feel like he could finally come out and just say it. "He's too young," he bit out. "He's on the team." Hell, George could totally fuck around if he wanted—he'd never thought about it this much, but he felt like he needed to say all of this, for himself, for them.

"I know," Joq repeated. He was focused on the road, but George could feel his reassuring presence fully in this conversation.

"Nothing happened. Nothing's happening," George finished. If he said it enough, he'd believe it. Because nothing was happening. Nothing was going to happen. That weird moment in the hallway was just a weird moment—they'd been drinking, and yeah, they were attracted to each other, George wasn't in denial about that, but that happened sometimes. It didn't mean anything.

"Babe," Joq said quietly. "I know."

George nodded sharply. Good. If Joq got it, George knew he'd be okay. And now he desperately needed to get back on familiar ground, to do something with this energy zipping under his skin.

"So what about you then? Another suit?" George asked as calmly as he could, in a way he hoped conveyed that he wanted to hear, in explicit detail, all about Joq's casual fuck, to let Joq wind him up so he could lose himself in the fantasy and forget everything else.

"Yeah," Joq replied.

"Any good?" George asked, his dick already taking an interest.

Joq smiled over at him. "Meh, he was alright."

George laughed.

"I was at his place when you called actually, had my dick in his mouth."

George groaned and adjusted himself. Yeah, this was good, this was what he needed.

"That's why you hung up so fast."

Joq huffed a laugh. "Yeah, he didn't stop. When I answered, he didn't stop. Just took me deeper."

"Jesus," George said and closed his eyes, squeezed his dick through his pants. He was suddenly accosted by the image of Finn on his knees, George's dick in his mouth.

"He was one of those guys who just loves sucking cock, you know?" Joq went on.

George could picture it—Finn absolutely losing it as he sucked George off, rubbing himself over his pants like he couldn't help it. "Yeah," George breathed.

He knew it was wrong, layering the fantasy like this, but it was like the horse he'd penned the night before had bolted and he was never going to catch it. All he could do now was lose himself in it.

"Oh, yeah..." Joq smiled over at him, quick and sly, "I came in his mouth so fast after that, but we had all night, so..."

"Jesus, Joq," George said and gripped himself.

They needed to get home. Now.

When they got in the door, he squeezed Joq's hip, told him: "I'm gonna have a quick shower, you shut everything off, then bed?"

Joq laughed at him. "Okay, geez, that one really got to you, eh?"

George felt a flash of guilt, but he wasn't doing anything wrong, so, "Yeah," he squeezed again and then ran up the stairs, Joq still laughing below him.

As the water hit his shoulders, he looked down at his half-hard dick and closed his eyes. It was Finn again, behind them. His soft smile as he looked over at George at the blackjack table—he had a section of hair at the front that was really white, bleached by the sun, and it'd hang near his eyes, hit his eyelashes sometimes, and when he smiled like that—private, really happy—it damn near did George in, made him ache, made his breath catch. Even George knew that was corny as hell, but it was what it was.

He opened his eyes and grabbed for the soap. He wasn't going to touch himself in here, he was going to save it. He thought about Joq waiting for him and felt his arousal dampen. It was quickly followed by a rush of guilt and he told himself to stop thinking like that.

Joq was lying in bed, chest bare, scrolling through his phone when George came out wrapped in his towel. Joq rolled over and placed his phone on the bedside table as he spoke, "Took you long enough," he was grinning as he rolled back to face George.

George shrug-smiled and dropped the towel. He felt awkward, which was really strange—he didn't know what was wrong with him.

He crawled over Joq and leaned down to kiss him. Joq met him and it was familiar—Joq's soft lips, his smooth skin—he always shaved and he wasn't a hairy bastard anyway—and he smelled like Joq, clean, well maintained, good.

It wasn't doing anything for George. And that made him worry.

He pulled back. "Did you fuck him?" he asked. It was a normal question for what they did, but it felt desperate this time.

"Course," Joq smiled, ran his fingers along George's cheek. "Put him on his hands and knees, took him from behind until he was begging."

George groaned and got frantic again.

He tugged the covers away, rolled Joq over and pulled his hips up with a rough grip, while Joq laughed and panted. "Yeah, kinda like that."

George squeezed his eyes shut and exhaled roughly. He saw Finn again, that look in the elevator, that look at his door in the hotel. He shook his head. Leaned over Joq so his front was pressing into his back as he reached for the lube in Joq's drawer.

He tried to imagine Joq's hook-up—he'd never met any of them, had seen pictures of some of them when Joq showed him guys on his app, and he tried to remember the last guy. He looked like one of those types you see walking down the street in the city at rush hour, nice suit, fresh from the gym and shower before they go and do whatever it is those guys did in the city every day. He imagined it as he slicked his dick up, rubbed lube around Joq's entrance, that guy shaking under Joq's hands, all riled up.

He slid his dick forward and rubbed it along Joq's crack, over his low back.

Joq huffed. "C'mon," he panted out.

George tried to laugh but he felt strange. He held his dick at the base, lined up and pushed inside. He was gripping Joq's hips, closing his eyes and shoving in quickly with a groan.

"Fuck, okay," Joq panted out.

George kept his eyes closed. He was horny, sure, his dick was rock hard, but he was flagging as well. He didn't get it. He was so keyed up and yet something was off.

He pulled out and pushed forward roughly, tried to get a rhythm going—it was sex, it felt good, but it wasn't great.

He thought about Finn asking to get a drink and a rush of excitement filled his chest, made his limbs tingle and he imagined taking Finn up on it. The images cycled rapidly through his mind—Finn sitting close while they shared a drink, Finn asking him to come to his room, George losing it once the door closed and pushing Finn against the wall, the way he'd tell him he was sorry, he knew it was wrong, but he had to kiss him, he had to, and Finn letting him, Finn pressing into the kiss and begging for more.

George was really pounding into Joq now, lost in the fantasy, lost in an imaginary kiss.

He came suddenly with a guttural sound and felt embarrassed.

He came back to the room. Joq panting underneath him.

George got some lube, a hand on him and got him off quick, Joq tightening up around his spent dick in a way that was uncomfortable.

George was off kilter as he pulled out. He got out of bed and went to the bathroom, cleaned himself up and looked in the mirror as he splashed water on his face, caught his breath.

Something in his chest ached in the worst way. He felt guilty and oddly depressed. He didn't know what the fuck was wrong with him, but he knew he needed to get it the fuck together.

18

♥

Finn collapsed face first on his bed with a groan. He hadn't bothered to turn any lights on. Fuck, he was so embarrassing. What'd he been thinking? Asking George to get a drink.

And then, and then—

He groaned when he remembered the way he'd looked over at George in the elevator—his heart had been pounding but he had this sudden urge to just stop pretending for a second, to look at George and simply say: *I want you, do you want me too?*

He flopped onto his back and scrubbed his hands over his eyes as he recalled the shock that went through him when George's hand landed on his wrist. He'd been replaying the feel of it for twenty-four hours, which was accompanied by the quick rush of embarrassment when he thought about how he'd gripped George back so desperately. And yet he couldn't have stopped himself from just looking once more, he couldn't seem to stop himself from wanting George even though it was impossible for him to have George the way he wanted.

George had a boyfriend.

Finn sat up and swung his legs over the bed.

George had a boyfriend who fucked around on him.

Finn got up, he was too angry to sleep. Who gets George and negotiates fucking other dudes? Seriously, who the fuck does that?

He shook his head, stripped, changed into loose workout pants and went into his kitchen. He wasn't hungry. He had that stupid tingly, crush feeling and food was the last thing he wanted.

But George seemed content in his relationship.

Finn opened all his cupboards one by one and had no idea what he was looking for.

George might be down to fuck if Finn pushed, but he'd been with Joq for twelve years, there's no way he'd be interested in fucking what?

Finn slammed the cupboards shut, got a water bottle from the fridge and went back to his room.

There's no way he'd be interested in leaving Joq to start anew with a stupid twenty-year-old. Even though, Finn took a sip of his water and felt the thought teetering there, a dangerous thought.

Even though, Finn made himself think it, *even though he'd be a better boyfriend than Joq.*

He looked around, spooked. He laughed at himself.

George wouldn't see it that way. George was taken and Finn really needed to let it go.

The problem was he liked George so much. He thought about him all the damn time, could barely sleep on the eve of training sometimes for the excitement at seeing him again the next day. He didn't know how to go and turn that off.

But he needed to. Because George had a boyfriend. A guy Finn actually liked when he wasn't thinking about him fucking around on George.

Seriously, who does that?

Well, someone who knows how fucking great they are, that's who. And maybe George really liked that? That kind of confidence.

Finn groaned again and lay down. That wasn't him. He would never be cool and suave, chill with George fucking other dudes if he wanted. The thought of it alone made him want to throw the world's biggest tantrum.

He needed to get over it. He really needed to get over it before George's party where he'd have to see Joq again. He didn't want to embarrass himself, to embarrass George by proxy. But it's not like he was going to do anything about it, and it's not like George wanted him to. He needed to remember that.

He probably needed to sleep more.

He was never going to sleep.

He got up and checked the soil on all his plants, he knew Rose from next door was coming over to water them while he was away, but it didn't hurt to check the soil was still damp.

Finn threw his shirt off in a huff. He'd changed three times for George's party so far. He'd almost broken and called Soph. She'd laugh at him, naturally, but she'd be cool too. She'd help him decide what to wear. Well, she'd tell him what she always did: '*Have you seen us, Finn? We look good in everything.*' Which always made him laugh. Man, he wished he had her confidence. He knew it wasn't all the way down, she got insecure too, she felt hurt when some douche-bro said her ass was too big that one time—Finn was going to beat the shit out of him, but that made her laugh and feel better because, '*Come on, you do not know how to fight.*'

Point for now was, she'd be cool, but she'd want to know why he cared so much and she knew he liked George, accepted he talked about him all the time and had a crush; but Finn wasn't going to out George. That wasn't his place. He reckoned Soph reckoned it was a harmless crush on Finn's part and he wanted it to stay that way.

Because that's all it actually was, he reminded himself, and with that thought he pulled on the last shirt he'd thrown off, his best dark jeans and went to get his shoes and jacket on. Because it didn't matter what he looked like. He wasn't the man of the hour and he wasn't, and never would be, the partner of that man. It was still a thought that hurt to think, but he had to accept it and move on or he was going to drive himself crazy.

When one of the wait staff from the bar below led him upstairs and through a roped-off area into a swanky private room overlooking the Yarra River, Finn noticed he was one of the first guys to arrive. God, he was so stupid, coming on time, but he thanked the guy with a gracious smile and the guy closed the rope with a clumsy hand and replied, "No problem, yeah, anytime. Shit, I mean."

Finn laughed in a way that told the dude it was fine. They were about the same age, and Finn wasn't sure he'd ever get used to people acting so weirdly around him. But he hated the idea of anyone being uncomfortable, so he did his best to smile and the guy responded with a grateful smile. It gave Finn a moment to focus on something other than how embarrassingly early he was.

"Finn!"

At least Les was in the same boat, Finn thought as he turned to his voice over by the bar. He was making his way across the room when he caught sight of George on the other side of the bar laughing, carefree and happy. Finn got stuck looking at him. Then he recognised the dude with him—Scotty O'Brian, ruckman, retired, legend and infamous loud-mouth—God, now Finn was really embarrassed.

George caught his eye and his smile faltered for a split second before he recovered and grinned. Finn was aware of Scotty following George's gaze in a peripheral way, but it was Scotty who yelled, "And this must be the great Finnegan Flynn!"

Finn blushed and waved awkwardly before dropping his gaze and beelining for Les.

"Hey," Les grinned at him like a madman. "Thank fuck you're here, thought I was gonna be stuck drinking on my own. I mean, it's not like I can just wedge myself between those two," he gestured over to George and Scotty, "or the rest of them," he jerked his chin around the room at the smattering of people—coaching staff, some guys and ladies Finn didn't recognise but looked like they were country people, all older than Les and Finn.

"Why not?" Finn shot him a cheeky smile, felt himself recovering into the familiar pattern of making Les feel at ease. "You're a league player, they'd be lucky to meet you."

Les honked a laugh, his eyes disbelieving. He was one of those guys that looked young. He was young, but there's guys who turn eighteen and you can already see the man emerging, while with others the boy is still firmly at the forefront. Les was the latter.

The barman came over. "What can I get you?" he asked, smiling warmly.

"Ah," Finn didn't know why he darted a look over at George, and he felt like his heart skipped a beat when he found George watching him back. George tensed for a second like he'd been caught before he recovered quickly and inclined his glass. "Whatever pale ale you've got on tap," Finn said, his eyes darting back to the bartender before meeting George's again. He could see and hear Scotty talking, and he could tell George was listening to him, but he was focused on Finn, half of his smile all for him. Finn felt a flutter of nerves and looked away.

"Coming right up," the guy said.

Finn had a feeling it was going to be a long night and he better keep them coming.

He was down to the dregs on his second when George appeared beside him.

"You two haven't moved," George said.

Finn cracked a grin, and Les cracked up and it was normal, totally normal—the coach saying hi to his players, and most of the team were there by now, current and former in attendance, and Finn realised George was just working the room, saying hi to everyone.

"Happy birthday," Finn said because he'd wanted to say it since he walked in, had toyed with the idea of getting George a gift all week, meandered in and out of the shops in Fitzroy after training, browsed online until he asked Cary what he was getting George and Cary looked at him like he couldn't comprehend the question. "You mean like, a gag gift?" he'd asked, then seemed to really consider that, and Finn had laughed, agreed, and moved away.

Of course players didn't get their coaches presents. That would be ridiculous, brown-nosing, inappropriate.

But he could say happy birthday.

"Yeah, happy birthday," Les chimed in. He was red-faced, tipsy, and a very happy drunk.

"Thanks," George smiled the coach-smile, layered with a few beers. "You boys alright? Getting enough to eat?"

"Yeah, it's awesome, I thought it'd be like, all swank and shit, but party pies!" Les replied. Finn could attest to the fact that Les had eaten a lot and raved about the food.

"Good," George clapped Les on the shoulder, the regular way the older guys did with the rookies. Finn looked at his hand and thought about the way George touched him and how it didn't feel like that at all.

George was saying something about a break from the nutrition plan every now and then was good for the soul, good for maintaining it long term.

"But I reckon Finn knows more about that than me," George was smiling at him again, warm and friendly.

"Oh, yeah," Finn smiled back and then didn't know what to say.

Thankfully an older guy in a suit came over and pulled George away. George excused himself and said he'd catch them later.

Finn ordered another beer then sank into dejection when he re-alised after hyping himself up so much to get there that was probably the most he'd see George all night.

Only, George kept drifting back to him. Checking in. Introducing him to his sister. Cara. Finn recognised her from the Brownlow Medal red carpet photos over George's career.

"Damn," she said as she pumped his hand, "you are even better in person." She winked.

Finn laughed, surprised, while George shook his head at her, "Cara, geez."

"What?" she smiled at Finn. "I'm sure you have a wonderful per-sonality and I shouldn't objectify you and so on."

Finn laughed again. "It's alright, I get it but it's just genes or what-ever. Reckon people should compliment my mum."

"Well said," Cara smiled at him, studied him. She looked like George—rich, thick brown hair with a slight wave; deep brown eyes that were wide set and expressive; clear skin. Only she was finer, smaller, her jaw sharp where George's was strong, likewise her bone structure was feminine and angled, whereas George had the cut and sharp edges of a man.

"George tells me you're close to your mum? Your sister?" she went on, sipped her drink, peered at him; friendly, yet intently.

Finn chanced a glance at George, who looked sheepish.

"Yeah, what can I say, I'm a mama's boy," Finn replied.

"No, it's great. This one," she bumped George, "barely called us that first year. Mum was constantly muttering and worrying about how he was. It's good. You should keep doing that."

"I was pretty busy," George said to her.

"I'm sure Finn is pretty busy too," she winked at him again.

Finn blushed and looked at his feet.

"Alright, come on," George nudged her, "Scotty wants to say hel-lo."

Cara scoffed. "Scotty does not want to say hello," but she went with him and told Finn, "We'll catch up again later, you can tell me all about these family dinners."

Finn darted a look at George; George rolled his eyes, but he was giving Finn an apologetic smile, which Finn didn't get.

"For sure," he said as they moved away.

He saw Lacy at the bar and decided another drink was a very good idea.

"Finny!" Lacy said as he came alongside him. "Pool? You play?"

"You mean can I kick your ass at pool?" Finn replied, oddly winded.

Some of the other guys rocked up and he and Lacy had a nice thing going with the pool, the beers flowing. Finn's gaze kept drifting to George—George standing with his old teammates and laughing, his smile so big, his eyes alight, and then, like he could feel Finn watching him, he'd look up like he'd just gotten a signal, tuned into a frequency, and Finn thought for a split second in those moments he should look away, not get caught, but then George's eyes would land on him and his smile would change, his eyes would focus, it was hard to describe, but it was like a look all for Finn.

Finn had to look away, his teeth digging into his lip, his heart rabbiting with excitement. He returned his attention to the game. Lacy was up again and so was Finn. Lacy was so hammered, Finn reckoned this one was his, easily.

Lacy stumbled over to him at the bar. "I gotta straighten this out," he said.

Finn didn't know what he meant, but he said, "Yeah," because Lacy probably should straighten out if he was going to make it much further.

"You want?" Lacy asked.

"Huh?"

"Some coke, gonna do a line, straighten out," Lacy went on.

Finn felt his eyes widen before he could control the reaction. He wasn't against partying, he wasn't judging, he just wasn't into that shit himself and he couldn't believe Lacy just offered, just like that.

"Uh, no, but thank you for offering," he said pretty fucking diplomatically he thought.

Lacy howled with laughter, the sound of it raining down on Finn even as he disappeared around the bar into the bathrooms.

Finn racked up the table while he waited for Lacy to come back. Les and the guys were talking about how badly Freo were using Jack. Finn agreed.

"Could be we knew how they were gonna use him," Finn said.

"Yeah, maybe," Cary replied, sipped his beer, his ass resting on the edge of the stool. "Plus Hiller's selfish off the feed sometimes."

Finn nodded at that, and Les said, "Yeah, that's weird as fuck, why not pass?"

Lacy reappeared as Finn broke. Lacy rubbed the side of his nose and inhaled sharp and quick. Finn snorted a laugh. Subtlety was not in Lacy's repertoire; he grinned, his eyes wide and alight, grabbed the pool cue and bumped Finn aside.

"Watch how it's done, ladies and gentlemen," Lacy addressed the players around the table. Everyone snorted, guffawed and cat-called him, which made him smile wider.

Lacy lined up, rocking the cue between his fingers; he had the cue aligned perfectly on white, all lined up to sink a red, big. Lacy pulled back, pushed forward and the cue crashed into the mat, ran along the ground like a plane that'd gone down, the horrible scratching sound as everyone laughed, then held a collective breath to see if he'd fucked the table.

Finn was laughing, the table wasn't fucked, and he was holding his hand out for the cue.

"I think I need to try that again," Lacy said.

"That's not how it works," Finn replied. Lacy darted away with the cue as Finn reached for him.

George plucked it out of Lacy's hand from behind.

"Oh, c'mon, Creed," Lacy said but he was laughing and wandering over to sip on his drink.

"You haven't sunk anything yet, right?" he directed at Finn as he rubbed chalk on top of the cue.

"Not yet," Finn smiled, "but I can let you go first, have a shot at it."

George smirked at Finn as he got ready to take the shot. His eyes flicked down to line up the white ball on the red, he was going to go for bigs, and Finn watched him, felt a buzzing under his skin, felt like George was taking the shot for the game, but taking the shot so Finn would watch. Finn didn't know what else he'd look at when George was in the room, but maybe George hadn't realised that yet.

George struck the white ball hard, the cracking sound sharply followed by the sound of two balls sinking. He was going bigs. He straightened and walked right by Finn to line up his next shot; and as George met his eyes, Finn met the look back, huffed a laugh at the indulgent smile George was giving him.

"You got lucky," Finn said.

George laughed and it rained down on Finn like something he wanted to dance in; whenever he got George to make that sound, he was just so damn happy. He needed to settle it down though.

George was lining up the next shot, his powerful body angled gracefully into it, and just as he was he about to crack the ball with the cue, he looked up, met Finn's eyes, winked and took the shot at the same time, eyes never leaving Finn's.

Finn cracked up, shook his head as George grinned at him.

"That was smooth, old man," Finn said. "Am I ever gonna get a turn?" He'd realised already George was one of those players—the players who take the first shot and sink the whole table.

George stood from his last shot, which finished off all his balls. Only the eight ball was left in play. He came and stood close to Finn, their shoulders brushing as they surveyed the table. George rested his hands on top of the pool cue and Finn liked it so much, how close he was, how warm it felt.

George pointed at the bottom corner pocket with his cue.

"You mighta told me you could finish a table, let me go first," Finn said.

George grinned. "You reckon it would've mattered? I'd get my shot eventually."

"Yeah, but if I'd known, I'd hold you off from taking a shot as long as possible."

George watched him for a second, he was still smiling, and Finn felt glad for all the beers he'd drunk.

"You ladies gonna finish this or should I have a shot?" Lacy asked.

George ignored him for a second. "You reckon you could hold me back long enough to win the game?"

Finn dropped his gaze, he felt embarrassed, and he didn't get why. He looked up, George was waiting; it'd only been a few seconds, but it felt like longer, and he felt a charge of certainty.

"Yeah, I reckon I could."

George's smile brightened. "Yeah, you could."

He moved away to take the shot. Finn shook his head, his smile disbelieving; he felt kind of breathless again.

George lined it up, focused, then sank the eight ball from a tough angle like it was nothing.

Finn huffed and shook his head. George tossed the cue on the table with a clatter.

"Alright, now we can really play," Finn said as George came over to him and ruffled his hair.

George smiled softly at him, was about to reply, when Scotty slipped into the crack of silence.

"No more taunting the rookies!" he shouted.

George laughed and the moment between them was broken as he watched George turn back into Creed. It was subtle, and Finn didn't reckon anyone else would notice it, and he wasn't sure if he was imagining it, but it felt like... It felt like George opened a side of himself for Finn—it was softer, quieter, it was attentive—and Finn liked it, Finn liked it a lot.

Finn went over to the bar, sat next to Lacy, and shook all that off. This was a team event, this was professional, this was not going to be happening.

"Yeah, he pantsed me the first time I played him," Lacy said.

"Huh?"

"Y'know, if you get a whole table sunk on you without a shot, you gotta take your pants off. Creed did it to me the first time we played 'cos I didn't know, you know? Didn't know how good he was, that he could do that."

Finn cracked up laughing imagining it. He glanced to the table and found George's eyes on him, smiling softly.

"There's no way you're breaking," Scotty said as he got his own cue.

"No shit," George snorted. "But," he pointed at Scotty with his cue, "those are actually the rules, I win, I break. So I want it recorded that I am being magnanimous here."

"No one's fuckin' taking notes, Creed," Lacy yelled.

"Well, maybe they should, like in a court because you're all dodgy as fuck," George grinned and pointed at the assembled players.

Scotty took his shot.

"It's true," Lacy said as they watched the play. Scotty had sunk two.

"What is?" Finn asked.

"We're all dodgy, but we're kinda not? Like, George is so straight, so clean, so by the book, you know? It makes the rest of us seem more dodgy than we actually are."

Finn was pretty sure snorting coke in the bathroom at a team event
with management present, getting blind drunk on the regular, and, if
the rumours were true, going to some pretty wild, high-class sex parties
in the city, not to mention, according to the rumours, fucking his way
through the bathhouses in Europe and North America, then it would
be tough to make that seem more dodgy, but he took the essential
point.

Scotty was calling George a filthy cheat. George was laughing at
him. Lacy was right. George was so good, a model player, and the face
of the franchise. Finn wondered for a second how much of it was who
George really was, and how much he'd developed out of fear; like Finn
had learned in Kenny's self-esteem workshop back when he was on the
Sharks. Kenny said a man can develop a characteristic to compensate
for a fear. Maybe George really didn't want to be so controlled, but he
had to be.

"Hopefully he'll loosen up a bit more now he's the coach," Lacy
finished up.

"Yeah," Finn replied, he didn't know what else to say—George
always seemed great to him.

"You wanna another one?" Lacy asked.

"Yeah, why not."

"Why not indeed," Lacy grinned and they drank.

Finn lost count of the number of beers they drank. Lacy disappeared. The other guys slowly dissipated until it was just George and
Scotty in high definition in front of him as he drained what he was
determined to be his last drink. He was going to piss and then he was
going home. He got up, only wobbling a little bit as he made his way
around the bar and into the bathroom.

As he came out, he bumped into a firm body blocking his path.

"Sorry, sorry," he said and looked up right into the cool blue eyes of Joq.

Joq's smile was friendly enough, but Finn felt a rush of annoyance go through him, his face contorting, which was embarrassing, so he tried to smile to apologise for it. "Joq, hey. Didn't know you were still here."

"I didn't know you knew I was here at all," Joq replied.

Now, Finn was drunk, but he was pretty sure there was an accusation of some kind in there.

"Well, it's George's birthday, so," Finn smiled, but it was weak—of course Joq was there, he was George's fucking boyfriend.

"It is," Joq replied firmly. He sounded really sober. "Heading out?"

Finn definitely felt like that was some kind of accusation. Maybe it was the alcohol because normally he just felt embarrassed and kind of ashamed around Joq—he was crushing hard on the guy's boyfriend, open relationship or not, that was awkward as fuck—but he'd also had this indignation—Joq gets George and fucks around on him? No, no fucking way.

So, he could hear the insolence in his own tone when he replied. "Uh, yeah?"

"George and Scotty will make this an all-nighter," Joq said.

Finn shrugged. He got the distinct feeling what Joq was trying to say was: *and it won't include you*. He shrugged because he needed to show he didn't care. He made sure to look like he didn't care. He felt a weird hurt at the thought of it though, at not being one of the inner crew joining the dawn patrol.

He watched as Joq placed his beer on the bar.

"What about you?" Finn asked.

"What about me what?" Joq met his eyes as he moved past him with the bottle.

Finn jerked his chin at the exit. "Heading out?" Because if Scotty and George were pulling an all-nighter, that didn't include Joq either did it?

"Yeah," Joq straightened up. "George knows where his bed is."

Finn felt like he'd just taken a massive body blow—Joq's bed was George's bed. They shared a bed. Of course they did.

And Finn fucking hated it. He was suddenly mad, really fucking mad.

Joq was looking over at George. Finn followed his gaze, and in that moment, in the midst of his drunkenness, he had this strong knowing that Joq wasn't good enough to be with George.

Joq looked back at him and leaned forward. "He gets a bit worked up after nights like this."

Finn jerked back in shock. He thought about George fucking Joq and something in him twisted painfully.

"You know how it is," Joq finished.

Finn was hurt, but he was indignant too. "You shouldn't be telling me this," he said; he tried to sound mad but curse it all, he sounded really hurt.

"You do know what boyfriends do, right?" Joq said.

Finn hoped he hid the flinch at the word 'boyfriends', but the indignation was still going strong. "That's George's business."

Joq raised both eyebrows; and yeah, okay, it was pretty rich for Finn, the rookie, to be telling George's partner of twelve fucking years what was George's business. But, fuck it, Joq was out of line.

"I think I know what George's business is better than you do," Joq replied—he was meeting Finn's eyes directly, and even though he was tilting his head up to do it, Finn felt smaller than him.

But then he wanted to fucking explode—Joq did not deserve to be with George if he was going to stand here spouting off personal details;

and Finn was fucking mad that Joq got to know George's business that well at all if he was going to behave like this. He balled his hands into fists and breathed noisily, unsure his voice was going to be steady if he spoke.

"Hey," George's voice drawled as he came over to where they were still standing near the service entrance.

George's eyes landed on him and sharpened. "Finn? You okay?"

The concern in his tone—it did Finn in, every time. But he was so aware of Joq beside him, and he wanted to give him absolutely nothing.

"All good," he said, smiling closed-mouthed. "Heading out."

"You sure?" George asked, his eyes never leaving Finn's face—searching, piercing.

"We should probably go too," Joq said and Finn could feel that couple comradery between them; how in the fuck no one else picked up on the fact they were together was beyond Finn, but there you have it.

But George was shaking his head at Joq, and that looked familiar too. "Me and Scotty going to the casino. Was gonna see if you guys wanted?" he looked from Joq to Finn.

"Yeah, sure," Finn replied as Joq said, "No, I'm beat—

Finn felt a thrill shoot through him. He liked Scotty too, so it'd just be the three of them, closing it down; if he played his cards right, he might get to sit next to George and they could brush shoulders.

Okay, Finn, you're drunk.

But George was grinning at him.

"Awesome," he said as he beamed at Finn. He leaned back to ask Joq if he was sure and Finn listened as Joq went on a lecture about how it was a bad idea, what with them being famous and drunk and out in public.

Instead of rolling his eyes, Finn said, "I'm sure it'll be fine."

"What'll be fine?" Scotty asked as he appeared, dragging George and Joq into his chest with an arm over each of them. "Joqqy!"

"The casino—

"Hell to the yeah!" Scotty cut Joq off.

"You wanna get your picture taken throwing up in a gutter?" Joq asked.

Scotty frowned.

Finn scoffed and felt Joq glare at him.

"We can go to George's! You still got the dart board?" Scotty said.

"Yeah!" George grinned at Scotty, then looked at Finn. "Finn?"

"Fuck yeah," Finn said.

Joq had driven, so they piled into his car and took off down the near-empty, wet streets to George's place. Finn felt a pang sitting in the back, seeing Joq and George together up the front as he listened to their murmured conversation.

"You settlin' in alright, rook?" Scotty asked from beside him.

He was pissed as all hell, but Finn could see it was a genuine question, like he could create a tunnel of seriousness between himself and all the booze.

"Yeah, lovin' it," Finn replied.

"Good. George said you were gettin' up in ya head a bit? Listenin' to what people outside the team think?"

"Scotty," George said and turned in his seat. "Don't interrogate him."

"Why would you tell him that?" Finn asked, more blunt than he'd normally be. It wasn't really a breach of confidence—it was hardly a secret on the team that he was a confidence player and had a tendency to look at his own press—but Scotty was up in Queensland now, which meant George would have to make a point of telling him on the phone.

"Sorry," George said though, really seriously, "I shouldn't have told him or talked about you but I needed some advice, wanted to see if Scotty remembered anything like that."

Finn shook his head and smiled softly at George's earnest face, at how he was twisted around in the seat to meet Finn's eyes.

"It's fine, I wasn't like, accusing you, I just don't know why you're wasting time talking about that when you got other stuff to talk about," Finn muttered.

Scotty laughed and tugged him into his side. "This one gets it! George wastin' my damn time, callin' up all, 'how would you manage this with a rookie? How should I talk to him??'"

The car veered sharply and Finn went crashing into Scotty's abdomen. Scotty held him close and laughed as he told Joq it wasn't the Indie 500 and could he settle down, please.

"Sorry, pothole," Joq replied, smiled at them in the rearview mirror.

Finn struggled to get a read on Joq. No doubt he suspected Finn's crush and was marking territory, which Finn got, but Joq was also just this nice guy; like, he seemed genuinely chill to drive his very drunk boyfriend and friends home and chat amicably to George about people at the party as they drove.

When they got there, George took everyone straight down to the basement-garage-bar set-up and Finn finally noticed George was treating Joq like a friend. George let them in the gate; he let them in the house; he took charge of getting drinks, while Joq acted, loosely, like he came there sometimes, but didn't, you know, fucking live there.

Scotty didn't know then.

Who did know? Finn wondered.

He was about to settle on the couch with a drink when George said, "Nope, we're playing first, I'm sick of playing this fatty," he pointed at Scotty.

Scotty cracked up. "Hey! I'm just enjoying garlic bread for a bit, then I'll be back in form."

"Sure you will, buddy," George said and tugged Finn over to the dart board.

His hand was warm through the material of Finn's shirt.

Finn was breathless, giddy again.

"Alright, you've played, yeah?" George asked as he grabbed the darts.

"No?" Finn asked.

"No?" George looked at him.

"When would I play darts?"

"I dunno," George scratched his head.

"We didn't all grow up on a farm in country Victoria," Joq said and Finn realised, one, he was listening and watching them, and two, he knew that, knew George well enough to know he probably played darts on his farm in the shearing shed or some shit every summer break. Joq probably played with him down there when they took holidays to visit George's family.

But Joq gave Finn a warm smile—impersonal yet kind—and Finn smiled back.

"Yeah, that," he said to George.

George rolled his eyes. "Right, well, I don't know what Joq's on about, he might be a city boy, but he's a damn good darts player," he smiled over at Joq, then came around alongside Finn, pushed right up against him so they were touching from shoulder to hip. He brought his hand up. "Here, like this, you wanna aim..."

Finn paid attention to every word, felt lit up by every touch as George taught him how to aim, throw, and spoke the rules against his ear.

"Got it?" George asked.

"Yeah," Finn replied.

George cleared his throat. "Well, alright then, twenty first."

Finn turned and focused on twenty. Two hit and one sailed past the board and ricocheted off the wall.

"Shit, sorry," Finn said, while George laughed.

"Everyone does it, you should see the wall behind our board on the farm," George gave him a gentle shoulder nudge and handed back the dart.

"Yeah?"

"Yeah, the wall's full of holes."

Finn smiled, imagining it.

"Are you two gonna actually get through a game?" Scotty asked.

"Right," George moved away and focused on the board. Three perfect twenties in the highest score band.

Scotty got up and joined them after a while. Every time Finn made a good shot, Scotty rubbed him on the head, he really dug his fingers into his skull and it felt kind of nice.

George nudged Scotty aside when he did it the first time, but didn't say anything. Scotty laughed and Finn blushed.

"You're up," George said to Scotty.

Scotty laughed again, but George didn't. He put his body between Scotty and Finn and they played.

Finn had to admit by the third time Scotty did it, it was clear he was doing it to piss George off. Finn batted Scotty's hands away, laughing, and George gave Scotty a gentle hip and shoulder, a friendly smile this time, but there was a warning there too.

Scotty cracked up and went to get a drink.

He didn't come back and Finn settled into playing against George. He reckoned he could've done this forever and been happy. He let one loose wide and hit George's framed jersey. It was his rookie year jersey.

"Steady on," George laughed, "how'd you even point it thataway?"

Finn shook his head and bent to pick up the dart, but he was drunk and big and clumsy and as he straightened, he hit the underside of the framed jersey and it crashed to the floor in a shattering of glass and material. Finn's mouth dropped open. He met George's eyes. George looked like he was trying not to laugh.

"Fuck, sorry," Finn said as he started laughing when George let loose.

"How does that happen in a game of darts?" George looked around, still giggling.

George crouched down to pick it up and Finn did the same.

"Fuck, sorry, I'll buy you another one," Finn said.

George laughed. "Yeah, you will," but he shook his head. "It's all good, I'll just get it framed again, doesn't matter, just funny, like how'd you manage that?"

"I reckon I don't realise how big I am yet," Finn replied.

"Might wanna get on top of that," George was still laughing, picking up the chunks of broken glass and layering them on top of the jersey, and Finn did the same.

"I'm working on it," Finn replied.

George was already watching him when Finn looked up, those eyes bleary with booze but warm and fond, and Finn couldn't help his huff of laughter at the situation. It felt like just them, but then he remembered it wasn't—it really wasn't—and he pulled back and dropped his focus back to the broken glass.

Finn was trashed by the time Scotty said he'd call him a car.

"Where's George?" Finn asked.

Scotty rolled his eyes, "Like I told you last time you asked, he's passed out on the couch. I'll get him to bed after I get you in a car."

It was dark, but it was going to be light soon. Finn took inventory of himself—yep, he was pretty trashed. He thought about playing with George all night, being up in his space and about the last time George walked him out to wait for a car. He wondered why he wasn't now.

"Where's George?" he asked.

Scotty groaned. "Mate, you are trashed. He's asleep. He's fine. You'll see him on Monday."

Finn sighed. Scotty had an arm around his waist as he trudged him down the driveway to wait for the car. Finn listed further into his side. "That's so far away," he said.

Scotty was laughing, Finn was pretty sure; he could feel his chest moving.

"Kid, unless you planning to be the first out player, you might wanna get a handle on broadcasting that while you're drunk," Scotty jostled him as they came to a stop on the footpath.

"Course I'd be out if I was with George," Finn said like Scotty was stupid. Because he was—if Finn landed George, he'd need to advertise that so everyone else stayed away. He was satisfied with this line of thought and glared at Scotty as he thought it.

Scotty cracked up. "Alright, killer, settle down. I'm just sayin', maybe check in with George first if you two are gonna go there."

Finn frowned, he was confused—Finn and George couldn't be a couple, did Scotty not know that? Maybe not. Finn pressed his lips together and looked at the street.

"How come George didn't wanna wait with me?"

"He passed out," Scotty replied. "I'm sure he would've if he could've and he's gonna be all jealous I got to do it, don't worry."

Finn frowned harder. "No, he won't, he doesn't want me like that."

Scotty chuckled, "Dude, you're fucking blind."

The headlights of the car washed over them as it crested the little hill.

"No," Finn shook his head and replied with quiet certainty, "he just wants a fuck, maybe, but I can't 'cos I want everything."

The car came to a stop and Finn went to get in.

Scotty grabbed his arm. "Hang on, what?"

"What, what?"

Scotty leaned down and opened the door, "Give us a second, mate?"

"Of course, of course."

"Thanks."

Scotty slammed the door, stood, held Finn straight and looked at him. "What do you mean George just wants a fuck?" Scotty asked quietly. "George is not like that, not at all. What makes you think that?"

"Oh," Finn dropped his gaze. So, George probably didn't even want that, and Finn was reading everything all wrong.

Scotty shook him. "If you're just interested in something casual, I don't reckon George will be okay with that, so maybe stop leading him on if that's what this is about. But I don't reckon it is?"

Finn met his eyes again. He was swaying slightly and Scotty's grip on his arms was doing a fair bit of work to keep him upright. But he heard that alright.

"Of course it's not," he said. "It's not me that's only down to fuck," he finished and he sounded like a child, all butt-hurt, and felt instantly embarrassed. Then he had a moment where he imagined himself waking up tomorrow and remembering all of this and he cringed.

Scotty was squinting at him, his face pinched, his head shaking, and Finn needed to cut his losses.

"Thanks for getting me to a car," he said and stepped back so Scotty let him go.

"Yeah, course, anytime," Scotty flipped the switch and smiled warm and big. "Any guy who's important to George is important to me."

And Finn felt that like a knife and a flash of hope all at once. He needed to go to bed. He looked at Scotty—his face only just decipherable in the dark against the back glow of a streetlight—and he saw he was sincere, he really meant that.

"Thanks, you too," Finn replied and got in the car.

When Finn rolled over in the morning, the sun was well past morning. It was early afternoon, he thought sleepily. Then the night before rushed over him and he groaned and threw the covers over his head.

Fuck, fuck, fuck.

Could he be any more obvious? So much so, Scotty was saying that? And what does it mean that Scotty doesn't even know about Joq and George? Finn got that they wanted to keep it private, but that private?

Then he remembered himself saying, '*Course I'd be out if I was with George.*'

He grabbed his pillow, shoved it on top of his head and wondered if there was a way to surgically remove the part of the memory for specific events.

He lay still and breathed, tried to reason it out—it was only Scotty... Who'd probably tell George!

Finn threw everything off and got out of bed.

He found his phone on the counter. He had a few texts from George at the top. He bit his bottom lip, rubbed his left calf with his big right toe, tried to breathe calmly.

It's not like George would text him: *Finn, you are being completely inappropriate!*

Or: *Finn, I told you that in confidence, if you make it so obvious you've got the hots for me people might have thoughts about me too. Therefore, I am ending this friendship.*

Okay, Finn, settle down, he told himself—since when would George text him so formally, like a lawyer?

He set his phone aside, got a bottle of water, chugged the whole thing, wiped his mouth, made a little growl sound to pump himself up and opened the goddamn text messages.

Scotty said he got u a car? U get home alright?

The first one said, time stamped 5:13am.

Im guess u sleeping, I hope? Text me when u get up so I know u okay.

That one was seven minutes later.

Sometimes I can't stop thinking about kissing you.

Finn dropped the phone. Like, he literally dropped the phone and made a series of acrobatic catches to try and save it before it crashed to the floor. He scooped it up, breathless, and read it again to make sure his brain wasn't making it say something he so desperately wanted.

Sometimes I can't stop thinking about kissing you was still waiting for him. Time stamped 5:37am.

It was 1:17pm now. Finn held his phone in his hand, stared at the words on his phone and knew he had to answer. The obvious reply was, *Me too*. Fuck, me too times a million. But, Finn couldn't stop thinking about kissing George as a boyfriend, as an exclusive boyfriend, whereas George must've been into him for a casual thing.

He rubbed his nose, scratched his leg, bounced on the spot for a minute. He needed to reply. He needed to get his reply just right. And he had to think seriously here—if George was down to fuck, and if that was all Finn was going to get, was he really going to turn that down? Was he that stupid?

He typed quickly, hit send, tossed his phone on the counter and ran into his shower, his heart pounding.

He really took his time in there, focusing on each body part—his legs, his feet, his toes, his ass and back, his chest, his dick—he washed each part thoroughly, relished the feel of the hot water and breathed in deep for a count of four seconds, held it for ten, then exhaled for six, and did not let the thought of George's face reading that reply overwhelm him.

He was getting out, wrapping the towel tightly around his waist when he realised—Christ, George was drunk! When he sent that, he was drunk!

He ran back to delete his message when he saw underneath his response: Read 1:18pm.

And no reply.

Just kiss? was hanging there lonely and mortifying.

19

*J*UST KISS?

George read it again and tried to keep his shit together.

It was under his own message: *Sometimes I can't stop thinking about kissing you*, which George didn't remember sending; he hadn't checked his phone all morning because Joq had been all systems go on being ready for his parents coming round for lunch. He now regretted that decision because that there was a message that should never have been sent. And yet now he had the flirtiest reply he could dream of and he was sitting there, trying to nod politely as Joq's mum talked about this new restaurant they needed to try while inside he was caught roughly between humiliation and straight up horny, no in between. He had a desire to shove Finn against a wall and kiss the shit out of him in response to *Just kiss?* He had so many feelings belting around in his chest like a frantic, caged animal.

He glanced at the thread again.

Just kiss?

He couldn't leave him hanging. Finn was damn sensitive. He was probably hyperventilating.

He tapped out, *No* and hit send.

He refocused on the conversation and did his best to appear normal. Joq's mum was giving him a pointed look, but George had gotten used to that. He knew she wasn't happy about George being in the closet while Joq wasn't. He knew she wanted more for Joq and George knew she was right. But he had a feeling his sudden and uncharitable thought in her direction—'*Do you know how much dick your son gets and I don't? Do you know about that?*'—was Finn related.

His phone vibrated.

All the willpower in the world couldn't have stopped him from looking at it.

Fuck! George!

He snickered.

"Somewhere you need to be, George?" Joq's mum cut into his little bubble. He looked up at her—she was sipping her wine, and even being in her early seventies did nothing to dim her beauty, she was classic, ice cold; she reminded George of Catherine Deneuve, which added another layer to how she terrified him.

"No, sorry," he put his phone down, smiled at her like he would someone in the media who asked a question he didn't want to answer but knew he needed to. "Just drinks with some old friends last night for the birthday, getting spammed with night-after gossip."

"Hmm," Janice replied and placed her glass down deliberately.

"Thirty-one," Joq said, ever the cool peacemaker. He smiled at George, his expression relaxed and familiar, at ease. "Getting old," he teased.

Joq's dad jumped into the conversation, regaling them with the story of when he was thirty-one and coaching the national swim team, his own career over and successful, and it was almost engaging enough to make George forget about the proposition on his phone. Almost. He grinned at Joq when his dad—Jim—got into detail about the training regime he had the guys on, the six hours a day, the nutrition plans for stamina.

"Something else happened that year," Janice said, her eyes beautiful and fond on her son. George's mum certainly loved him, but he was always envious of how much Janice adored Joq, it was candid and she managed to keep it on the right side of overbearing.

"This one," Jim said and rubbed Joq's head like he was still a boy; Joq laughed good-naturedly, ducking his head. The beautiful spread he'd prepared in the glass house dining room with fresh cut flowers at the centrepiece, the baked fish and roasted vegetables, delicately prepared starters of dip and olives, the wine glasses and the bottles chilling on the side—it was all lit up by the afternoon sun, the room warm and glowing. Joq had made this atmosphere, created it out of nothing, and George felt a mix of gratitude and guilt.

"A very pleasant surprise," Janice said, her eyes so fond on her boy.

And George's phone buzzed with a call. Finn.

There was no universe in which he wasn't taking this call.

"Sorry," he said and stood. He hoped he appeared normal. "Excuse me, I better take this."

He strolled down the hall and hit answer.

"Hello," he said softly.

"Hi," Finn breathed down the line.

And George got himself through the door to the games room, shut the door, and down the stairs as he replied gruffly, "You all good?"

"Yeah, you?" Finn asked.

George stood in the middle of the games room, ran a hand through his hair, exhaled roughly, aware of Joq and his parents upstairs, consumed by Finn breathing down the line down here.

"Yeah, bit hungover, but got people for lunch, so..."

"Oh, shit, sorry, I'll let you—

"I answered," George cut him off.

Finn didn't say anything, but George could hear him breathing.

"I wouldn't have answered if..." *if I didn't want to talk to you so badly* sounded like too much, "if I didn't want to."

"Yeah, I... I know," Finn replied quietly.

Just kiss? Flashed through George's mind and his dick stirred, his heart fluttered; Christ, but what were they doing? He couldn't be doing this with Finn.

He couldn't not be doing this.

"So, you think about..." Finn trailed off.

"Yeah," George breathed out the word. Because he did. Constantly. "You?"

"All the time," Finn replied quickly, but his laugh was hesitant, shy. "Sorry, I got like zero chill about this."

George barked a laugh. "Me neither."

"So, you think maybe, I mean, it's not just me then?" Finn asked. God help them both, God help George, he was so sincere, so hesitant—this was a guy with a fanbase and social media following other players found staggering, women and men fell over themselves to get near him, and here he was, asking like some nerd asking the jock to prom in one of those cheesy American movies. George almost wanted to laugh.

"I think, if you mean, am I attracted to you? Then, yeah, Finn, yeah, I am," he took a deep breath, "I shouldn't be."

"Why not?"

"Because," he heard the sound of murmured voices upstairs and decided this was not the best time for this conversation. "We need to talk about this, but I better get back to lunch."

"Oh, course, yeah, who's round? Is Scotty still there?"

George cringed. But he wasn't going to lie to Finn. "Joq's parents actually."

"Oh," Finn said then rambled on in a way George was getting to know was his way of trying to cover something he just did and felt embarrassed about, "cool, that's so cool, yeah, I shouldn't have... We'll talk tomorrow."

"It's really fine," George said, but he felt awkward. "Like I said, I answered."

"Yep, you did, but now you better go and I better.."

"Okay, later, Finn."

"Later, George."

And he was gone. George squeezed his phone and clenched his other fist. He had no fucking idea what he was doing. He felt unsettled and anxious in a way he hadn't in over a decade.

He jogged back up the stairs and re-joined the lunch. He didn't miss Janice's pointed subject change nor her disapproving look, but what could he do? It's not like she was wrong. He did his best to ignore it all—her looks, Finn's what? Proposition?—and focused on Jim, on Joq, on enjoying this perfect afternoon, the cake Joq had ordered him from his favourite bakery, the champagne. It was a good lunch.

And once Joq's parents left and George pulled him into a tight hug to say thank you, he decided this thing with Finn couldn't go any further, he couldn't risk this. He needed to talk to Finn but not about just kissing, about letting this thing go before they did something reckless.

And the best laid plans or whatever the hell they say was all George could think when he jogged up to the coach's box the following Saturday night and they still hadn't talked about it.

They hadn't texted about it. Nothing.

George got settled in his seat and surveyed the ground.

They'd had opportunities to pull each other aside and say something, but it was weird; when he got in on the Monday morning, all ready to have a talk, he saw Finn and something about the way he looked at him told him he didn't need to say anything. Then he got the distinct feeling all week during training that they were both spooked. Like they'd admitted something they really shouldn't have, and now both of them were trying to pretend they hadn't.

George focused on Finn now—kicking to Lacy, taking a quick mark from Cary, booting it through the middle as they finished warming up—and affirmed it was for the best.

They were here to win a Premiership. That's all that mattered. Everything—including relationships—needed to work in service of that.

They were looking good going into the fourth, one point in it, and it was clean football—marks hitting chests, kicks sailing through for goals—with Finn and Lacy working beautifully together. The whole building was buzzing like it was braced for them to do it, to pull it off.

The siren sounded and the ball-up at centre opened the final quarter, and Finn got it and kicked it to Lacy, where his opponent gave him an illegal hold.

Lacy got the ball and was lining up for his free kick, a side shot on goal he'd probably make in his sleep.

George's eyes wandered back to Finn—off ball, looking lazy—while his opponent, Marcus, decent defender, bit of a shit talker, was really giving it to him—shoving, nudging, mouth constantly moving. George was about to look back at the play—Lacy was about to take the kick—when he saw the hit happen with disbelief.

Marcus swung fast and quick, an uppercut to Finn's jaw, and Finn toppled to the ground.

George was up and out of his seat—he heard a roar from the crowd, thought he heard Kurt saying something—but he was already jogging down the stairs and hitting grass.

Finn's body was completely still on the far side of the oval.

George ran straight for him.

He glared daggers at Marcus, but decided to leave the spray for later.

He knelt down beside Finn and slid his fingers along his chin, his cheek. Finn's eyes were closed; he was breathing, but he was definitely unconscious. George kept his touch gentle, ran his fingers along Finn's jaw.

"Finn," he said softly like it was just between them.

Finn's eyes cracked open and yeah, George remembered this part, he'd been here—waking up on an oval in a packed stadium with thousands of fans screaming and wondering where the fuck you were and what the fuck just happened.

Finn winced, but his eyes stayed on George and his lips curved into a smile. "Your timing is shit," he mumbled.

George huffed a laugh, he stroked Finn's jaw briefly before he slid his arm around his back and helped him stand.

"Can you walk?"

"Yeah, just, fuck, my head," Finn said quietly like he was ashamed, like he was about to be sick.

"We got him if you want," the head trainer, Carson, was saying.

Finn leaned heavier into George's side and yeah, George didn't want to let him go either. "Let's get him to the tunnel," George said and walked Finn off the field to the roar of fans.

Another trainer, Trina, met them at the top of the tunnel.

"Got the doc here," she said as they got there.

Finn groaned.

George pulled him in close for a second and spoke against his ear, "I'll come see you as soon as the game's done, do as they say in the meantime."

Finn nodded, his eyes on his boots, but his fingers gripped George's shirt tightly before he let go.

George ran out, up the stairs, and back up to the box.

"He good?" Kurt asked and George didn't miss the incredulous look he was giving George—yeah, coaches did not run out onto the oval when their players got injured, but he was ignoring that.

George shook his head. He didn't trust himself to speak.

Shortly after, they got a radio message that Finn was being transported to hospital. George drew on his years of professionalism to focus on the game, on addressing the locker room afterwards, on focusing on the goddamn road to get him to the hospital and up to Finn's room.

Finn's eyes were closed and he was alone when George walked in, but he knew Finn wasn't sleeping. George dragged the chair next to his bed and sat down.

Finn sighed, deep and profound and George snickered.

Finn's eyes snapped open. "George," he breathed out, winced, looked like he was trying to smile.

"Who'd you think it was?"

"Ugh, Carson, he's great, but he's too positive," Finn replied. "How'd you get here so fast?"

"Never mind about that, what's the verdict?"

"Concussion," Finn said and shrugged like it was nothing. "Should be outta here soon."

"Ah, no," the doctor said as he came in, "twenty-four-hour hold, at least, then..."

And George knew all this, so he sat back, studied Finn surreptitiously to see how bad it was, really.

Once the doctor left, Finn said, "Stop it. It's not that bad."

"It's not that bad that you ended up out cold in a split second? I was gonna kill that wanker Marcus, but the boys took care of him," George seethed.

"Yeah?" Finn brightened. He looked awful against the white hospital sheets, in the white hospital gown, his eyes taking on the black bags that seemed to accompany a concussion for reasons George didn't understand.

"Oh, yeah, reckon there'll be a few suspensions all round, but it'll be worth it."

Finn smiled; he looked like he was about to cry.

"Don't bloody cry over it, it's normal," George said to get Finn to laugh. Finn did and George settled back in his chair.

"You can go if you want, Carson is gonna check in and my mum'll probably come down."

"Do you want me to go?" George sat forward.

"Well, no, but I know you got—

"Finn," George grabbed his hand and squeezed. "I'm where I wanna be, alright? So unless you want me to go so you can get some sleep, I'm gonna sit for a bit and do the concussion protocol with you."

"Yeah?"

"Yeah, if that's alright with you?"

"Yeah, course," Finn sank deeper into his pillow. "Fuck my head hurts. Shoulda stuck with surfing."

"You could hit a reef and then you'd be under water, concussed. Drowned. Dead," George shot back.

Finn laughed again. "Stop making me laugh. It hurts."

"I'm not trying to make you laugh, I'm serious, footy was the right choice," he realised he was still holding Finn's hand. He was about to let go when Finn squeezed.

"It was."

George smiled his taking-the-piss smile, which transformed to the soft one, the just-for-Finn one, and as Finn rolled his head to look at him, George felt like he was taking it in, looking his fill and not caring what it meant for the moment.

George dropped his eyes, felt himself blushing. "You wanna hear how the game ended up?"

"Yeah, we won?"

"Yeah, we did. Lacy belted another one, you know how he gets after fights..."

George told him about the game, about the likely suspensions, about the tribunal on Monday, and he felt it when Finn slipped off to sleep. George readjusted himself in his chair, freed his hand for a second so he could get his phone out.

He messaged their HR managers for Finn's emergency contact numbers. His mum's phone was off—probably on a flight—but his sister answered.

"Yeah?" a young woman's voice answered like, *who the fuck is this?*

"Sophie? I'm not sure if you remember meeting me when I was on a video call with Finn—

"George? How's Finn? Is he okay? Mum's on a flight, but I can't get out of here until tomorrow. That fucking asshole."

George agreed. "He's alright, concussion, I'll sit with him 'til your mum gets here then."

"You're with him?"

"Yeah," George didn't know why he suddenly felt self-conscious.

"Can you put him on?"

"He's asleep, but I can, if you want, I mean," he was flustered, he knew they were twins—did twins have some weird energy healing shit? He needed to ask Finn about it.

"No, don't wake him, but get him to call me as soon as he wakes up," she said.

"It could be late, I've got to wake him in a few hours—

"I don't care, I'm gonna yell at him 'cos he never fights back."

George smiled, gruff and pleased. She was right.

"Think he's tryin' to avoid a suspension," he said.

She scoffed like that was an absolute ludicrous assertion. "He can defend himself and not get suspended, come on, you know that."

George did.

"Anyway, maybe you should tell him, he won't listen to me and Mum," she went on.

"We'll have a chat about his defensive work when he feels better," he replied, rather diplomatically he thought.

Soph snorted. "You do that, but you're definitely gonna stay with him now?"

"Of course," George looked at Finn's sleeping face, heard the quiet whistle of his breath through his parted lips.

"Good, thanks, it's stupid but I hate the thought of him hurt and alone, which is super embarrassing and don't tell him I said that but you know what I mean," she said.

"I do, yeah," he agreed.

"Good," she said.

They ended the call soon after and George sat forward and took Finn's hand again, gave it a good squeeze, loosened his hold, then rubbed his fingers back and forth on Finn's knuckles.

When the doctor came back in for the concussion protocol, he glanced at George's hand and away quickly, his face schooling to professional, but there was a split second of recognition there, a seeing it for what it was and not what George was saying it was. Because George might tell the world, his boyfriend, and himself this was a coach taking care of a rookie he was particularly fond of—which happened, coaches and managers had their favourites—but in that doctor's expression, in that flash of recognition, was the truth: this wasn't a player George was protecting, this was a man George would launch a thousand ships for.

"How long's he been asleep for?" the doctor asked. He was pulling out the little torch they used to torture you when you had a concussion.

"A couple of hours," George replied. He squeezed Finn's hand and was about to let go, when Finn gripped him back.

The doctor was shining the lights in his eyes and Finn was groaning and rolling his head to the side, looking for George.

"Hey, I'm here," George said softly.

"Sorry, Finnegan," the doctor said fondly, "you know the drill. How you feeling?"

"Sick," Finn mumbled. "Head hurts."

"Yes, well, you took a haymaker like you were in the ring, not on the football field. In fact, if it had happened anywhere other than the field, good old Mike Marcus would be facing an assault charge," the doctor said.

George looked at him, he felt Finn doing the same. He was an older guy—maybe fifties—fit, but tired, and he had an agitated yet bored energy about him.

"He'll get suspended," George said.

The doctor wrote something on Finn's chart, shook his head. "There's a bowl if he needs to vomit, and if he needs the bathroom you need to help him get there—I don't want him taking a fall and I don't trust what I saw on the scans."

"Alright," George nodded readily enough; he knew all that, except the bit about the scans.

The doctor left shortly after and Finn opened his eyes and looked at George.

"You're givin' me ideas," he said and gripped George's hand.

George snorted. "You already had those."

Finn's smile widened but it turned into a wince.

"Go back to sleep. I spoke to Sophie, she said your mum's on her way."

Finn's eyes opened. "You spoke to Soph? What did she say?"

So George told him.

Finn laughed, then sobered. "That's it?"

"Yes?"

"Good."

"She didn't regale me with any embarrassing stories about you if that's what you're worried about," George said. "Not really the time."

Finn smiled, his eyes still closed. "She wouldn't care about timing. Nah, it's all good, Soph can just get ideas about how things are based on what she thinks she's seeing, that's all."

"So," George said slowly, "she's a woman."

Finn cracked up. "Stop it, it hurts to laugh. Oh shit, I'm gonna be sick—

George got the bowl and rubbed Finn's back as he heaved up a lot of liquid.

He helped him rinse his mouth out with a glass of water and got him settled back against the pillows.

"Fuck, this is so embarrassing," Finn said around an exhausted breath.

"This is a concussion, I've seen it and done it all myself before," George said as he stroked the sweaty hair back from Finn's forehead.

"No, but," Finn shook his head. "I didn't want you to see me like this."

"Like what? Hurt?"

George settled back down in his chair. Finn flipped his hand over, palm up, an invitation. George took it and slid their fingers together.

"No, disgusting and sick," Finn replied.

George laughed. "Don't worry, you still look good and I'm sure your milkshake's still bringing all the boys to the yard."

Finn snorted a tired laugh. "Don't, I'll be sick again."

"Go back to sleep," George tightened his hand; Finn gripped him back.

"You look like you," George said softly. "You could never look bad, not to me," he finished quietly and felt embarrassed but it was true—even vomiting with red eyes and bleary tears, his big body reduced to lying down and staying still because Finn couldn't trust he wouldn't fall over if he got up—he was the best thing George had ever seen. And George needed to examine that and ignore it and accept it would never be his in the way he wanted.

Finn stroked his fingers alongside George's. "Really givin' me ideas."

"And you really already had 'em."

Finn huffed a soft laugh and drifted back to sleep.

Finn's mum arrived just before dawn. She was both what George expected—where Finn got a lot of his arresting good looks, but he knew that from TV and video calls—and not—she met his gaze steadily, spoke like she was talking to an equal, and she gave off the vibe of being friends for decades. She sat on the end of Finn's bed and took his hand, while George dropped his hold and stood, uncomfortable.

"He hates being sick," she murmured. "How bad is it?" she looked up and asked directly, her gaze sharp yet friendly.

"It's..." George thought about the vomiting, the dizziness, the words he didn't want to think—post concussion syndrome—and the doctor's grim face. "It's not conclusive yet."

She tilted her head to the side. She was so much like Finn and yet not, it was uncanny. Beyond the obvious—she was a very beautiful woman—she was also solid, grounded in a way Finn wasn't, she was the earth and Finn was like the wind, like the ocean, in constant motion and unpredictable, a calm breeze or a ferocious storm. George felt the contrast and felt himself liking Finn even more, which shouldn't have been possible.

"So, bad," she leaned forward and brushed Finn's hair off his face. "Do you need to go?"

George didn't want to, but yes, he really should. "I probably should, yeah."

She smiled over at him. "Thank you for staying with him. I got delayed and Sophie said you were here, it was better, it made me feel better, knowing he wasn't alone."

"I'd never let him be left alone when he's sick," George said gruffly and regretted it instantly, but her smile softened and her eyes never left his.

"I appreciate it."

He jerked his chin. "Tell him to—

George was about to say text, but Finn might be banned from screens for a few days.

"I'll tell him you stayed," she said warmly.

George wanted to tell her not to say that and he wanted to tell her to tell him a lot of things, but none of them were appropriate, so he just said, "Thank you," and then, once she looked at him quizzically, even confused, made his feet move towards the door. Because, yes, what was George still doing there?

"Nice to meet you," he said as he went out the door. He glanced at Finn, dead asleep. "Later, Finn," he said quietly, and got the fuck out of there.

It was sunrise when he got home. Joq was in the kitchen getting ready to go to work. George soon discovered Joq was also in the kitchen getting ready to give George hell for staying with Finn all night.

"I gotta go to work," Joq said after they exchanged a greeting and it was so frosty it might as well have had snow on it.

"He's gonna be alright," George said pointedly—where did Joq think he'd been? Out fucking half of Melbourne? Hardly, he'd been sat by a hospital bed all night until his injured player—a player Joq himself insisted they look out for—had family arrive to take over.

"Yeah, I don't give a shit," Joq said as he went by.

"What?" George couldn't believe what he'd just heard.

"Seriously?" Joq spun back to face him, his normally icy features contorting and okay, George got it then, he was really mad. "Since when does a coach sit at a player's bedside all night? How do you think that looks?"

"I don't give a shit how it looks," George replied because he didn't—Finn needed him, he wasn't going to bail because of how it might look.

"Well maybe you should," Joq shot back. "Oh, and by the way, the phone is a thing."

"You knew where I was," George was utterly confused—they didn't live in each other's pockets, there was no reason for George to call. "I don't get why you're so mad."

"Just, I'm gonna be late," Joq shook his head and then he met George's eyes, his expression serious, reprimanding, and sad all at once. "Just, twelve years is not nothing, you know."

George sucked in a breath, he had no idea what to do with that—of course twelve years together wasn't nothing, but he didn't get the point. Even if he did something with Finn—which he totally could if they pursued this attraction—he wasn't going to break up with Joq. That was absurd. Finn would be looking for a fling, a casual fuck, he wouldn't be looking to marry George for fuck's sake.

"I know," George said to Joq, held his gaze. "But what's that got to do with anything?" Because he would really like to know.

Joq recoiled, his eyebrows went up. "A phone call," he said like George was dense. "I think it means I deserve a phone call if you're not coming home."

George nodded, Joq was right; they didn't live in each other's pockets, but George would normally shoot Joq a text or something if plans were changing. He'd honestly just not thought of it and when he had, idly, he'd genuinely dismissed it because Joq knew where he was.

"You're right, I'm sorry. I was just, he was—

"It's fine!" Joq yelled.

George startled. He couldn't remember ever having a conversation quite like this with Joq.

"It's fine," Joq repeated, calmer. "I gotta go. See you tonight."

He headed for the door.

George debated not saying he might not be here but after this conversation he thought that was a terrible idea, so he called after him, "Okay, but I might not be here, but I'll call—

The front door slammed.

George was bewildered. And chastised. But more bewildered.

Did Joq think things between George and Finn could ever be more than fucking? George wasn't stupid—he was more than attracted to Finn, he fucking liked him, really liked him—but he was in a relationship with Joq and Finn was twenty, hardly looking to settle down and there was just no way George was blowing his life up for a fling, no fucking way.

Joq had nothing to worry about; even if George and Finn did fuck, which was beginning to feel more inevitable by the day, and more like a bad idea at the same time, but even if they did, that's all it would be; fucking.

Just kiss?

No, not just kiss.

But just fuck? Certainly.

George felt resolute about that as he headed upstairs to shower and get ready for a postgame meeting with the assistants and management.

BY THE FIFTH TIME his mum wouldn't let him check his phone and offered to do it for him and he yelped, "No!" Finn decided he needed a new strategy.

"If you've got a boyfriend, I can't see why you wouldn't want me to see that," his mum said casually, relaxing back in her chair and rearranging her scarves.

"I don't have a boyfriend," Finn replied, breathless and a little crazy-sounding. "I've just got some private texts with friends on there, that's all."

He focused on his fingers clasped over his stomach, began rubbing his thumbs up and down each other, totally chill.

His mum was quiet. She laughed suddenly.

"What?" he asked, shooting her a quick look.

"I'm sure a few minutes won't kill you," she handed the phone over.

Finn tapped it so it lit up, punched in his code and went straight to his messages. The glare did hurt his eyes, and if he was staying on here for longer, he'd dim it, but he was only looking for one thing. His mum had said George was here when she arrived. When he asked, "What time did you get here?" and she said, "Around five?" Finn nodded like his stomach wasn't doing somersaults, while he also berated himself for sleeping through a whole night with George. His concussion could fuck right off!

He found George's name, two unread messages.

Had to go, but waited for your mum.

Finn knew that. He liked that George wanted him to know that.

Later in the day there was: *I'll drop by tonight if you want. U prob cant check ur phone?*

Finn tapped out his reply: *checking phone. Come now.*

He hit send, locked his phone, and handed it back to his mum. She was smirking at him.

"What?" he asked.

"Nothing," she replied as the phone buzzed in her hand. "Do you need to check that?"

"No," he said, everything in him screaming—yes!!—but she was onto him and—although he talked to her about everything, literally everything—he didn't want to talk about this. Not yet.

She'd tell him it was a bad idea—it was.

She'd tell him not to go anywhere near a committed partnership, open or not—and she'd be right.

She'd tell him if George was serious, he'd leave his partner, and that's the kind of guy Finn deserved—and on the last point, she'd be wrong. This was George fucking Creed; hell, even Finn didn't know why he'd contemplated saying no to a casual fuck if that's all George was offering.

She smiled at him. She looked tired, she'd been up all night getting flights; of course she looked tired. But she still looked great, she always did, and he wished he had her Zen. But her smile right now said she knew, as she went to put the phone back in the top drawer, that he would—

"Give it to me," he said, not meeting her eyes.

She laughed at him and handed it over. "You've got ten seconds. I don't want your doctor to tell me off. That man looks like he needs somewhere to unload and I don't want to be in the firing line when he's right."

Finn nodded vigorously and opened the message.

A laughing emoji and: *be there soon as this meeting finishes*.

Good, he tapped out and hit send. He did not have time to craft sexy responses—his mum was right: his doctor was terrifying.

He handed it back. It buzzed again. He closed his eyes and shook his head. He heard his mum placing it in the drawer and closing it.

"So, George seems like a good coach, very attentive," she said.

Finn held in his reaction. She didn't know that's who he was texting. "Yeah, he's great."

"I'm so glad you've got him, I wasn't worried, I know you'll do well wherever you go, but you know," she said.

Finn opened his eyes and looked at her. She was meeting his eyes, smiling knowingly at him.

"You know I get lonely," he finished, heavy on the sarcasm.

"I know you do best when you've got people on your side around you," she corrected.

Finn closed his eyes again. She was right of course, but he didn't like it—he should be tougher than that.

"Get some sleep," she said.

He didn't want to sleep in case he slept through George's visit.

"'M alright," he murmured.

"Finnegan," she leaned forward and rubbed his arm, "you need to sleep and heal."

"Alright, but wake me up if I get visitors," he slurred.

The last thing he remembered was the sound of her laughter and the promise to do just that.

"No, don't wake him," George's voice drifted into his consciousness.

"He'll throw the world's biggest fit if I don't," his mum said as she shook his arm. "Finnegan."

"George," Finn said and looked in the direction of his voice.

He was there, dressed in the club polo and classic pants, his hair messy like he'd brushed it quickly; he looked tired, but his eyes were warm and wide awake on Finn.

"How you feeling?" he asked. He was standing. Finn wanted him to sit.

"I'll be alright," Finn replied.

"I know you'll be alright," George smiled, "but how you feeling now?"

Finn smiled up at him. He wanted to tell him to sit down.

The conversation was brief and then George had to go. He never sat down. He never stopped looking at Finn with anything other than fondness. Finn felt pissed off after he left.

"He seems very fond of you," his mum said after George left.

"I guess," Finn replied and sat up. He needed to drink something.

"Well, you'll tell me about it when you're ready," she said.

Finn shook his head. There was nothing to tell. "Maybe you could bring Stimpy down for a visit?" He knew it was ridiculous—Stimpy was their dog and Finn missed him as much as he missed his mum and Soph. But there was no way they'd fly him around—he was too old—but he was going to miss seeing him since he was banned from travelling with the team that weekend and having a cry over not getting to see his dog seemed better than having a cry over George coming and going so quickly and thinking stupid things like: I can't train, I can't travel—when will I see George again? He was pathetic. He was aware.

"I know you know that would upset him," she said and sat back. She was knitting. She was an incongruous figure to be knitting—she was forty, but she looked around thirty-five, and she was stunning, fashionable—but she was always knitting. She told them once it was because she used to smoke. Finn almost fell over—her? Health nut extraordinaire? She laughed and said, "You have no idea."

Anyway, so she was knitting and telling him there was no way she'd be putting Stimpy on a plane and he knew that, but she accepted that he didn't want to talk about George and that was fine, so let's talk about Sophie instead. Finn agreed. He liked talking about Sophie. Apparently, Sophie was seeing a new guy, but, "It won't be serious, you can see she's working through something on this one," and Finn nodded, and then he wondered what his mum would say to Soph about Finn if she knew Finn wanted to bang George, marry him, and live in domestic gay bliss with him and their kids.

'*Daddy issues.*'

Eww. Also: no. Finn chatted to Kenny about all that—absent father figure—and Kenny reckoned he was fine, even said, '*Just 'cos the psychobabble is out there, doesn't mean it applies to you.*'

If they knew it was casual and George had a boyfriend? Well, there would be concerned fucking looks shooting all over the place. Finn was yet to get into the whole casual thing. But he could. He totally could. He'd fucked a few guys casually—a tourist in Maui, a couple of tourists in Byron—and yeah, he'd felt, kind of hollow afterwards, but that didn't mean he couldn't do casual like it was a done deal. He totally could.

One thing was for sure, he wasn't letting his mum and Soph get wind of it, not until he was sure it was all working for him and he could show them he was honestly fine.

Finn was back training with the team the week after the Brisbane trip. They won that game and Finn was pleased—team first and all that. Plus, the more games they won, the more likely they played finals and thus, the more games Finn would get to play after being sidelined with this bloody injury. George was right: *rest and get better so you're good when we need you.*

That was the last text he'd received from George. He'd visited him again before the Brisbane trip, but since Finn went home with his mum to his apartment, since the team went to Brisbane and won, Finn had heard little other than messages like that.

George was coming into the locker room now, stopping to chat with each player, his notepad tapping against his thigh. Finn was aware of him as Lacy got dressed beside him and continued a monologue about this antique road trip he wanted to take.

"You mean, like, antique furniture?" Finn asked, looking up at him.

Lacy was focusing on doing up his pants, his chest bare—he had so many tattoos, Finn often felt himself getting lost in them, trying to work out what they all were.

"Yeah," Lacy glanced at him and pulled a face. "Like what you see?"

Finn laughed. Lacy shoved him.

"Yeah, you want a piece of this, eh?"

"You wish. Anyway, antiques?"

"Yeah," Lacy grabbed his shirt—it was a classic cut button-up, designer—and went on about some places in the Blue Mountains. Finn thought he could make out a lion eating a snake or was the snake coming around to eat the lion wrapping around Lacy's hip.

Lacy flicked him with his towel in the head and Finn laughed and then George was there.

"Lacy, fuck's sake, he's got a head injury," George said.

Lacy put both palms up, "My bad, didn't know cotton was so bad for the skull."

Finn laughed and George shooed Lacy away telling him to focus on not getting suspended, everything else was fine.

"Right, Finn," George said. He glanced at Finn, then down at his notes, then tapped them against his leg, expression serious. Coach to a player. "You'll be back when you're back, in the meantime, keep up the conditioning without pushing it, got it?"

"Yeah," Finn smiled.

George cleared his throat and gave him a blank look. "Good."

He walked off.

Finn was left feeling confused and yeah, he checked in with himself, hurt. He got the need for professionalism, but that was damn clinical. Add to that there'd been no real communication between them since the *'Just kiss?'* message and Finn was confused as fuck.

If George didn't want to do anything, fine, but Finn needed some clarity either way.

He shoved all his shit in his bag, shoved his feet in his sneakers and stormed out.

21

♥

GEORGE SAW THE HURT look in Finn's eyes like a slideshow on repeat as he went about finishing up for the day, as he drove home. He knew he was being confusing. He knew he was broadcasting mixed signals.

But just before he left for the Brisbane trip everything between him and Joq felt so awkward, so strained—Joq didn't give him a lift and George readily accepted his lie about being too tired—it was a caricature of how they normally were, it left George unsettled, and he just couldn't have that in his life.

Coaching first year under the stream of shit scrutiny was enough. He could not handle blowing up his home life. He knew it was selfish, but he also knew if the time to pull back was any time, it was now.

He got home and found Joq in his office. He went over, kissed him, leaned back as Joq smiled and said, "Hi."

"Wanna go out for dinner?"

Joq tilted his head to the side in that sexy way he had sometimes. "Yeah, sounds good. Just gotta finish some tax stuff."

"Take your time," George said and went out, smiling at him over his shoulder.

Yes, this was good, this was what he needed.

They had a nice dinner at the place Joq's mum recommended—private, fancy—and when they came home, they fucked, and it was good. Familiar, practiced. George caught his breath and watched the ceiling as Joq drifted off beside him.

George was still watching the ceiling an hour later and his heart was pounding. His heart was pounding like it had when that article came out and every time it came out and did the rounds in the ten or so years since.

He grabbed his phone off the bedside table and went into the ensuite. He put the toilet lid down, sat, and tried to get his breathing to settle, to calm his rabbiting heart.

He was going to call Scotty. Scotty would be cool. It was embarrassing as fuck when this happened, but Scotty was always cool.

He tapped the screen and saw it light up with a text notification from Finn. He'd had it on silent.

He took a deep breath and decided he'd look at it after he called Scotty.

He was hovering over Scotty's contact when he closed it and opened the messages.

If u want to pretend we never talked about hooking up, that's okay, but please tell me.

George breathed out roughly.

'*We never talked about hooking up.*'

And there it was, in words.

George got up, went downstairs, opened the patio doors, went outside and hit the contact he never dreamed he'd call in all the years he'd had the number.

"George?" Alistair sounded surprised.

"You sound like a yank," George replied.

"Oh my God, George! How are you? Tammi said you look great whenever you're down, but I can see that for myself on TV," Alistair said and George could hear the grin in his voice.

"Man, your accent," George laughed. It was so damn good to hear his voice though. "How you been?"

"How've I been?" Alistair laughed, it was deep and rough, and George remembered that too; Alistair had a great voice, husky, and he loved to talk. "Seriously? I haven't seen you since the draft party back home and you want to know how I've been at... it must be after midnight there."

"Yeah, well," George rubbed his head and sat on the pool lounge. "Better late than never. Sorry. I meant to call, but..."

"Yeah, I get it, what was there to say, right?"

And Alistair said it like it was the truth, that George bailing the morning after and never speaking to him again after they'd been together for most of high school was totally cool.

"Still," he said now, "I am sorry."

Alistair chuckled. "It's really fine. I was fine with it then, I'm fine now. I reckon you could've kept in touch as friends, but I always got it."

"Yeah, fuck, I'm such an asshole."

Alistair snorted. "Nah, you're just a celebrity and an athlete—narcissism comes with the turf, I'm now surrounded by them, how've you been though, for real?"

So, George told him, something deep inside him loosening and unwinding as he told him about that first year, about that article coming out, the years after, winning it all, and Alistair listened and laughed and said all the right things before telling George about his life in LA, about working his way up as a chef, about finally getting his own place.

"You'll have to come see it," Alistair said like he expected George wouldn't. "I've called it The Last Stop."

"I'd love to," he found himself answering honestly and thinking of Finn. "Fuck, I, yeah…" his voice cracked on the 'yeah' and he was instantly embarrassed.

"You okay?"

"Yeah, I'm just," he blew out a breath and looked around his backyard. "I never fucked around," he said quietly, "and now I'm wondering if I, you know, didn't live life right or something."

"Didn't live life right?" Alistair laughed. "Man, you had a fuck tonne to lose if it came out, but please tell me you at least got some since back home."

"Yeah, fuck, I'm not a monk, I got a guy, but…"

"But?"

"But I dunno, I never played the field or whatever."

"Ah," Alistair said on a breath. "So now you're wondering what's out there. Makes sense, since you're retired now, kinda."

"Yeah," George breathed out. That was kind of it. Really what he was doing was searching for a way to make this okay.

"Well, if your guy's cool with it?"

"Yeah, we're open."

"Nice, so what's the problem?"

George wondered what the problem was as well, since Alistair made it so normal.

"Yeah, I dunno, you settled down?"

"Just finished a long-term thing, seeing a new guy, don't change the subject," Alistair said—it was a gruff tease and George had a flashback to fucking Alistair in his bed back home, Alistair teasing him, laughing, until George nailed him right good and laughed at his stunned face. "What's the problem?" Alistair asked again.

"I dunno, you know how fucking awkward I am with all that," George said.

"Shy maybe, at first, but it's like riding a bike," Alistair said seriously and George laughed.

"Yeah, okay, I'm just not sure I can do it without the feelings," George said and felt really spooked—that was the crux of it.

Alistair cracked up. "Now you tell me."

"What? You knew I loved you, man."

"How would I know?"

"You just ... you didn't?"

"Yeah, I mean, I figured? But, we were kids, so..."

"Yeah."

"Look, I gotta go," Alistair said, his footsteps loud through the speakers. "Dinner prep."

"Oh, course, sorry—"

"Never apologise for calling me. It's fucking awesome to hear from you and do me a favour, yeah?"

"I'm scared to hear it, but alright."

Alistair laughed. "Go and get laid for fun. You were always too serious, have fun."

George huffed a laugh. "Yeah, alright."

They ended the call and George felt lighter.

He opened Finn's text message. *If u want to pretend we never talked about hooking up, that's okay, but please tell me.*

George read it a few times, glanced at the pool, read it again, then started typing.

I don't want to pretend we never talked about it, I meant what I said. Just don't know if it's a good idea with the footy.

He hit send.

It was honest.

The read receipt appeared immediately.

George swallowed as the text bubble came up.

I get it, but u cant be mean to me if u change ur mind.

George laughed under his breath. George was terser with Finn at training; he thought he was being professional, or at least, that's what he told himself. Finn was calling bullshit and that was fair.

I don't know if I was mean, he wrote anyway and hit send.

U know what I mean, not friendly, cold.

Which is why maybe we shouldn't do anything, he wrote back because if it meant having conversations like this in the middle of the night then it was a terrible idea.

But who was George kidding? He thought as he watched the text bubble—he was loving every second of this, he felt alive.

So u want to forget about it?

Jesus, George thought, Finn was so direct, it was disarming. George didn't think he could forget about it. But it was the right thing to do. Alistair was right—George did need to loosen up, to fuck around—but maybe George needed to do that with someone whose every reaction and feeling he didn't feel himself living and dying by.

I don't want to hurt you, he wrote, hesitated, then hit send.

So don't, came back right away.

George didn't know where to go from there. His heart was pounding again, but it wasn't bad this time. It was good. It was life.

We should get some sleep, he sent.

Okay, but don't shut me out like that again, no matter what else happens.

George squeezed his phone. The last thing in the world he wanted to do was hurt Finn. *I won't. I promise.*

Good. Came back immediately and George snorted. Then: *Night, George.*

Night, Finn.

George sat in the dark for a while longer. He had no fucking idea where he was going to go from here. This was the last thing he expected his first year coaching, the last thing he needed.

And yet, he thought as he got up and headed back inside, he wouldn't trade it for the world.

Finn smiled sheepishly at him in the locker room the following morning. George grinned broadly back and Finn laughed and ducked his head.

As they made their way out to the oval, George jogged by and leaned in close, "Is this friendly enough for you?"

Finn laughed and met his eyes and George regretted opening the Pandora's box before Finn even spoke, "It could be friendlier."

George felt himself blush, but he was laughing, and he gave Finn a gentle shove as they headed out for training.

It was better after that, George felt like he could breathe. Yes, he was attracted to his rookie. Yes, he could admit, finally, that he probably needed to fuck around a lot more than he had, that he was kind of fucked up in that area and had a few issues on account of that damn article. But in the week since that text exchange, he felt like he found a safe middle ground with Finn—flirty yet not crossing the line. It was good. It buoyed him up.

Of course, he'd be a fool if he thought that could last.

They were playing a home game against an inner city team that weekend, then an away game in Adelaide the following weekend. Both called for trying some different tactics, and George was about to head to a meeting with the coaching staff and leadership group—Lacy and Cary—when there was a knock on his office door.

"Yep," he called out.

Finn stuck his head in. "Got a minute?"

"Yeah, course," he said. He didn't, but he always did for Finn.

"I umm," Finn stepped inside, shut the door behind him, then looked at George, he skittered his eyes away, fiddled with the drawstring on his pants before rubbing the back of his neck in a way that looked painful.

"What is it?" George asked and came around his desk.

"It's umm, I was thinking—

George's door opened and Travis stuck his head in. "You comin'?"

"Yeah," George came over to him and herded him out, "be there in a sec."

"'Kay. Hey, Finn," Travis called as the door was closed on him.

"Hey," Finn replied, his voice cracking. "Sorry," he shook his head, clearly embarrassed. "It's not important." He went for the door.

George grabbed his wrist, his body alongside Finn's so his chest brushed Finn's arm. Finn spun his fingers clumsily in the grip and gripped George back, his eyes on their joined hands.

"Text it," George said quietly. "You're good at giving me what for when you text."

Finn huffed a laugh at himself that was more like discharging pent up energy than laughter. But he nodded. "Okay."

George squeezed his hand and Finn squeezed him back.

Lacy yelled down the hall and they pulled back.

Finn disappeared out the door.

George's phone vibrated in his pocket throughout the meeting. He wanted to take it out so bad, but he made himself wait until he was back in his office. He couldn't have said what was decided in that meeting even if you put a gun to his head.

He sat in his desk chair, pulled out his phone and looked at all the message notifications. He made himself tap and open like ripping off a band-aid.

In case it wasn't obvious: if u want to hook up im interested in that.

George felt his heart thud, his stomach flip and his dick take interest. There it was. Out there.

I mean, ur open and he does and we could.

George frowned. It was true enough, but he didn't like it for some reason.

I mean, fuck, sorry.

George snorted. He was used to Finn's texting style by now. He had a hesitancy in person he abandoned completely in text.

I just mean, I can't get laid and I'd like to.

George actually laughed at that one. He didn't know why, but that was the one that made him think it could work—Finn wanted to get laid, George was available. Okay.

But we can forget I said anything and just be friendly if ur not into any of this.

The speech bubble was coming up again as George replied: *I'm into all of this* just as Finn's '*sorry*' came through, rapidly followed by, '*yeah?*'

George laughed. *Yeah.*

Thank God, Finn sent. *U busy now?*

George's dick really took interest because yeah, technically, why not? He could go round to Finn's, pin him against the wall, kiss him until they were desperate for it, and fuck him in the entryway with their pants around their ankles.

But, no, he needed to get it right in his head, he needed to tell Joq. And most important of all, he needed to make sure they did it right; it was stupid logic for a hook-up, but George felt like he needed to make sure he treated Finn right.

He also desperately needed to diffuse this pent-up sexual energy, this anxious desire, this feeling that he was going to go crazy if he didn't have Finn now.

Jesus, he wrote and hit send.

Then: *Keep it in your pants rook*, to make Finn laugh and break that tension.

He got back a series of emojis that now looked different in the new context, laughed, and debated taking a cold shower in the locker rooms.

Soon? Finn sent back.

Yeah. Don't reckon I can hold out much longer. George almost felt embarrassed by that, but it was the truth.

Fuck!!!!

George snorted a laugh.

Away game next Saturday, he wrote and hit send.

Yeah, fuck, okay, I'll come to ur room?

Yeah.

He hit send on the last one and tossed the phone on his desk. He spun and looked out at the oval, the sunset, the seagulls. His heart was pounding, his dick was hard, and he was getting into something way over his head; but he could do this if he remembered what this was for Finn—he needed to get laid, he was too famous to get some outside the bubble, George could give that to him.

George liked that logic, it meant he could make it special for Finn, good, and once Finn was older and he met someone else, someone more suitable, he'd know how he could expect to be treated.

It was just fucking and George could work with that. Like Alistair said, George needed to loosen up, to have fun. This could be that.

And one day, Finn would meet the right guy for him. George let that feeling land properly—he needed to remember that above all else and not lose his head here.

But Finn's play wasn't right that Sunday. On the Monday in training, something still wasn't right. George heard the TV blaring in the hallway as he headed for the locker room. One of the talking heads dissecting Finn's play: "*Rattled. Kid's rattled. He needs to get over it. He's playing with the big boys now, he needs to learn to shake it off.*"

George caught the eye of one of the physios coming towards him, "Can you turn that shit off?" he gestured at the TV.

"Yes, I think it's in Travis's office," he looked around—Adrian, George was pretty sure his name was Adrian—"but I'll find it and turn it off, Mr Creed, sorry."

"George, call me George," he pushed into the locker room, "and thank you."

The door swung shut behind him and he was caught on what those wankers were saying; they were missing the point; Finn wasn't having a problem with playing with the 'big boys' and he wasn't rattled. George had a sinking feeling he knew what he was looking at when he replayed Finn's movements in the game—the hesitancy, the reactions being off by a fraction of a second.

Finn wasn't at his locker.

"Doc came and got him," Cary said.

George met his eyes—Cary was fresh from the shower with a towel around his hips, and his expression told George he saw it too.

"Thanks," George said and went out again.

He pushed into the doctor's room. Finn was slumped on the bed with his head down. He was alone.

George walked over to him and Finn didn't look up—his breathing was loud, his eyes fixed on the carpet. George brought his hand up and slid his fingers onto Finn's chin, slid them along his jaw until Finn looked up.

Finn's eyes were wet with unshed tears. His lips parted as he looked at George. He was hurt, defeated, but the longer George held his face gently, caressed his forefinger along Finn's cheek, the more Finn's expression transformed.

This wasn't to make Finn feel better, this was because George couldn't hold out for another second.

He leaned forward and pressed his lips against Finn's. Finn's lips parted immediately under his and George caressed Finn's tongue softly with his own, and Finn met him, pressed into it urgently.

George pulled back but stayed close. When he spoke, his lips brushed Finn's, their breaths combining in the tight space. "Footy's not all you are, you're so much more than this," he smiled against Finn's lips, felt Finn's breath against his mouth as he went on, "and I'm gonna show you this weekend."

He stepped back. Finn watched him—his lips parted, his eyes widening, he was the perfect picture of dishevelled shock and then he started to smile—a radiant, joyous explosion on his face—and George grinned back.

He could hear the clock ticking on the wall, each tick loud in the room, and it felt like an eternity of just them, smiling insanely at each other.

The door opened behind him.

"Creed."

George turned to the voice of Dr Miller. "Take good care of this one," he said gruffly but he smiled the familiar smile of knowing the doc since he was a player.

"I take good care of all my players," Miller said around a fond smile. George nodded, and left.

Im not cleared for footy but im cleared for other activities.

George read Finn's text as he got home that night and laughed.

Good, he typed back quickly, *I knew about the footy*.

He wondered if Finn had asked the doc about 'other activities' and didn't know whether to laugh or squeeze his dick.

"Joq?" he called as he took his boots and jacket off, tossed his keys into the bowl at the door.

He found him outside by the pool. He was about to tell him—he needed to tell him—but after saying hi and checking in, because it was weird for Joq to be sitting out here drinking soda water, instead of pushing or saying anything, he said, "Alright, well, I'm gonna cook, you want anything in particular?" kind of breathlessly.

"You only know how to make stir-fry," Joq replied.

George laughed, it felt nervous. "I can always order something."

Joq sipped his water. "Stir-fry's fine."

"Cool, give me thirty, just gonna shower," George said and felt a rush of adrenaline leave him.

He'd tell Joq after. They always talked about Joq's hook-ups after. The thought of divulging what he did with Finn felt wrong, but regardless, that's when they'd talk about it, that was the pattern.

George got in the shower, nervous energy skittering everywhere, and thought about that kiss. It'd been fucking electric. He braced himself against the tiles, let the hot water hit his shoulders and just breathed in the warm memory of it.

22

F INN SHOOK HIS HANDS out as he waited outside George's door
after the Adelaide game. He'd been on the bench all game, exchanging thoughts with George during the breaks, and it'd felt like the
biggest build-up; every smile, every word felt loaded, felt like he was
going to burst. He was so fucking nervous. He was so fucking excited.

He knocked, three soft raps. Too soft, Christ, George wouldn't
hear him.

The door opened.

George looked nervous too, but then he smiled, shy but inviting,
and Finn relaxed.

"Hi," Finn said.

"Hi," George's smile widened and he stepped back to let Finn in.
He reached for Finn's waist as he went past like he couldn't stop
himself, his fingers caressing Finn's side.

Finn met his eyes and smiled. He felt like he was going to fall
forward and not come up for air until the next day as the door closed
softly behind him.

George gripped his hip to still him.

"Joq's gonna call, but after..."

Finn pulled back. Right, Joq.

"Oh, course, cool, cool."

"Sorry, we always, on the road, we always—"

"No, of course, it's fine, I'll wait in the bathroom."

"You don't have to do that, just make yourself—"

He cut off as the sound of a video call started blaring from his laptop.

Finn went for the bathroom.

"Finn," George said after him, "you can sit out here, it's fine; we're not doing anything wrong."

"All good," Finn said quickly and shut the bathroom door behind him. He heard George answer the call and had to shove down a mixture of incredulous hurt. He hadn't forgotten about Joq, but there was a part of him that didn't get Joq and George at all. A part of him that felt angry at Joq for fucking around on George, and a part of him that was angry at George for not instantly leaving Joq now that he'd met Finn. He knew the last part was insane, but a part of him couldn't help but think if George loved him like he knew he already loved George, then George would just be with him.

He leaned against the sink and listened to George's voice, Joq's tinny replies through the speakers. He bit his thumb nail and waited. He was still dialled right up but he felt kind of shit now too. This wasn't what he wanted, at all.

He turned and looked at himself in the mirror. God, he was so fucking young. And so fucking stupid. *If this is all you can get*, he berated his reflection, *then you better fucking take it and not fuck it up*.

But, God, he wanted so much more. And he had a feeling Kenny would say that was bad logic. So would his mum. And Soph.

He listened and heard nothing. He opened the bathroom door a crack.

"He gone?" he asked and winced internally—he could've asked nicer than that.

"Yeah," George said on a breath. He was moving to the other side of the bed, his gaze heavy on Finn. "C'mere."

Finn forgot all about Joq. He forgot about everything outside of this room. His heart was in his throat and every step felt heavy as he padded from the bathroom to stand in front of George sitting on the bed.

George placed his hands outside his thighs, slid them up under his shirt and tugged the hem. Finn didn't need to be told twice—he ripped the shirt off and stood, panting, as George ran his hands back down, watched their path, watched Finn.

"What do you want?" George asked.

Finn heard his voice shake, but it was a genuine question. Fuck, Finn wanted everything George would give him.

"What do *you* want?" he asked and placed his hands carefully on George's shoulders, felt them firm and strong under his weight.

George was lifting his head and Finn bent to meet him. Their lips touched in the most hesitant caress; Finn heard and felt himself panting into it. His heart was pounding and his nerves felt overwhelming. He felt George's tongue touch his, tentative, and he responded, feeling him out agonisingly slowly. It was the softest kiss Finn had ever had. But he wanted so much more, he was so turned on he thought he was going to come the second George touched his dick, but he wanted to make George feel good first, to show him how much he wanted him.

"I want to suck you off," he said against George's lips.

George groaned and kissed him harder.

Finn would've laughed if he wasn't so busy getting kissed so thoroughly, meeting George for more. He broke the kiss and met George's eyes. George flicked his eyes back and forth on Finn's—he was hiding nothing, it was all there, his naked desire, for Finn. He surged back in and kissed George hard, tried to tell him with his mouth, his tongue, his lips, how much he wanted him, how much he liked him, loved him.

He pulled away and sank to his knees, George's hands sliding over his back, up his sides, onto his shoulders before resting one big palm on his nape.

George's dick was straining against the fabric of his pants. It looked thick, long, and it was so hard it bobbed and flexed the longer Finn watched.

"The idea is to suck it," George said breathlessly around a nervous smile.

"George," Finn cracked up and dropped his head against George's abs, his face right near his big dick as he laughed. George's hand was a steady weight on his nape, squeezing lightly, tugging gently on his hair.

Finn sat back.

"I want," he said as he looked up at George.

"Whatever you want," George replied with quiet conviction. Finn looked at him—his tousled hair, his eyes wide and sincere—and he felt the impact of those words like a body blow.

He leaned forward and rested his head on George's thigh to hide his reaction, which was pure adoration; he wanted George so much he thought he'd choke on the heavy breath he let out. George's hand went into his hair and his body surrounded Finn as he leaned down, kissed the top of his head.

"You want to stop," George whispered against his hair, "you tell me."

Finn jerked up. "I don't want to stop." He never wanted to stop, that was the problem.

George kissed him, found Finn's hand and slid it to his dick.

Finn would've teased him if he wasn't so turned on by the idea that he was turning George on so much he had to have Finn's hand on him now. He rubbed, squeezed, did his best with the angle.

George tilted Finn's head back and kissed him roughly. Finn felt him losing control and he let go into it, went slack in George's hands. George brought his other hand down and under Finn's, freed his dick and got Finn's hand back around himself.

Finn broke the kiss and leaned over George's dick. He gave it a firm stroke—of course it was a gorgeous dick, he thought hysterically for a moment, thick and smooth, the head glistening with pre-come as it stretched out of his foreskin. Finn stroked, inhaled the musky scent and leaned forward and licked around the head. He saw George's abdomen ripple. He sucked the head into his mouth, got it nice and wet, felt himself moaning like the world's biggest slut as George's hand gripped and released in his hair, his hips rocking up in tiny movements, his breathing loud above Finn.

Finn had sucked cock before. Exactly three times. He liked doing it, but he was no expert at it. He so desperately wanted to make this good for George though, so he focused on doing everything that would make himself feel good and watched carefully for George's reactions. He slid down, slid up, licked around the head. George sucked in a sharp breath, pushed up, and then Finn stopped thinking altogether. He was moaning, sucking, licking, trying to take as much of George as he could, trying to make him feel as good as George was making him feel.

He sank all the way down and felt George's guttural groan. Finn controlled his gag reflex as George thrust into his mouth like he'd lost control. Finn held George there before sliding up, meeting George's eyes with only the tip in his mouth. He watched George pant, wild eyed, and sank all the way down again.

"Fuck, baby, Finn," George panted, his hips rocking into Finn's mouth.

Finn moaned at the endearment. Fuck, but that was the hottest thing that'd ever happened to him—hearing George losing it.

"Can I fuck your mouth?" George asked.

And scratch that, Finn was pulling up; now he'd heard the hottest thing.

George was rolling his hips, so turned on, his eyes roving all over Finn as Finn pulled away from his dick.

"Yeah. Please," Finn said, his voice husky.

George groaned and gripped him by the hair, moving him so his mouth was back at his dick as George drove inside Finn's waiting, panting mouth.

God, Finn's moaning had turned into continuous whining as George fucked his mouth with powerful yet measured rolls of his hips. Finn could tell George was losing it, but that he was trying to be careful.

Finn didn't want him to be careful. He rubbed George's thighs, ran his hands under his shirt, revelled in touching him. He relaxed his throat while tightening his lips around the shaft driving in and out of him. He met George's eyes as his saliva coated George's dick in a slick slide, and his own eyes leaked with tears as he took the assault on his mouth and his throat. He loved every second of it.

George never broke eye contact, his breathing was so loud and his hips were getting faster. "Can you swallow?"

Finn moaned desperately—he wanted that so bad.

"Oh, God," George bit out. "You can swallow," he slammed in and Finn felt his cock jerking and releasing down his throat. He groaned, swallowed, watched George the whole time. George panted, thrust into his mouth, his eyes wild on Finn's as he came deep down his throat.

Finn was so turned on, he felt like he'd lost complete control of himself as George slid out of his mouth and yanked him into his lap. George kissed him hard. It was a kiss full of passion and gratitude. Finn whined into it, writhed in George's lap, he slid his hands under George's shirt again and dragged his fingers over skin in rough movements; he needed to touch, he needed to come.

George pulled back and ripped his shirt off. He got his head free and kissed Finn again—it was a bruising kiss, punishing—and then his big body was lifting Finn and shoving him back so he was stretched out on the bed.

George pressed alongside him, rested his head in his hand as he propped himself up on his elbow and ran a rough hand over Finn's trembling body.

"Geez, Finny, you wanting somethin'?"

"George," Finn whined, but he couldn't stop himself from laughing. "Please."

"I dunno," George said in a deep voice, a rumble against Finn's side, his hand a tease as he ran it down and cupped Finn's dick. "I don't reckon you need me, reckon you got it covered."

Finn was thrusting into that hand, giggling, his eyes never leaving the fond, teasing smile George was giving him.

George looked sated, content, but Finn didn't miss the heat in his eyes as he watched Finn, the little catch in his breath as his smile broke into a huff.

George slid down the bed, tugging Finn's pants down and off as he went. He pushed his thighs open in one smooth motherfucker move. Finn was going to tease him, but he was shaking too much, and he needed to hold on. He slid his hands into George's thick hair like he'd been wanting to do since they met, held his fingers in the strands against George's skull as George sucked his straining dick into his mouth and took him to the hilt in one go.

Finn gasped and arched; his blow job had been the work of an amateur compared to this—George was taking him root to tip in a slow, methodical, tight rhythm—each plunge downwards was careful, while each time he dragged up, it felt reverent, his tongue laving Finn's dick. Then he felt George add a finger against his perineum—just a soft drag of the tip against his skin, from the root of his dick to his hole and back again, careful and teasing. Finn panted, his hands tightened in George's hair—he was going to come, they'd barely started and he was going to come.

George pulled off.

"No, please," he gasped.

George wrapped his palm around Finn's dick and stroked him slowly, but tightly. He shifted under Finn and when George's tongue caressed his hole, Finn felt like he'd been electrocuted. George was tentative but getting firmer, then aggressive as he pushed inside with his tongue and started to fuck Finn's hole at the same speed as his hand stroked his dick.

Finn felt like he was getting played in the best possible way. He was a livewire, right on the edge of the mixed sensations, right on the edge of coming. He pushed his hips up to try and get more, shoved them down to try and get more.

"Please, please," he begged and didn't recognise his own voice, "George, please..."

George breached him with a finger and Finn gasped. He felt it moving inside him next to George's tongue, deep and agonisingly slow, the hand on his cock so measured, so perfect.

The need to come wound so tight in him and went deeper; he felt it building against that measured pace, getting stronger. His whole body went tight. He stared at the ceiling as it crashed over him.

George's mouth came back to envelope his cock as he started to come, while he drove into Finn with two fingers, thrusting so deep inside he was hitting him right there. Finn came and it was unlike any orgasm he'd ever had, it felt deeper, it felt like it would never end—a steady, blindingly good stream of sensation. And George just sucked him through it, fucked him through it with his fingers.

By the time he sagged back into the mattress, he was so wrung out he wasn't entirely sure what'd just happened.

George released him and pulled his fingers out, slid up the bed and tucked himself tight against Finn's side. Finn sagged further into the mattress and relished in the feel of George's hand stroking his chest, playing with his nipples. He felt giddy, warm, and so fucking good.

He cracked his eyes open. He was still panting. He smiled up at George and basked in George's answering smile.

"Fuck," Finn breathed out. "What was that?"

"An orgasm?" George grinned down at him. The smug bastard.

Finn huffed a laugh. He moved closer for a kiss and George met him immediately.

George kissed him deeply and Finn responded. The edge was gone but the deep pleasure remained as Finn brushed his lips against George's, met his tongue with his own and caressed him there, savoured the feel of George's hands roaming over his body, appreciated every second of his own doing the same. He didn't know how long they made out for, but it felt like a long time. It felt like they said a lot with those kisses—Finn felt like George wanted him as much as Finn wanted George with those kisses.

Finn pulled back an inch. George was watching him, smiling softly.

"Ten out of ten, will fuck again," Finn said.

George laughed. "We haven't fucked yet."

"But we will?" he asked, smiling.

George stroked Finn's cheek. His eyes never left Finn's, and Finn couldn't believe for a second that George didn't want him as badly as Finn wanted him.

"We will," George said.

"Just fuck?" Finn asked and felt his heart rate spike with hope.

George frowned and Finn hated that, wished he'd never said anything.

The moment stretched and Finn wanted to fidget.

"Just fucking," George replied.

Finn searched his eyes—George was watching him seriously, but there was something guarded there, something that wasn't there before Finn asked—Finn reckoned he knew what it was too. George was trying to let the stupid rookie down easy, remind him he had a boyfriend he fucked out of love and Finn was just that, a fuck, just for fucking.

"Okay," Finn said because what else could he say? He wasn't about to stop. Not after what they'd just done.

George rolled away and got up.

Finn felt bereft.

"Order something, no junk," George said, his voice moving away.

"Okay," Finn said, eyes closed.

"Then meet me in the shower."

Finn's eyes flicked open and landed on George. He was gloriously naked and giving Finn a cheeky smile, but it was shy too, like there was some universe in which Finn would turn down shower sex with George.

He smiled—delighted and out of control—and did as he was told.

23

G EORGE WAS ABOUT TO lather up when he felt the shower door open, felt the warm presence of Finn behind him. His heart was in his throat and he didn't trust himself to speak. Finn pushed against his back and draped himself there. George relaxed. His arms came up and gripped Finn's where they wrapped around his torso.

It was exactly what he needed and he exhaled roughly, let his weight sink into Finn behind him, sink into all the places their skin slid over each other. Finn's broad chest pressed into his back, his groin and dick snugged in tight against George's ass, and his thighs pushed against George's own, his shins brushed George's calves, his feet slid outside George's on the tiles, and his toe caressed George's in a way that tickled. He felt held, he felt like the shaking inside could settle.

"Just fuck?" Finn had asked, so hopeful, so fucking beautiful.

George wanted more than fucking with Finn. He wanted it more than he wanted anything else in the world—he wanted it all—but it was impossible. He was in a relationship, a good relationship, a bloody long-term relationship. And Finn was just so bloody young—he didn't get it yet, but he would, he'd realise soon enough he was so turned on by George because he was fucking one of his footy idols, but soon, sooner than George would like, he'd realise he needed an actual partner, a real boyfriend, someone infinitely cooler and smarter and hotter than George.

Anyway, he thought as he sighed gruffly and melted into Finn's touch, it was a lot to be torturing himself with after the best goddamn sex of his life. Which was the other problem—that was not just fucking, not even close. He squeezed his eyes shut and let his head fall back on Finn's shoulder.

Finn kissed his throat, kissed a line up to his jaw, his breath warm. George let his head fall to the side and Finn kissed his mouth. George pressed into it, turned fully and pressed Finn against the wall and kissed him, ran his hands all over his body, caressing his sides, brushing his fingertips over his stomach, and teasing his nipples.

He broke the kiss and dropped his head to Finn's shoulder, danced his fingers over Finn's abs. Finn kissed his head, ran his hands up and down George's back.

"Fucking seriously?" George ran his palm over the cut of Finn's abs.

Finn laughed and George pressed his palm into the vibrations.

"You know how hard I work," Finn said.

"Yeah, but," George tilted his face up. Finn was watching him, smiling softly, self-consciously, the spray of the water leaving little droplets in his eyelashes as it lashed George's back. "There's knowing and then there's this," he ran his fingers over Finn's torso but never looked away from his face.

Finn's lips parted—he looked like he was turned on and trying not to giggle.

George slid his hand down and found his dick hardening. He stroked it with his knuckles.

"What'd you order?" he asked.

"Ah, fuck, food," Finn said.

George laughed and kissed him.

He wrapped his palm around Finn loosely, "What kind of food?" he asked against Finn's lips as he stroked him with a loose grip.

"Fuck, burgers, but. C'mon, more, please," Finn pushed into George's hand.

George loved how needy he got and how he didn't take over. He trusted George to give him what he needed.

George tightened his grip. "Burgers are junk," he said and let go as he reached back and pumped the soap.

"I got it from the healthy heart section and don't fucking stop!"

George laughed. Finn was laughing too, but he was also giving him an incredulous look.

George took Finn's dick in a firmer hold, the soap making it nice and slippery, and started to jerk him off in a way that'd get him there really quickly.

"Didn't you just come?" George asked as he kissed the corner of Finn's mouth gently, a direct counterpoint to the firm way he was working his dick over.

"Fuck," Finn panted, "try bein' twenty and George Creed's givin' you a hand job."

George huffed a laugh. Finn angled his head for better kissing and George kissed him properly, got him off.

Finn's come was washing down the drain as he reached for George.

"I better get the food," George said and kissed him hard. He was hard again, but he needed to save it; he didn't want to remind Finn he was so much older he kind of needed to save it if he was going to fuck Finn after they ate.

"You sure?" Finn asked. He seemed unsure. The water was hitting the tiles loudly, the room full of steam, and George saw the insecurity flash in Finn's eyes. He couldn't stand that.

George grabbed Finn's hand and wrapped it around his rock-hard dick.

"I need to fuck you later, yeah?" he asked.

Finn squeezed. "Yeah," he replied on a breath.

"I'm gonna need this," he smiled, tried to make it a joke, but now he felt self-conscious. God, Finn could do so much better—George remembered that fucking Brazilian barman, that dude could probably get rock hard and fuck Finn all night. It's not like George was old—he could certainly go a few rounds in a night—but he wasn't twenty.

Finn though, Finn keened and pushed into George's space and kissed him like he'd lost control again, kissed him like he kissed him when he crawled into George's lap after the blowjob. It was a lot and it did George in something crazy. Finn was squeezing and releasing on George's dick. George groaned into his mouth and let Finn push him up against the wall, the water hitting them side on as Finn rubbed his abs against George's dick, jerked him in a tight fist, and George couldn't believe it as he rubbed up against Finn and started to come.

"Shit, fuck, sorry," he panted hoarsely as he watched his dick shoot rope after rope of come over Finn's stomach, watched it drip down his groin, slide over his dick.

"Good?" Finn asked.

George met his eyes as he caught his breath. Finn was beaming at him.

George laughed, breathless. "Fuck." He panted. "Yeah."

"Good," Finn said and kissed him. He pulled back. "We'll get to the fucking," he smiled, cheeky and beautiful. "When we get to the fucking."

George smiled, disarmed by Finn taking control; he liked it, he loved it.

"I really better get the food," he reluctantly got out.

George took a final bite of the burger Finn had ordered him—grilled steak and salad, from the healthy heart section indeed, even came with sweet potato fries, which George wasn't a fan of, but it's not like they could eat regular fries.

He ran his hand up and down Finn's back as Finn sat forward and ate his grilled fish and salad burger, his spare hand rubbing up and down the inseam of George's pants. They'd both put trackies on to eat, their torsos bare, and George savoured all that glorious tan skin as he splayed his fingers wide and dragged his palm down before running it back up with light fingers.

They were watching a replay of another game and Finn was commentating, making some pretty good points about how every team was using all their players wrong. And well, Finn wasn't wrong.

When Setter, an ex-player recently made coach, but he'd done years as an assistant first, came on screen, Finn said, "Wow, Setter's really let himself go."

George snorted, squeezed Finn's hip. "Benefit of coaching and not playing." He resumed the caress.

"Yeah?" Finn looked over his shoulder, his smile was mischievous. "You planning to?"

George wasn't, couldn't imagine it, but, "I dunno," he ran his hand down Finn's back, "I do like pies."

Finn scoffed.

George sat up so he could tickle Finn's side. "Will you still like me if I tub out?"

Finn wriggled out of his grasp, laughing manically, his hair wild, his eyes shining. He made George's heart clench.

"You won't?" he asked faux-seriously and grabbed Finn around the waist.

"I might," Finn replied, breathless with laughter.

"Might?" George asked incredulously. He got both hands onto Finn's sides then and started to tickle him.

Finn tried to get away, choking on his laughter.

"Alright, alright, I'll still like your fat ass," he gasped out through his laughter.

"I'll give you a fat ass," George hauled Finn up and rolled them so he was straddling him, pinned his hands over his head. Finn was watching him, laughing, wriggling, trying to get free. He bucked up and George let him take the upper hand. George was pushed under him with his powerful thighs and he laughed as Finn pinned him, smiled smugly, his hair falling down around his face.

Finn leaned down and kissed him, but he was laughing and George was laughing and it was kissing with giggling. George used the moment to push up and get Finn onto his back again, kiss him properly.

There was a roar from the TV and they both looked up.

"See?" Finn said. "I told you."

George agreed. Finn's earlier assessment that they were using Carr all wrong, they needed to play him in a position in the pocket and let his 'mad skills' shine, was coming to fruition with that stellar mark.

"Yeah, alright," George said and focused on kissing Finn's Adam's apple where it was taut and stretched below him as he reclined his head back to see the TV.

"No, seriously, watch the replay. I'm tellin' you, he needs to play Carr in the pocket."

George watched the replay. It was a fucking beauty of a mark—Carr soaring out of the bodies and using his defender as a ledge for his knee as he took a screamer. George grunted—yeah, he was impressive, he was older than George and still going strong too.

"What? He's good," Finn's eyes were still glued to the screen where they were replaying Carr pulling up a bit of grass, flicking it in the air to check the wind—ostensibly; all guys knew it was a habit to settle the nerves—before he lined up for a shot on goal. "I'm telling you, forward pocket."

Carr took the shot on screen and it sailed through for a perfect goal. They cut away from him getting mobbed by teammates to replay the mark in slow motion from another angle.

"See?" Finn said. "Fuckin' beauty. Man, he looks good. Still."

"He's alright," George replied and rolled to sit up, dragging Finn with him and resituating him between his outstretched legs. "I met his girlfriend at the Brownlow's last year—she's nicer than him."

Well, met was a stretch, they'd been on the red carpet together at the same time and Cara had complimented her purse and George had shaken Carr's hand, said hello to his girlfriend, smiled politely and moved on with Cara. But his point stood—in that few seconds, she seemed like a very nice lady.

Finn laughed. George ran his hand up and down his back again.

"Real smooth, old man," Finn said and squeezed his inner thigh.

"What?" George raised both eyebrows. He had no idea what Finn was talking about.

Finn glanced back at him and George tried to maintain his oblivious look. "I'm just saying, she's a nice lady."

"Oh, that's all you're saying is it?" Finn asked playfully.

"Yes," George doubled-down. "And they seem very happy."

"Okay, I'll stop myself from trying to get in on that then," Finn started to giggle.

George broke too and tickled his side. "Damn right you will," he tackled him down and tickled him and he knew there was no way Finn was going to what? Hit on Carr? But he liked the reassurance of having him here in his arms, giggling at his hands, his words. He kissed his throat, his pulse point and then dragged him back to sitting to finish watching the game. He felt annoyed whenever Carr came on, but he didn't say anything because even he realised that was fucking ridiculous. He was pretty sure Carr was going to marry his missus soon anyway, which was also fucking immaterial and a stupid thought to be having.

They watched the game and it was nice, comfortable.

He noticed Finn's caress on his thigh change subtly—it went from a reassuring touch, a touch to touch, to something that felt like an intent as he swept higher and higher, almost but not quite brushing up against George's dick with his long fingers.

George cocked his leg out and Finn took the invitation—sweeping his fingers higher, lightly brushing. George stroked lower on Finn's back, down to his ass, and Finn sat forward asking for more.

Finn continued to tease him—his hand skimming the base of George's dick as George got harder, started to strain against the fabric.

George slid his fingers further down Finn's lower back, teased where he could reach. Finn made the lightest touch over his dick and George pushed down, slid his forefinger along Finn's crack and pushed inside gently. Finn wriggled forward and George worked it in and out of him as best he could with the angle, his breathing turning rough.

Finn finally made full contact with his dick—his hand rubbing, stroking, squeezing inside his pants—and George thought he was going to come, just from this furtive, fumbling touch.

Finn looked over his shoulder, giving up all pretence of watching TV and met George's eyes. He gave George's dick a deliberate squeeze, his eyes searching George's; so blue and so guileless—a question there.

George pushed his finger in deeper and leaned forward. Finn kissed him, a warm brush of lips, a gentle caress of tongues, a heated exchange of air. George worked that finger in and out of Finn in time with the way they kissed and Finn did the same to his dick—pumping him slowly, firmly. The kiss deepened, got wetter, more out of control and their hands followed pace.

George knew they were going to fuck and he felt eager and nervous. He was so aroused the nerves became excited fuel as his heart thumped loudly in his chest, as Finn's hair caressed his cheeks and his nose rubbed gently against George's.

George brought his arms up and hauled Finn around to face him, to get him into his lap. He didn't stop kissing him. He couldn't. He got his fingers in his waistband and shoved his pants down, continued to kiss Finn as he got each leg free, kicked his pants away before wrestling with Finn's pants until Finn was giggling into his mouth, "Let me," he said and got them off before he let George haul him into his lap properly, their naked chests slamming together as their kisses went frantic.

He needed to be inside Finn yesterday. Last week. Last year. Hell, two years ago.

George broke the kiss, grabbed the remote and clicked off the TV. He was leaning down to get stuff from his bag and Finn touched him like he couldn't not—he stroked his chest, kissed a line up George's throat, massaged his pecs with his long fingers, sucked a kiss under his ear, and rubbed his rock-hard dick into George's abs with a constant roll of his hips.

George tossed the condoms and lube next to his hip and wrapped one arm around Finn's back. He met Finn's eyes and watched him meet George's look; he didn't say anything but he said so much with that look. George wanted to crush him into his chest and never let go. He exhaled roughly, grabbed the condoms and gave them to Finn. He got some lube on his fingers, eyes never leaving Finn's as he reached around and pushed into him with two.

Cradling Finn with his other arm, he worked the lube inside him, never ceasing in his look roving all over Finn's beautiful features—his parted lips, and the way he was in constant motion, rolling his hips back to meet the touch, his tongue darted out to wet his lips, his breaths panted between them and his eyes searched George's, asking him for so much more.

Finn ripped the condom open and rolled it down George's dick, stroked him firmly. He dropped his gaze to watch.

George pulled his fingers out, gripped Finn's hip with one hand and slid his other one up into the hair at Finn's nape, wrapped his palm possessively there. He lifted him until he was hovering over George's cock; Finn angled his hips so he was poised at his entrance before rubbing the tip over himself. George couldn't hold out any-more—he thrust up and Finn met him, pushing down, gasping as he was breached.

George had to kiss him. He used the hand in his hair to tug him forward, to take his mouth as he drove into him as deep as he could go.

He planted his feet on the mattress and used the leverage to fuck into Finn steadily, his hands cradling Finn in his arms at the hip and nape, his cock sliding in and out of that warm, tight heat. God, but it felt amazing, not only where his cock was warm with intense pleasure, but everywhere, his body was alight and overwhelmed with feeling.

He relaxed his grip and let Finn take over.

Finn rolled his hips down, let his head fall back as he gasped and rode George's cock.

"Look at you," George breathed out. "Fuck, look at you."

George couldn't believe Finn was real—all that toned, perfectly sculpted manliness, stretched taut, rolling down to take George's cock as deep as he could get it, his throat a long line, his breaths punching out of him, the keening sound he made when George spoke.

George looked past Finn's shoulder at the mirror above the desk and his heart stuttered. His dick felt like it got harder at the sight. Christ—the picture they made! Finn's beautiful back, all toned muscle stretching and flexing as he ground his hips down, and George's cock like steel as it drove inside him. George looked at his expression—he was lost, he was only desire, his hair a mess, his eyes shining, and his hands roving over Finn's back.

He watched himself kiss up Finn's neck, focused back on Finn as he spoke. "You have to see. Have to see how good you look."

Finn gasped and slammed down on George's dick, riding him frantically.

George held him still. He thought he was going to come right then and there, his lips and breath wet as he spoke against Finn's ear. "Turn around."

Finn gasped, small and broken, and tried to roll his hips, to get more. He turned his head and kissed George frantically. His little cries out of his control as he took George's mouth. George kissed him back roughly.

He pulled away. "Turn around, baby," he said shakily against Finn's lips. "Hands and knees."

Finn groaned, but he got moving when George pulled out and lifted him, spun him to face the mirror, pushed him down gently with a hand on his back. Finn came up onto his hands and knees and George heard him gasp when he looked at himself, looked at George going to his knees behind him.

George ran both palms over Finn's back, steadying himself. He left one on Finn's shoulder, while he placed the other one on Finn's hip to hold him in place.

He met Finn's eyes in the mirror.

Finn was watching him back and his lips parted. His eyes never left George's. A heartbeat of time passed between them and George pushed in. He watched Finn as he entered him, watched Finn arch and pant but never break eye contact as George slid all the way to the hilt. He paused, luxuriated in the feeling. But he was suspended too—caught in those wild blue eyes staring at him, trusting him, giving him everything. For a crazy moment, George wanted to take it all, to have Finn completely.

"Look at yourself while I fuck you," he said.

Finn gasped. George watched the blush rush up his chest, his throat, he saw the shy look in his eyes—he had looks and a body that would put Apollo to shame and yet here he was, split open on George's cock, loving every second of it, begging for more with every ripple of his body and looking shy?

He did George in, he really did.

George pulled back and then slammed in again, pushing Finn forward.

Finn closed his eyes like he couldn't watch anymore.

George plastered himself to Finn's back, wrapped his arms around his torso and hoisted him up.

He kept Finn's back snug against his chest, brought his thighs outside Finn's so he was bracketing him and used his arms to hold him up taut.

He brushed Finn's hair aside with his nose, brushed the skin there softly, kissed the exposed skin. "You look so good like this, so good," he said. He kissed Finn's cheek. "Look," he said again.

Finn whimpered in his arms and Christ, he was going to be the end of George, but he did as he was told—opened his eyes, lifted his head, and George watched as he took in the sight they made together. George holding him, his dick inside him, his hands running up and down Finn's chest before he let one palm rest over Finn's heart.

Finn made a little broken sound.

George kissed his ear, whispered, "But this is the most beautiful part of you," he kissed the shell of his ear and pressed his palm firmly against his heart, "No one can touch this."

He couldn't believe he'd just said that—he had no right to say that—but Finn melted into him and George let go. He fucked into him, kissed him everywhere—his throat, his shoulder, his cheek—he fucked him deep and close, held him tight.

As he slid his hand down to grip Finn's dick, he flicked his eyes up and met Finn's. He was almost scared to do it after he'd gone and said too much. But Finn was waiting for him. George wrapped his hand around him and jerked him off in time with his thrusts.

Finn went tense in his arms, his eyes widened, and George sped up, willed Finn to let go. He didn't trust himself to speak anymore—but he saw it all in high definition as Finn let it crash into him, his dick coming in George's hand, his ass tightening on George's dick, his body going lax as he came and let George hold him through it.

George kept fucking him, jerking him off, kissing his neck as he watched him. He couldn't tear his eyes away as he pressed his words into Finn's skin, "You look so good," he whispered, "you're so perfect, baby, coming for me, so perfect," he kissed his throat, "I'm so lucky to be with you like this, so fucking lucky."

Finn slumped in George's arms.

George went to pull out, to rip the condom off and finish himself when Finn reached back and held him close.

George groaned, buried his face in the crook of Finn's shoulder and neck. He felt Finn's other hand in his hair, felt him hold him there, his lips moving in George's hair as he whispered, "I'm the lucky one. Christ, George, I'm so lucky," he kissed his hair, pressed his words at George's hairline, "Come in me, c'mon, want to feel it."

George's thrusts went erratic—he couldn't believe what he was hearing, it was the hottest thing that had ever happened to him, he was losing control, he couldn't stay upright.

Finn held him, took his weight, took everything George was pounding into him, his body strong, taking it, there for him.

When George started to come, he let go completely, let go of what felt like decades of repression and let Finn hold him. He trusted Finn could hold him together as he flew apart.

The physical release was phenomenal, but as he came back to himself, to Finn's hand in his hair, to Finn holding him; as Finn kissed his way up his throat and took his mouth, took over—getting him onto his back under the sheets, getting rid of the condom, going away and coming back and cleaning his skin, then kissing him and kissing him and kissing him—George felt like something else got released, something deep and unnameable.

George didn't want to let Finn go the next morning. He felt off-kilter at him leaving and yet he was centred from being with him. With Finn beside him—out of the bed now and looking around for his clothes—he felt good, like something had clicked into place.

They'd fucked again that morning. George woke with Finn plastered to his chest—front to front—their dicks hard and rocking against one another, half asleep, and George wasn't sure who initiated the kiss, but they were kissing, then they were fucking and as George fucked into Finn underneath him, kissed him as he cradled his head in his hands, he woke up slowly and never wanted the moment to end.

But it was ending.

Finn was dragging his pants on, smiling sheepishly. "Go back to sleep," he whispered.

George scoffed. "And miss this show?" He waved a hand at Finn's bare ass before it disappeared under the material.

Finn laughed and bent to find his shirt.

George didn't want him to go.

He needed him to go.

"Bit rumpled," Finn said as he straightened, "but I don't reckon Les will notice."

"Hmm," George didn't really care—which was a thought that drew him up short. Yes, he did bloody well care—no one could know about this, nobody could know they were buddy fucking, which, not only did that sound ludicrous in George's head, it wasn't anywhere near the truth.

But, they were just hooking up. And no one could know.

"It's still early," George said.

"I know, go back to sleep," Finn repeated as he got his shoes on, left the laces undone.

He grabbed his key card and ran a hand through his hair as he came over to George, then hesitated.

"C'mere," George sat up.

Finn did. George pulled him down and kissed him. Finn kissed back—all of him into it, all of him in it. George wanted to drag him back into bed and fuck him again. Hold him. Keep him.

He broke the kiss. "See you on the bus."

"Yeah," Finn replied and pulled back. He stumbled, laughed at himself, then went for the door. "Later, George."

"Night, Finn," George said.

The door clicked shut softly and George felt his heart clench painfully.

He got up and went for the shower. He needed to review the game anyway.

He was back in his office in Melbourne that night, all his meetings done, everyone gone home for the night. He needed to go home. He'd texted Joq not to pick him up from the airport because he'd organised the postgame meetings before leaving Adelaide.

The guys seemed surprised but acquiesced—they knew he was anxious about doing well this year, proving all the haters wrong—and he knew they'd think calling a meeting after they got off the plane was probably a quirk related to that.

But he couldn't drag out discussing their offensive holes any longer than he had. They needed Finn back and that was all there was to it.

Finn. He'd seen him get on the bus, met his eyes, nodded perfunc-
torily, then returned his gaze to his notes. Finn had done the same—a
nod of acknowledgement, all business—and taken his seat next to
Lacy near the back and that was that.

George pulled out his phone.

He thought maybe Finn would text, but nothing.

Should he text?

And say what, George? He asked himself belligerently. *Hey, Finn,
great fuck last night and this morning, want to do it again some time?*

Christ, no.

He wanted to do it again more than he wanted air, but he didn't
want to seem needy, he didn't want to seem like he thought this was
more than just fucking. Because, world shifting feelings aside, it was
just fucking. It could only ever be just fucking.

And besides, he needed to get home, he needed to tell Joq. That
was the deal. They were open on the condition they were open with
each other about fucking around. He wasn't looking forward to the
conversation and not because it felt like a hell of a lot more than just
fucking, but because it felt... private.

He shook his head. He needed to get it done, like ripping off a
Band-Aid. He grabbed his small backpack, shouldered it, grabbed his
case, switched the lights off and headed for the carpark.

He was crossing the asphalt when he heard him.

"Took you long enough," Finn said and emerged from the darkness.

"Finn," George replied, his face stretching into a grin. "What're you
doing here?"

Finn came over to him, his hands stuffed in his pockets, his head
down, but his smile was shy yet cocky. He shrugged. "Waiting for you."

George wanted to ask: why?

But the truth was if the situation was reversed? Yeah, he'd be waiting for Finn too.

"You need a lift?" he asked.

"Yeah, thanks," Finn replied and went back to the building and George saw he had his case there, his footy bag even though he wasn't playing.

"You should've texted," George said as Finn came alongside him. "If you were waiting, you should've texted."

"Nah," Finn smiled at him, bumped him, "I know you're busy, I can wait."

"I wasn't though, I was just," he bumped Finn back and grinned, "fucking around."

Finn laughed and dumped his stuff in George's boot.

"Okay, next time I'll text."

"Good."

They got in and George wanted to lean over the console, push Finn against the window and kiss him, touch him, suck a hickey into his collarbone.

He took a shaky breath, grunted like he was clearing his throat and started the car.

"You okay?" Finn asked.

George glanced at him as he reversed. Finn was smiling, sinking into the seat, but George was getting to know him now too—he was nervous, he hadn't casually waited, he'd put himself out there. Again. One of these days, George thought, he was going to do that for Finn.

"Yeah," George replied and spun the tyres right, looked ahead, "just really want to kiss you."

"Oh," Finn said like he was genuinely surprised. "You should. Do that. You should definitely do that."

George huffed a laugh. "Not in public I can't."

Before Finn could reply, George asked him what the hell he'd been doing out there all that time to occupy himself and Finn regaled him with the conversation he'd had with his sister on the phone, then how he was killing the competition on his language app—he was learning Portuguese, which pissed George off because of that bartender, but Finn said it was for surfing, so, okay, George, settle down—and apparently there were leagues, and Finn was "crushing it."

By the time they pulled up at Finn's building, George felt relaxed. It was late and he really needed to let Finn get inside and get some sleep. He needed to get home and talk to Joq.

He found himself parking, helping Finn with his bags. He found himself following Finn inside and when Finn dropped the suitcase and spun to George as the door shut behind him, he let Finn push him up against it and kiss him.

He brought his arms up and tugged Finn close and kissed him back. His heart was pounding and he was surrounded by Finn—his smell, the soft skin of his nose as he rubbed against George's when he kissed him, the minty taste of his breath like he'd chewed something before George came out—and he deepened the kiss, lost himself.

He pulled back for a second. "I should go," he said and tugged him closer with the hands he had snug on Finn's ass.

Finn huffed. "Okay."

George smiled. Finn smiled back.

George kissed him again and Finn met him.

George didn't know how long they kissed for, but they were both hard, rubbing off against each other through their suit pants.

George broke the kiss and nudged Finn's head up with his nose, kissed his throat. "I really better go," he said into Finn's skin.

"Yeah," Finn slid his hand down and squeezed George's dick through his pants.

George bucked into the touch. Finn undid his pants quickly and got a hand around him.

"Jesus, Finn," George said and forced Finn's mouth to his, kissed him roughly.

He was reaching for Finn's dick when Finn broke the kiss and dropped to his knees.

"Shit, Finn," George gasped. "You don't—

But Finn was pulling him out, sucking him down and worshipping his dick before George could finish the thought. George wrapped Finn's hair in his fist and held on.

He was surprised and yet he wasn't when he felt his orgasm rushing up.

"Finn, I'm gonna—

Finn made this little whining sound and shoved down until his nose was pressed against George's pelvis, his eyes wide as he looked up and met George's, swirled his tongue around George's skin.

"Oh, God," George started to come.

Finn stayed where he was, swallowed it all, and as he tucked George away his panting breaths were harsh, and George dropped to the ground, grabbed Finn and yanked him close, kissed him quickly before pushing him to his back right there in the entryway of his door.

Finn keened when George got his mouth on him, sucked him off deep and deliberate; and when Finn started to come, George held his hip down, held him still so Finn was forced to let George drag it out of him.

He rested his head on Finn's thigh after, caught his breath. Finn's hand scratched lightly at his scalp, ran through the strands.

"I better go," he said again.

"Yeah," Finn sounded wistful.

George looked up, his chin resting on Finn's thigh. Finn looked down, his eyes meeting George's in the darkness. He was sated, he was happy, but there was something sad there, George was sure of it. But he knew it was for the best—he couldn't stay, they couldn't what? Become a couple?

George rubbed his forehead against Finn's pant leg and then heaved himself up, reached down for Finn and yanked him to his feet.

They got their pants done up, arms brushing, and George leaned forward and gave Finn one last kiss.

"See you tomorrow," he said and then got the hell out of there.

"Bye, George," Finn said softly at his back as the door closed.

Joq was asleep when he got into bed, but he woke up and rolled over as George slipped in beside him.

"Sorry, go back to sleep," he whispered.

Joq slid his hand over George's stomach, slid lower.

George's stomach dropped. It felt wrong. He stopped Joq with a hand over his.

"Not tonight, go back to sleep," he said again and placed Joq's hand on the bed, rolled over and faced the wall.

He wasn't even close to feeling sleepy. He could feel Joq rolling over and facing the opposite wall and he knew he was wide awake now too.

They needed to talk. He needed to tell him. Just fucking, he needed to say it—*I'm just fucking someone now too*. Totally normal. Totally fine.

He felt like his breaths were too loud. He felt confined and out of sorts. He felt like Joq was lying wide awake right beside him but couldn't have been further away.

The following day was a blur. The out of sorts feeling he'd had the night before carried into the day and he was off during training, and when he spoke to the players before the video review, he felt like his words weren't syncing with his brain.

He managed a polite interaction with Finn.

Kurt asked him if he was feeling alright.

Todd told him to go home and get some rest when George suggested they discuss their strategy for the game that weekend.

As he drove home, George realised what was bothering him. Joq had been his steady place for over a decade. Everything could crumble and go to shit 'out there' but he could always come home and Joq would be there—calm, steady, available and willing to talk and listen to whatever George said without judgement. He felt at ease with Joq in a way he didn't with anyone else.

And for the first time that was out, like a door left ajar when it should be closed. Things with Joq weren't perfect—they never had been. Joq wanted to be out and George never, ever wanted that. Joq readily agreeing to it when he was twenty was just that—a certainty at twenty that waned by thirty. By thirty you knew you deserved better. Sometimes George got the feeling Joq damn well knew he deserved better and it was only George's fear, his pride, that kept him from having it.

But as he pulled into his driveway, cut the engine and saw Joq wasn't home yet, the familiar sensation of panic rippled over his skin at the idea of being out. It wasn't even the shift from 'one of the greatest players of all time' to 'one of the greatest gay players of all time' that bothered him. He was ashamed to admit it, but what bothered him was people treating him like he was less of a man because he was gay. He couldn't bear the thought of it, never mind the reality.

And they would, he was sure of it. He knew what was said in locker rooms and pubs, shearing sheds and sporting clubs—'faggot' and 'pussy' were synonymous. And in the league, implied in the sledges, in the comments about showers if a 'faggot' was on the team, it was a known undercurrent that gay men were weak, less than, not quite men. George didn't want to deal with any of that.

He got out, went inside, took off his shoes and coat and was about to go and get something to drink or even cook when his nerves prevented him. Or he was afraid if he let himself get into something, he'd lose the courage to talk to Joq.

He needed to tell him. He needed to close that door again. If things with him and Joq weren't right, nothing was right.

He sat on the couch and waited.

It was a good hour before Joq came home and it gave George time to think. Things with Joq were far from ideal—they wanted different things in a pretty crucial area, but George always thought they'd made their peace with it by being open. In George's mind, Joq got that in exchange for George getting to keep them completely private. Now he was wondering if this thing with Finn would throw the balance out.

Contrary to how good it was with Finn, it was just fucking, it could only ever be just fucking. Finn might look at him like he wanted more; hell, George wanted more, but it was unrealistic that a twenty-year-old knew what signing up for a committed relationship meant. See his point above about Joq. About him and Joq agreeing to this when they were nineteen and twenty respectively.

He heard Joq's car pull up.

They weren't perfect, not by any stretch, but they had a comfortable home here, they had a partnership. George wasn't going to blow that up.

Joq came in the front door and George stood.

"Hey," Joq said when he saw him. He was flushed pink on his cheekbones from the cold—he had the look you got when you'd been out in the world being your public self and now you've walked in the door prepared to let that drop.

"Hey," George replied. "Can we talk?" He was nervous, God, he was so nervous he just wanted to be on the other side of this.

Joq looked nervous now too. "Yeah, course."

"Okay," George sat back down. He couldn't remain standing for this. He was anxious, ashamed and he didn't get it—Joq did this all the time, he wasn't doing anything wrong.

George waited as Joq kicked his shoes off and came into the room. He felt him take a seat in the armchair, felt his energy dialled up as tensely as George's. He needed to say this to get them back on even ground.

He sat forward, clasped his hands together and focused on them.

"I..." George managed. "I decided to..." he cleared his throat. Fuck, why was this so hard to say?

"We're open," he finally settled on and glanced up at Joq. Joq was watching him back, expression cool, but wary. "So, I fucked around," George finished. There, he said it, that was enough.

"Okay," Joq said slowly, "Is this your attempt at foreplay?"

George felt like he did when a journalist asked him an obviously invasive personal question—disgusted and shocked all at once. He couldn't think of anything worse than saying what he did with Finn as a preamble to fucking someone else.

"No, definitely no," he shook his head. "I don't want to..." he couldn't even get the words out, "like you do. If that's okay."

Joq shrugged. "Of course."

There was something off about that 'of course', but George was going to take it at face value. "Cool," he breathed out and looked at Joq. "It's just. I can't... talk like you do." Not like that, not about Finn.

"It's really fine," Joq said, and George could hear it kind of wasn't, but he'd be damned if he was going to give an inch on this. Joq did the open thing his way, George was going to do it his own way.

"Cool," was all he said though, looked at his hands.

"So, we're cool?" Joq asked. He sounded nervous.

"Course, why wouldn't we be? I mean, if you're cool that I'm, you know, doing that now too, then of course," George stood. He wanted to get out of this conversation now, he wanted everything to be calm and easy like it was before.

"Uh, yeah, but I mean..." Joq trailed off.

George waited. What did Joq mean? That he was going to have a problem with George getting some other dick when he'd done it for over ten years? Or, worse, George thought anxiously, was he going to bring up the fact it was Finn?

"You mean?" he asked. He didn't want to know what Joq meant and he heard it in his voice.

"Just, you know, be careful or whatever," Joq said.

"What's that supposed to mean?" George was affronted.

"Nothing," Joq shook his head.

"I'm using protection," George replied because if Joq thought he was that fucking stupid then what the hell else did he think George was stupid at?

"Good, I knew you would. Good," Joq said quietly. George didn't understand why he seemed so cut up about this. This was the deal. But he could see it was making Joq uneasy, hurt even.

George shook his head, "Okay, well, I just wanted to tell you 'cos that's what the agreement was. So, yeah," and he went to leave. He'd told Joq, he didn't know what to do if it bothered Joq this much; he didn't want to have a fight about hypocrisy.

"I'm just saying," Joq said before George had left the room. "If it's Finn, be careful."

George's step faltered. Just the sound of Finn's name out of Joq's mouth in this context made his heart speed up and his stomach flip. But Joq had nothing to worry about if he was telling George to be careful because it might be more than just fucking, but George knew what the deal was.

"I know what the deal is," George said softly. He looked at the hallway, at all the pictures of him with his family artfully framed and hung haphazardly down the corridor. And for a second he thought about how he'd never have that—a family of his own, a hallway with pictures of his own line, instead it'd just be him as the son, as the brother, never the husband, never the father.

He didn't know why he was suddenly thinking it now. He shoved it down. Gave Joq a tight smile and left the room.

24

*T*ONIGHT? 8PM?

The message was burned into Finn's brain. He'd gotten butterflies after he'd seen it waiting for him on his phone after training. He'd texted back asking George if he should wait, but George said he'd come over and that was that.

Finn had changed his outfit three times. He shook his head at himself. George was coming over to hook up—there was no reason for Finn to shower, do his hair, put on nice cologne and carefully select a good outfit—though he'd done all those things. He was standing there in his best faded black jeans, a white cashmere hoodie with a white shirt underneath—it was a local designer in Byron and she made all this fancy-as-fuck clothing look worn in, but it sat on the body just perfectly. Finn was looking at himself in the mirror and remembering the day in her shop and how delighted she was when he tried everything on and let her take polaroids that now hung around the shop.

But as he ran a hand through his hair, he reminded himself, painfully, that it was just fucking, George was coming by at 8pm to fuck, which was awesome, great even, but it'd be weird if Finn was all dressed up.

He tore his clothes off, pulled on his trackies and an old Sharks shirt and club hoodie and put all his clothes back.

He'd just finished when there was a knock on the door. George was early.

Finn went out and opened the door. George was there in a really fucking nice button-up shirt, jacket, perfectly fitted jeans, his winter coat turned up at the collar so his tousled and styled wavy brown hair brushed the edges, his smile shy and a little surprised.

"Hi," he said gruffly. "Can I come in?"

Right, because Finn was standing there staring at him. "Hi. Course," he stepped back and George went by him. Finn closed the door and felt fucking stupid.

But George grabbed his waist with a clumsy hand and Finn pressed up against him and kissed him. George kissed back, messy and a little frantic.

"Sorry," George pulled back to say after a second, his hand still on Finn's waist, holding him close, "I thought we'd go out to eat, but if you just wanna..."

Finn pulled back. "Oh, no, I wanna, hang on," and he untangled himself and darted back into his room, heart pounding.

He was yanking off his clothes, pulling on his jeans and fastening them when he heard George huff a laugh at him in the doorway.

Finn glanced up, smiled self-consciously.

"I was ready before but I thought maybe you'd just want to, you know," Finn flicked his hair out of his face and waved his hand at the bed as he went for his shirt.

"Yeah, I know. But it weirds me out a bit," George said as he watched Finn pull on his shirt.

"What does?"

"You know," George said and came into the room, slid his hands around Finn's waist and kissed his nape while Finn pulled out his fancy cashmere hoodie, "just coming round to fuck. I like hanging out first."

Finn rolled his head to the side to let George get more of his throat. George kissed down, kissed the skin at his shoulder above his shirt.

"Same," Finn replied, his voice airy—that felt fucking good. "But it's been a few days, you wanna? First?"

George groaned, ground his hardening cock against Finn's ass.

"Yeah, but I made a reservation."

Finn's heart just about exploded in his chest with excitement. "Yeah?"

"Yeah, nothing too fancy and a bit out of the way 'cos, you know," George went on, his lips travelling back up Finn's throat as he continued to rub his dick against Finn's ass.

"Yeah," Finn rocked back on George's cock. He did know—they could explain why they'd be out to dinner together, a coach and a player, it wasn't totally weird, but it'd be better not to.

Though at this rate, Finn thought as he rubbed his ass against George and George got a rhythm going, his kisses on Finn's throat finding Finn's mouth, the whole thing getting out of control, at this rate, it wasn't going to matter.

George pulled back with a little groan, dropped his head on Finn's nape and kissed the skin there firmly before letting him go.

"Dinner," he said gruffly.

Finn laughed and pulled on his jumper.

George was waiting outside his door when Finn came out. Finn smirked at him. George gave him a sheepish smile. Finn got his boots and coat on, grabbed his phone, keys and gave George a giddy smile as he stepped into the hallway.

George smiled back, took Finn's hand.

Finn slipped his fingers between George's awkwardly and held on.

Finn had never been to a dinner where he had to adjust his dick so often. George wasn't even doing anything special, but for some reason the way he talked about the team, about his past as a player, all of it the normal shit they talked about, and Finn knew at the end of the dinner he would get to touch George and George would touch him, it turned him on.

And George looked at him like he knew it too.

So when he said, "Looks like we'll secure that new ruckman from Tassie for next season," Finn heard the words but he had to shuffle in his seat and try to downplay his blush.

And bloody George just smirked at him.

Finn laughed at him.

"Eat your bloody eggplant," George sipped his glass of red wine.

It was a nice place in Northcote; people gave less of a shit about football players around this way, and George knew the chef. He'd got them a private table upstairs, ordered them the five-course chef's selection tasting menu.

Finn stuffed the eggplant, some broccoli and kipfler potatoes into his mouth in one go.

George speared an oyster, looked at it, his face was a little red, but his voice was smooth when he said, "At this rate, I'm gonna have to fuck you before we go anywhere."

Finn almost spat his food across the table.

"Can I get you anything else?" the waiter came over to ask.

"Maybe just the bill," George said, smiling warmly. "We'll pay it now so we can duck out once we're done."

"Of course," the guy said smoothly and disappeared back into the darkness—the top floor lit by a few strategically placed dim lamps.

"Bastard," Finn whispered around his laughter when they were alone again.

"What?" George asked, faux-innocent, and ate his oyster.

"You better fuck me the second we leave this place for that comment," Finn said and winked.

It was George's turn to choke. "You like exhibitionism?" he asked a little shyly.

"Never tried it," Finn replied.

"Here you go," the waiter reappeared and placed the bill folder on the table and left again.

George sipped his wine. He looked around the darkness of the empty room. Finn thought he'd ignore it, and he didn't meet Finn's eyes when he said, "Add it to the list."

Finn felt his blush deepening. He ducked his head, and ate his dessert as quickly as possible.

George laughed at him, eyes shining and fond.

Finn chewed and smiled, mouth closed.

George placed his card in the bill folder and the waiter reappeared.

"I'll go halves," Finn said after he swallowed.

George shook his head. "I'm taking you out."

Finn's heart fluttered again. He had no idea how he was eating at all.

"When I take you out then," he said.

George was looking down, but he was smiling, he was nodding. "Yeah, I'd like that."

And Christ, did he know what that side of him did to Finn? The side that wasn't the calm, commanding captain and coach people knew him as; but the side that was unsure, that was delighted when someone wanted to do something for him just because he was George?

The waiter slid the wallet back packed with mints and George's card. George thanked him and Finn stuffed a whole parfait into his mouth.

George laughed heartily, his whole face lit up, brown eyes dancing as he watched Finn. "Can't take you anywhere."

Finn shook his head, swallowed. "You can take me home."

George finished his wine and stood. "Let's go."

Finn did not need to be told twice.

They kept a careful distance and a professional air as they left, waved at the waiter and thanked him, and Finn thought he was being very good as they got in the car and he pulled his seatbelt on. He glanced over at George, who was looking around before giving Finn a shy smile, a 'what're you gonna do' smile. Finn wet his lips as he watched him. George made this annoyed-whine and then surged over to kiss him.

It was rough and quick and Finn chased him for more.

"Okay," George said and started the car. "Hold on."

Finn laughed as George tore out of there.

Finn thought it'd be frantic when his door clicked shut behind them. And it was—the kissing, the peeling out of clothes without wanting to stop kissing as they stumbled to Finn's bed—but by the time they were naked and George was pushing in, they slowed down.

George fucked him with deep, deliberate rolls of his hips while he traced Finn's bottom lip with his thumb. He kissed him gently and met Finn's eyes every time Finn gasped or moaned.

Something about it felt fragile. Finn wrapped his legs around George's hips to urge him closer, to keep him deep. George rubbed his nose over Finn's in a careful brush, ghosted his lips over Finn's in the same careful caress.

"God," Finn panted out, he was feeling it everywhere.

"Yeah?" George asked, his lips quirking.

Finn huffed a laugh.

"Good?" George asked seriously as he pushed in deep, rocked out gently, pushed in again.

"So good, God, George, you make me feel so good," Finn rushed out, his words pouring into George's mouth as their lips touched while they spoke.

George groaned, dropped his face into the crook of Finn's shoulder and upped the pace.

Finn grabbed his ass with both palms and urged him on. "Your dick feels so good in me," Finn whispered against his ear, his words punctuated by George's thrusts.

"Fuck, Finn," George said into his skin, his lips wet, his breath warm.

Finn felt it before George was about to come—felt his ass clench, his abs tighten, his body tense. He had a moment to wish they were doing this bare—he'd love to feel George coming in him like that.

"Come in me," he said anyway. George groaned, made a broken sound and started to come.

Finn snaked his hand between them, out of his mind with a need to get there.

"Let me—

But Finn cut him off as he started to come over George's abs and his own.

George got them both cleaned up and Finn dozed in his bed as George went into the bathroom. He cracked his eyes open to watch George wiping down his dick—still half hard, still fucking glorious—and George smirked at him as he came over and wiped Finn down.

"If I had a dick like yours, I'd never wear pants," he slurred.

George laughed. "I think it's a pretty regular dick and you're no slouch."

"Hmm," Finn replied and reached for him.

"Hang on," George said and left the room.

Finn sat up.

George came back in with his clothes.

"Oh, you gotta go?"

"Huh?" George looked at Finn. "I was gonna stay, but I can—

"No, stay, but why?" he waved his hand at the clothes.

"Gotta hang them up," George said like that was obvious.

Finn laughed and slid back down under the covers.

He was wrapped in George's arms, his bare chest against George's, the feel of their hearts slamming together a relief in his ears as he drifted off.

It was early the next morning when George's alarm went off. George hit it and went to get up.

Finn rolled on top of him. "No," he said and kissed his bare chest.

George made a throaty sound, like a laugh, and rubbed Finn's back.

"I gotta get home, shower, get ready," he said, his voice rumbling through Finn, his hand caressing Finn's ass.

Finn wanted to tell him to leave some clothes here. But George had been clear it was just fucking.

And well, Finn thought as he leaned up to kiss George, if it was just fucking...

George left an hour after that, left Finn dozing after he'd put him on his stomach, tongue fucked his ass, then fucked him hard and deep into the mattress all the while kissing his nape, his jaw, telling him how fucking beautiful he was.

Finn groaned and went back to sleep as he heard the front door shut.

When the doctor told him he could play again that weekend, Finn knew that should've been the best bit of news he got that day, hell, that year.

But when George texted him a link later—a link to a local surf comp at Bells Beach and an attached booked and paid for chalet with the message, *just for the day?*—scheduled for their off day later that week?

Well, his heart was in his fucking throat. That was the best news he'd gotten in his life. And it made him think, *Maybe*. A part of him felt terrible about Joq, but another part didn't—how much could Joq really love George if he wanted to be open?

Regardless, Finn wanted to talk to George about it. It might be early days, but he felt like this could be something, something a lot more than just fucking.

And Finn wasn't into sharing.

25

♥

GEORGE HADN'T HAD THIS much sex since he hooked up with Joq when he was a teenager. Possibly not even then. Finn was stretched out on his chest, catching his breath after their latest round in the little chalet near Bells Beach. The place was artfully decorated to feel like the beach—clean white walls against brown accents, shells everywhere, paintings of the beach, photographs of seagulls—all of it cast in the forceful blast of the setting sun behind them, the waves crashing in front visible from the floor-to-ceiling window. George thought it'd be nice to wake up there, to watch the sun rise over the ocean.

They couldn't stay overnight with training and their lives in the city, but they were sure as hell making the most of it, George thought as he stroked Finn's back, brushed his fingers lightly over his gorgeous ass, ran his hand back up the expanse of his muscled back, slipped his fingers through the strands of his unruly blonde hair and leaned down to kiss his head.

"Mm," Finn replied and kissed George's chest, teased his nipple with a lick of his tongue.

George tightened his hold in Finn's hair. He'd just come but he could feel himself swelling again the longer Finn kept that up, his hand wandering aimlessly up and down George's side. And to think he'd almost decided not to do this, to finally fuck around, to take advantage of being in an open relationship.

He kissed the top of Finn's head again, let his lips linger as he felt them both breathing, moving, syncing up.

"George," Finn said. He brought his head up and rested his chin between George's pecs.

George traced his bottom lip with his thumb, stroked his jaw—he'd never get over how gorgeous Finn was. His striking eyes, light blue like a summer sky, his perfect bone structure, full lips, full bodied hair; he truly was an Adonis, but as George got to know him better, and in the carnal sense, it was the stuff under the surface that was even more beautiful. The way his eyes would look unsure when he wanted to ask something he wasn't sure if he should—would George stay? Would George come earlier so Finn could cook and they'd have dinner? Would George let Finn rim him? The way he'd laugh out of control when he teased George and thought he was being subtle.

"Yeah?" George replied softly. Finn was looking at him with the 'I'm not sure I should ask this look.' It always made George simultaneously light up and fearful.

"This is good right?" Finn asked but he sounded like he wanted to ask something else.

"Yeah," George breathed out and smiled encouragingly at him. "This is great."

"Hmm," Finn rubbed his face against George's chest.

George traced the shell of Finn's ear.

"Do you ever think..." Finn said into George's skin.

George felt his heart rate pick up. He had a feeling he knew what Finn was going to ask. It'd only been a month, but yeah, George thought about it all the time. And he reminded himself it was impossible.

Finn rested his head on George's chest and met his eyes. He was terrified, George could see that, but he was putting himself out there, again. "Do you ever think you could be with me? Properly, I mean. Just me. I know you're with him, but I feel like—

"Did you study *Romeo and Juliet* at school?" George cut him off. He thought about being with Finn constantly. He thought about how it would never work just as much.

The terror fell away from Finn's face and he brightened. So, George was guessing he didn't.

George wasn't great at school, he was too busy with football, but he was one of those students who got right into something if it caught his interest—the endocrine system; the Night of the Long Knives; inertia; *Romeo and Juliet*.

He leaned down and kissed Finn hard, it was a bruising kiss, a kiss that was meant to tell Finn he wanted this more than anything but Finn didn't know what he was asking.

He pulled back and slid out from under him, got out of bed. He pulled on his pants and didn't look at Finn as he finished. "I'm your Rosaline."

They didn't talk about it again. Finn let it drop when George came back with food, they ate, fucked again, stayed as long as they could without making it ridiculously late when they got back to Melbourne.

But George would have to be blind to miss the angry, hurt look Finn shot him the next day at training; he ignored it, and he ignored the buzz of his phone in his pocket too when he saw Finn look at him pointedly after he'd typed something on his phone, his face still devastated.

George looked at it when he got home.

Ur not Rosaline to me. The first one said. George sighed.

Then a few seconds later: *U don't get to tell me how I feel.* George had a feeling that was the one that accompanied the devastated look and he felt like the world's biggest asshole; Finn might be young, but he wasn't fucking stupid.

And anger must've come ten minutes later because the last one said: *U can go fuck urself with that teenage infatuation crap. If u not into smethng serious, just say, but don't tell me wat I feel.*

George laughed at the beginning of that last one—Finn certainly never held back when it came to texting and letting George have it—but on the whole, it wasn't funny. Christ, but the last thing he wanted to do was hurt Finn.

"George?" Joq called from downstairs.

He threw his phone on his desk and stood.

"Up here," he called out.

The last thing he wanted to do was hurt Joq as well.

He had a feeling he was getting himself into a big fucking mess and he had no idea how to get himself out of it without hurting everyone.

He went back and picked up his phone and shot off a quick message: *Pick u up Wednesday night at nine, wear workout gear.*

He hit send just as Joq came into his office.

"Hey, busy?" Joq asked, he was smiling but it was guarded. George hated that he'd done that, put that look on his face, but he didn't know how to make it better. Well, he did—stop fucking Finn—but beyond the blinding attraction and feelings he was barrelling head first into was this indignation at Joq for the last ten years. Why should he have to stop? He was aware it was childish, it was quid-pro-quo, but he was beginning to think he might've repressed a lot of feelings over the years and they were bubbling up.

"Not right now," he smiled.

"Cool, I was hoping we could sort our schedules for the summer? See where we can fit in a holiday? If I'm gonna book, now's the best time," Joq said, relaxing against the doorframe. He looked good, still in his work pants and white shirt, the collar unbuttoned, his feet bare. His hair was shorter, like he'd recently been to his monthly hair appointment.

"Oh, yeah, course, meet you in the kitchen?"

"Yep," Joq gave him another weird smile, but it was thawing, it was hopeful, and George smiled back. This was normal, this is what they did every year—found a stretch of weeks between George's commitments and Joq's work and disappeared to a tropical island for a break.

He picked up his phone once Joq was gone.

Fine was waiting for him.

George had to snort. God, but he loved Finn's tantrums. He felt guilty for hurting him, but he wasn't wrong. Finn would get over this. He would move on. And George had a life with Joq, a history. It was foolish to try and make this anything other than what it was.

But they could have some fun until it ended.

In the meantime, he had a good evening with Joq—there was a week in December just before Christmas they could both get free and Joq was keen for Thailand. They had some good memories the last time they went and George acquiesced.

He was sitting up in bed, reading a book when Joq came in. George smiled, a little surprised—Joq normally watched the news, then the analysts discussing the news, then the news that'd happened since the last news.

"Hey," George smiled and returned to his book—he was trying to read *The Art of War* with mixed success. He was finding nuggets but struggling to concentrate.

Joq slid onto the bed beside him and ran a hand up his thigh, cupped his dick over his boxer briefs.

George set his book aside and tried to smile. "Oh, hello," he said with forced interest.

"Yeah?" Joq asked, a hint of uncertainty again.

"Yeah," George said to make that go away, to get back on even footing here. He realised, somewhat stupidly, that in the month since he'd started fucking Finn, he hadn't done anything with Joq. He didn't think they'd ever gone that long without fucking.

He needed to fix that. Joq pulled his boxers off and George wriggled his hips to accommodate him. He leaned back against the headboard as Joq took him into his mouth.

Joq was working him over expertly—he knew the exact suction, pressure, speed George liked, he wasn't unsure and checking in like Finn did, or overly enthusiastic and messy like Finn got—George got hard at the thought of it, of the way Finn did it.

Then he felt fucking terrible. Mortifyingly, his dick went soft.

Joq pulled off. "Have you been drinking?" he asked.

George appreciated the sentiment but he'd been with Joq all night and he'd been drinking water.

"No," George groaned and rocked into Joq's hand—Joq was working him over, his saliva slicking the way.

George couldn't remember ever losing his hard-on. He wasn't about to now. He was getting hard again as Joq jerked him off. Joq took him back into his mouth and George thrust his hips up, tried to lose himself in the feel of that wet mouth. He reached for Joq's head, went to sink his fingers into hair and hold on, but his fingers slipped, scrabbled against scalp and ended up clumsily gripping at Joq's scalp.

He felt himself going soft again. "Ah fuck."

He slipped out of Joq's mouth.

"I can't turn my head off," he said as Joq sat up, wiped his mouth with the back of his hand; his expression was weird—hurt, certainly, but like he'd expected George to fuck up somehow.

George covered himself with the blanket. He ran a hand through his hair, flicked his eyes up at Joq and then away as he apologised.

He saw Joq shrug in his periphery. "We haven't fucked in a month. Don't reckon that's ever happened."

George snorted. "It hasn't." Not to him, not ever.

Joq got up and pulled his pyjama pants back on. George realised he hadn't even noticed Joq had come in naked, which meant he'd come in with the full intention to fuck. He felt terrible.

Joq got back into bed and George slid over to give him more room. He was breathing heavily and he knew he needed to say something.

"It's the season, it's, you know. A lot," George said, which was true enough—it was a lot coaching for the first time, keeping himself free from the criticism by never looking at it while also knowing it was still there whether he looked or not. And he certainly copped it at every press event. Win or lose.

But Joq was shaking his head. "It's not the season," he said quietly.

George rubbed his face. Joq was right of course. And he deserved some kind of response. George was nervous as fuck but he had to tell the truth. "It's just... new. You know?" he started. Because that was true—it was new, and it was exciting and good, so fucking good; no wonder Joq fucked other guys so much.

"I get it," Joq replied calmly and George picked up steam because yeah, Joq did actually get it.

"It's just fucking, but," he glanced at Joq.

Joq tipped his head in acknowledgement, open and willing to listen, happy almost to finally be hearing about it.

"It's..." But George didn't know how to put it into words that would be palatable for Joq. He didn't think he'd want to hear it if Joq felt this way about a hook-up.

"It's?" Joq asked.

George huffed. "You know," he said and broke the moment, stole back the truth before it had even found air. He waved his hand at Joq. "I mean, *you* know. You do this all the time."

"Yeah," Joq replied, sagging like he knew George wasn't saying everything. "It'll wear off."

And George reckoned it'd hurt less if Joq slapped him. Because that was the truth, wasn't it? That was the truth George knew and why he couldn't, even feeling what he did, really go for it with Finn.

"Yeah, he'll get sick of it soon enough. And I'll, you know..." he couldn't even fucking say it, "as well," he finished lamely and got out of bed, scooped his pants off the floor. "Nothing to worry about," he finished as he dragged a hand through his hair and went for the door. He needed to get the fuck out of there, he needed to get away from the crushing feeling in his chest, the confirmation.

"Where're you going?" Joq asked.

"Water," George said over his shoulder and jogged down the stairs, went into the garage, flicked on the lights and randomly picked up his darts.

He needed to do something, he needed to exorcise this awful feeling.

He played. He played against himself. He played round after round until his world narrowed to the soft thudding sound of the dart penetrating the soft cushion of the board.

Finn slammed the car door as he got in just before nine on the Wednesday.

George had to hold in his smile. Finn's tantrums were endearing, yes, but they made George nervous; he had a feeling his laughter every time it happened was nerves.

"Don't laugh at me," Finn said softer than George expected. He was hurt.

George reached over and squeezed his thigh. "I'm not laughing at you."

Finn snorted, but didn't look at George, he kept his eyes fixed outside the passenger window.

"I'm not," George reiterated. "It's just, you..."

Finn looked at him then, his expression hurt but pleading with George to explain to him why they couldn't be together.

George had to grow a pair here, he really did. "You scare me sometimes."

"I scare you? Me?" Finn raised both eyebrows.

"Yeah, you do," George took his hand back and started the car. "I fucking like you too, alright? That's pretty obvious. But I'm older, I know," he shook his head and accelerated down the road, "I know what it's like to be young and think something's more than it is. To make a commitment you maybe shouldn't have, wouldn't have if you were older. I don't want that for you."

He let out a deep breath, proud of himself for getting it all out; terrified to look at Finn.

Finn was in motion beside him, shuffling around in his seat. "I, fuck, George," he said and George glanced at him. He was looking out the window again, chewing his thumb nail. "I reckon I can't convince you, can't make you believe me. But I reckon he's not nothing either."

Part of George wanted to reassure Finn that, in fact, since they'd met, Joq hadn't been as much of a factor as he should've been. And George reckoned he should've felt worse about that. But he was in love with Finn in a way he'd never be in love with anyone else.

"Where are we going anyway?" Finn asked, like he wanted to change the subject, change the tone, let them forget.

George was a coward. He took the out.

"To play," he accelerated for the stadium, a cauldron of concrete in front of them, dark grey against the night sky.

"Wait there," George said to Finn once he walked him to the centre of the oval. He placed the football in his hands.

"Okay," Finn replied.

George was giddy as he jogged to the tunnel to get the lights. He'd watched Finn train, he'd watched Finn play—he'd never played with Finn himself.

He flicked the switch and the grounds exploded with light. Finn was at the centre of the oval, which looked greener, sharper in that way it always did under lights, and George watched his face brighten as he looked at him.

"You ready to get your ass kicked?" George asked as he jogged over.

Finn gave him a blinding smile, bounced the ball once and then took off unexpectedly, his explosive speed propelling him down the ground.

George gave chase. Normally, a guy bouncing the ball while you gave direct chase with no one bumping you off course would be an easy catch—not with Finn. He was booting it and the ball sailed through for a perfect goal as George finally tackled him. Finn laughed in his arms as George pushed him into the grass.

"Alright, looks like we're taking this seriously," George said and tickled Finn's side.

Finn cackled and pushed up.

George got to his feet and gave Finn a hand. Finn took it and let himself be yanked up.

"Is there any other way to take it?" he asked—his chest heaving, his eyes dancing, and his mouth curved up.

"Good point," George jogged over to get the ball.

They played.

George tore down to the other end and Finn knocked him to the ground embarrassingly easily. George laughed as he ate grass and Finn rolled him over, gave his ass a good pat, then a lingering squeeze. George grinned at him. He let himself be pulled up this time.

"Let's see how you're lining up from fifty," George tossed him the ball.

"No wind? No crowd? No pressure?" Finn bounced the ball and jogged to the top of the line.

"None of that's ever been your problem," George jogged alongside him. "Your problems are all in your head."

Finn scoffed, but he lined up, focused on the shot and took the kick. It sailed through for a beauty of a goal.

"Fuck yeah, Finny," George cheered and lifted Finn off the ground and crushed him to his chest.

Finn cackled into his shoulder. "Bit effusive, but okay," he said.

George spun him. "Not if it's the game winner."

They played one on one. They played kick to kick. They took shots on goal from weird angles and teased each other.

"Hey! This is private property!" came from the sidelines.

George looked over and made out a large man and a torch. He jogged over.

"Hey, sorry," he said as he approached, "I probably should've let you guys know I was using the place tonight?"

"George Creed?" the guy asked and shined the light in George's eyes. George winced. "Sorry, sorry," the guy said and dropped the light. "George Creed," he breathed out.

George could hear Finn jogging over behind him. "Hey," he said warmly.

The security guy swallowed. "Finnegan Flynn."

"Hi," Finn smiled and held out his hand. "We're just running some drills," he said as he pumped the guy's hand.

"Of course, sure, yeah, sorry to bother," the guy rambled.

"No bother," George said. "We better call it a night anyway."

"Can I get your autograph," the guy blurted out.

"Sure," George said and Finn did as well and they signed an old receipt and the back of the guy's business card and wished him a good night.

"'S'pose we should call it," Finn said as they watched the guy walk off, looking at the signed bits of paper in his hand.

"I was thinking of getting something to eat?"

"Yeah?" Finn brightened.

George bumped him. "Yeah, I'm feelin' one of those heart healthy burgers again, what about you?"

"For sure," Finn fell into step beside him. "There's a good place that delivers to my place if you don't wanna eat out?"

George bumped him again as they went down the tunnel to hit the showers. "Yeah, sounds good."

Finn ducked his head and hid his smile, still panting from the workout or from the conversation.

"I reckon you gotta work on your stamina," George said as they stripped in the locker room.

Finn cracked up. "Fuckin' serious? How long did I ride you for at Bells? Thirty minutes?"

George gave a shocked laugh. Finn just said that, out loud, here. "That's a fair point, sonny," George replied, mock serious. "But I reckon you could put your back into it a bit more next time, give me forty."

Finn shook his head, giggled. "I'll give you fucking forty alright."

They headed into the showers, a careful space between them, even though George was using extraordinary willpower not to shove Finn against the tiles and kiss him.

Finn smiled over at him as he got under the showerhead beside him and turned on the water. That smile said he was exercising some serious willpower too.

George exhaled roughly and focused on the water, on the soap, on the sound of water splashing on the tiles, on the steam billowing. He heard Finn's shower turn off and thought he should probably do the same when he felt Finn press up against his back. Their wet skin slid together as Finn's arms wrapped around George's waist and held him close. His lips ghosted warm on George's nape.

George leaned into him, craned his head back to whisper, "Here?"

Finn kissed his throat, the line of skin exposed as he arched into the touch.

George pulled him in front and pressed him back against the tiles.

Finn watched him back—eyes full of desire, but adoring too—it broke George, it really did, how much Finn didn't hide from him.

George kissed him, deep and full of feeling, full of everything he couldn't say.

Finn brought his hand down, his fingers trailing lightly over George's abdomen until he reached his groin.

George stopped him before he touched his dick. "Let's go home," he said against Finn's lips. He leaned past him and turned the tap off. Finn's breath ghosted over his jaw and George just managed not to kiss him.

As they got dressed, George tried to get them back onto ground that wasn't—I want to throw you on the ground right here and fuck your brains out—by talking about how Kenny was doing in Sydney this season.

Finn smiled knowingly at him, a smile that said—please throw me on the ground and fuck me senseless, but if not, hurry the fuck up and get dressed—and George grinned at him as Finn talked about Kenny's method, about his self-esteem workshops for players, and about how Sydney were always going to be contenders while Kenny had a heartbeat.

They ambled up the tunnel, still chatting, still bumping each other fondly when George stopped and turned the lights off. He came back over to Finn and grabbed his hand. Finn laced his fingers with George's immediately and George brought that hand up and kissed his knuckles. He did it like breathing. Finn watched him, breath caught, and even in the dark George could see in his eyes that burning question—how can you act like this isn't fucking more? How can you act like this isn't fucking everything?

George was beginning to wonder the same thing.

But later that night after they ate, after they tumbled into bed all ready to fuck, Finn steadied George's hand before he could penetrate him. "Do you ever?" he asked and slid his hand between George's crack.

"No, never," George shook his head. Then for reasons that will always elude him, he went on, "Maybe save it for your next partner."

Finn's face contorted; he covered it quickly, but it was there, like a broken moment frozen in time.

"Yeah, for sure," Finn said quickly and rolled out of bed.

"Where are you going?" George asked.

"Need to piss," he replied and slammed the bathroom door.

The truth was, George reckoned if Finn wanted to do it that way, he'd totally do it. But he didn't know how to say that now, how to bring it up again without it being forever tainted with something George didn't even want to think about—Finn having another partner? The thought alone just about killed him.

He heard nothing from the bathroom.

He got up. "Finn," he said against the door.

"Just a sec," Finn replied.

The water turned on, there was splashing, the water turned off.

Finn emerged and barrelled into George's chest.

"You okay?" George asked, his hands gripping Finn's biceps.

"Yeah? Why wouldn't I be?" Finn asked. "You ready?"

"Yeah, but..."

Finn wriggled out of his hold and George let him go.

He followed Finn back to the bed and slid alongside him. Finn grabbed his hand and placed it over his semi. "Maybe you can show me how good you are, give me something to remember you by before I get a real partner," Finn said—a little breathless, a little snarky, a lot hurt.

"Jesus, Finn," George said and squeezed. "I don't want, I just mean, someday—

"Okay!" Finn rolled on top of him. "I get it, so make the most of it, okay?"

George grabbed him and rolled him under him again, kissed him roughly, cruelly, and Finn arched into it, angry too, eager.

The sex had an aggressive edge to it and as George pushed in, he asked Finn, "You want this cock or some other cock?" He was surprised it was coming out of his mouth, but he was so pissed off his jealousy was finding words.

"Fuck, just yours," Finn said and arched and shoved down and took George to the hilt and begged for more.

"Yeah, just mine, baby, just fucking mine," George recited like a litany as he pounded into him, his dick like steel, his orgasm a possessive claiming he forced Finn to take before he dragged Finn's out of him with a rough hand on his dick.

He felt better after. He left Finn sleeping and drove home and he felt better until he stepped inside.

He heard Finn's words, '*A real partner*,' and threw his keys in the bowl, toed off his shoes, and headed upstairs for the shower.

'*A real partner*,' he thought again as he looked at Joq's products everywhere—like what George had here, with Joq.

George left the stadium earlier than usual the following night. He stopped at the shops and got everything he needed to cook. He'd been paying attention when Finn cooked from those healthy meal boxes and George 'helped.' Finn recommended a cook book, so George bought that, and decided this marinated and baked fish dish would work. He got all the stuff and the sauvignon blanc Joq liked, then he saw a six-pack of the ciders Joq had been ordering when they went out and grabbed those too.

'*A real partner*' was echoing in his brain. George had a real partner. He needed to make an actual effort with his real partner. Finn was going to move on. Finn was going to get a real partner too. And George had a real good thing here.

He got home and got to cooking. Well, marinating.

He heard Joq come in and called out to him.

Joq came in and surveyed George, the benches, said "Hey," and George looked up and smiled.

"Hey, babe," he replied.

"What's all this?" Joq asked as he cocked his hip against the bench and folded his arms over his chest.

"Thought I'd try and cook you something different," George winked over at him.

He felt it when Joq started to thaw, which was also when he realised Joq was freezing him out.

"Yeah?" Joq asked with some real interest in his expression.

"Yeah," George smiled warmly and then went back to marinating these fillets—which he realised meant turn them, just turn them in the sauce he'd made after a while, and then coat in breadcrumbs, which he did. "It might suck balls, but I can always correct next time."

Joq snorted at him and went for the fridge. "Okay, coach."

"I got the wine you like." He nodded approvingly when Joq went with a cider. Joq drank it at the window, looking out at the blustery night, the palms swaying erratically against the blackening sky.

George started talking about the team, how it was going, how he was feeling now they were certain to make the eight, how he didn't think it'd get rid of the haters but it was a good start for his first year, should secure him a contract for the following year and Joq watched the night coming in and made sounds to acknowledge he was listening.

George set the inside table, made it as nice as Joq always made it for him and then set the food down.

"Looks good," Joq smiled.

George smiled back. It did look good. And this was good.

"You been holding out on me," Joq said when they finished.

George laughed and cleared the table, drank his water.

Joq went in to watch the news and George did another workout. A standard evening, but better because he'd cooked, he'd pulled his weight more. This could get better if he put in more effort, he thought as he did a cool down with some yoga, took a quick shower.

Joq was already in bed when George got there. George slid in behind him, pressed his hardening dick against his ass.

"Not tonight," Joq said.

"Really?" George was honestly shocked.

It was totally fine, of course it was, but it was fucking strange. He let Joq go quickly, rolled onto his back but kept one hand on Joq's hip to maintain the contact, gave him a squeeze.

"Yeah, long day, management, you know?" Joq said.

Joq started telling him about this need for security scanners for bag checks at the stadium and George felt his eyelids getting heavy as he responded, "Hmmm."

He could hear Joq speaking softly, his voice calm and barely animated as he detailed how he didn't get the sudden urgency, and it was the last thing he heard before he was asleep.

26

FINN WAS LYING ON his couch, staring at the ceiling, ostensibly resting after a brutal workout. No George tonight, he thought bitterly.

'A real partner.'

He'd tell George to go fuck himself if he wasn't so into the prick.

His phone rang on his coffee table.

And who the fuck was calling him now?

He rolled his head to the side, slapped the table, looked at the photo on the screen and sat right up.

"Jackie!" he said as he hit answer.

Jack groaned. "Are you ever gonna let that drop? How's things?"

"Yeah, good, good, you?" Finn asked and got off his ass to get some dinner started. He felt energised just hearing Jack's lazy drawl.

"Same old," Jack replied.

Finn scoffed. "You and Hiller are killing it."

"Yeah, I guess," he replied and Finn could almost see him rubbing the back of his neck, blushing, looking down—man looked like an All-Australian full forward in any year—tall, built, handsome—and yet he was almost cripplingly shy once you got to know him. Finn liked to tease him that it was because he was from Western Australia. But then that made no sense, look at Hiller, Jack said when he stayed with Finn in Byron, "Man's madder than a cut snake. Still won't tell me what I did to him."

Which brought them to now—Jack liked talking about Hiller and he didn't at the same time. Finn wasn't in the mood to tease him about it. Jack was gay, but "who knows" was his answer on Hiller. He didn't have a girlfriend. He never went home with anyone. He seemed to put most of his attention into giving Jack a hard time.

"How is Sean?" Finn decided to ask as he got his latest meal box out.

"You know, the usual," Jack said kind of weirdly. Last he'd heard, Sean Hiller was still being the bane of Jack's existence, but that there sounded almost fond.

"I didn't call to chat about Sean," he stated and Finn did not miss the use of 'Sean' instead of 'Hiller.' Huh.

"What's up?"

"Oh, nothin', just gonna be over there in a few weeks, thought we could catch up? George still won't take my calls," he tacked on the end.

Finn shook his head. Bloody George. Man acted all calm and collected, but he held a grudge over nothing for years.

"Yeah, George can be a bit emotionally constipated," Finn replied and got his stuff on the bench. "But I'm down, for sure."

"Oh, it's George is it?" Jack laughed at him.

Finn laughed too to cover it. "Yeah, shut up. We were talking for a while before, you know that."

"Yeah, yeah, I get it, George is actually a great friend when he's not convinced you've crossed him," Jack replied.

"He'll get over it," Finn said.

"He probably won't, but what can I do? I've apologised for it even though I didn't do anything wrong," Jack said.

Finn could imagine him running over the story again: wanting to go home; being transparent about that; requesting and getting the trade; George never speaking to him again for 'abandoning' them.

George really was a lot more emotional about some things than he let on.

"Yeah, I know," Finn just stopped himself from saying he'd talk to George—that would be fucking weird. Him and George weren't anything.

"So, how about you? Seeing anyone?"

Finn snorted. "Well, just come on out and ask why don't you?"

"What? Are you?"

"Are you?"

"Touché," Jack said. "I don't kiss and tell."

"Oh, wow," Finn grinned. "You so are! Good for you man."

"Yeah, well, early days, what about you though?"

"I also don't kiss and tell," Finn focused on frying his weird looking chickpea patties.

"So, that's a yes," Jack said warmly.

Finn sighed. "Yes and no, it's complicated."

"Any guy doing complicated with you is not worth your time," Jack replied gruffly.

"Aww, thanks, Jackie," Finn laughed.

"I'm serious. How can it be complicated?"

Finn groaned. "It just is."

"Do you like him?"

"Like him?" Finn shook his head and turned his patties and spoke without thinking. "I fucking love him."

"So what's the problem?"

"I dunno if he's..." Finn swallowed. "He might not feel the same."

"Then he's insane," Jack replied, kind of animated for Jack.

"Thanks." Finn was honestly touched.

"Seriously, I'd get an answer on that one, have you asked?"

"Kind of? Also, I can't believe we're talking about this," Finn laughed, kind of embarrassed.

"Why shouldn't we talk about this? Straight guys talk about this," Jack said.

"Do they?"

Jack hesitated for a minute.

"I dunno, I assumed?"

Finn shook his head, blew out a breath. "Probably, anyway, yeah, I'm gonna sort it." He thought that, but the truth was he'd keep accepting seconds until George told him to fuck off. He realised he needed to take Kenny's self-esteem workshop again if that was the case.

"Hang on," Jack said and Finn could tell he was muffling the phone to talk to someone.

"Hey, I gotta go, but we'll talk more when I get there alright?"

"Is that your boyfriend?" Finn teased.

He was surprised when Jack answered seriously. "Yep, and he's giving me a look like I better get off the phone now."

Finn laughed. "Too much information, but good for you."

"Yep, and I'm serious, we're gonna talk, but I gotta go."

"Get it, Jack."

"Bye, Finn," and the line went dead.

Finn looked at his phone, tossed it on the counter and got back to cooking. That was weird.

But fuck it all, Jack was right, he needed to talk to George.

Training was good the next day. Finn was playing again and while he wasn't having blinders every week, he was putting in a solid showing, his possessions were good, he felt good, he felt like he could relax into his confidence a bit. He had physio and ice baths in the afternoon and he sank into both, let his muscles release into gravity.

George came over to talk to him at the end of the day: how was he feeling? Good. He was probably going to get tagged that weekend, he needed to be ready for it, watch some of Simpson's games? Finn told him he'd watched enough. They exchanged a quick smile and that was that. A coach and a player.

Finn marvelled at how well they did that as he turned to finish packing up and getting dressed.

There was a message from George waiting for him.

Wanna come round for a swim? Pool's heated.

Finn scrunched his face up, his heart flipped and his stomach got butterflies. But he was annoyed with George too. And this was the other thing they did, he thought dryly.

"Hey, Finn, you in?" Les asked from beside him.

Finn startled and swiped his messages closed.

"In for?" he asked.

"We're goin' to get dinner and game, some of the boys from the Colts are comin' round," he said as he pulled his flimsy white shirt on, tucked it into his pants.

"Ah, yeah," Finn was nodding. He liked the Colts' kids—farm team—and it was always good to hang out with them because it made rapport easier when they got called up.

But then he thought of George, his gruff smile, the way he was fucking this up spectacularly but Finn could see in every look, feel in every touch, that he didn't want to be. He was just perpetually fucking stupid or something.

"Yeah, nah," Finn said.

"No?" Les asked as he got his sneakers on, looked up through his wet hair. "You got plans?"

"Yeah, loose dinner plans with a friend down from Byron. I better check in, but if he cancels..."

"Yeah, for sure," Les stood and smiled at him. "We'll be at mine."

"Cool," Finn smiled and watched Les leave.

He sent George a thumbs up and went to wait in the carpark.

Finn sank into the heated pool. The night was dark and still around them, just the bubble of the filter, the occasional flap of a palm in the soft breeze, the soft lighting from the cabana and kitchen, the pool lights.

"Fuck that's good," he said as he watched George slide into the water on the other side.

"Yeah, I love it, best thing I ever did with this place," George replied.

The drive had been fine—polite—and the arrival had been the same—polite and pleasant.

Finn felt like he was going to explode because who were they kidding at this point? Even their polite and pleasant pulsed below the surface with a desire that felt uncontainable, scary even. He watched George drop below the surface, re-emerge with wet hair and a soft smile as he blinked the water out of his eyes. He ached with how much he just bloody liked him—too much, way too much.

He pushed off the edge and swam into George's space. George's arms encircled him immediately and they were kissing. Their lips brushed a little roughly, tongues met and tangled between harsh breaths. It felt a lot like relief, it felt urgent.

George yanked Finn closer with his hands under his thighs and rubbed his dick against his abs, took his mouth desperately.

Finn moaned and scrambled at George's back, tried to hold on, to get more, to get closer.

"Shit, Finn," George said against his mouth, "I need more," he sounded almost sorry about it.

Finn brought his head back an inch and searched his eyes. George looked overwhelmed, but he looked sad too and Finn fucking hated it.

"You can have everything," he said sincerely, his legs tightening.

George groaned, kissed him, and crushed him tighter against his chest.

"I can't fuck you in here," George pulled back to say.

"Why?" Finn asked between kisses.

"Condom," George pulled away and released Finn enough to make some room to grab his hand and tug him out of the pool.

Finn wanted to tell him they didn't need condoms. He wasn't fucking anyone else. He was clean. But George fucked Joq, presumably—a thought that almost made Finn lose his erection—and Joq fucked everyone. Finn wanted to scream about the last bit, but George was pulling him into the cabana, pushing him down, bracketing himself over him and kissing him again and Finn let it go.

He shoved at George's boardshorts enough to get his dick free and stroked him.

George bucked into it as he worked Finn's shorts off. He reached for his wallet and fumbled to get a condom out.

Finn laughed. "You only got one in there?"

George smiled sheepishly at him. "I stash a few around now."

Finn giggled but stopped laughing when George pressed a finger into him.

"You want me to get lube?" he asked against Finn's lips.

"No," Finn shook his head and tightened his legs around George's waist, "there's enough on the condom."

George groaned again but got it on and pushed inside.

Finn arched, gasping.

George kissed down his throat and then started fucking him harder, more erratically than he normally did.

Finn held on. He could feel his shorts hanging off one ankle, felt the top of George's shorts as he dug his fingers into George's ass, tried to get him impossibly deeper. He felt him everywhere, in his chest, in his throat, in the frantic beating of his heart.

George seemed like he wanted to bury himself inside, tattoo his touch everywhere. He brought his face back so he was looking down at Finn, traced his thumbs up and down Finn's cheekbones, his hips pounding into him, the sound of their skin slapping loud in the still night air, their mixed panting breaths harsh against the cool breeze.

George leaned down and kissed Finn so gently, it made him ache, rock up for more. His eyes were wide open, watching Finn's breath stutter out of him with every thrust of his dick deep inside him.

"Good?" George asked so softly it made Finn gasp—such a gentle question in the midst of an absolute pounding.

"So good," Finn panted.

"Yeah? Love that dick, baby?" George asked as he nailed Finn right where it felt so good and Finn lost all thought.

"Yours," he gasped out between thrusts. "Just, fuck. Yours."

"Yeah," George's face lost the smile; he looked at Finn with the heat of a man possessed. "Just mine," he ground his hips in deep, shoved into Finn, the combination of his thrusts and Finn taking it winding them both higher, deeper.

Ah, fuck, but it was wrong, Finn thought—he wasn't George's and yet, when they were like this, when George said that and looked at him like that, how could he be anyone else's?

"Yours," was punched out of him as George fucked him. "Just yours," he said over and over again, winding George up higher, winding himself up.

"Fuck, please," Finn said and threw his head back.

George kissed his collar bones—still so achingly gentle—as he brought his hand between them and started to jerk Finn off.

"Gonna come on my dick, baby?" George asked against Finn's lips.

Finn brought his hands onto George's ass, tugged him in; he rocked down onto George's cock, looked him straight in the eyes and said through panting breaths, "Just yours."

George groaned and buried his face in the crook of Finn's shoulder and neck. He punished him with a brutal pace, jerked him off with the same pressure, the slap of skin obscenely loud in counterpoint to the soft sucking sound as he kissed his skin, whispered "Just mine" in a broken voice against Finn's skin. He shoved in as far as he could go and stilled. Finn felt him coming and let himself go. His dick pulsed in George's hand as he cried out, pushed up, and tried to get more.

"Jesus," George said against Finn's throat as they came down, George's hips still rocking into him.

"Just Finn," Finn gave George's dumb joke back to him.

George giggled—giggled!—the sound of it vibrating through Finn's chest where they were pressed together, where George was still inside, half hard.

Finn smiled and carded his fingers through George's hair.

"At least we can just clean up in the pool," he said.

"Yeah," George rubbed his face back and forth on Finn's throat before heaving himself up, pulling out slowly with his fingers wrapped around his dick.

Finn arched and made a little whine.

"Sorry, sorry," George ran his hand up and down Finn's inner thigh.

"All good," Finn replied, eyes sleepy on George as he tied off the condom and tossed it on the patio next to his wallet.

Finn laughed, he didn't know why, but he took George's hand, returned his sated smile and let himself be pulled up. He kissed George's collar bone as George leaned in and wiped the come into Finn's skin, whispered, "Let me."

He shook his shorts off and followed George into the pool, wrapped his legs around his waist again and lost himself in deep kisses, kisses that weren't going anywhere, kisses they were doing to be close, because it felt damn good.

"Hi," came from behind them—sharp and shocking—and Finn leapt away.

He spun around and saw Joq standing on the threshold, his expression annoyed but polite. Finn had a hysterical moment where he realised he knew Joq about well enough to know he was a guy who could pull that off.

"Joq, hey," George said, a little breathless. "That was quick."

"Cancelled," Joq replied, clipped.

Finn figured he must've been meant to be at something at work and George had invited Finn over knowing they'd have some time to themselves; presumably, more time.

Joq looked at him. Finn could feel his flush, and his smile felt guilty—these guys might be open but Finn was fucking human, okay? And in his mind, he'd just been caught making out with the love of his life by the boyfriend of that guy and it was a weird, uncomfortable and embarrassing situation to find himself in. Under Joq's cool, slightly irritated look, he felt himself wilt.

"Hi, Joq," he said though, forced an ease into it like all was well and he was just enjoying the open thing like some cool hippy from the seventies—free love, oh yeah! Even though he couldn't have been further from that at his core, but he could act, he could fucking well act!

"Hi," Joq replied. "Mind if I join you?"

Finn frowned and then quickly hid it but it was too late. Joq saw it. Because uh, *fuck no*, he wanted to yell in that stupidly handsome face.

"Course," George said though. "Nice and warm."

Finn could hear the false cheerfulness and he wondered for a moment what the fuck the three of them thought they were doing, like, really, what the fuck were they doing? Who were they kidding?

"Cool, I'll go change."

Joq disappeared inside the house and Finn wanted, in that moment, more than anything to just leave. But that would look even worse, wouldn't it?

"Hope that's cool?" George asked him, horribly unsure.

"Yeah, course," Finn lied, his voice airy and stupid.

George blew out a breath. Finn swam away from him, putting a careful distance between them.

"Joq's cool," George said.

"Yeah, I know," Finn replied and watched his hand on the water. The most awkward silence descended and Joq reappeared in his board shorts. He was lean, not an ounce of fat on him but he had the body of a cyclist—like he worked out to keep anything, including muscle, off his body, anything that could slow him down. He was mostly hairless too—just a faint wisp of blonde hair at his happy trail.

As he stepped in at the steps near George, he smiled at them, and it looked painful as he said, "Warm."

"Can't believe you've got a heated pool," Finn said to George because he needed to say something, he needed desperately for everything to feel okay.

"I like to swim all year round," George replied, eyes warm on Finn like he couldn't completely turn it off.

"Yeah, same," Finn said and leaned back. He rested his head on the edge and looked at the sky—he couldn't look at George if George was going to look at him like that and have his boyfriend at the same time.

He saw it out of the corner of his eye when Joq leaned in to kiss George though. He saw George respond a fraction of a second later. It was a perfunctory kiss, a boyfriend kiss.

Finn felt his heart shatter in his chest. He was moving, he was getting out, he heard his voice saying, "I better go."

"No, don't go, I've defrosted steaks—

George was cut off as Joq cut in, "You got a problem with a bit of PDA between boyfriends?"

God, that was a vicious slap. Finn fumbled around for his clothes, or a towel, where was a fucking towel? He was stark naked and about two seconds away from bursting into tears.

"Joq," George said, but it sounded far away.

"What?" Joq asked, his hands up.

"Course not," Finn mumbled and decided he didn't need a fucking towel. He grabbed his shorts and yanked them on.

"Why the rush then?" Joq asked. "Stay for dinner."

"I've got, I forgot," Finn mumbled and hiked his shorts up over his ass, focused on tying the laces, his fingers as clumsy as his voice as he finished, "plans."

He grabbed his hoodie as George got out of the water. "I'll walk you out."

Finn kept his head down but felt George's naked body beside him as he yanked his own shorts on and tied them quickly.

Finn waited. He didn't know why. He should've just walked out and told them both to go fuck themselves with their weird fucking relationship. But he waited, horribly aware of Joq watching him, disliking him, and that made him angry, but he waved awkwardly and smiled at his feet as Joq said, "Later, Finn," and then cursed himself for smiling at all, for being so embarrassing.

He got his feet moving and felt George next to him. Their feet were wet on the tiles in the kitchen, in the hall; Finn's eyes focused on his phone as he opened the ride sharing app and got a car. Ten minutes away. He felt George breathing beside him.

"I'm sorry about..." George trailed off.

"It's fine," Finn whispered.

"Jesus, Finn," George huffed, angry and maybe hurt too.

But Finn didn't get it.

"I just," he looked at George and found him watching him back, his expression so torn up. He lowered his voice. "I just don't get it. I feel like you want me too, I feel like this is *something*."

"This is just fucking," George replied but if ever a sentence sounded hollow, sounded like a fucking lie, it was that one.

Finn shook his head though, he couldn't force George to see he was sincere, that he was capable of committing in a forever way; twenty or seventy, he knew what he was fucking well feeling.

"Okay," Finn shrugged, defeated. "But I just don't buy it, you and him."

"You know we're together. And someday you'll find some-one—

"Stop saying that!" Finn exploded—he kept his voice down but it swelled with rage inside those quiet walls.

"It's true," George insisted, also quiet but very firm. "You're still so young, you don't get it."

Finn couldn't believe this bullshit. "You were eighteen when you got together with *him*," he hissed.

"It's different," George replied, his eyes pleading with Finn to get it. But Finn didn't get it. "We were both young. Someday you'll meet someone your own age and you'll..." he trailed off.

Finn was furious. All he heard when George said that was George didn't love him enough to care whether or not he fucked other dudes. When for Finn it broke his heart to think of George with Joq.

"Yeah, okay," he said. "Go fuck your boyfriend then."

He opened the door and it slammed shut from behind him as George pushed him up against it, spun him and kissed him. Finn yanked him in and kissed back. It was an angry kiss, it was a hurt kiss—Finn pushed into it and tried to berate George with it, to get him to stop using Finn's age as an excuse.

George pulled back, but stayed close, his eyes on Finn, searching.

"I just..." George whispered.

"You just what?" Finn begged him. He searched his eyes back, pleading with him to tell him he loved him too, he wanted to be with him, just him.

George breathed heavily and Finn watched the moment he swallowed down the words.

Finn's heart sank, but what could he do? He couldn't force George to see he was settling, he couldn't make him see they were the real deal.

And he was beginning to think he might have to let George go.

"You should go," George said.

Finn watched him for another moment, then left without another word.

It was cool out and he should've felt colder in wet shorts with damp skin, but all he felt was numb.

His car was waiting and as he got in, he apologised for his wet clothes, and the guy got him an old bomber jacket to sit on. As they headed for his place and he listened to the guy talk about the problems with his homeland all he could think was he needed to text George and end it.

Back home, he took a long, hot shower, planned the message, went over the words again and again in his mind—*I think we should stop.*

But he couldn't send it.

He sat on his bed, spun his phone in his hands and willed himself to send it.

His phone buzzed.

He opened it.

One line from George: *If you want to stop, we can stop.*

Finn sucked in a breath. So George was going to do the leg work for him.

He thought of George's kisses.

He thought of the feel of George inside him when they fucked.

He thought of the way George really looked at him like he bloody loved the view.

He typed. He hit send.

I don't want to stop.

27

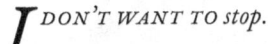

I DON'T WANT TO stop.

George was hit with a wave of relief so profound when he read the reply, he had to sit down on the couch for a minute.

He was in the living room, the house dark and turned down for the night save for a few lamps.

Joq had gone to bed after they endured the world's most excruciating evening. After George had walked back into the kitchen from the heated exchange with Finn, he'd seen Joq standing there, fridge open, evidently hearing enough by the look on his face.

"How much did you hear?" he'd asked.

Joq had slammed the fridge. "Enough."

George figured. He was ashamed, he was embarrassed, but he was oddly resigned too. He shook his head and folded his arms over his chest ready for Joq to let him have it—he deserved it.

"Are you in love with him?" Joq asked, point blank.

George did not expect the question, and by the look on Joq's face, he hadn't expected to ask it either.

George was at a loss. *Yes*, a part of him answered immediately, a part of him that knew fundamental truths. But another part, the part that knew it was impossible, shouted that idea down.

"I..." he started, stopped. There was no way he was telling Joq the truth of what he was feeling. "No," he said firmly. "It's a crush," he went on, which it was, for Finn, he was sure of it. "It's just fucking," it was certainly that too. "It's the season, it's intense," which was also true.

Joq nodded along, but he'd shut down and gone distant when George hesitated. He wasn't fucking stupid. "I'm gonna shower," he said and went to go past George.

George had the feeling he was about to lose him and he panicked. Joq was a fundamental part of his life; he wasn't going to fucking lose him over a passionate affair with a rookie—what was he? A character in one of his mum's soap operas?

He placed a hand on Joq's bicep. Joq stopped.

"It's just fucking," George said again.

Joq jerked his chin in acknowledgement, but he was like ice when he looked at George, and George knew what that meant—he was hurt, really hurt.

"You might want to tell him that," he said and left the kitchen.

George responded—"Yeah"—too late.

He might want to tell himself as well, a snarky voice said.

But he took Joq's point to heart and worked himself up to text Finn. To remind him what this was.

How he ended up on: *If you want to stop, we can stop*, was another mystery in his fucked-up head.

I don't want to stop stared up at him.

He rubbed his temples, he smiled, and then he started laughing hysterically. The hardest part of this year was supposed to be the coaching debut—not this... this... what was this?

Love, a voice whispered to him.

He sobered and shook his head.

It wasn't, because it couldn't be, and he just needed to get them to the end of the season and then they'd go their separate ways for a few months over summer before preseason. It'd be good.

But in the meantime.

Good, he hit send.

28

FINN SNORTED WHEN HE read George's reply, *Good*.

He shook his head. *Good.* Fuck's sake.

One word and his dick took interest.

Fuck his life, seriously.

The next day at training, he jogged out onto the oval and George was already there, aviators on, whistle around his neck, frowning as he watched everyone warm up.

Finn accidentally got caught staring but instead of giving him nothing, George smirked, and Finn huffed a laugh, which made George smile wider. It was like last time—it was like this place was separate and fun and they both got that.

He shook his head and started on the suicides.

In between all the drama, Finn had forgotten he was booked onto one of the talking heads footy shows that night. Lucky for him Ally grabbed him before he got to the showers and asked if he was ready.

"Ready for what?" he panted out.

She looked at him like he was insane. She said the name of the show. "You're a guest. Tonight. You're a guest on the show tonight. Did you read my email?"

He had not.

George went by and she corralled him.

"Finnegan is on tonight, can you give him a rundown of what to say and more importantly, what not to say," she looked at Finn. "Get ready, suit. I'll meet you out the front in forty-five minutes."

Finn decided to wait until she was out of ear shot. "I didn't bring a suit."

George chuckled. "Didn't you know you were on?"

"Yeah, but I forgot! Fuck!"

Lacy strolled by. "Ladies," he said and tipped an imaginary hat.

"Lace," George grabbed him. "Can you go to Finn's and grab his suit? He's on TV tonight."

Lacy looked at Finn, said the name of the show, rolled his eyes and said, "You owe me. Also, Haddy is a wanker."

Finn snorted, thanked him and ran and got his keys.

George reappeared as Finn got dressed.

"Okay, you gotta give 'em something personal, so make it personal cute, but not real personal," he said.

"Yeah, like, talk about your dog," Lacy said.

"I don't have a dog."

"No shit, dumb-ass," Lacy went on, "but you got a dog equivalent, yeah? A sister? Mother?"

SASHA AVICE

"Did you just call my mum and sister a dog?" Finn asked around his laugh as he buttoned up his shirt.

"It's a compliment. Have you ever met a dog that's a shit cunt? No, you haven't, Finny, you have not."

"Can't believe you brought the blue suit," Finn said as he pulled on the jacket George handed him.

"I can't believe you have that many suits!" Lacy shot back.

"It's not that many," Finn mumbled as he pulled his shirt collar over the suit jacket collar, shook his hair so it tumbled down his neck.

"It's so many I couldn't even count them. And all that other shit as well, your wardrobe is more extensive than any woman I've met," Lacy said, smiling his shit-eating grin.

Finn just stopped himself from asking what Lacy knew about women because as far as he knew, George didn't know—and he was still hovering and smiling indulgently at Lacy—and he also didn't know if Lacy was gay or bi.

"Right, well, you look good and I think that's the main thing—nothing personal," George said.

"And don't let them bait you into something," Lacy added.

"I have kinda done this before," Finn said.

George and Lacy shared a laugh.

"What?"

"Believe me, this ain't like a boundary interview or surf cam or whatever you hippies call it," Lacy said and pointed, smirked, "and you've already got a profile and they'll want a soundbite they can leverage into clickbait. Believe me, they'll ask a curve ball to try and get it. And they'll make you think you're friends first, soften you up."

Finn couldn't do anything other than frown at that—what could they possibly try and get him to pipe up about?

George smiled reassuringly, told him it'd be fine, and walked him out, while Lacy told him it probably wouldn't be fine but they'd all confessed to doing coke in Amsterdam in the offseason at least once.

"Ah, no, we haven't," George replied and got Finn out of there as he laughed.

They were right about softening him up first. They asked him about his family, brought up a nice picture of him and Soph on the beach, then made the mistake of believing his Wikipedia page—Soph had edited it to say she was his older sister. She was, by a few seconds. The presenters seemed to think she was older-older. Then they played a game where he had to handball footballs into a spinning wheel and compete against the presenters.

It was when they started talking about George, or started to shit-talk George, that Finn got worked up. But surely this wasn't what they were trying to get him to break on? If so, it was a soft target.

Fortunately, Finn wasn't alone.

Old Billy Mac, a legend of the game from the late seventies and eighties, was also a guest. He knew his shit. He was someone Finn could have a genuine spirited debate with. The other two were as Lacy warned—producing entertainment, looking for a soundbite.

Old Billy Mac got the questions started, but he seemed sincere in it. "There's been a lot of talk about Creed's ascension to Head Coach."

Finn felt his spine straighten with the subject change. He shifted his body on the couch, angled himself in Mac's direction.

"Now I know Creed," Mac said. "Hell of a player, hell of a player," he shook his head and smiled, his eyes going distant before they sharpened again, "but coaching ain't playing and while he's got you boys as finals contenders, I gotta wonder if you'd a done it without him anyway. You got the side for it."

Finn had started shaking his head halfway through. "It's all George."

"Come on now," Mac sat forward, lifted his hand to start counting on his fingers, "you got Lacy down there makin' those same plays he's been doin' since he was playin' with George last season—

"Sorry," Finn had to cut him off; he smiled apologetically, but enough was enough, "but look closer. George put Lacy down there. He's moved me and the rest of the mid-field to work with Lacy without taxing Lacy all over the ground."

"Yeah, but, you get a player like Lacy, like yourself, you're gonna do that anyway," Mac said, his old eyes crinkled and sure.

Finn shook his head. "You don't get it."

The TV men scoffed at him. Finn met their eyes. They were looking at him like he was young and stupid, like he was out of line talking to Mac like that. They were looking at him like they were the kind of guys who penned that article about the way he goes about his business, saying he wasn't '*taking it seriously.*' They looked at him like they'd shake his hand, smile nervously in awe of his fame, but use up any mileage in an established relationship to further their own careers.

Let them. Finn thought of George—it was one them, or their ilk, hunting George quietly every few years with that article.

He looked at them again and thought—come after me all you like, but try and touch George and I will burn your studio to the ground.

He smiled at them, his gaze sharp. "George sees every player. He like, sees us. And he's not afraid to go old school if he sees that'd work better for that player."

He sees us, he thought in their direction, unlike you.

"Okay, okay," Old Mac nodded. "I can see that. I can see that."

"He's still a bit green to be Head Coach though," Haddy—the TV man who'd never played a sport in his life but memorised stats like that's all there was to a game of anything—decided to pursue it further.

In Finn's mind, the conversation was dead. But *Alright, Haddy*, he thought and shot him a mean smile. "And when we make final four? Is he still gonna be too green then?"

"With you on the side, Finnegan, you were always gonna make final four," Carson, the guy whose show it was, old newsman, bit of a dick but seemed like less of a dick because he was sitting next to Haddy, said.

"And that's where George gets what you don't," Finn replied. He put some authority into that—these guys weren't going to shit-talk George, not on his watch, and if they wanted to make a soundbite of him defending his coach, then so be it. Everything else between him and George aside, George was a bloody brilliant coach. Not as good as Kenny yet, but he would be once he got some years under his belt.

"Oh yeah?" Haddy asked, smirking, delighted—he knew he was about to get his quote.

Finn smiled at him again, nothing friendly in it. "It's about the team. We're a team," he said, calm and even; he knew his shit, unlike this joker. "George sees each of us as individuals and then puts us together like a single organism that works. Sure, I'm a valuable piece, but you're playing to lose if you build an entire team around one player. George doesn't do the favourites stuff like you do. He knows all of us, and he values all of us. We all feel it, and we all respect him because of it. It's not fake, it's real. He's a bloody brilliant coach, and I'm honoured to play for him."

Finn felt a little winded as he finished—it was all true, but he was worked up because he was just sick of it, sick to fucking death of them coming at George for the sake of a story. All they had to do was look at the facts and see he was doing a good job, but they didn't want to do that because that was no fucking story, was it? *Young Head Coach Does Good Job.*

"Finnegan makes a good point," Old Mac said, oblivious to the other two raising eyebrows and looking a little taken aback by Finn's outburst. "It reminds me of Hawthorn in the eighties, and we really saw the truth of a great team versus a great player in that Grand Final against Geelong..."

Finn focused on Mac. He could feel his skin flushing, felt his breaths coming a little fast. But he didn't regret it, not one bit.

Once the show was over and they were all untangling their ear pieces and mics, Haddy—focused on his shirt mic, smirked—said to Finn, "Gotta a bit of a thing for Creed, eh?"

Finn flinched before he barked an awkward laugh and rubbed the back of his neck. He wanted to punch the guy in the face, but worse, he couldn't come up with a response.

"Knock it off," Old Mac said from beside him and then started to lever himself off the couch. One of the cameramen came over to help him and he shook his head, got up and stared Haddy down. "Some of us here have actually played a game and know what it's like to be playin' and seein' ya teammate or ya coach coppin' it when they're a fuckin' good bloke. Makes the blood boil," he finished.

Finn forgot how tall Mac was—even old and stooped, he was intimidating.

"I didn't mean it like that, Mac, come on, I'm just having a laugh."

Mac shook his head. "You're bein' a fuckin' dick."

And then he left.

Finn stood, followed, and gave the presenters an obnoxious head tip as he did.

He caught up to Mac outside the dressing room.

"Thank you," he said.

"Nothin' to thank me for," Mac said and smiled at him. "I reckon you're really gonna be somethin', ya know that?"

Finn blushed, dropped his gaze and rubbed the back of his neck.

"Thank you," he said again.

"Ah, get over yourself," Mac said around a laugh and Finn looked up and met his eyes, laughing.

"It's just a game at the end of the day, isn't it?" Mac said.

"Yeah," Finn grinned. "It is."

"But sticking up for ya mates? That's real," he clapped Finn on the bicep. "Good for you. That was good."

"Thank you," Finn said again and smiled shyly but maintained the eye contact this time.

"Good boy," Mac grinned. "I got the missus around here somewhere to drive me home," he said as he dropped his hand.

"I'm here," a classy-looking old lady said from behind them, "I see you managed to work the 1989 Grand Final into the conversation again," she winked at Finn and held out her hand. "Edie Macdonald," she said as Finn took it, "you made him look good," she winked again.

Finn laughed. She was tiny, but as she looked up at Old Mac watching her adoringly from his height, he felt like she was the real mountain.

"Well, come on, woman, have you got the keys?" he grinned at her.

"I better, since you've been declared illegal to drive," she retorted with a smirk. "Nice to meet you, Finnegan. Hopefully we'll see you at the Brownlow's? This one is getting honoured."

"Oh, yes, I should be there, yeah," he looked at Mac. "Congratulations."

Mac snorted. "You're probably gonna win it another year since ya did ya head in. Maybe Lacy, unless he gets a suspension. Pity about that injury Jack got, and Hiller's suspension—"

"Alright," Edie cut him off, "we'll pick this up at the ceremony. Good night, Finnegan."

"Edie," he smiled at her. "Mac." He turned to him.

"Sonny," Mac shook him again with a hand on his shoulder, gave him a big grin, and then let his wife herd him down the hallway, his arm going around her waist and tugging her close.

Finn stood there long after the back door exit had shut, his smile fixed on his face, but he felt sad; he didn't get why or maybe he didn't want to examine why.

But then Ally found him and told him he'd done well, "Sort of," she gave him a look caught between a question and a reprimand and got him out of there and he forgot about it.

29

♥

GEORGE GOT HOME, HIS face stuck in a permanent smile as he thought about Finn charging around getting ready for his interview. He'd check out the replay. In the meantime, he knew it was important to do something with Joq. Things were way too tense; everything was so far out of balance, George was actually starting to feel at his best when he was with Finn at the stadium with the other guys around. It was a happy place. Safe and easy. And he'd been an athlete long enough to know that wasn't sustainable—the home life had to be good, supportive, whatever that looked like. The first year of him and Scotty living together was an example of good and bad—good because, support system, bad because, they hit the piss too much and let each other off the hook with it. George had a feeling living with Finn would not be like that.

Which was an insane, random thought; he shook his head and called out for Joq.

"In here," Joq called from the upstairs office.

George jogged up the stairs, stopped in the doorway. Joq was sitting in the office with no lights on, no computer, just him, spinning in the high-back chair.

"Hey," he smiled, it felt awkward. "What're you doing?"

Joq shrugged. He was giving George absolutely nothing.

"Well, ah," he ran a hand through his hair and felt uncomfortable. God, ever since Joq almost caught him and Finn fucking and overhead that conversation, George felt like he was doing something wrong whenever he was in Joq's presence.

And he kind of was and yet he wasn't, he reassured himself. He was allowed to fuck other guys. But he had a sneaking suspicion he should be doing everything in his power not to fall in love with the guy he was fucking. If he was falling in love with the guy, he probably shouldn't be fucking him. They were open, not fucking poly. The thought alone made him shudder.

"Did you want something?" Joq asked—it wasn't rude, it was carefully neutral.

"Just wanted to see if you wanted to go see a movie. I've got that away game, then Freo the week after and they've got Reaver back, so I'm gonna be all systems go thinking how to shut him down—

"Jack's back?" Joq cut him off.

"Yeah," George grimaced. He'd never minded Joq's flirting with Jack, but what bothered him was how much Joq defended Jack after he left and dismissed George's '*man pain*.'

"Looks like the season-ending injury wasn't so season-ending," he said anyway.

"Huh, good for him," Joq replied.

"You know, I'm really beginning to wonder whose side you're on this season," George smiled and hoped Joq would defend his love for the team but he just shrugged and defended Jack's decision. Again.

"Yeah, well, he could've waited another season or two. And what's he done since he went home other than get spectacularly injured?"

"And play some spectacular games with Hiller before that," Joq pointed out.

Now that made George snort—Hiller's silent rage at Jack almost made George feel vindicated, like someone was doling out his retribution for him.

"What?" Joq asked, finally taking genuine interest in the conversation.

"Nothin', movies; yes or no? I feel like some mindless action."

"Uh, yeah, okay. But what's the deal with Hiller?"

George tapped his knuckles on the doorframe. "I mean, yeah, they team up well, but watch closer next time. I know you know Jack," he said pointedly—*yes, I didn't miss the flirting, Joaquin*—but Joq scoffed and George went on. "Hiller's got a hate-on for him so hard," George shook his head and backed out, "sometimes I think it's taking everything Jack's got not to cry about it. Movie starts at eight-twenty."

And then he left Joq to it to go and get changed.

Yes, movie night, this was good.

Doesn't this feel good? he asked himself as he got changed.

Yes, it did, he nodded to himself.

"George sees each of us as individuals and then puts us together like a single organism that works. Sure, I'm a valuable piece, but you're playing to lose if you build an entire team around one player. George doesn't do that favourites stuff like you do. He knows all of us, and he values all of us. We all feel it, and we all respect him because of it. It's not fake, it's real. He's a bloody brilliant coach, and I'm honoured to play for him."

George was in bed when he listened to Finn end his point with that little speech and he had to swallow.

The conversation moved on—thank God for Old Mac classing this shit up and making some decent points—and George felt a rush of gratitude for Finn. He looked at him on screen when the shot flashed back to him—he was calm if a little red, breathing incrementally faster, which was only really noticeable because George knew him so well—and George's heart felt warm.

He gripped his phone. What he was feeling had nothing to do with Finn personally. He was just beyond grateful to have a player come out in support of him so wholeheartedly. And he could tell Finn said all of that as a player, not as a guy in George's bed, but as a guy who played for George.

The show finished up and he fired off a text.

Thanks.

He got a thumbs up in return.

You did good, you looked good.

He got a smiley face and an eggplant.

George chuckled, got up, got ready and went downstairs.

Joq was sitting by the coffee machine.

"Oh, hey," George said. "You're up early."

He went to the fridge and got his stuff—water, smoothie—went to pack his training bag.

"Couldn't sleep," Joq replied. He sounded off.

"Hmmm," George wondered what was up with him but he didn't have time to get into it, so he just said, "Thought you were gonna fall asleep in the cinema."

He zipped up his training bag, mentally went through his morning checklist—his keys and phone were on the table near the door, he'd already put his case and laptop bag at the door—he was good to go.

Joq huffed a laugh but it sounded forced. George just didn't have time. He was about to leave when Joq said, "I caught the footy show, with Finn."

George shouldered his bag and frowned. "Did you come to bed at all?"

"Have you seen it?" Joq asked, ignoring the question.

"Uh, yeah," George replied—literally thirty minutes ago—he ran a hand through his hair. "Thought he did well. Those things always suck, you know that."

"You didn't think he was a bit, you know..." Joq said with an inflection in his voice that told George he should know what Joq meant.

Maybe George did, but he didn't think so, and he felt uncomfortable criticising Finn.

He raised an eyebrow. "A bit what?"

Joq shook his head like he was done with George's bullshit. "You know, George, come on," he got up and refilled his coffee, every line of his body defeated.

"I reckon you're gonna have to tell me," George said anyway, because he had a good idea what Joq was implying and he didn't agree, not this time.

George watched Joq as he glanced at him—Joq searched his expression, really checked in with those icy blue eyes; they'd thaw when he knew you, liked you, was willing to let you in. George always liked that about him—he was closed until he let you in, so when he did, it made you feel special.

He liked it a lot less right now as Joq turned, his expression shuttering as he leaned against the bench and sipped his coffee. "It was a bit much, he might want to tone it down."

Fucking seriously? George thought. Finn was publicly supporting him. It was exactly what George needed—the highest profile player in the competition this season coming out in support.

"After all the shit I've had thrown at me this season," he said to Joq, "I reckon having my star player come out in support is a good thing. I'd have thought you'd agree."

Joq looked at him like he was insane, which George was getting used to, but he was not prepared for his words. "I might if you weren't fucking him."

George was taken aback. "What's that got to do with it?"

"Really?" Joq asked, bewildered and belligerent.

"Yeah, really," George hoisted his bag up his shoulder and prepared to leave. "We can separate this stuff," he finished because that was absolutely true.

"Really," Joq said sarcastically.

George shook his head, smiled as he thought about training this week; after all the drama, they were still player and coach on the field. Sure, Finn might be his favourite thing to look at on said field, but George did his job and Finn did his.

"Yeah, really," he said to Joq and hoped it'd reassure him. "Look, I gotta go, I'll call you when we get there," he came over and kissed Joq's temple. "You're reading too much into shit," he said quietly against his skin.

Joq sighed, his whole body sagging with it. "Yeah, maybe," he said, his voice whistling over George's collarbones.

"Yeah, definitely. Finn's got a good eye for the game and even if we weren't, you know," George moved away—he couldn't say it, couldn't cheapen it and couldn't embellish it—"I'd be interested in what he thinks."

"He should still tone it down," Joq muttered.

And George had enough. "Christ, why?"

"'Cos you don't want to be out!" Joq exploded at him.

George recoiled at the words and at Joq—he never lost it, never. He was so calm, always. He hated that this had upset him so much but he had no clue how to make it better.

"I really don't think that's gonna happen," he said quietly after a minute. He really didn't. "I gotta... Don't worry about that, alright?"

"I'm just trying to protect you," Joq said into the weird space between them. And George got that; hell, twelve years Joq had been in this bunker with him and done everything right to keep them secret. But George really thought Joq's fears were misplaced on this one.

"I know," he said and he wanted to say more, but he had to go. "I'll talk to you later."

He left and felt off-kilter the whole way in.

The room was amped when he walked in and it was good—everyone ready to fly, pumped up to take Sydney.

He jogged up to his office to get his notebook, clocked the time, and decided he had a minute.

He pulled out his phone, pulled up Joq's number, hit call.

"Hello?" Joq sounded surprised.

"Hey. Just wanted to call before we left," he said brusquely. He didn't have much time.

"Oh, okay," Joq replied, still surprised but chiller than he was earlier. "You good?"

"Yeah, all good. Just…" he shook his head, "thought that was kinda shitty this morning."

"What was?"

"That conversation."

"Yeah," Joq breathed like he was relieved. "Well, maybe I'm reading too much into it—

"You are," George cut him off and told him firmly—he was sure of it.

"But," Joq went on forcefully, "I meant what I said, I'm just trying to protect you."

George shook his head again and smiled. "And I appreciate it, but, and I can't believe I'm the one saying it this time…"

He smiled wider—it was actually nice being on the other side of this for once. "But you're being paranoid," he finished.

Joq didn't say anything, but George could hear him breathing down the line.

"Joq?" he asked finally.

"Yeah, yeah, I'm here, sorry."

"Just, go have some fun while I'm away, okay?" George hoped Joq actually did, more than usual.

Joq snorted and it made George smile.

"You too, I guess," Joq muttered.

George sobered at that; he didn't want to discuss that with Joq. He sighed. "I gotta go. We're good, yeah?"

"Yeah," Joq said. "Call me from the hotel."

"I will. Later."

"Bye."

By the time George got off the bus at the airport, went through check in and waited at their gate, he was wondering if maybe Joq was right—maybe he should be more paranoid. All the guys seemed to be looking at him, then quickly glancing away.

He *was* being paranoid. How on earth anyone could go from Finn publicly supporting him to '*they must be fucking!*' was insane.

He excused himself from the huddle he was in with Kurt and Todd and went to the bathroom to get some privacy and take a breather.

He felt Finn behind him, didn't even need to look to know it was him.

He went into the men's room, checked the stalls were all empty, listened to Finn's footfalls on the tiles behind him, and then wheeled on him.

Finn's hands went up, but George could already see it in his face—it was something, it was something bad.

30

♥

Finn's hands went up. "I'm not gonna jump you," he said wildly.

It broke the tension and George snickered, but he still looked hunted.

It was in his voice too when he asked, "What's going on?"

Finn dug his phone out of his pocket, tapped it, pulled up the article and handed it over.

"Dropped this morning. Another list. You're on it," Finn did his best to just state the facts, but he was angry. And worried. He wouldn't have cared if it was him, but George was so bloody private he kept himself shut up in a closet with a boyfriend who fucked around on him in exchange. And no matter how many times George said it wasn't like that, it bloody well was as far as Finn was concerned. George was a romantic partner kind of guy—what fool wouldn't see fucking other dudes would hurt him?

George was scanning it. He muttered the name of the publication. Finn nodded—London edition, but it was a mainstream masthead.

George shook his head and handed the phone back. He was putting his best stoic face on it, but Finn saw he was rattled, probably mentally going through all the looks he'd gotten that morning and re-examining them.

"Thanks," he said and went to leave.

Finn stopped him with a hand on his chest.

George stilled and met Finn's eyes.

Finn splayed his fingers and pressed down, dropped his eyes to his hand over George's heart. "They can't touch you here," he repeated George's words back to him, flicked his eyes up and met George's watching him back. "Not unless you let them."

George smiled then, a real smile, a grateful smile, a smile like the young boy in him was peeking around the clouds of the scared man he'd become.

"Thank you," he said and placed his hand over Finn's on his chest.

"'S alright," Finn said stupidly.

George cracked a lopsided grin. "C'mon, I better face the looks now I know what it's about. At least it's not—

He stopped abruptly. He squeezed Finn's hand and then tugged him to follow. He let go as they stepped into the throngs of people meandering up and down the tunnels.

"At least it's not?" Finn asked from beside him as they walked.

"Nothin'," George said, his smile gruff but warm. "It's really nothing. And really," he bumped Finn, "thank you."

"Ah geez, it was nothing, I just hate the thought of you feeling like shit about this of all things," Finn said because it was true—it bothered him that George seemed to, if not hate, then not fully like, the fact he was gay.

"I don't feel like shit about us," George said quietly and seriously.

Finn shook his head. "Good to know," he answered, mirroring George's tone, "but I meant about liking the 'D' in general."

George cracked up for real and Finn smiled at him, pleased.

They re-joined the guys and every time Finn looked over at George, he saw he was smiling for real, at ease, his head lifting to meet Finn's gaze as if he could feel it on him, and it made Finn duck his head and smile for real too.

31

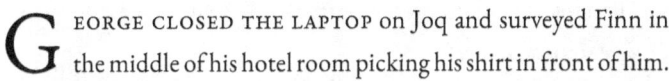

GEORGE CLOSED THE LAPTOP on Joq and surveyed Finn in the middle of his hotel room picking his shirt in front of him.

He snorted a laugh at him. "Where're you going you need something fancy? You boys finally discover there's life beyond going out for soy lattes?"

Finn laughed and shoved him gently. "Shut up. For your information, Skelly booked us a private room at some bar on The Rocks."

"Private room, eh?" George rubbed Finn's head. His touch slowed as he ran his fingers gently down the side of his face and Finn leaned into it.

Right, shirt.

George stepped back.

"I've got the blue button up?" He knew it'd look perfect with Finn's eyes, but he wasn't going to come out and say that.

"Yeah, nice. Thanks," Finn replied.

George could hear him unbuttoning his shirt behind him.

He focused on the suits and shirts he'd hung up when they arrived earlier and pulled out the shirt. He turned to see Finn pulling the last cuff down and tossing the shirt on the bed.

Christ, every time, George thought, and hid his reaction to Finn's washboard abs, the cut of his hips, the expanse of tan skin. He'd touched, sucked, and kissed every inch of Finn by this point and it still did him in, every time.

"Here," he said and handed it over.

"Thanks," Finn took the shirt, his finger stroking over George's in a quick caress, like the ones he did when they were out in public and George handed him the ball, handed him a water bottle.

George cleared his throat.

Finn smiled, crooked and disarming, and pulled on the shirt. He was looking down, doing the buttons up from the bottom when George stepped closer.

Finn glanced up from under the fall of his hair.

When George leaned in to kiss him, Finn craned the last inch to meet him. Their lips met hesitantly, and yet it had already started to feel familiar. The burning desire was there, but so was the comfort of knowing what Finn felt like, wanting so much more of it, knowing more was coming once they got going.

George pulled away and focused on the buttons. He did up Finn's shirt, ran his hands up his arms, and rested his palms on his shoulders.

"You better go," he said.

"Yeah," Finn breathed.

George pressed forward for another kiss.

Finn kissed him back and pushed for more.

George broke away.

"Have fun," he said.

"Yeah," Finn stepped back. "Later."

He headed for the door, his step stuttering.

"Thanks for the shirt," he said and then disappeared out the door with a soft click.

George groaned, sat down on his bed, and dropped his head into his hands.

He needed to review the Sydney game. He needed to go over his pre-game remarks. He needed to decide whether or not to play Lacy forward or use him to tag Guido.

There was a soft knock on his door.

He lifted his head and got up.

He opened the door and Finn barrelled in, kissing him hard before the door had even closed. George wrapped him up, pulled him in, kissed him back and took his weight as Finn pressed him back against the wall.

"I cancelled," Finn pulled away to say against George's lips.

"No, you've gotta see your—

"I'll see them all summer," Finn said. The rest of that left unsaid—*but I won't see you, not for months.*

George spun them, pressed Finn against the wall and deepened the kiss.

By the time George had Finn naked and under him, his dick rock hard as it slid over Finn's abs, his fingers sliding in and out of him leisurely and loudly with the lube, Finn's mouth panting wetly against his own, George felt his mind finally catch up with a decision his heart had made a long time ago.

Possibly years ago, when he was watching the draft and a few texts were exchanged.

He pulled his fingers out and rested his forearms on the pillow beside Finn's head, kept his knees outside Finn's hips so he hovered. He could feel Finn's warmth, but they weren't touching.

"Finn," he started and his voice shook.

Finn's gaze sharpened on him.

God, George thought as he stroked his thumbs over Finn's cheekbones, he was beautiful—and not just physically, though he was certainly that; but in his honest expressions, his hurts that he wore openly and angrily, in how much he cared about his people, in how he was the warm and relaxed sunshine in any room he was in.

"Are you..." George cleared his throat and tried again. He zoned in on Finn's pulse rabbiting wildly against his skin, kept his eyes there so he could get the words out. "Are you... with anyone else?"

"No," Finn replied on a breath, quiet but vehement. "No, never."

George met his eyes again, licked his lips. Finn tracked the movement, held his breath.

"After the season," George said into the space between them. "I'm, I haven't, Joq and I haven't, since ..."

Finn sucked in a breath.

George lined up his bare dick and Finn spread his legs.

"After the season?" George asked again.

"God, yes," Finn panted out, his smile radiant.

George pushed in and Finn angled his hips down to meet him.

They fucked deep and close, slowly, their lips lingering on every place they could reach while fused together. When George came hot and wet inside, Finn arched his back, let his eyes open and meet George's as he smiled, as he gasped, "Fuck, George, I—

George cut him off with a kiss, jerked him off until he was coming too.

He was wired after, Finn sleepy in his arms.

"Would you ever come out?" he asked. Finn had implied as much when they spoke about it when Finn came out to him, but George wanted to know what that meant.

"Course," Finn replied like it was nothing as he rubbed his face back and forth on George's pecs; his voice dreamy as he went on. "If I was with the right guy, I'd never hide that." He dug his chin in and met George's eyes.

George watched him back. '...*the right guy.*'

Finn dropped his gaze. "I mean, if he wanted to as well," he mumbled.

George tightened his hold, kissed the top of Finn's head.

Later, as Finn slept beside him, and George traced his fingers up and down each knob on Finn's spine, he thought his heart would be pounding in anxious fear. It wasn't.

He was in love with Finn. He wanted to be with Finn. He didn't care who knew about that. And it was about time he did something about that.

He'd get to the end of the season first—a few more weeks plus finals—and he'd end it with Joq. It was painful—of course it was, Joq had been in his life for twelve years and it was foolish to think they could be friends after this—but he couldn't be with one man when he was in love with another.

George felt sure in his decision all the way through the rest of the trip, the flight, the milling around baggage claim and the debriefing.

Joq was idling on the curb, a ways down from the bus, and George got in and it was as if with that door closing, the air sucking in and forming the Joq-and-George bubble, within that, he started to waiver, started to wonder if he was about to make the world's hugest mistake.

Joq was in good spirits, pointing out all the highlights from the game and making suggestions for what could be worked on—"Don't ever use Lacy as a tag again."

George found himself laughing. He felt the recognisable rush of being at ease, of being home. "No, I know. He's bloody good at it but he's gonna get suspended for sure."

And by the time he was turning in, Joq staying up to watch the news, his heart was pounding, and he was anxious. He replayed every look Finn had given him since that morning when he rolled over and met George's eyes in bed, to the slightly pissed look he gave him when George left everyone at baggage claim to meet Joq.

A lot of that could still be a crush. Infatuation. Puppy love.

He might be in love with Finn, but was he going to blow up his life for a guy who might leave him in a month because he realised he could do better than this old man?

George reassured himself: nothing had been made concrete yet, nothing had even been said explicitly.

Just get to the end of the season, he told himself, it'd become clear what the best course of action was at the end of the season.

32

F INN FLOPPED DOWN ONTO his bed.

'*After the season?*'

He felt giddy.

After the fucking season, alright! He jumped up and went to his fridge where he had the schedule pinned. He ticked off the weeks with his fingers.

He wondered what they'd do. Would George maybe want to come home with him for a few weeks? After George met his mum and Sophie as Finn's boyfriend, they could rent a house, one of the big places with the floor to ceiling windows on the edge of the rainforest, overlooking the ocean—George could press him up against the glass and fuck him while they watched the sun rise.

Finn laughed, shook his head.

But then he remembered George leaving him at the baggage carousel. He saw Joq idling down the road, his expression difficult to discern behind the sunglasses but probably blank or chill.

Finn wanted to grab George and beg him to come home with him instead. If they were going to be together, why was George going home with Joq? And what were they doing right now?

Finn looked out his little kitchen window at the trees, watched the street where a couple walked by with a little dog.

George said they hadn't—at least, that's what Finn thought he meant, but what if he was wrong?

If George did anything with Joq from this moment on, Finn didn't know if he'd ever forgive him. It was petty maybe, but George was his. He didn't get why he couldn't just be his now.

Things were totally normal at training, which Finn was more grateful for than he knew he would be. It was calm, fun, and professional. He grinned at George when he made a good play and George gave him an approving nod back.

Later in the week, George asked him to stay back and Finn readily agreed; he hoped George would want to come round, maybe have dinner, make out, go to bed.

Finn shook his head at himself as he shoved everything in his bag.

George came in after everyone had left. He looked nervous; that was the first thing Finn noticed and it made him nervous.

"What's up?" he asked casually, thankful they were in the locker room for this because it felt safer.

"Look, sorry, this is awkward, but... Joq wants, well, he reckons it'd be good if," George rubbed the back of his neck and Finn felt his heart start pounding. A smattering of shitty things raced through his mind: Joq reckoned it'd be good if Finn broke up with George; Joq reckoned it was cool if George and Finn were together if he could join them and they could be poly; Joq reckoned George should break up with Finn.

"Dinner?" George asked.

"Sorry," Finn shook his head; he hadn't heard anything George just said.

"No, I'm sorry, it's just, I've been with Joq a long time and if we could all get along that'd be... even though I know, fuck," George shook his head; he looked defeated.

"Dinner?" Finn asked because he thought that's what this was about.

"Yeah, Joq's asked if you want to come round for dinner again, so, I get it if—

"No, that's fine?" he asked. It really wasn't fine, but he didn't like how fucked up George seemed over it. He could deal with Joq for one more evening if it meant George was okay. So long as they didn't touch. Or kiss. Or talk to each other. Or basically interact at all.

Fuck, what had he agreed to?

"Thank you," George said in his gruff way, which meant he was grateful, beyond grateful, and Finn knew he'd have to suck it up.

Not long to go now.

He smiled and George smiled back and gripped his wrist, squeezed, and let go.

"I've got a meeting, but if you get a car, I'll be like thirty minutes behind you," George said.

Finn didn't like the idea of being alone with Joq, but alright. "Alright," he smiled again. "Then maybe after the Freo game?"

"Definitely," George grinned.

"Oh, shit, I'm catching up with Jack, but maybe you could come and then after?"

George shook his head, but he was still smiling. "Alright, for you, I'll make the effort with fucking Jack."

Finn beamed. "Fuck, yeah, and definitely after?"

George started walking backwards, his smile turning sly. "Finnegan, there is no universe in which I am not fucking you senseless after."

Finn laughed. He wished he could run over there and kiss George senseless right now.

But George winked and disappeared out the door.

33

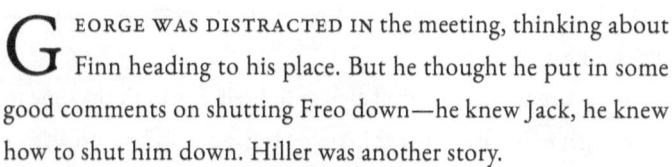

G EORGE WAS DISTRACTED IN the meeting, thinking about Finn heading to his place. But he thought he put in some good comments on shutting Freo down—he knew Jack, he knew how to shut him down. Hiller was another story.

As he drove home, the nervous energy ramped up. Finn had texted him as the meeting ended, it was a nothing text: *I'm here, you be here soon?*

And George replied that he was on his way.

So Finn would already be there and everything would be fine—George was being ridiculous. He imagined Joq would've offered Finn a glass of the sem sav he liked and Finn would've declined, but accepted a low-cal beer. They were probably making small talk around the kitchen bench, there was nothing to worry about.

As George turned onto his street, he told himself again there was nothing to be nervous about. He wasn't sure anymore how this was all going to shake out—was he leaving Joq for Finn or wasn't he?—but he'd decided to put it out of his mind until after the season ended. He was sure the answer would become clearer then. But a part of him, a tiny, excited, hopeful part, knew he'd already chosen Finn. It was always going to be Finn and loving Finn meant blowing it all up. And he was finally feeling okay with that.

He pulled up at his gate and hit the open button, waited, and realised that's why he was so fucking nervous about this. He had to act normal in a situation that was anything but.

He parked, took a deep breath, looked up at his two-storey, white brick townhouse, the imposing figure it cut against the Melbourne winter sky, the warm lights from the living room, and had the strangest sensation that this wasn't his home. He thought of that Talking Heads song and an uncanny ripple went through him—how did he get here? And whose home was this? And was that his beautiful partner?

Okay, George, he huffed a laugh at himself, it wasn't the time to be losing it to some esoteric thinking. He got out and headed across the driveway. His boots crunched in the asphalt and then tapped quietly on the steps. He opened the front door, pushed inside and didn't hear anything, then he heard movement coming from the living room. He took a step, poked his head inside and balked.

Joq was leaning over Finn—one arm on the back of the couch with his head tilted down; he'd only need to move a fraction and he'd be kissing Finn—and Finn was flushed, breathing heavily. They hadn't seen George come in and George spoke without thinking.

"What the fuck?"

Finn startled back so violently he almost fell off the couch.

Joq leaned back and gave George an easy once over.

Finn got up. "It's not, George. It's not..." Finn's voice cracked at the end and then just stopped.

George didn't understand. He was furious—he was pretty sure he just walked in on... but that made no sense, that made absolutely no sense, Finn wouldn't do that.

"Finn?" he pleaded with him to tell him that's not what he just walked in on.

Finn looked like he was about to cry—his eyes were going red and his big body was cowering. Something was wrong.

George was about to go to him when Joq stood and planted himself between them. "Finn and I were just getting better acquainted. Right, Finn?" He said in the voice he used with his hook-ups—casual and sexy—and he looked over his shoulder and met Finn's eyes.

George couldn't see Finn's face but he got what Joq was suggesting and he still couldn't believe it—but why wasn't Finn denying it?

"I have to go," Finn said—his voice shook, but he sounded firm too.

"Probably a good idea," Joq replied, smooth and casual. "Some other time maybe."

And really, George thought it'd be better if Joq just hit him. There was no way, no fucking way.

Finn's eyes were on the carpet as he stumbled around the coffee table, and he wouldn't look at George as he made his way to the front door.

"Hang on," George said. He wanted some fucking answers. He wanted to know why Finn was so upset. "Finn, what's going on?"

Finn shook his head and kept his face covered with his hair—his whole body was trembling.

"Let him go, babe," Joq said from close behind him. "We didn't think you'd be back so soon."

And if George thought he'd been hit before, it was nothing like that—he felt like he'd just been shot. Finn was going to fuck around with Joq?

And he wasn't denying it? He wasn't fucking denying it. George heard Finn suck in a sharp breath but he didn't fucking deny it.

"No," he said to Finn as he went to him. "No, Finn. What's he... what..."

But Finn straightened, kept his head down, and George could hear his wet breaths; he could tell he was crying, and then he was opening the door and slamming out of the house.

"What the fuck was that?" he turned to Joq.

Joq shrugged, his casualness even more pronounced in counterpoint to Finn's devastation.

"Fucking around?" Joq said. "I dunno, it just kinda happened. Or started to."

"No," George shook his head. There was no universe in which Finn would cheat on him. "He wouldn't..."

Joq went into the living room and grabbed his laptop off the coffee table. "I'm sorry," he said, his tone heavy. "He did."

But there was just no way. "Did you..." He looked at Joq. Joq hooked up with a lot of guys—did he put some moves on Finn? "What did you—

"Tread carefully, George," Joq said, his tone turning cold. "You've known me a long time. You think I go around hitting on kids who don't want it?"

George watched him—in his white shirt and casual jeans, his classic features fierce but clear—and he knew Joq was right. George did know him. Joq would never hit on someone who didn't want it, and he read those cues better than anyone.

But that meant...

It was unthinkable.

"You're right, I'm sorry," he dropped his head because he just couldn't hold it up anymore—Finn had given Joq a sign? Why?

He heard Joq sigh heavily and go by him to head upstairs as he said something about dinner being ready.

Had George been right all along? Was Finn really just infatuated and ready to leave him for something better if better presented itself?

He just couldn't believe it.

And why was Finn so upset? If he was fucking another guy, why not own it? Or if he wanted to fuck another guy. The thought of it alone made George's heart ache in his chest, but he didn't think Finn was the kind of guy who'd hide it either. He'd own it. He'd own it embarrassingly sincerely and possibly even angrily, but he'd own it.

George lifted his head, he was angry, he felt like his heart was breaking, but his anger energised him. He grabbed his keys and slammed the door on his way out.

He thumped on Finn's door a few times.

There was no sound from inside, but George didn't know where Finn would go if not home.

He knocked a few more times.

Nothing.

He dropped his head against the wood and breathed in for a count of four, out for a count of five. His eyes stung. He couldn't remember the last time he cried.

He slapped his palm on the door and heard movement inside.

"Who is it?" Finn's voice drifted through the wood.

George sucked in a relieved breath. "It's me."

"George," Finn sounded far away.

"Can you let me in?" George asked after Finn didn't immediately do so or say anything.

He heard his footsteps coming closer and straightened, waited for Finn to open the door.

He didn't.

"I can't talk right now," Finn said right on the other side of the wood.

"What do you mean you can't talk right now? We have to talk. What was that, back there?" George asked. He still couldn't believe it, but, "You can talk to me, tell me the truth."

"I can't," Finn said and his voice broke. "Please, can you go away?"

George knew Finn was crying and he didn't fucking understand.

He pressed his hand against the wood. "Finn, please don't send me away. Please talk to me. I'm not mad."

He heard Finn plant his hand on the other side of the wood. George splayed his fingers.

"I'll talk to you tomorrow," Finn said, his voice rough.

"Why can't you talk to me now?" George murmured.

"Tomorrow, I promise," Finn replied. His voice was shaking.

"Okay, but I'm going to sit out here for a while in case you change your mind."

George expected Finn to tell him to go away; he didn't.

George could feel him on the other side of the door, heard him sliding down and sitting and so George did the same. He pictured their backs against one another through the wood.

George had so many questions and a very bruised heart, but his instincts told him not to push Finn right now—something wasn't right and George needed to be patient, to let Finn come to him.

"I've gotta go to bed," Finn said after a while.

"Are you sure I can't come in?" George asked.

Finn huffed a laugh, it sounded wet. "Yeah, sorry. Tomorrow," he finished, his voice airy. "Go get some sleep."

"I won't be able to sleep," George said.

Finn didn't reply but George could hear him getting up, moving to stand against the door. George did the same.

"George?"

"Yeah?"

Finn huffed a wet laugh. "Nothin', just glad you're still there."

"I can be here as long as you like... be better if you let me in, told me what's going on," he said.

Finn sighed on the other side. "Tomorrow."

George dropped his head on the door again. "Okay."

He heard Finn do the same, could hear him breathing through the wood.

"George?"

"Yeah?"

"Night," Finn said softly, his voice cracking.

"Jesus, Finn, just let me in," George replied.

"I gotta go to bed," Finn said his voice moving away. "George?"

"Yeah?" George asked.

"I think we gotta..."

George sucked in a sharp breath against what he knew Finn was about to say.

"No, Finn, we can talk about it."

"We can't," Finn said, his voice cracking. "We gotta end it."

"Why?"

But Finn didn't say anything else and after another hour, George had to accept that he'd gone to his bedroom. He'd talk to him tomorrow. If Finn wanted to end it, fine. But he needed to tell George what had happened, what was going on.

George felt lost when he got home. He went into the kitchen, braced his hands on the bench and dropped his head. If Finn was serious... then... it was over.

He heard Joq come into the room behind him and made himself say the words, test how they felt in his mouth. "It's over."

"What happened?" Joq asked. George could hear in his voice he was trying, and George appreciated it, he really did, but Joq was the last person he wanted to discuss it with, especially since what he felt for Finn would only hurt Joq.

But he shook his head and gave the only answer he had. "He wouldn't let me in."

Joq didn't say anything and George didn't blame him.

Eventually Joq said, "Sorry."

George dragged in a deep breath. That made him feel even worse. "No, I'm sorry," he looked up and out at the pool, thought about fucking Finn out there. "It was more than fucking. For me. It was unfair to you."

George's eyes felt wet.

"It's okay," Joq said calmly. "It's over now."

"It is," George replied and thought of Finn ending it, in his own way, tried to think it was better now than later, better than if George blew up his whole life for what was a passing fling for Finn.

He stood, went to the fridge, grabbed a beer and avoided eye contact with Joq. He'd deal with the fallout there, he would, but first, he thought as he crossed to the cabana and took a swig of his beer, he needed to try and process what the fuck just happened.

He sat, he drank, he got up and got more beers and drank some more.

His phone was ringing. He slapped at the coffee table, found it, held it over his face, blinked and then sat right up when he saw the contact for the club President.

"Jim?" he asked.

"Do you know what's going on with Flynn? He's put in a trade request; Sydney's made the bid," Jim heaved in a deep breath, "do you know about this? Can you talk to him?"

"He what?"

"Trade, Sydney, it's going through now, all I'm getting from a contact over there is something about mental health issues and wanted to get closer to his family," he sighed heavily. "Shit, Creed, did we know anything about this? The problems? This is gonna be a nightmare if we failed to get treatment."

George was stumbling up, casting around for his shirt, his pants. "I'll talk to him."

"Good, get him to reconsider, he's gonna be the new face. I just can't believe he'd make this call so suddenly. What the hell happened?"

"I'm on it," George said. "I'll call you back." He couldn't listen to any more of that.

He hit Finn's contact and cradled the phone between his shoulder and ear as he did his pants up.

"C'mon, Finny," he whispered desperately.

The call rang out. He tried again. Same result.

He went and pulled his boots on.

"Did he tell you?" Joq asked as he came downstairs.

"He won't take my calls," George replied and realised then it must've already been all over the news. He headed out.

George pounded on Finn's door.

Nothing.

A girl in workout gear jogged up the stairs with her little dog and looked at George banging on Finn's door.

"I think he left last night, like maybe midnight?" she said as she stopped at the door down the hall.

"Are you sure?"

"Yeah, I reckon it was around then. I was up 'cos I was watching the new season of *The Bachelor* and then I got in this fight on twitter about it. Then I heard his door slam and I got up and looked out and saw the taxi pull up and he was out there, like loading some cases into it," she was chewing gum as she talked—her jaws snapping in between her streaming monologue. She picked up the dog and held him at her chest. She was probably the same age as Finn. "Reckon he must've been going to the airport but he never said, normally he tells me," she blew out a bubble in her gum. It was absurd for a moment.

Then George caught up to what she said. "He tells you when he's going on the road?"

"Yeah, I water his plants," she replied, chewing away. "But he didn't say this time so I reckon he's either not going for long or gone for good. But even if he's going one night, he's got a temperamental fern in there," she nodded her head at his door, "so she always needs watering at least once a day. So he's probably getting them shipped? 'Cos like, he didn't ask me to water her."

Now George thought about it, Finn did have a lot of house plants.

"Can I give you my number and you let me know if he calls?" George asked.

She gave him a look like he was sketchy then. "You got his number?"

"Yes, but he's not taking my calls," George said desperately.

"Hmm," she unlocked her door, "then I reckon he doesn't wanna take your calls and I ain't getting in the middle of all that," she waved her finger up and down. "I seen and heard you two," she winked and then disappeared inside her apartment.

"Fuck," George said under his breath. And then he realised why he said it: not because someone knew he was gay and banging his rookie, but because he couldn't get in contact with him, even indirectly, and he was obviously already gone and not coming back.

In fact, the last thing he cared about was whether or not anyone knew about him being gay and them fucking like rabbits for months. He just wanted to see Finn in front of him. To hear his voice. He just wanted to talk to him.

It was evident after a day of heated meetings, attempts at negotiation with Finn's 'management', not the young man himself, Finn was gone, and he was not coming back.

In between the meetings, George tried to call repeatedly.

When it cut out after one ring in the late afternoon, George realised Finn had blocked him.

He was outside the conference room, leaning against the wall when it happened. It was difficult to put into words what that felt like—like all the wind had been taken out of his sails and his heart had plummeted to the deepest point in the ocean all at once.

As George walked inside, Joq stood from where he'd been watching the bullshit about it on TV.

"Did you speak to him?" he clicked it off and asked.

George shook his head. "He's gone."

"Whaddya mean he's gone?" Joq asked.

"He left last night," George said, exhausted. He couldn't do this with Joq, not right now. "Flew home."

"Fuck," Joq said on a breath.

That was the gist of it, George thought as he went upstairs. He went into the bathroom, turned the water on full blast and stripped. He stepped under the spray and felt it hit his shoulders; he placed his hands against the tiles and hung his head. He felt a ripping sensation in his chest, like something was breaking apart. It took an embarrassing second before he realised he was heaving, he was crying.

He stood like that for a long time.

By the time he turned the water off, he was drained all the way through and he did not feel better.

He pulled on pants and a shirt and got into bed.

He heard Joq come in some time later.

"Freo tomorrow," Joq said.

"Yep," George replied on autopilot and rolled over to face the wall. He was wide awake and he didn't sleep.

34

Freo destroyed them in the game the next day. George knew he should feel, well, anything about it. He didn't.

He'd walked into the locker room before the game and the conversation had turned down. He'd caught the scent of it though—confusion, concern, a fuck tonne of questions—and no one bothered to hide the manly hurt looks when they turned to George for answers.

"So, you've probably heard," he'd said and then couldn't bring himself to say more. He coughed, cleared his throat a few times.

"Did he say why?" Les asked, a desperate plea in his voice.

George hadn't realised it, but until Les asked that question, he'd been hoping one of them could tell him.

Instead of pretending all was well and he had all the answers, he decided to just come out and ask.

"I haven't spoken to him directly. I only know what his management said and that's all over the news. Has anyone spoken to him?" He was proud of himself for getting that out without his voice shaking.

"He won't answer," Les said.

The rest of the guys muttered similar versions of that. Except Lacy, who suddenly looked very busy with retying the laces on his boots.

"Lace?" George asked.

"Huh?" Lacy looked up, stood tall, jumped in place for a few beats. "Nope, haven't heard from him."

He was lying. George knew it. George knew Lacy knew he knew it.

Lacy gave him a look that said, *Don't push me on this.*

They'd been friends and teammates a long time, lot of respect and love there. For the first time, George felt like breaking it just so he could get some answers.

He punched out a breath, looked away, shook his head. "Right, Freo..." He gave the remarks he'd prepared, aware of Lacy watching him curiously the whole time.

But losing Finn had rattled them all the way through. *It wasn't just his play*, George thought as he followed the team down the tunnel after the thrashing, *it was him—he was a real team man, a warm heart at the centre of wherever he played. And now he'd gone and taken that heart and given it to Sydney without so much as a phone call.*

George caught sight of Jack coming down the tunnel beside him. Jack caught his eyes and smiled, looked like he was about to say hello. He was still the same old friendly-looking bastard, huge and shy, and for a split second George entertained talking to him because he knew Jack and Finn were friends. Maybe he'd spoken to Finn.

He broke the look without a word and went into their locker room. He caught the hurt look Jack shot him and he felt bad, but he just couldn't deal with that right now.

The team were slumped in defeat back in the room.

George sighed. "Fuck, guys," he said, not loudly, but everyone turned to look at him. He rubbed the back of his neck, twisted his mouth to the side. His chest still hurt from his breakdown the night before—he had an ache lodged in there, a deep, dull pain that seemed to throb in time with the laborious beating of his heart.

He looked around at the team and realised Finn had kind of broken their hearts too.

"I want everyone to take a few days, go do what you gotta do, okay?"

A murmuring of assent rippled through the room.

"Okay, see you on Tuesday," he left them to it.

He stopped at the bottle shop on the way home and got himself a carton of full-strength beer. When he arrived, he parked himself in the cabana by the pool and started drinking. He pulled up his thread with Finn and started rereading their messages. Unlike Finn, he hadn't created a file, he hadn't bothered to try to hide anything so he had the whole lot—from the first one at the draft to the last one where Finn had said he was at George's place and George replied that he'd be there soon.

He frowned at that last exchange for a second.

Why had Finn messaged him? George knew he was there. Did Finn want to get an idea how far away George was so he could fuck around on him?

But see, George just couldn't buy it. It was ludicrous. Something about the whole thing felt wrong and he couldn't put his finger on why.

He scrolled right to the top and read them all. He read them slowly, remembering each one—where he was, how his face had wanted to split into a grin every time his phone dinged. He got up to get more beer, then sat down and read the one he was on again but slower, reliving it.

He thought about the last time they'd fucked, how Finn had said, '*No, never,*' about other guys.

George felt that choking sound rising up again and shook himself. He hacked up nothing to make himself stop it.

He remembered Finn telling him how he'd hidden their messages in a folder, and George had been surprised, not that Finn had hidden them, but that he was keeping them too. George had thought at the time he was the only one who was hoarding them, revisiting them every now and then just to smile. And now, revisiting them like they were the only things he had left in the world.

He got to the end and paused over that exchange again.

I'm here, you be here soon?

Then George's reply: *on my way.*

No matter how many times he tried to splice it, he could not read into that the desire to know how long he had before George got there. It read how Finn always read—an endearing open-book who didn't realise how his honesty about where he put his heart caught George off guard every time, even in the most innocuous exchange.

'*No, never,*' he'd said so vehemently—his blue eyes shining, bright and alive, and the way he'd arched when George had pushed in, the way his tongue had darted out to delicately touch George's thumb when he rested it on Finn's bottom lip while he pushed inside, got as deep and close to him as he could.

Finn watched him the whole time, Finn never wavered in welcoming him in.

George shook himself and finished his beer.

He got another one, sat and spun his phone in his hands, stared at the water.

He knew what he had to do. He had to have a break with Joq. He'd move into the spare room. He got up, suddenly energised and charged up the stairs; he realised he was still in his winter coat but he didn't bother to take it off. He opened his drawers and pulled out underwear, socks, shirts, took it all in handfuls to the spare room. Then he did the same with his clothes, his shoes, and finally his toiletries—he picked them up in clumsy hands and dropped them all over the counter in the bathroom attached to the spare room.

He looked at the politely made bed, the clean bedding, the complete lack of personality to the space—washed and made nice since Scotty had stayed. He felt a tightness in him ease when he thought about coming in here at the end of every day. He didn't want Joq to see how he couldn't sleep. He didn't want to explain that he couldn't fuck, he couldn't function.

'*We gotta end it,*' Finn's broken voice on those last words; George replayed them now and sucked in a sharp breath. He went back downstairs, got another beer.

He finished that one and got another one.

He looked at the water shimmering, breaking the pool lights into fractured lines, and kept hearing it—'*We gotta end it.*'

"Hey," came from the other side of the pool and George startled.

He looked up and squinted at Joq standing there.

"Oh, Joq. Hey," he said.

"Havin' a party?" Joq asked, his head inclined towards the empties scattered around George's socked feet.

He realised then it was late and Joq must've gone out; George wondered idly if he'd hooked up with someone, if that's why he was coming home so late. He realised how thoroughly he didn't care anymore.

"You went out?" he asked.

"Obviously," Joq said, a little belligerently, a little drunk. He was flushed with it, his collar open and skin glowing with the red hue.

"Sorry," George shook his head, focused on his phone in his hands.

"You comin' to bed?" Joq asked and George couldn't think of anything worse; he was grateful he'd moved to another room. He needed to tell Joq, but he didn't have the energy.

He rubbed his eyes, shook his head.

"Look," Joq said. "I know Finn leaving sucks, but you'll rebuild. It'll be fine, maybe not this year, but you're a rookie too, you know? Just get through the season."

George started laughing. It was small at first, but then he was heaving with it—the season? His coaching gig? Who gave a shit, he thought hysterically.

"What's so funny?" Joq asked.

"Nothin', sorry," George met his eyes. "Nothin'."

Joq smiled at him; it was kind, inviting, like he really wanted to share the joke, like they'd always shared in each other's jokes.

What the hell, George thought.

"You think I give a shit about the season?" he asked.

"Well, yeah..."

"Look," George got serious. He needed to say this. "I know this is not fair to you, I know that. But I'm gonna need some time, okay? It wasn't... nothing."

Joq seemed to sober as he looked away, focused on the gardens, immaculately kept by the gardener Joq found and George contracted.

"I didn't mean for this to happen," he barreled on; now that he was on a roll, he needed to come out and say everything. "So, if you want out, I get it."

Joq looked back at him. "What're you saying? You want to break up?"

George shook his head because he didn't think he wanted that. "No, but I'm saying I get it if you do 'cos I'm asking for some time to, you know," he looked at his phone, "get over him."

"Are you still speaking to him?" Joq asked.

George flinched. "He blocked me."

A silence descended, broken by the palms swaying in the cold night breeze.

"Just," Joq said finally around a sigh like it was all too much, which was fair enough—George had no idea why Joq stayed with him normally, never mind now. "Let's talk after the season ends."

"Okay," George nodded along; he didn't think that'd help, but if he got hold of a little patch of stability that had to be good, but, "I've moved into the spare room, so, you can have some space while I..."

While he what? Got over losing the love of his life? He couldn't finish that sentence. And as Joq turned and went back inside without another word, he got the feeling Joq knew what the end of that sentence was and was done fucking hearing about it.

Fair enough, George thought and swigged on his beer, he'd be done with it too if he could be.

35

THE MOST IMPORTANT GAME of the season arrived: a win meant they finished at the bottom of the eight; a loss meant they were out of finals contention. They'd been top four before Finn left. Now they were reduced to this.

"Knock, knock," Lacy said from outside George's office door and came in without waiting for an answer. He was carrying two take-away coffees. "Here," he said and put it on George's desk.

He'd been doing this once a week since Finn left.

George eyed it, looked at Lacy, and wanted to ask, so bad, but—

"Drink your fucking coffee," Lacy said and left.

George cracked a smile and did as he was told.

They lost the game and that was it, season done. They still had games to play, but they were not going to be in the finals. The media cycle wound up but the wheel felt tired as it cranked along—*Losing Flynn Ruined Creed!*—and ran the same thing they'd been running since

Finn left: the presence of Finn hid the reality of how shit George actually was, obscured the fact he should never have been given the Head Coach gig.

George wanted to care, he really did, but he just didn't.

He looked at his players after the last loss and their looks mirrored his own feelings back to him, albeit muted—losing Finn over some "mental health" explanation they, rightly, called bull-shit on because they'd been messing around with Finn literally the day before, all season in fact, and the dude was a bastion of good health and sunshine vibes; not only that, but as Cary rightly put it, "Kid was an open book with all that psych shit, he'd have said."

George agreed. But how could he say: '*No shit, it's actually my fault, I drove him away because I wanted more and once he knew that, he ran.*'

Because what else could it have been?

There's just no way Joq would hit on Finn if he didn't get a clear sign.

And there's no way Finn would invite that unless he was trying to let George down without having to come out and say it.

But it made no sense.

And George had played this over in his head so many times.

He got home after the game, greeted Joq politely and then headed to his room. Because this is what they did now—carefully tiptoed around one another; George heart sore and Joq stoically enduring the latest pile of shit his boyfriend had dumped in his lap.

He'd get over it, he told himself firmly, once the season ended, he'd just... He breathed out and collapsed face first onto the bed. He felt like Finn when he did it and it made him laugh—Finn did shit like that, fun shit like dramatically throwing himself on beds.

George rolled onto his back, his smile splitting his face when his thoughts caught up with him. The smile fell away and he had to rub his chest, rub at the ache that just wouldn't abate.

The season ended and Jim took him aside and assured him he'd be getting another offer, and George went home and decided it was time to make a fresh start.

He found Joq in the kitchen, sipping a wine while he watched a video with a recipe and followed along.

"Hey," George said.

"Hey," Joq replied but didn't look away from what he was doing with a garlic clove.

"You still thinking Thailand for the break?" George asked.

Joq looked up. "Yeah?" His whole face lit up and George felt like an absolute prize fucking asshole because it was clear how much what he was doing was dragging Joq down with him.

"Yeah, I think a holiday would do us good if you still want? I mean, I get it, I've been—

"No, yeah, that'd be great. I hadn't booked, but yeah, I will," he smiled and immediately brought up a different page on his tablet. It looked like flights. Right, because it'd be December, busy, and they needed to book that shit yesterday.

George smiled back, although he didn't feel it. But he remembered what he got taught when he first started playing in the juniors' farm team that'd lead to the league, and he felt like an imposter: fake it until you make it.

"Cool" he said and went to go lie down.

Baby steps.

George was still lying on his bed the next morning when his phone rang.

Lacy.

"Lace? Shouldn't you be—

"Not now, I'm gonna send you a link—open it and then fix it."

He hung up.

George sat up. His phone pinged. Lacy's name, a message with just a link.

George opened it, the page loaded and as George took in what he was looking at he felt his heart stop in his chest.

He sucked in a shocked breath.

His heart restarted and his breaths went shallow and frantic.

A wave of feelings hit him all at once—hurt, seething jealousy, anger at the privacy invasion. Heartbreak.

It was Finn—no doubt about it—he looked really drunk and he had some burly guy pushing him up against a wall, it looked like a nightclub; the guy's lips were fused to Finn's neck, their bodies wound tightly together; Finn's eyes were red and bleary as he looked unseeing into a phone camera.

George read the caption: *And that was before he got railed in the bathroom...*

George's heart seized again.

Fuck, he couldn't breathe, he couldn't be here, he couldn't be anywhere.

He stumbled out of his room, down the stairs and into the kitchen. He still had his phone clenched in his hand. He heard a tinny sound coming from the living room and went in, saw Joq in front of him on the couch, heard what sounded like a woman telling people to "Fuck off!" coming from his phone.

George came up behind the couch and saw the video. Finn trying to leave his home, his mother and sister on either side of him, and Finn's face. He was stoic, yet terrified. But George knew him so fucking well; as he watched Finn's eyes drop, watched him shrink in on himself—he was ashamed.

He made a guttural sound, completely out of his control. That was his Finn and he was hurting.

"He'll—

"Don't," George cut him off. He went for the door; don't tell me he'll be fine, he thought viciously as he pulled on his boots, his coat, grabbed his phone and keys. He left and headed straight for the airport. All of his own feelings were shoved aside—he needed to see Finn, hold him, tell him it was all going to be okay.

This wasn't about him anymore; this was about protecting Finn.

He'd once thought he'd launch a thousand ships for Finn; well now he reckoned he'd slay a thousand reporters if they so much as looked at him wrong, and if he found the shit cunt who took the picture and posted it online, he'd kill them too.

He got his phone on speaker and made a few calls: a one-way ticket to Byron Bay leaving in two hours; Finn's address from HR; and Lacy.

"Yeah?" Lacy answered.

"What did he tell you?"

Lacy didn't need clarification; George knew Lacy knew he meant when Finn left.

"Are you going to see him?" Lacy asked.

"On my way now," George replied, weaving in and out of shit drivers on the highway.

"Good. He just messaged me when he left that's all."

"Yeah? And?"

"And he said 'Take care of George'."

"That's it?"

"That's it," Lacy said. "But that's kind of everything, isn't it?"

"Yeah," George breathed out. "Thanks."

"No dramas, just take better care of him this time, eh?"

"I'll do my best."

"Good, I gotta go—coke to snort, cocks to ride!"

"Jesus, Lacy, too much information," George huffed.

"Ah, like you don't know all about it."

Thankfully he hung up before George could reply.

Adrenaline got him on the plane, Finn's address and a car from the airport booked on arrival. Now he needed to think about what he was going to say.

His palms tingled. His chest felt lighter.

He had no idea what he was going to say, but the first thing he was going to do was crush Finn in the world's biggest hug.

And then he was going to punch him for fucking another guy.

He was done pretending it was okay for either of them to be doing that.

He was done pretending.

36

♥

GEORGE'S CAR PULLED UP at the address he'd been given. There were media vans there, which surprised him, but maybe shouldn't have.

"Go down the driveway," he said to the driver.

"Gonna be hell to reverse out," the guy said.

"I'll give you a hundred bucks to go down the driveway."

"Sure," the guy said, "can make the turn, no problem."

George didn't actually care if the media saw him at this point—he was past all that—but he wanted to get a read on what Finn was okay with before he made any bold moves.

He pulled his collar up and turned his body against the window, sunnies on. As they descended the steep driveway flanked by a thick, luscious, rainforest line of trees, he saw a few reporters stir, but the car disappeared before anyone could react.

"This'll do," George said and tapped out the tip. Then he got out.

He fiddled with his collar again and realised he was wearing the clothes he slept in, he had nothing on him except his wallet and his phone, and he hoped he didn't smell bad.

Well, there was nothing for it now, he thought as the guy reversed back out easily, and all he was doing was trying to avoid his nerves.

But Finn was in there and he'd walk through fire to see him, so beating back some nerves was nothing. As he made his way to the front door, he wondered why he didn't just come here straight away when Finn left.

He knocked.

He heard rapid footsteps and a voice he recognised as Sophie's shouting, "If that's a reporter get the fuck off my property or I'll call the fucking police!"

"It's George," he called back.

The door swung open.

"George," she breathed out. "Oh, thank God, come in, come in."

George stepped inside. "Is Finn—

She slammed the door and cut him off. "What the fuck happened?" she demanded. God, she looked so much like Finn it was uncanny—she was just the female version—but her energy was completely different. Where Finn was gentle sunshine, she felt like a storm being unleashed.

"I don't know," George said gruffly. "But if he'll see me, maybe I can..."

She was shaking her head, her blonde hair flying all over the place. "I don't mean with this latest fuckery, I mean when he left. What happened? One minute he was all 'George this, George that' and so happy. And the next, he was flying home in the middle of the night crying his fucking eyes out. Mum said he hardly leaves his room anymore and the one time he did 'cos the Sydney crew convinced him, he goes on a bender and lets some fucking asshole fuck him. Finn doesn't do that," she spat at the end. She was really mad—and that was like Finn. Sunny until he got mad.

But all he could think about was what she was saying—he left to come here to join Sydney and he's been depressed? Why? What the fuck happened?

"Is he here?"

"Of course, but you have to make him talk to you, he won't tell us what happened," she went ahead and George followed. She stopped at the entry to the hallway. "He's the door at the end, just bang on it a few times in case he's asleep—he sleeps all the time now," she said, emphasising it bitterly, but her voice cracked like she was going to cry.

Jesus Christ.

"I'll talk to him," he said and went to Finn's door.

He stood there for a second and caught his breath. He knocked softly.

"Yeah?' Finn asked.

"Can I come in?" he asked.

"George?"

He heard movement from inside and opened the door.

Finn was rolling over in bed, swinging his legs over the edge as George pushed the door open and stepped inside. A little white dog sniffed his legs, tail wagging, and distantly he heard Sophie calling, "Stimpy" and the dog went by him, but all George's attention was fixed on Finn.

Objectively, Finn looked terrible—his eyes were red rimmed, lifeless, and flanked with shadows so dark, he looked like he'd been punched or turned into a creature of the night; his hair was a chaotic mess; and his shirt and pants were old, worn and tragic.

But he was still Finn, and George's breath caught at seeing him again—he was magnificent, a carving of muscle in repose with his perfect skin and gorgeous face, a loveliness on the edge of his bed that encased the best heart George had ever known.

"Can I come in?" he asked again, his voice gruff.

"George," Finn stood, "what're you, why're you... You're here."

George shut the door behind him, watched Finn for a moment; then he crossed straight to him and swept him into his arms in a bone crushing hug. God, but that felt good. As their chests ground together and Finn's arms came up to grip him back, his head tucking into George's shoulder, breath fanning his throat and pressing in, George felt all his pieces come back together.

"Fuck, I missed you," he whispered against Finn's hair, kissed him there.

Finn squeezed him harder.

George crushed him closer and held on. Finn seemed content to do the same.

But then Finn was wriggling out of his hold. "You have to go," he said.

George let him out of the hug but gripped his biceps. "I'm not going anywhere until I know you're okay."

Finn's head was down and he wouldn't meet George's eyes. His head was shaking. *He* was shaking George realised. "If he knows you're here..."

"Who?"

"You have to go, I'm sorry, you have to go," Finn shook George off and stepped back.

"I'm not leaving," George said.

"Please, if he knows you're here," Finn's voice was shrill and terrified.

"Jesus, Finn, who? What's going on? I'm not leaving until you tell me what happened. Why did you leave?"

Finn looked up at him and he was a picture of shame.

George couldn't stand it. He dragged him in again.

And Finn just broke. His sobs started small and then he was heaving with it, holding George tightly and saying he was sorry over and over again.

George had no idea what he was apologising for—fucking that bruiser? Leaving? Something that happened with Joq?—but he held him, rubbed his back, reassured him again and again that he had nothing to be sorry for and George wasn't going anywhere.

Finn eventually petered out, rubbed his face against George's shirt.

George huffed a laugh. "I'm gonna need to borrow a shirt."

Finn cracked a smile—George could feel it against his chest.

He slipped his fingers under Finn's chin and made him lift his head.

"I'm not leaving until I know you're okay," he watched Finn take that in.

"I'm trying to protect you," Finn whispered.

George wanted to ask him what he was protecting him from exactly, but that seemed to set him off, so he tried a different tact.

"Okay, but nobody knows I'm here," he answered Finn's earlier assertion.

Finn sagged in ... relief? What the fuck was he afraid of?

"Okay," Finn said more to himself. "Okay, do you want something to drink?"

George smiled at him, then he leaned down to kiss him.

Finn looked surprised, but when George's lips brushed his he kissed back like nothing could've stopped him.

George broke the kiss way sooner than he wanted to. "Hi," he said against his lips.

"Hi," Finn smiled into it.

But then he pulled away, went for the door, something still off. "I'll get us something to drink, eat, where's your stuff?"

"You're lookin' at it," George said and ran a hand through his hair.

Finn opened his mouth. Closed it.

"I saw," George waved his hand at the front of the house. "I got a flight."

"Why?" Finn breathed out.

"Because if anyone's gonna hound you, they're gonna come through me to fucking do it," he replied.

Finn blushed, shook his head, smiled and looked at his feet. "Okay."

"Okay?"

Finn looked up, met George's eyes, and for a split second the sunshine-Finn he knew and loved peeked through the clouds and smiled at him.

But then he dropped his gaze, went back in on himself and left the room.

"Jesus," George said on a breath. What the fuck was going on? George got the distinct feeling someone had threatened Finn—but who? And why? And why couldn't he ask George or, hell, anyone on the team for help?

He stood there, feeling helpless, until Finn came back with two bottles of cider in one hand, a bag of seaweed chips and some kind of dip in the other.

"I can cook, but will this do for now?" he asked.

"Of course," George took the drinks and allowed Finn to keep the careful distance between them. "I can cook, or order us something too. Are you hungry?"

"I think I should be asking you that," Finn smiled sadly and sat on his bed.

George looked at the chair and then thought, fuck it, he hadn't touched Finn in over a month, he was cuddling.

"Scoot over," he said and Finn hesitated but did as he was told.

George sat on the edge of the bed against Finn's hip, placed the ciders on his bedside table dressed with a sarong and piled high with surf magazines; he pulled his coat and boots off, brought his legs up, stretched them out and then pressed his whole body alongside Finn's. When Finn didn't push him off, he leaned in for more, slipped an arm over Finn's waist and rested his head against his chest.

Finn brought his hand up and brushed his fingers through the strands of George's hair.

"No one knows I'm here," he said again into the material of Finn's shirt.

"Okay," Finn said again softly, his grip tightening and releasing in George's hair.

George breathed in his scent—a hint of sweat, musk, all Finn—and closed his eyes.

"Don't you want your drink?" Finn asked, his fingers still carding through George's hair.

"In a minute," he said into his shirt and tightened his hold.

"George," Finn breathed out as he bent his head to kiss George's hair.

George pulled him closer; he didn't sleep, but he finally relaxed.

"You won't tell anyone you're here?" Finn asked after a while.

"No one," he frowned. "Oh. Lacy knows."

"Lacy's alright," Finn ran his finger over George's ear. "But no one else."

"Okay," George said and sank into the worn material of his shirt, felt the warmth of his skin under it. He needed to know what the fuck happened, who'd scared the shit out of Finn so thoroughly, and he wasn't leaving until he had the answer.

In the meantime though, he dragged his fingers up and down Finn's side in a caress, synced his breaths with Finn's and felt himself let go and recharge at the same time.

"I need a shower," George said. Judging by the light outside the closed blinds in Finn's room, he guessed it was late afternoon.

"Oh, course, I'll get you some towels," Finn tried to get up.

George tightened his hold, rested his chin on Finn's sternum and looked up. "Come with me?"

Something flickered in Finn's eyes—guilt, George was sure it was guilt—George squeezed him harder.

"I don't care what you've done," he said and frowned. "Well, that's a lie, I want to find that guy you fucked and kill him, but I'm being a hypocrite, so I'm just saying, I don't care about that if you're thinking you can't join me 'cos of that."

Finn was shaking his head, the guilt multiplying to a weird shame all over his body. "I barely remember it, just flashes."

"He raped you?" George went to sit up.

Finn tugged him in, lips twisting to the side. "No, I was just really drunk," his voice dropped to a husk and his eyes went to the bedspread. "If I can't have you, I just don't care anymore."

George had to clear his throat a few times, try to swallow. "Okay," he said gruffly—it really wasn't okay, he was so jealous he wasn't sure what to do with it, and he couldn't bear Finn treating himself like that. "But it's not like you're seeing this guy ... Are you?"

Finn laughed. His body shook and it was the best thing George had heard since he arrived. He was almost glad for the burly fucker. Almost.

"I don't even know his name," Finn smiled. "And he left me sore, real jack hammer—that, I remember."

George groaned and shoved his face into Finn's stomach. "I'm tryin' here, I really am, but too much information. I already want to kill him for touching you, never mind touching you badly."

Finn shook George's shoulder. "Yeah, well, now you know how I feel." He said it softly, not a hint of malice in his voice; it broke George's heart anyway.

He sat up and Finn let him. "Christ, Finn," he ran a hand over his head. "I'm so sorry, if I had it all to do over again, I would do it all differently. I'd be honest, I'd just be with—

"I get it!" Finn cut him off and shuffled forward to sit next to him. "But this is why you can't stay. Please George," Finn grabbed his hand, "trust me on this, it's not safe if you stay."

George managed, barely, to bite his tongue on demanding Finn tell him what the fuck he was on about.

Instead, he asked, as calmly as he could, "Not safe how? Is someone going to hurt me?"

Finn dropped his eyes. "Yes," he whispered. "They've got..."

"What have they got?" George pulled Finn closer with his hand.

But Finn shook his head and pulled away. "I'll get you some towels," he crossed his room and added, "I think there's a red eye to Melbourne."

That's good, Finn, he thought, *but I won't be fucking on it.*

When Finn returned, eyes downcast, and said he'd show him where the bathroom was, George got up and followed.

Finn held his arm out as if to say, 'there you go, all yours,' his body preparing to turn and leave George to it.

George crowded him against the door. "No one knows I'm here," he said again.

Finn sucked in a breath, and George could see his pulse in his throat pounding, just from that, just the invitation—George got it, he was exactly the same.

"We shouldn't," Finn said. "If he finds out."

Who?!

"He won't," George whispered.

Finn lifted his face, his eyes searched George's—frightened, honest, turned on—and George saw the second his desire won and he kissed Finn and dragged him into the room, closing the door behind them.

The water pelted onto their backs in the wide shower recess—it was a beautiful space, done in the tropical style, huge and open—and they kissed desperately, hands touching everywhere, then their kisses went soft, and George traced the cut of Finn's abs, his hip bones.

"You still been workin' out," he said against his lips.

"At night, can't sleep," Finn replied and rested his head on George's shoulder.

George gripped his hip. "You need to eat more."

Finn nodded, his nose trailing up George's throat until his mouth found George's again and his, "Yeah," was lost in a kiss.

"Do you want me to drive you to the airport?" Finn asked once they were back in his room, sated and dressed in team tracksuit pants and clean shirts, Finn's eyes anywhere but on George.

George heaved a sigh and sat on the edge of Finn's bed. He clasped his hands together and focused on them. It was dark out, and the lamp Finn had turned on made the room glow soft and warm.

"I'm not going anywhere," George said quietly but firmly.

"I can't tell you what happened," Finn said, his voice animating, frightened but impatient.

George was already nodding. "I know, I hear you. So, don't tell me," he glanced up, "but I'm staying anyway."

"But," Finn shook his head, he was still standing on the other side of the room, "if anyone finds out you're here..."

George shrugged. "They're gonna hurt me?"

Finn jerked his chin, eyes on the wall.

"So, they can fucking hurt me then, but I'm not leaving unless you want me to leave—

"I do—

"I mean, really want me to leave, not leave because you're scared, leave because you don't want me anymore," George found himself breathing hard at the end there, every line in his body tensed. If Finn didn't want him anymore then, okay, he'd deal, but by God, it'd fucking hurt.

Finn kept his gaze on the wall. He opened his mouth. "I don't," he broke off and shook his head; he met George's eyes, his expression awash with bitter self-pity. "I can't even say it to protect you, I can't even say it, I'm fucking useless."

George got up and pulled him off the wall, hugged him. "You're fucking perfect."

"You really should just go," Finn said again as he gripped him tighter.

"I'm never leaving you again, so long as you'll have me."

Finn tightened his hold so much, George thought he might burrow down inside of him. He'd let him.

"I'd have you forever if I could," Finn whispered.

"You can," George said. He kissed Finn's throat, the shell of his ear. "I'm all yours."

George didn't care what happened anymore; Finn could tell him or not, either way, he wasn't going anywhere.

37

FINN'S MUM RAISED AN eyebrow at him when he brought their empty dishes back to the kitchen close to midnight. He'd left George stretched out on his bed, told him to stay when he offered to help clean up—he looked like hell.

"You look better," his mum said.

Finn sighed, shook his head and rinsed the dishes.

"I'm glad he's here," he whispered, ashamed.

"Finnegan," his mum tutted at him and pulled him away from the sink and down into a hug. "You love him and there can't be anything wrong with that. Talk to him. I'm pretty sure there's nothing you can say that'll make him stop loving you too."

He squeezed her hard and she made a joking "oof" sound.

He pulled away and smiled down at her. "Okay," he nodded his head. "Okay." He realised then he just needed permission—he'd accepted he was useless and pathetic and was going to get George outed and destroy his life, why not just tell him the truth? Because it was awful and shameful, his mind answered.

"Good boy," his mum brought him back to here and now, her smile warm and amused, "and just remember, the house is big, but not that big," she finished as she went to the other side for her room.

Finn laughed, embarrassed, but well, it was with George—how embarrassed could he be?

"All good?" George asked when Finn came back.

He took a deep breath, crossed the room, and slid onto the bed alongside George. He tucked his head under George's arm, pressed his face against his ribs. "Yeah," he breathed out. Here goes nothing, he told himself. "You remember that night I came round for dinner?"

George tightened his hold, but his voice was very careful when he answered, "Yeah, kind of hard to forget."

"Joq showed me something before you got there, he said he'd show everyone if I didn't leave you alone, but I swear, when you walked in? I swear I wasn't, I'd never, with him," he rambled out.

George ran a soothing hand up and down his side. "I know," he replied. He sounded absolutely certain and it made Finn relax. "I reckon I always knew that."

"Good," Finn pressed his face into George's side. He'd hated the thought of George thinking he could ever do that almost worst of all. "But I couldn't say because if I did, he'd show everyone and it'd be my fault. And you don't want that, you don't ever want to be out."

George hugged him closer and breathed evenly. "Can you tell me what happened from the start?" he asked so gently, Finn almost laughed. He was a hysterical nightmare. But the truth was, it was going to be hard to get the words out. The incident had haunted him when he slept, terrorised him when he was awake.

He sat up, moved so he was in front of George. George read the play and pulled his legs up and Finn sat in front of him cross-legged, his head hanging down.

"Okay," he nodded his head. "I came round and Joq said he wanted to show me something, but I wouldn't go with him. Upstairs, I mean. He wanted me to go upstairs," Finn glanced up to check in. George's jaw was clenched, but he was trying really hard to look calm—Finn appreciated it.

"I don't think he wanted to, you know," he waved his hand.

"What did he want?" George asked evenly.

"Well, like I say, I wouldn't go with him and he kind of made fun of me like, 'as if I'd jump you', but I didn't care, and he went and got his laptop and I texted you 'cos I felt like something was off, you know?"

He took a deep breath, checked in again; George was watching, his expression tight but reassuring. This bit was hard—he wasn't sure he could put into words what it felt like to see him and George together like that on grainy security footage, to see that moment violated by the sound of Joq's voice threatening to release it as Finn watched.

"Finn," George had taken his hand, "take some deep breaths, okay? You can finish telling me later."

"No," Finn shook his head, he was panicking, he hadn't realised, but he was back there and he was panicking and he had to get it out. "He had his laptop and he said he had something to show me," he sucked in a breath, blew it out and spoke with the rush of air: "It was us, it was security footage of us in the shower that night we played. I got in with you, I kissed you. Fuck, I'm so fucking sorry."

George was pulling him in and hugging him over their crossed legs. "Don't you ever apologise for kissing me, for touching me, okay?"

"Okay, but," Finn untangled himself and met George's eyes, "he said if I don't leave you alone, if I don't stop, he's going to release it. And it'd be all my fault, don't you see? 'Cos I let you in now and fuck, do you think he knows? Do you think he's already released it? I've got my phone off." He went to grab it to check the news.

George was grabbing his hands and stopping him. "Finn, no one knows I'm here remember?"

"Yeah," Finn nodded his head, kept nodding it, his breathing panicky. "Yeah, okay, but you see I had to leave, I couldn't let him do that to you. I didn't want to, but I had to."

"Yeah," George said slowly, calmly. "I get what happened, you didn't do anything wrong."

"But I did. I am," Finn whispered. Because he loved George. The whole time they were together, he ignored the boundaries he shouldn't have crossed—George had a boyfriend; George wanted privacy and to not be out above all else; George did not fuck in public places—and Finn crashed all over those lines, got in the shower with him in the first place. He was such a fucking asshole.

But the worst part, the part that rang in his ears and made it so he couldn't sleep at night, was Joq taunting him.

"He said," he whispered now, his voice hoarse like sandpaper, "he said, 'I thought you'd fight more for him' when I just agreed to leave you alone. When he said he'd release it if I didn't, I agreed and he said, 'I thought you'd fight for him more than that.'"

"Finn, you did," George said, his voice getting mad. "You really did."

"Fuck, I'm so sorry, I'm so fucking sorry," he repeated and he started to cry.

38

GEORGE TUGGED FINN AGAINST his chest as Finn repeated: "I'm so sorry, I fucked up, I'm so sorry," and all George could think was: he was going to kill Joq.

And once he'd done that? He was going to marry Finn in front of God and country and the whole goddamn world because Finn was the love of his life and no one was ever going to come after him and make him feel like this again.

Finn's bleary eyes looked up at him, "Sorry," he said again.

George kissed him gently, smiled against his lips, "Was it hot?"

"Huh?" Finn asked and pulled back.

"The footage of us in the shower. Was it hot?" George asked.

Finn laughed. "George," he whacked his head against his chest.

George slid a hand into his hair, shook him lightly. He was a little shaken up—footage of him fooling around in the showers at the stadium floating around out there was no joke—but he wasn't as frightened as he thought he'd be.

In fact: "What? If it's gonna be out there, I better look good."

Finn giggled. "It's hot," he murmured and squirmed a little.

George ran his nose along Finn's hair line, smiled against his skin as he pressed his lips there.

Finn made a small space between them. "You're not mad?"

"I'm mad but not about that. Hell, I want him to release it so everyone knows you're mine..."

"Really?"

"Fuck, yeah, really, gotta stake my claim," he smiled.

"But what're you gonna do, for real?"

"Well, first," George leaned in and kissed him, pulled back and met his eyes, "I reckon I'm gonna marry you."

Finn's eyes widened comically.

"But I'm gonna ask better than that, but just so you know it's coming."

Finn laughed. "I'm gonna say yes."

George let out a nervous huff. He hadn't realised he was nervous about that.

"Good, that's, yeah, that's really fucking good."

"You thought I'd say no?" Finn gave him the sly smile and then climbed fully into his lap, his legs crossing around George's back.

George brought his arms up and hauled him in. "Can't ever be sure with a solid fucking ten."

Finn laughed, delighted. "There's no universe in which I'd say no."

"And there's no universe in which I'd marry anyone else," George said. "I'm really sorry it took me so long, that this had to happen to you."

But Finn was shaking his head. "I was alright, I was just so scared for you."

George didn't believe Finn was totally alright. Getting extorted is going to leave a mark on a man. But he was going to deal with that. He was going to fucking deal with that alright.

In the meantime? In the meantime, he thought as he pulled Finn into a deep kiss, he was going to fuck his soon-to-be husband deep and hard, so fucking deep and hard there was never going to be a memory of any other guy inside him ever again, he was going to bury himself so deep in that body he loved more than anything else in the world and forget he'd ever been with anyone else too.

The sun was peeking under the blinds when Finn drifted off to sleep beside him, his naked back and ass on full display, a sheen of sweat coating him, a trickle of lube and come on his ass and thighs. George ran his hand up and down, dipped into the mess to watch Finn huff and wriggle in his sleep, murmur, "George," his face caught between a smile and a frown.

"Sorry, go to sleep," George whispered.

He kept one hand on Finn's low back and grabbed his phone with the other.

He pulled up his messages and tapped out one line: *I know what you did*.

Then he blocked the number and called his lawyer.

39

FINN WOKE UP IN their rented house in Byron Bay, rolled over and took in George sleeping beside him. He smiled, reached out and ran his fingers lightly over George's bare chest, spread his fingers over his stomach and watched his hand rise and fall.

George's hand came up and slipped over his.

Finn glanced up.

George's eyes were cracked open, crinkling at the corners, his smile warm and indulgent.

Finn smiled back and leaned up to kiss him.

George's hand slipped into his hair and reeled him in, kissed him deep and wet.

He broke the kiss and whispered against Finn's lips, "Happy birthday."

Finn grinned. "Thanks," he slipped his hand lower and stroked George's cock, already hard and straining upwards, "could be happier?"

George laughed, rolled Finn under him and then spent the better part of an hour taking Finn apart with his tongue, his hands, and his dick.

"Where are we going anyway?" Finn asked once they'd eaten the lavish breakfast George had prepared, showered, and gotten dressed 'smart casual.'

"It's a surprise," George winked and unlocked the latest model Range Rover he'd bought since they moved in together up here.

Finn grinned; he loved surprises. George had surprised the shit out of him that first morning back at his mum's place. He'd fallen asleep after their marathon fucking session, every inch of him reclaimed by George, and when he'd woken up, George had told him he'd ended it with Joq; taken a leave of absence from the club; put his house on the market; and had no plans to leave Finn's side so long as he'd have him and he was happy to stay at Finn's family home if he wanted, but there were some nice beachfront properties for rent if Finn was interested in moving in together?

Finn had just stared, lips parted, eyes gritty from crying and then sleeping.

"Sorry," George had said, "if this is going too fast, I can get a place—

"No," Finn busted out, "yes, house, us, together, please that."

George had smiled, shy and pleased, and they'd found this place. Now it was his twenty-first and as he got in the passenger's seat, watched George start the car, he thought he didn't need any presents, he'd already gotten everything he ever wanted. He told George that as they headed out and George snorted a laugh at him.

"You still gotta win at least one Grand Final, one Brownlow, one Norm Smith and be an All-Australian to even compete with my record, Finny," he grinned.

"Mate, I'm gonna do at least two of each just to shut you up," Finn grinned back.

"Good."

They drove and talked, George reaching over to squeeze Finn's thigh intermittently whenever he laughed or felt like it—Finn loved it, how tactile he was, but he worried too. People knew about him now, wasn't George worried that one day—probably really fucking soon since they now lived together and went out a lot—someone would get a photo, put two and two together, and George would be forced to come out?

But Finn was too scared to bring it up; he was almost superstitious about it, like if he didn't mention it, it wasn't real, and if he did, George would suddenly remember all of his fears and end things immediately. Finn was aware how stupid it sounded. Which is why he never voiced his concerns, just soaked up every precious moment like it was all he'd ever get.

By the time George parked next to an open field with a little building, a tiny plane, and some people in parachute gear milling around, Finn was ready to explode with anticipation.

"No fucking way," Finn said.

George laughed. "Way," he leaned over and kissed him—and Finn thought, Jesus, it's like he wants to get caught—and pulled back as he said, "Happy birthday."

Finn laughed. "Thank you."

They got out and made their way over to the building; Finn tried to keep a space between them, but George stayed close, grinning and bumping shoulders.

Once inside, Finn looked around and realised it was just them and the people who worked there.

"Mr Creed," the guy pumped his hand, "nice to finally meet in person."

They got suited up, everything explained, which is when Finn realised George had booked the whole skydiving facility for them.

"Just a sec," George said as they made their way to the plane; he jogged back to speak to one of the guys inside.

Finn was too giddy to think much of it. He'd never skydived before; but he'd always wanted to.

He really wanted to hold George's hand, to do the cheesy hold-hands-and-fall-together-on-the-way-down thing, but George jumped first with his instructor and Finn went after.

It was exhilarating, terrifying, and when they pulled the parachute and drifted the views over the ocean and the bay were magnificent.

His instructor nudged him, "Think someone wants to ask you something."

Finn looked down and gasped.

An enormous sign had been raised on the landing spot—*Will You Marry Me?*—emblazoned in rose petal red against a white back drop. And there, next to it, on one knee was George—looking wind swept and sure.

"Oh my god," Finn exclaimed.

Once he got to ground, his instructor couldn't unclip him fast enough.

"Finn—

"Yes!"

George laughed. He was still on one knee and he had a ring in his hand, a classy white gold band, and he tried again. "Let me ask," he smiled, shy but joyful. "Finn, will you make me the luckiest man alive and marry me?"

"Fuck, yeah!" Finn grinned.

George slipped the ring on, stood, and pulled Finn into a deep, passionate kiss, right there, in front of people.

Finn pulled away, but George stayed close, smiled against his lips. "Fuck, yeah? Really?"

Finn laughed. "Yeah, well, I'm all amped from the dive and then this."

George laughed. "I think that's the point."

Finn became aware of the guy filming them. "Umm."

"For the wedding video," George beamed at him.

Finn shook his head but he couldn't stop smiling. "Okay."

In the car on the way to lunch—and that's all George was giving him—George seemed nervous. Finn struggled to fathom this—shouldn't the nerves come before the proposal? He looked at his fancy wedding band—engagement band?—and decided to just ask.

"You're nervous," he said.

George glanced at him. "Kind of. I want, well," he focused on the road and blew out a breath. Finn waited, nervous now too. "I want to do something, well, a few somethings, and I want you to be okay with it but I can't force you and I won't if you're not."

"Jesus, what is it? Now I'm nervous," Finn turned in his seat to face him. He'd been giddy from the proposal and now he was just anxious.

"It's," George tightened his hold on the steering wheel and Finn saw the moment he decided to say it. "I don't want us to hide. I want," he shot Finn a look, "I want to come out with you," he looked back at the road, "do a press conference before the wedding, have one of those weddings some of the guys have where it's in the magazines and shit."

He was red. George was bright red and his voice was embarrassed at the end. Finn laughed because what else could he do?

"Uh, yeah, that sounds fucking amazing?"

"Yeah?" George looked over at him, surprised and yet not at the same time. Exactly. Did George know him at all? Had he seen his social media?

"George Creed," Finn shook his head at him and smiled, "who knew you were such a celebrity whore."

George laughed, loud and free, and squeezed Finn's thigh. "Yeah, well, now you know. Back seat, the paper bag," he went on and Finn twisted around.

He pulled it onto his lap and started pulling out—

"Oh my God," Finn laughed.

"Yeah?" George asked. "I love the château but maybe beach?"

Finn couldn't stop smiling—it was magazines and brochures with all the packages for the best places to get married in Byron.

"Definitely fairy lights," George continued.

"Definitely," Finn beamed at him as he went through them all.

"Or there's this place," George said as he parked in front of one of the most exclusive rainforest resorts in the area.

The car park was full, so they'd have to keep their distance until this press conference—Finn assumed that's what George wanted—but no one was around so he leaned over and kissed him.

"Thank you," he said.

"It's nothing," George replied, his smile so happy you'd think it was his birthday.

"C'mon," George said and got out, took Finn's hand as Finn came around the front of the car.

Finn laced their fingers together and figured they'd part once they were inside.

"Now the smart casual makes sense," he murmured.

George grinned. "Yep, and you picked the perfect shirt."

He nodded at Finn's classic white button-up, covered in raised white shells.

They went through the lobby, and the receptionist greeted them by name, which should've been Finn's first clue, but he was honestly shocked when he stepped into the restaurant and everyone shouted "Surprise!" He saw his family, his teammates—old and new—all his friends, everyone standing at the artfully decorated tables, the wall of rainforest behind them, 21st ornaments and banners tastefully adorning the place in silver and gold against white.

"Oh my God," Finn covered his mouth, dropped his hands, and laughed high and delighted. He turned to George, watching him back, smiling. "You did all this?"

Before George could reply, Lacy shouted, "Did he say yes?!"

George was still looking at Finn, his smile widening, but nervous too, "I thought it'd be okay to tell our friends and family? You said, if you were with the right guy you'd come out. I think I'm the right guy?"

Finn shook his head—George was a moron; everyone knew about Finn since he'd been so dramatically outed, and he'd never cared, George knew that, the point was, did George care?

"I'd have told everyone if I could," Finn replied.

George grinned and leaned in to kiss him. Everyone cheered, and Finn broke away to laugh and hold up his hand, "Getting hitched!"

And then there were hugs, champagne, food, cake, and when his mum told him George had booked the resort for all of them for the week, had her pack Finn a bag of clothes and toiletries and leave it in their suite, Finn looked over at George in an animated discussion with Lacy and Sophie, saw the moment George felt his gaze and looked up to meet his eyes and smile softly just for him and he thought, *I'm the luckiest guy in the world.*

They tumbled into their room at the resort—the exclusive honey-moon suite, "so we can get an idea if this is what we want," George said pragmatically, which made Finn giggle—full of champagne and good food and sand in his crack from their early morning beach walk with the team. His old team. He owed them an epic apology for leaving and royally fucking over their finals chances.

"We get it Finny," Lacy had said, drunk and high so quite articulate, "but you gotta make it up to us, you didn't just bail on George."

"Yeah," Les nodded along, a sheen to his eyes, and Finn swore he'd make amends. He was an asshole, he knew it.

But then George told them to leave him alone and herded Finn back to their room and finally Finn remembered to ask:

"What were the other something's?" he was focused on unbutton-ing his shirt, it was hard work.

George was laughing at him and then he was in front of him.

"What something's?" he asked as he undid Finn's shirt, slipped it off his shoulders.

"You said you wanted to do a few something's," Finn held up his hand, "press conference, celebrity wedding, that's two."

"It's not a celebrity wedding," George shook his head, "I just want you know, the *Vogue* spread or whatever."

Finn cracked up. George grinned at him, a whole other side to him—playful yet shy, enjoying his celebrity for once but so unsure if he was allowed to.

"I'm all for the *Vogue* spread, and whatever else you want," Finn undid his pants, "you just gotta tell me."

"Yeah, okay," George took his hand and led him out to their private deck and spa.

"A fucking spa," Finn cackled but got in as George turned it on.

He watched George openly as he got naked, leered at the view.

George shook his head, smiled gruffly as he got in. "You're gonna be looking at it for the next fifty years or so, no need to stare."

"I'll stare all I want," Finn replied. "Where's the champagne?"

He was mostly being a shithead, but George actually got out and brought back a chilled bottle in a bucket with ice. "I had everything stocked," he said as he popped the cork, poured and handed Finn the glass.

Finn sipped. Grinned.

"I want to tell Joq to release the footage," George said.

Finn almost spat the champagne everywhere.

George smirked at him.

Finn laughed.

"You were kidding," he said.

George shrugged. "Kind of, I do want to confront him about it, let him know it's no threat, let him know it's not cool, what he did. In fact, it's fucking illegal. It's eating away at me, knowing he hurt you like that."

"Hmm," Finn just wanted to let it go. But, "I reckon he hurt you too."

"Not as much, not the same way—

Finn sunk down in the jets. "No, but, I reckon that's when you must've realised he never loved you."

George focused on him like he'd made some big revelation.

Finn was pretty drunk, but he thought this was obvious. "You know," he waved the champagne glass, "if you love someone let them go, if they're yours, they'll come back? It's like this," he took a big sip, "would you do that to me? Threaten my lover so you could keep me?"

George's jaw clenched.

"We're never going to be open," George said and Finn could tell he was trying to remain calm.

"No shit," Finn snapped, "you're not fucking anything but this until you die," Finn waved up and down himself, "but wind back a few, you hear what I'm saying? If, as in big fantasy land hypothetical, I had a lover and you were threatened by them, would you threaten them so you could keep me?"

George was already shaking his head. "Never, I'd never hurt you."

"Same," Finn replied and drained the glass. "So, I'm just saying, I don't think he really loved you like in an unconditional way."

George frowned. "Well, I don't really care either way, but what I want to know," he nudged Finn's thigh with his big toe, "is if it's okay with you if I confront him about this."

"You can do what you want," Finn replied. He didn't like the idea of George anywhere near Joq, but he wasn't about to be his keeper.

"I know that, but I want you to be okay with it. Maybe you could come too?"

"Yeah?"

"Yeah," George was nodding. "Wait outside for me."

"Don't hit him."

George hesitated.

"Oh my God, you were gonna hit him," Finn cracked up and got more champagne.

George grabbed him around the waist and hauled him against his chest as he got back in.

"He hurt you," he said against Finn's ear.

"I forgive him," Finn replied and leaned back. "We got here, it's all good."

George kissed down Finn's throat, slid his hand down and gripped his cock.

"We did, we were always going to, but I want to close this," George said against his ear as he began to stroke his dick.

And Finn had been keyed up all day and night—from the skydiving, the proposal, the birthday party—it didn't matter how much he'd drunk, he was going to come from nothing but George's voice at this point.

He thrust up into George's hand. "You do what you gotta do, so long as I can come with," he panted out.

"You gonna come for me?" George asked.

"Yeah, fuck, we should get out."

But George was on it, lifting him, spinning him, pressing his hips against the edge of the spa so he could suck Finn off and pull his orgasm right out of him.

Finn rested his hand delicately on George's throat and felt him swallowing; he gasped when George's eyes flicked up to meet his, a vulnerable expression there, a desire to be good, to be so good for Finn.

Finn sunk down and straddled him, kissed George until he tasted nothing but him, urged him to fuck him there and then, gasping into his mouth when George did.

"God, I love you so much," George panted in time with his thrusts.

"And now you're gonna marry me," Finn tipped his head back; George kissed up the line of his throat, thrust up into him.

"Yeah, fuck, I can't wait, was gonna spring it on you this weekend I want it so bad," George replied.

Finn stopped moving. "Really?"

George stilled, but he looked pained. "Yeah? Sorry, I didn't 'cos not cool, plus it was your birthday, so—

Finn laughed, kissed him and got his hips moving again; he honestly didn't think he would've minded.

In the end, the meeting with Joq in a dive bar in St Kilda was over and done in less than twenty minutes, and when George rejoined Finn on the sidewalk, he was smiling, relieved and happy, smiling like a man who'd shed a mental burden.

"All good?" Finn asked as they fell into step with each other.

"All good," George replied and bumped him.

In less than a month, George would be able to take his hand and they'd walk down any street as a couple.

B UT IT WASN'T ALL smooth sailing: George had a communication problem and Finn had a temper and a tendency to bolt. This all came to a head in the chaos between planning the wedding and sorting out where they were going to live.

Sydney had given Finn a spectacular offer. George wasn't surprised—Kenny always wanted him, and now he had him, fuck the cost.

And George was surprised to find he wouldn't mind chilling at home for a while after they were married, supporting Finn, but when Kenny called him up and said he'd spoken to George's old coach, who was now coaching the other Sydney side, mentioned George would be moving to Sydney and would he be interested in taking George on as an assistant? Waugh had said hell to the yeah, and George figured, why not?

They were still in their Byron place, but George had feelers out on Sydney real estate; he loved the look of an old Mediterranean-inspired mansion, the Villa Biscaya, surrounded by massive gardens in Rose Bay. He loved it even more when Finn's eyes widened and his smile went disbelieving when George took him to see it.

But they were still in Byron for now and George had told Finn he had a week free in December before he'd need to start the new job and they'd get the house sorted and take a quick holiday.

"So if you want to pencil that in, that'll work with my schedule," George finished.

"But there's going to be a huge swell, so I was thinking maybe the week after—

"But I've got one week in that gap," George cut him off, eyes on his phone calendar; he was thinking about going down to Sydney, then maybe up to see Scotty. "So, we'll go down to Sydney on the Sunday, which will work 'cos I got meetings on the Monday."

"Oh, you've got meetings?" Finn asked.

George looked up. Finn was giving him a pissy look. "What?"

"You do realise I've got shit on too, right?"

"Yes?" George was baffled. Of course he knew that. "So if we fly then I can get to this meeting and—

"So, I have to fit in with your schedule, is that what you're saying?" Now Finn was giving him a belligerent look. "You're the super star and I fit in with you? 'Cos that's how you're talking to me."

"No," George said slowly, baffled, "I'm saying I have a week free and we need to get the house sorted, take a break, maybe see Scotty, so if you could pencil that in—

"Don't, don't fucking," Finn cut him off; he was red, his hands waving everywhere. "Don't treat me like the fucking wife! It's what you did to him! It's why you broke up!" Finn yelled the last bit then stormed out of the room, down the hall, slamming the bedroom door behind him.

George was dumbfounded. And fucking hurt. He broke up with Joq because he didn't love him. It wasn't even comparable to what he felt for Finn.

He went to the bedroom and opened the door.

Finn was sitting on the edge of the bed, his chest heaving, his eyes glassy.

"Go away."

"No," George said as he came in.

"I don't wanna talk to you," Finn said to his feet.

George saw a tear roll down his cheek and his heart clenched so painfully, he didn't know what to do with it.

"Finn, talk to me, please, what did I do? If you don't tell me, I can't fix it," George crept closer, but stayed standing, a good metre between them.

Finn exhaled roughly. His voice shook when he spoke. "You, you dismissed me, you acted like what I thought didn't matter, like I need to put my routine second to yours. Like I need to, need to," he looked up and met George's eyes, his expression seething yet hurt, "you treated me like some footy wife. But I'm not! I'm a player too, I fucking matter! That's why you broke up with him, you did that to him!"

George swallowed. Well, all that fucking hurt to hear.

"Okay, I... I hear you."

Finn snorted. "Great!"

"No, Finn, I didn't realise I was... But, you're right, I'm sorry."

Finn glanced up, watched him warily.

"I'm not here to facilitate your dreams," he said harshly.

George nodded. That hurt too. "I know. But, babe, you gotta."

"I don't gotta anything!" Finn spat.

George couldn't help it; he cracked a smile.

"Why are you smiling?"

"Sorry, it's just, sometimes you get..."

"I get?"

"Really fucking mad," George said, his smile helpless.

Finn huffed, but he turned his face away to hide his smile.

"I saw that," George said and crept closer, sat down next to him. "I hear you, I didn't know I was doing that. I'm gonna stop, but Finn?"

"What," Finn said, eyes back on the floor.

"You gotta talk to me, pull me up on shit, not run away. Don't," he took a deep breath, "Don't shut me out," he said shakily. It was his biggest fear: Finn shutting him out, leaving him, ghosting him.

Finn let out a blustery noise and whacked George on the thigh.

"Okay, but you gotta call me out on it. This is who I am."

George smiled and grabbed his hand.

"I know and I love you, all of you, but you gotta tell me when I'm fucking up. I really don't want to fuck this up."

Finn shook his head. "I'm fucking it up too."

"You couldn't," George said firmly. "You could never. You could do anything and I'd stay."

Finn shook his head again. "Then you need to do Kenny's self-esteem workshop."

George laughed, relieved.

"Or one of the other ones, my mum sent me some links."

George pulled Finn close and Finn went to him, pressing into his side.

"I'll do that," George pressed a kiss to Finn's forehead.

Finn brought his face up and George met him, kissing him roughly. God, every time he thought he was going to lose this, he went insane; he had to touch Finn, have him, prove it was all still here, still his.

But he needed to say something first.

He pulled back.

Finn whined and leaned in for more.

George obliged before pulling away again.

"Just a sec, I need to say this," George panted.

"What?"

George met Finn's eyes, so close, so blue, a tinge of red from his tears.

"I broke up with Joq because I didn't love him."

Finn dropped his gaze and nodded his head.

"No, babe," George slid his hand under Finn's chin, lifted his face to meet George's again. "You need to hear this and get it through that thick skull."

Finn snorted, but he wouldn't meet George's eyes.

"He wasn't my guy."

Finn glanced at him.

"You are. I left him in my heart as soon as I exchanged one text with you."

"Why?" Finn asked, his eyes searching, his breathing fast, like he couldn't believe it, still couldn't believe it.

"Because you're my guy. Only you. I was always yours, we just hadn't met yet."

"Yeah?"

"Yeah, babe. Always."

Finn kissed him.

Then he broke the kiss to say against George's lips, "Same. You're mine. Always be mine."

George groaned and tackled Finn to his back on the bed.

The strangest part about the fight, George thought as he got Finn undressed, kissed every inch of his skin, touched him with fingers that wanted to memorise just in case, was that he'd gladly take a backseat to Finn's dreams if Finn ever asked. But Finn wouldn't, and George needed to get better at letting him know they were in this together.

41

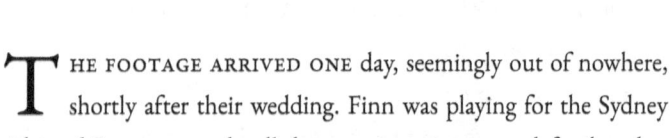

THE FOOTAGE ARRIVED ONE day, seemingly out of nowhere, shortly after their wedding. Finn was playing for the Sydney side, and George seemed really happy as an assistant coach for the other Sydney side.

They'd been publicly out since the press conference, though Finn was pretty sure it was the world's worst kept secret with the number of pics of them 'hanging out' floating around online; and with the way George smiled knowingly when he got asked about his '*friendship with Finnegan Flynn?*' at a footy breakfast event with a camera in his face, and he'd replied, '*Yes, we're very good friends*,' his smile smug.

And Finn would never stop laughing at the stunned look on the reporter from *The Sun's* face at the press conference when George cleared his throat and began, "I've got a few announcements. One, I'm gay. Always have been, always will be," he said it calmly, clinically; but Finn detected the faint tremor.

That evaporated when he went on, his voice suffused with warmth, "And I've been lucky enough to start a relationship with Finnegan Flynn."

There'd been murmuring around the room, camera flashes, and some awkward throat clearing.

"Finn has agreed to marry me," George said, and it was clear he'd been trying to remain professional, but he smiled, overjoyed, "and we'll be doing that next month before we both relocate to Sydney to work for different sides."

More tittering, and then George's face went hard and his voice scary. "This is all I'm going to say on it, but if I hear even a rumour of someone coming after Finn over this, over any of this, over who he loves and who he is, I will hunt you down and you will be sorry. I have a great legal team and deep pockets."

The room was silent. George smiled, cleared his throat like the moment before hadn't happened. "Thank you," he got up and left to a chorus of questions—"When did it start?" "Was there a conflict of interest?" "When's the wedding?" And so on.

Finn liked to re-watch it on his phone and George always told him to turn it off, but he was smiling so much Finn knew he was full of shit.

Then there was the wedding, which had been the *Vogue* wedding spread come to life in beautiful high-definition. Finn didn't think he'd come down from that high anytime soon, and he was decorating their new place in Rose Bay with framed photos from the wedding when a delivery arrived from his post office box that he needed to sign for.

He looked at the USB and knew what it was.

He put it on the kitchen bench, finished hanging the pictures of them in their white pants and shirts on the beach before he started on dinner.

George came in an hour later straight from preseason training.

"I was gonna cook," he said to Finn as he came into the kitchen and tugged him into a kiss.

Finn sank into it, moaned a little when George caressed his ass; Finn reciprocated with a hand on George's dick.

He broke the kiss. "You can cook tomorrow, I'm making faji-tas."

"I was gonna make you those petit farci you liked in Nice," he said and sounded genuinely disappointed. But also:

"Could you butcher the pronunciation anymore?" Finn laughed into his mouth and continued to rub his dick.

But then he remembered he was cooking.

He let George go and got back to the stove. "Oh, that arrived," he pointed at it with the spatula.

George picked it up.

"From Joq," Finn said, eyes on turning his strips of meat.

"Oh," George turned it over in his hands. "Did you watch it?"

"No," Finn shook his head.

"Do you want me to throw it out?"

"Do you want to throw it out?"

George shrugged. "I don't need to see it, just morbidly curious."

"We can watch it after dinner then," Finn said and winked.

He winked to hide how it gave him anxiety, just thinking about it, but maybe it'd be for the best, like exposure therapy.

In the end, it was better than that. They were sacked out on their enormous sofa in their open air living area on the top floor, the laptop streaming onto the TV and as Finn watched himself on TV kissing George, he felt embarrassed, but then real life George was touching him like he couldn't help himself, like he was so turned on he was out of control, and before Finn knew it, he was getting railed deep and so good, the image of himself and George leaving the tunnel with hands entwined etched onto the screen.

"We need to make more home movies," George said against his lips after.

Finn laughed. "We do. And send Joq a thank you note."

George huffed a laugh and kissed him again.

42

♥

I T WAS A YEAR later, on the eve of their first anniversary and George was relaxed. Finn was relaxed. Scotty's place was super relaxing.

Scotty snorted.

"I get it, you're so *relaxed*," Scotty laughed, kicking his legs out from where he was sitting on the car seat he'd converted into lounges in his bar shed.

Finn had already turned in for the night. Begging off, he'd told George he wanted to watch some shit on his phone and catch up on his socials. "Besides, you need to catch up with your friend, gossip about me," he'd winked.

George grabbed him in a hug, kissed the top of his head as he shook him. "We don't gossip."

"Sure you don't," Finn said, giggling while George tickled him.

"Alright, you got a room, I gave you a real nice room, private," Scotty said as he came into the bar shed, arms full of a carton.

"I'm out," Finn grinned as he extricated himself. "Night, babe," he leaned in to kiss George. "Wake me when you get in if it's late."

George kissed him harder for that. "Yeah?"

"Oh yeah," Finn replied and kissed him back.

"Okay, seriously, happy for you dudes, but please don't fuck in front of me," Scotty said.

"You heard the man," George grinned and let Finn go, his hand lingering on his low back as Finn moved away, his head ducking as he pulled out his phone.

"Night, Scotty."

"Night, rook."

"Ah, shut it," Finn laughed and wandered back to the main house.

They were on their third beer, bourbon for Scotty, when George said how relaxed he was.

Scotty kicked his foot after mocking him for being "so relaxed."

"Serious for a second," Scotty said. "What's up?"

"Nothing?"

Scotty sipped his drink. "You and him seem good, real good."

"We are," George sat forward and drank his beer in one go. He got up to get another one. He sat back down, glanced at Scotty. "We're so fucking good I'm terrified."

He took a long drink of his beer after admitting that.

Scotty laughed.

"That's funny?"

"Sort of, you're just," Scotty shook his head. "You always take shit so serious. Just enjoy it, man."

George huffed and sat back, cradled his beer in his hands. "I'm terrified he's gonna get older and realise he's made a huge fucking mistake. I'm this old man, and he's, you know, twenty-two and perfect."

Scotty cracked up. George looked at him—his manic hair sticking up everywhere, his big mouth wide and toothy as he grinned.

"George, I hate to break it to you, but he's far from perfect."

George scowled. "Yes he is." In all the ways that mattered, Finn was perfect; even his imperfections like his temper were perfect, he kept George in line.

Scotty snorted. "He throws tantrums and sulks. He speaks in that pop psychology bullshit vocab all these kids got going on nowadays, and he talks to his mum every day. I know you know he's not in there watching TV right now. He's on the phone to his mum."

"She's his best friend," George defended.

Scotty laughed again. "Not the point."

"And he's young, he's still learning how to manage his anger."

Scotty snorted. "Yeah, okay, but I'm gonna bet you a thousand dollars he's still the same tantrum throwing, hippy pop psych, mama's boy when he's forty, but also not the point."

"Well, what is the point?" George was getting pretty mad at Scotty running his boy down. They'd been friends for a long time, but he would hit him.

"Calm down," Scotty grinned. "Serious talk?"

George was nervous, but he jerked his chin.

"I reckon, from what you've said, Joq opening that up fucked you up a bit."

"No, it didn't, it wasn't fair on him, I wouldn't come out—"

"Let me finish," Scotty cut in, expression serious. "You were already ashamed 'cos you like the cock, yeah? And then you land this hot guy and you think it's safe, yeah? But then he's all like, is it cool if I bang a bunch of other guys?"

"Yeah, but, I didn't love him."

"Still a knock to the ego," Scotty replied and finished his bourbon. Then he finished the point. "Whether intentional or not, it would've made you feel not good enough, not enough. Now you believe that and you're missing what's right in front of you."

"Yeah? And what's that? Also, I dunno why you're ragging on Finn for being Mr Pop Psychologist," George said.

Scotty laughed as he poured himself another shot. "That kid? Balls to the wall in love with you, ass to the grave committed to you. Has been since I met him."

George's heart fluttered. He still couldn't believe it though; he knew they were happy, but he was always waiting, in the back of his mind, for the other shoe to drop.

"But he's so young."

Scotty sat back down with a flourish. "Yeah, you were his age once too. Younger I reckon when you fell in love with Alistair. You reckon if it'd all been different, if you hadn't gone into the league, stayed on the farm, he stayed too, you reckon you wouldn't have been committed?"

God, it was like imagining a world without Finn, which was impossible now.

But he took Scotty's point. He'd have been committed—he'd loved Alistair, maybe not in the way he loved Finn, which was all consuming, but it was real.

"All I'm saying is you're gonna fuck this up in your own head."

George nodded—Scotty was right.

"You're right."

"No, shit."

George rolled his eyes. Modesty was not in Scotty's arsenal. "What about you, then? I thought you were straight but that was damn weird with the neighbour the other day? Finn said he spoke to him. He said he was having issues with your lack of fencing, something about station boundaries—"

"Nope!" Scotty got up; he was uncharacteristically shy as he went to the fridge and got George another beer, which he didn't need.

"Definitely not talking about that psycho," he went on and George decided to drop it. Scotty would talk when and if he wanted to.

Besides, George had other things to think about, like his anniversary in Thailand. About a question he wanted to ask Finn, had wanted to ask since before they got married and now, finally, he thought maybe he could. Scotty was right—this was real, Finn had never given any indication he wasn't committed, and George was not going to fuck it up in his own head anymore.

GEORGE HAD BEEN DIFFERENT, Finn thought. Ever since that night at Scotty's and onto this trip to Thailand—he'd been different.

More sure. More relaxed.

Finally, Finn thought dryly—they'd only been married a year.

It seemed confirmed when he lay sprawled on Finn in their bungalow on their final night. George was tracing Finn's nipple with his finger, sated, humming something to himself.

"You ever think about having kids?" he asked—it felt like it came out of nowhere, and yet, it also felt like it was meant to be asked right at this moment in a humid bungalow as their sweaty, naked skin cooled under a lazy spinning ceiling fan.

"Yeah, course," Finn replied.

"Really?" George propped his head in his hand and met Finn's eyes. "You say it like it's a given."

Finn shrugged. "Well, I've always wanted them, so..."

"Yeah, but, we're gay?" George smiled his indulgent smile.

"Surrogate, duh," Finn replied. "We probably should've discussed this before we got married, but it wasn't a deal breaker for me, so..."

George grinned at him. "What was a deal breaker?"

"Being open," Finn scowled.

George laughed. "But seriously, you've thought about kids?"

"Haven't you?" Finn asked. He sat up and reached for his glass of champagne. They were going to have to up the intensity when they got back—sure, they'd been diving, surfing, hiking, and rafting since they got there, but they'd also been eating and drinking like kings. George reckoned they fucked so much, they were covered, but Finn wasn't so sure—he liked to be perfect for his skinnies—he was starting his third season in the league, second season with Sydney, and he was going to win the fucking Grand Final this year if he had to near kill himself to do it.

"I have," George replied slowly and accepted the champagne Finn handed him. "But I always thought it wasn't gonna happen."

"Do you want it to happen?" Finn asked and he was nervous, just a bit, because it wasn't a deal breaker, but it'd be nice.

"Well, yeah, if we use your ... stuff," George replied and took a big drink.

Finn cracked up. "How much of my stuff have you had in your mouth and up your ass now? I think you can say it."

George dropped his head on Finn's chest. "Finny."

"Also, it'd be one of each, duh."

Those serious brown eyes met his again, curious and kind of excited. "One of each?"

"Yeah, two kids, one of each of us."

"Oh," George breathed out; you'd think Finn had just successfully explained string theory to him, it made Finn cackle again.

"Ah, shut it, we weren't all raised by new age hippies," George said as he laughed at himself.

"No, well, I guess I haven't seen many gay dads around the place when we visit your parents," Finn mused.

And then George was really laughing—Finn could almost see him picturing it, a couple of dudes walking down the main street of his hometown with a baby strapped to each of their chests—yep, that would be something to talk about.

"Anyway," George said after a while, "I think that'd be good, when you want to do it, that'd be good."

Finn smiled, he took George's glass and placed it next to his, took his hand and made him get up and follow him out to the private pool for a night swim, and later, for a night fuck.

It was bizarre bumping into Joq the next day, but Finn saw no harm in saying hello while George checked them out.

When Joq said he was there with his boyfriend, Finn felt genuinely happy for him—he didn't think he was a bad guy at all, and he actually empathised with what he'd done; George wasn't the kind of guy you let go of easily.

"Well, I better," he waved a hand toward the lobby. "Nice seeing you."

"I can't say the same," Joq said suddenly, his tone switching from friendly to cold in a second.

Finn paused, stopped smiling and sized him up.

"Yeah, what I did was shitty and I'm sorry, I really am," Joq said and Finn believed him. "But you stole my boyfriend and no one seems to care about that part."

Finn cracked up, surprised. He looked at Joq and realised he was serious. "Oh, Joq. You still believe that?"

"I know that," Joq shot back.

"How could I steal something that was already mine?" Finn asked.

Joq frowned and went on, "Twelve years, me and George—

"He was never yours," Finn stated. He was surprised Joq didn't get this yet. "He was always mine, you were just keeping him company until I arrived." He smiled warmly at Joq because George did belong to him and that was just a fact.

Joq shook his head at him. "Well, keep telling yourself that if it makes you feel better."

"I don't have to," Finn said, he smiled and felt the confidence of George's words behind him—'*because you're my guy, you've always been my guy*'—and finished, "He does."

Joq flinched, and Finn had a moment to feel guilty because yes, things with him and George started out messy, and yes, Joq was a casualty in that, but he was hardly an innocent party, Finn thought—he could've left George at any point since he knew, surely he knew deep down, they weren't meant to be, they weren't really in love.

But he couldn't say all of that, and he was pretty sure he was the last person Joq wanted to hear it from; so he bid him farewell and went into the lobby, slid alongside George, who slipped an arm around his waist and tugged him in. Finn met him when George leaned in to kiss him.

"All set?" George asked against his lips.

"Yeah," Finn replied, his smile radiant as he looked at George. "I reckon they'll have better magazines at the airport."

"Why don't you just get a subscription on your phone?" he said as he ran his hand up and down Finn's back.

Finn rolled his eyes. "Because then how will you read them?"

George laughed and kissed him again.

"Here you go, Mr. Creed," the cashier said and George focused on him handing him his card and receipt, pointing to their waiting chauffeured SUV.

George held Finn tight and Finn didn't mention Joq; he leaned into George's embrace, accepted another kiss just before they got into the car and headed for the airport, headed for their home in Rose Bay, headed for another epic season.

Epilogue

In the end, it took Finn another two seasons to win the elusive Grand Final. He was playing in his third when they finally won it all. He'd won a Brownlow, he'd won a Norm Smith for best on ground in a losing Grand Final, and he was a two time All-Australian, but as that final siren sounded in his third and he knew they'd won it, they'd won it all, he started to cry; he dropped his hands to his knees, dropped his head as he was mobbed by his Sydney teammates and bawled his eyes out.

"Pull it together, man, we got kids present," George's gruff voice cut into the huddle.

Finn straightened. He wiped his eyes and laughed high and thrilled as George came at him. He had Amy strapped to his chest with her brown curls and serious eyes and Laine was holding his hand and doing his best to toddle over, his uncertain blue eyed gaze sharpening and his face breaking into a grin when he locked eyes on Finn.

"Dada!" he let go of George's hand and Finn scooped him up, hugged him tight, kissed his cheek and then leaned in to kiss Amy's forehead before leaning up to kiss George deeply; he was happy, and so fucking relieved.

"Took you long enough," George said against his lips.

Finn laughed. "Shut up, how long did it take you? Seven seasons?"

George grinned. "Something like that," then he smiled his private smile. "Congratulations, you were incredible; you'll get the Norm Smith for that."

"You reckon?" Finn asked and bounced Laine on his hip.

"Absolutely, I'm so proud of you, reckon I'm the luckiest WAG here," George grinned—he'd taken to retiring and staying home with the kids with relish, called their little family his new team.

Finn laughed again. "Yep, and you'll get lucky for it later," he winked and leaned in for another kiss, but then Laine was hitting his face, and the team were circling, and George was taking their kids—their kids!—and telling him to go have fun, to celebrate, he'd see him once he got the kids settled with Finn's mum, with George's mum back at the house and Finn looked at him against the backdrop of the crowd going wild and couldn't believe this was his life, that he got everything he ever wanted and then some.

"Love you," he mouthed at George and watched George blush, but he mouthed it back and Finn looked forward to getting railed by that later.

Acknowledgments

First and foremost, my beta team: I cannot thank them enough for reading this lengthy novel so quickly and giving me concrete things to fix—as always, it is a much better story for their input. Special thank you to Ana for talking to me every day and dealing with my angst so graciously; her sense of humour and sage advice makes for a great journey, every time. Huge shout out to my dad—without him, there would be no published book: he covered all the costs as I couldn't bear delaying due to some financial problems. Thanks as well to Cate Ashwood for another perfect cover turned around in a single weekend, and to my editor Kath for prioritising my book and getting it back to me so swiftly. Finally, to my Sasha, my mighty staghound and namesake; she died suddenly during the writing of this book and her absence was a glaring, daily hole. I hope it does her justice, in spirit if in no other way—she would never have behaved as dramatically as these men; she was far too self-possessed!

About Author

Sasha Avice is the author of nine novels (and counting!) and one PhD (which is enough). She lives in Western Australia with a changing cast of birds. When she's not writing, she's working with wildlife and thinking about life. She loves hearing from readers! Email direct at sasha@sashaavice.com or sashaavice@pm.me or join her mailing list at sashaavice.com for regular updates.

Also By

Contested Possession

"... possession is achieved as a result of winning a contest." *Australian rules football.*

Each book features a football player whose possession of the guy he wants is... contested.

Need more George and Finn in your life?

Because He'll Always Be My Guy

A Contested Possession Novella

These Bonus Scenes will take you back into their world as George explores his sexuality, and Finn reveals a hurt he can't get past. There's a trip to a bath house, a baby, a memorable Best & Fairest red carpet interview, and a George grand gesture to heal all Finn's wounds.

If you ever wondered how they navigated life after their shady beginnings, here's 30,000 words of just that.

Available at sashaavice.com

His Boyfriend's Rookie

A Contested Possession Novel

How far would you go to keep your boyfriend?

This is the debut season of the second greatest rookie of all time: Finnegan Flynn.

This is the season the greatest rookie of all time, George Creed, takes his position in history as the youngest person ever to coach a league team.

And this is the season Head of Stadium Security, Joaquin Nord, watches his boyfriend, the deeply closeted coach, fall in love with his superstar rookie...

Joaquin watches this mutual attraction unfold with patient horror, certain his boyfriend will get over his crush. But a moment of aching intimacy caught on camera forces him to intervene.

Will his desperate act of sabotage be enough? Or will it cement George and Finn as the first in Australian Football history at something else?

Available at Amazon.com

This Is My Church

A Contested Possession Novel

"Church boys don't come out of the closet to marry cocaine snorting dudes who like to take it up the—"

Mates with everyone and beholden to none, Lacy is a twenty-seven-year-old football superstar who parties as hard as he plays. It makes no sense for him to become best mates with their new ruckman, the bible reading, softly spoken celibate, Thaddeus Clay.

But from the moment the freshly traded twenty-three-year-old walks into the locker room, they do everything together.

Well, almost everything.

When Thad stumbles upon Lacy's extracurriculars—a drug-fuelled gangbang where Lacy loses consciousness to the number of men who take him—he knows they can't do *that* together.

But what Thad does next will change the course of their relationship in irreversible ways. Except Lacy doesn't remember. And Thad is left with a secret that threatens his friendship and his faith.

Lacy knows he never stood a chance with a church boy, but when Thad avoids eye contact he's left with one question—what the hell happened on the weekend?

This Is My Church carves a path through gangbangs, benders and a whole lot of praying to find out what it means to be truly loved.

Available at Amazon.com

Perimeter

Set in Western Australia at the turn of the millennium, each book is a standalone featuring guys who don't want love, don't seek it.

They drift, they work... and then some guy turns up and the dull isolation goes bright, blinds them like a splinter of sun caught in the eyes.

Shop now at Amazon.com for current books and future releases in this series.

www.ingramcontent.com/pod-product-compliance
Lightning Source LLC
Chambersburg PA
CBHW021119260626
47169CB00005B/1347